REBELS OF EDEN

ALSO BY JOEY GRACEFFA

Elites of Eden
Children of Eden
In Real Life: My Journey to a Pixelated World

REBELS OF

EDEN

A NOVEL

JOEY GRACEFFA

New York Times Bestselling Author

WITH LAURA L. SULLIVAN

Keywords

PRESS

——

ATRIA

New York London Toronto Sydney New Delhi

First published in Great Britain in 2018 by Keywords Press,
an imprint of Simon & Schuster UK Ltd
A CBS COMPANY

First published in the USA in 2018 by Keywords Press,
an imprint of Simon & Schuster Inc.

1 3 5 7 9 10 8 6 4 2

Simon & Schuster UK Ltd
1st Floor, 222 Gray's Inn Road
London
WC1X 8HB

www.simonandschuster.co.uk
www.simonandschuster.com.au
www.simonandschuster.co.in

Simon & Schuster Australia, Sydney
Simon & Schuster India, New Delhi

A CIP catalogue record for this book is available from the British Library.

HB ISBN 978-1-4711-6733-1
eBook ISBN 978-1-4711-6734-8

This book is a work of fiction. Names, characters, places and
incidents are either the product of the author's imagination or are
used fictitiously. Any resemblance to actual people living or
dead, events or locales is entirely coincidental.

Printed and bound by CPI Group (UK) Ltd, Croydon, CR0 4YY

MIX
Paper from
responsible sources
FSC
www.fsc.org   FSC® C020471

Simon & Schuster UK Ltd is committed to sourcing paper
that is made from wood grown in sustainable forests and support the Forest
Stewardship Council, the leading international forest certification organisation.
Our books displaying the FSC logo are printed on FSC certified paper.

Dedicated to those whose imagination makes this world a more beautiful place, never stop dreaming. And to my readers, who turn my dreams into reality.

SOMETIMES I THINK running away is what I do best.

As I run through the forest, my bare feet hardly make a sound on the dew-damp leaves. That's not the case with my pursuer. His feet crash like the paws of an infuriated bear, snapping branches and crushing tender new growth. I can hear him cursing.

"Doesn't matter how fast you run, or where you hide. I can smell the city stink on you. You can't escape. This is *my* home."

I shift my pace to leap over the thick trunk of a fallen tree, then remember Mira's advice: snakes hide under the crevice of fallen trees. If you step or jump too close on the far side, you'll be in perfect range of a strike. Snakes are calm and docile creatures, she added, unlike the malicious serpents many pre-fail humans believed them to be. "But if you stepped on me while I was sleeping, I'd bite you!" she told me, flashing her teeth so white in her dark, freckled face. With her good advice ringing in my memory, I instead jump on top of the fallen trunk and then leap far clear of any disgruntled rattler.

I'd almost rather face the rattlesnake than Zander.

He's getting closer, and I clutch the stolen strip of fabric tighter in my fist. I'd rather die than be captured, I think . . . then burst into laughter through my panting breath. I've said that kind of thing before, in much worse circumstances. I meant it then. Somehow my body and brain, recalling those past dangers, feel it even now. It has become second nature to me. I won't yield. Zander will never catch me. He's bigger and stronger than me, far meaner, but I'm lithe and fast. My tireless legs will carry me to salvation. As long as I have the great open Earth before me, I'm safe.

And then, the Earth ends.

I should have known. Zander knew—I realize now that he was chasing me here, herding me. I thought I was running on dewy ground, but of course it is far too late in the day for dew to remain. It burned off hours ago in the strong late-summer sunshine. No, the damp leaves were caused by mist from the waterfall.

It's swirling around me now, heavy enough to look mystically silver up here on the high elevation. Unfortunately not nearly thick enough to hide me from my enemy.

For he made it clear on my first day in Harmonia that I was his enemy. The place of my birth ensured that before he knew a thing about me.

"Give it up, City." He won't call me by my name, only insults about my origin. He lords his natural birth over me and the other refugees from Eden. I bear the brunt because I'm the only one near his age.

I whirl and face him, the sound of the waterfall raging behind me. I don't want to look at it. Not from up here. I've seen it from the bottom, where the rushing water cascades into a rock-lined pool in a never-ending crashing tumult. It is a scary enough force of nature seen from safe, dry, level land. If I look at it now, I might lose my nerve. And I'll need all the courage I possess to face whatever Zander as in store for me.

I'm used to heights, but that just means I know enough to be absolutely sure I don't want to fall off of them. Or be pushed.

When EcoPan set me free from Eden, and my mother and the others took to Harmonia, I was sure that life in nature must be a paradise. Isn't it what mankind has been awaiting for generations? And in many ways it is. But after three months in the wild, I've discovered that people are still people, whether they are in the city or the forest, no matter if they are trapped or free.

"Just don't be alone with him," Mira's boyfriend Carnelian once advised me. Easy for him to say. He spends as much time indoors as an Eden resident, tinkering with the small bits of tech we're allowed to help us live harmoniously with nature. Zander hates technology, so it's easy for someone like Carnelian to avoid him. But Carnelian took his Passage Test last year, and got a high ranking. I take the test tomorrow, so I've had to devote all my waking hours to the outdoors, learning how to navigate this strange, wild world.

I thought I was doing pretty well, until Zander started in on me. So far, it's just been with cutting words. But I see the way he and his brothers look at the Eden-born, like we're decadent, corrupt, weak. I'll always be an outsider.

Now, standing about ten feet away, he gives me a slow, malicious grin. I'm trapped, and he can take his time.

"Hand it over." He extends his hand, as if he's the most reasonable person in the world.

I take a tiny step back and shake my head. The small, loose rocks grate worryingly beneath my feet. If I'm not careful, I'll fall before he even decides to push me.

No, he couldn't be that terrible, could he? Just because I was born somewhere else? EcoPan chose me for liberation. Shouldn't that make me worthy in his eyes?

When I don't hand over the flag, his outstretched hand slowly balls into a fist. "Now," he says. "Before I lose my patience."

I just clutch it tighter. This is a bikking game! Two teams of athletes, each guarding the flag at their home base, each trying to steal their opponent's flag. It's supposed to be fun, build camaraderie, and train us for life in the wild—an excuse to run, hide, and stalk through the woods. But Zander, his brothers, and his friends have turned it into a war. They never expected an Eden-born girl like me to exceed them in speed and stealth. Now Zander sees it as a direct battle between Eden and Harmonia. A battle he apparently intends to win at any cost.

"You're going to fail tomorrow, too," he snarls at me. "Might as well get used to it today."

He's also in the Passage Test tomorrow.

"You know I'm going to get that flag one way or another. Tell you what, if you hand it over, I'll only break your arm. How about that, City? With a broken arm you might squeak by with the lowest passing rank . . . if your city-scum mother helps you."

I catch my breath, and my jaw tightens. "Don't you even mention my mother!" Until three months ago I thought she was dead, gunned down by Eden Greenshirts as she tried to help me escape to a better life. I was overjoyed to find her alive here in Harmonia. She's the most precious thing to me.

He ignores me. "But if you make me take it from you, I'll break your leg. You won't be able to take the Passage Test. Maybe not ever, if I break it badly enough."

"You wouldn't!" I gasp, overwhelmed by the unfairness of it all. "We're supposed to live in harmony here. What have I ever done to you, Zander?"

He shrugs. "Do you ever watch the wolves, City?" There's

a pack in the mountain range nearby. Sometimes they skirt close to Harmonia, but mostly they avoid us. The elder named Night took some of us to watch the pack at its den.

"They work together, sure, but every pack has a leader. The other wolves don't dare disobey him, or . . ." He mimes slitting a throat, and I wince. But he hasn't ever plunged a knife into another human being. He doesn't understand what it really means. I do. Maybe he's all talk.

Or maybe he just hasn't had a chance to be as cruel as he is capable of being, yet.

"When Night took you, did you see that scrawny little black wolf? Every time another wolf looked at him he rolled on his back and pissed on his own belly. Do you know why? He came from another pack. Kicked out, just like you. The other wolves hate him. He'll always be an outsider.

"We're a lot like wolves," he goes on. "I'm coming in top in the Passage Test, and working my way up from there. Someday I'll be leader—the alpha wolf of this pack—and when I am, I'll make the decisions, and all the corrupt city scum will know their place. Until then, I start with you!"

He lunges for me, and in that instant I make a split-second decision. Better to choose my own destiny than to let someone else choose for me.

I whirl, and leap into the roaring, misty void. The glimpse I get of Zander's utter frustration is enough to make me laugh like a lunatic as I fly off the cliff into the waterfall. I know that only adds to his rage, and that makes this suicidal leap almost worthwhile.

It's just a game, my mother's voice seems to whisper to me as I fall.

No, I think. *This is life. Life and death. Everything in Eden, everything out here, has serious consequences. The smallest decisions matter.*

But falling and philosophy don't mix . . . at least not for long. I'm a climber, with skill gained from scaling the high wall that was my childhood prison. Falling is a climber's nightmare, but for just a moment, my nightmare is beautiful. In seemingly slow motion I feel like I'm flying more than falling. The waterfall is lovely and savage, viscerally real in a way Eden simulations never could be, and I glory in the roaring sound, the chill. Beneath me, in a flash of clarity through the mist, I see my friends and teammates: vital, dark Mira like a lithe wild animal, and shy but earnest Carnelian, most visible of all with his shock of orange hair. They're looking up at me, their mouths open, shouting something I can't hear over the surging water.

Then time catches up with me and the beauty becomes terror as I merge with the crushing waterfall. It knocks the wind out of me, blinds me, and I brace for impact on the rocks below, thinking, crazily, *We won! I still have the flag!*

The landing is terrible . . . but not as bad as I'd thought. I miss the rocks and smack with an agonizing thunderclap into the water, but my situation isn't much better. The endless waterfall is pushing me down. I'm stuck in a swirling eddy under its crushing weight. Time and again I see light at the surface through the swirling bubbles, but I can't reach it. I learned to swim as soon as I got to Harmonia, but all this water is still alien to me. In Eden, all water was precious, rationed and recycled. Here it is bountiful and wild . . . and deadly.

My lungs are on fire with the ache to breathe. I tumble, disoriented, losing hope, until at last my feet touch the solid, slippery rock below. I shove up with all my strength and burst to a place that is free of the cascade's terrible push. Suddenly everything around me is calm. The water is clear and still, and I see the silver bellies of fish as they dart away from me. In that moment of peace everything seems possible, and I smile.

I swim to the shore, and my friends are holding out branches for me to grab, making a human chain to pull me to safety.

Gasping and shivering, I stagger away from the water's edge. Mira holds me up on one side, Carnelian on the other.

"Great Earth!" Carnelian says. "Did he push you?"

"No," I say with the faintest smile, and hold up the sodden flag, symbol of our victory, and my determination. "I jumped."

High atop the waterfall I can just make out Zander's ferocious scowl before he stalks back into the forest. The only good thing about having an enemy is beating them.

But somehow I have a feeling that Zander isn't finished with me. Tomorrow, when the Passage Test begins, he'll have plenty of opportunities.

As soon as I catch my breath, we jog back to our base at the edge of the city. It's just a formality at this point, though. We've won. Zander's brothers and other teammates are far behind, and there's no way he himself can get down from the waterfall in time to intercept us.

Unless he jumps, too, I think with a stifled giggle.

The rest of the team, the ones who'd stayed behind guarding our flag, greet us with cheers, and in a moment I'm swept up with Mira and Carnelian onto their shoulders, reveling in their cheers. It still feels so good to have friends, to be able to go out into the world freely. I spent almost all my life hiding, and when I was finally a member of a community, I wasn't myself, but Yarrow, a programmed product of the Center scientists.

Bits of her voice come uncomfortably back to me in my head sometimes. *What are you doing with these losers?* spoiled, selfish Yarrow sometimes whispers to me. That subliminal voice makes me deeply uncomfortable, and I have to remind myself that though the programming still lingers in my brain, it isn't me. Because it sure feels like me. In fact, the more she talks inside my head, the more like me she feels.

Sometimes there's another little voice, too, a low murmur of approval or concern that hardly seems separate from my own conscience. Yet there is an alien quality to it, a fascination that makes me want to both shut it out and listen harder.

No matter who is talking in my muddled brain, I make my own choices in this life. I'll never let society's programming dictate right and wrong to me.

Or a computer's programming.

I look at all my friends, and smile. The people carrying Mira and Carnelian come together so the happy couple can kiss, and I make myself smile even more broadly to hide the pain seeing their happiness causes me.

I've kissed two people, and I love them both.

Both of them are trapped in Eden, maybe captured, maybe tortured, maybe with their minds wiped and reprogrammed. Maybe dead.

Here in Harmonia, they tell us not to think about what we left behind in Eden. That was nothing more than a trial. Those lucky enough to pass now have the whole world in front of them. Look forward, not back, Elder Night says to the newcomers.

Here I have my mom, and a lot of new friends. I have fresh breezes and real rain, plants and rich damp earth and squirrels frolicking in the trees. The food is authentic, not synthesized from algae. No one is controlling me. I should be completely happy.

But I can't stop thinking about those I left behind. Lark. Lachlan. My twin brother, Ash. Rainbow and all the other second children. Even strangers, the anonymous people trapped without even realizing they are in a prison. Most citizens of Eden think they live in a sanctuary that keeps them safe from a deadly, poisoned world. All of those people should be free.

I said I can't stop thinking about them all, but I lied. More and more, as the weeks and now three months pass, I find myself forgetting about them. First it would be for a few minutes. I'd be relishing the novel enjoyment of some new fresh fruit, and only be thinking about what a wonderful place the outside was. Only thinking of my own luck, my own pleasure. Later the forgetting would last longer. I'd be chatting with Mira for hours as we walked in the woods, then go to bed tired and happy. Only when my head hit the pillow would I think of Lark, imprisoned in the Center. Of Lachlan and Ash, hunted, their whereabouts unknown.

Then the guilt hits me. I should be thinking about them all the time! I should be convincing all these natural-borns to help me break into Eden and free the trapped residents. Or if they won't help, I should go myself. Why should I be the one to enjoy the outside, just because EcoPan chose me?

Then I get lulled by some sport, some friend, by the fascinating agricultural practices by which we grow our own food, by some new animal I'd only seen in vids . . . and for a few moments I forget again.

Mira hops down from our teammates' shoulders and throws an arm around me, hugging me tight. "Well done, Rowan! I'm so glad you joined us in Harmonia!"

I hug her back, and try to fight the sadness that lingers behind all the happiness as we make our way back to the village. I need to keep my head clear. Tonight is the Wolf Moon ceremony. Tomorrow, I compete with other newcomers and those who have just come of age, to determine my position in this society.

When we're almost to Harmonia, a sweaty and angry Zander blocks our path. He had to be running at top speed to catch up with us, and his face is red, his arms scratched by thorns.

"You're deluded if you think this scum from Eden is anything but trouble for Harmonia," he shouts to the group.

"Shut up, Zander," Mira snaps.

"Shut your own mouth, dead-eye's daughter," Zander growls. Mira recoils. Dead-eye is a derogatory slang for first-generation people from Eden, referring to the dull, flat color of their lens implants. Mira's eyes are a beautiful, vibrant honey-brown flecked with gold. Is this just the worst thing Zander can think of to insult her with?

Mira is bristling, looking like she's about to hurl herself at him, but Carnelian holds her back, murmuring calming words.

"We've seen it before," Zander goes on. "You know the story is true. Nothing that comes from that stinking city is good. I don't care if EcoPan picked her out. If she's the best of the worst, she's still corrupt. But think about it—what if she was just clever enough to fool EcoPan. Those city people would stop at nothing to get out here and destroy what we have, just like their ancestors did."

A few people scoff at him, but I hear murmurs of agreement, too. Some of my friends look at me with new suspicion in their eyes. I remember from being Yarrow how a charismatic, loud absolutist can sway popular opinion. It happened with Pearl, and it looks like it is happening again now.

"Rowan isn't dangerous," Carnelian begins in his soft-spoken way.

"She wanted to go back," Zander says, eyes narrowed at me. "If she just wanted to go home, I'd say good riddance." He spits derisively on the ground. "But she wants to bring them out! Didn't you hear her when she first came? She wants all that filth to spill into our paradise."

"They're not like that!" I shout back at him. "The people in Eden are just like the people out here. We're all human."

"People from Eden are filth," he sneers. "Weaklings at the mercy of technology. Just like you. Just like your mom."

I can take him insulting me, but not my mom. I launch myself at him, not liking my odds against his strength and bulk and meanness, but not caring. If I can get one good punch in, I'll be happy. Smash the smugness off that face, and I'll take whatever beating follows.

But it's not to be. Mira, Carnelian, and the dozen others with us close around us, pulling us apart. We break into two groups, Zander with the larger contingent, and after a few more shouted curses and threats the conflict is over. For now.

2

"I'M SORRY THAT happened to you," Mira said. "Zander is a world-class jerk. Believe me, not all of us feel like he does."

"Yeah, but some of you do. I heard the others agreeing with him. They think everyone in Eden is somehow sub-human. Weaker, less evolved than the people of Harmonia. Sure, we have a lot of technology, but that doesn't make us bad people. How else could we live in a closed system without the efficiencies technology brings?"

"Yeah, but a lot of people here are suspicious of it," Mira says.

"Not Carnelian. And you have more technology than I first realized. Anyway, Zander doesn't understand! If everyone inside had the chance to live like this, I know they would!"

"Easy there," Carnelian says. "You might be right. You know the city people better than we do. But since it isn't going to happen, why worry about it?"

His words serve to shock me out of a complacency I've slowly, almost unknowingly settled into. I've been seduced by the peace of Harmonia for too long. I can never let myself forget that inside of Eden, a struggle rages, even if the brainwashed victim-citizens don't know it. It is a war for their freedom and self-determination, and I have to fight for my family and friends inside. They would do the same for me.

"If you don't stop worrying about Zander, you're going to be too stressed to do well tomorrow," Mira tells me as we stroll toward Harmonia. We've fallen back from the others, and now we three walk alone. "You need something to distract you. Let's do something special."

"I thought that's what the Wolf Moon festival tonight is for," I say.

"Yeah, but that's for everybody. We should do something special, just us two."

"Hey," Carnelian protests. "Why not us three?"

"You already passed your test last year. You're a grown-up." She says it in a mock-solemn voice, as if he's decades older than us instead of just one year. "Come on, Rowan, what shall it be? After tonight we'll have all kinds of responsibilities. We'll have—ugh!—*jobs*!"

I'm actually pretty excited about getting my "job" after the test tomorrow. Life in Harmonia is idyllic. With no money, no conflict, and an abundance of food, most people's workday is down to about two or three hours of absolutely necessary tasks. Some of it is tedious, the household and community tasks we used to assign to bots inside of Eden: cleaning, tidying, refuse collection and recycling, and building maintenance.

Other things are more interesting: gardening, gathering, textile work, and cooking. I've found I have a knack for cooking. In Eden, all of our food was either created from algae grown in skyscraper-like urban farms, or chemically synthesized proteins, carbohydrates, and fats. Everything was ready-made in factories, or assembled swiftly and efficiently by domestic bots, so there was no real need to cook at home. I thought everything tasted pretty good back when I was still a prisoner in Eden. Then I came here.

Oh, great Earth, when I think of those poor people in their desert-ringed prison knowing nothing but the artificial taste of synthetic strawberry, it makes me want to cry. For my first real meal in Harmonia, Mira (then unknown, just a friendly face) brought me a dish of oats topped with the tiniest, sweetest wild strawberries. It made everything I'd eaten so far in my life suddenly taste like dust. With real ingredients, grown in our own gardens, harvested wild from trees, cooking was a pleasure. Mira and some of the older women taught me how to use the communal solar cookers, and I always volunteer to help whenever I can.

But it is other jobs that really pique my interest. Harmonia may seem like a truly natural place, with its orchards and gardens, but there is technology here, too, mostly subtle and hidden.

When EcoPan first released me from Eden, when I awoke in that flowery meadow on the edge of the forest and was greeted by my mom and a few other representatives from Harmonia, I was practically hysterical, insisting that they help me back in to rescue Ash, Lark, Lachlan, and the others.

They're just right over there, I kept shouting, pointing across the meadow to the scorching desert, beyond which the thicket of giant synthetic bean trees were a smudge on the horizon. *If we get the right equipment maybe we can get back inside. At least send them a message, let them know the outside world is alive and ready for them!*

Oh, how I ranted and pleaded with them. They were patient with me at first, but after I broke away and tried to run back into the desert they tranquilized me. I remember being carried, a sense of almost imperceptible movement . . . and then I was in Harmonia. I had no real idea how I traveled, or how far.

Once in Harmonia, I couldn't settle down. How could I

be happy when loved ones were still in Eden? How could any of the outsiders be content when their fellow humans were imprisoned and experimented on?

I found sympathy, but no help.

The natural-born outsiders couldn't see how I could think about going back, even to help my friends. *You earned your way out, they didn't*, I was told. They seemed to think the residents of Eden were some kind of subhuman, base and unworthy. People in Harmonia didn't like to talk about Eden at all, except as an object lesson. *That's what we will be forced into if we ever cease to respect the Earth*, they said. If we can't be self-governing and respectful, we'll have to be prisoners.

Even those few who EcoPan had freed from Eden seemed to have no real desire to help their friends and family stranded inside. They just seemed grateful to be free themselves.

I didn't let that stop me. No one would tell me where Eden was, so every time I went out, I explored as far as I could. I found no signs of it. As far as I knew then it could be ten miles away . . . or thousands. I had no way of knowing.

The elders put up with it for a while—it was usual in newcomers—but after I ran away for two days seeking any signs of Eden, they put me in intensive counseling to help me get over what they called my unnatural obsession with my damaged past. It was a form of psychosis, the counselors told me.

Maybe they didn't put wires in my brain. Maybe they didn't change my vision so I couldn't see the truth, or implant new memories. But I could see the intention was fundamentally the same: *Accept the way things are now, or else we make life here very unpleasant for you.*

No one ever spelled it out. There are no formal laws in Harmonia. For the most part, there don't need to be. There is plenty for everyone, and it is such a close knit community that everyone would know instantly if someone stole. The rare conflicts are quickly settled by the elders. Yet it was implied that some kind of punishment would certainly await me if I didn't give up my quest to return to Eden for my friends.

So after a struggle, I now play along. *Enjoy being one with the environment. Forget everything that happened to you, the people you left behind. Be a good little member of our idyllic society.*

I've had a taste of utopia before, and it wasn't as perfect as it appeared. Now cracks in Harmonia are showing. Still, it is far, far better than Eden, and my friends should be here.

I remember something that Zander said. "What did he mean *we've seen it before*? What story was he talking about?" It didn't sound like he was just talking about a thousand years ago when humans almost destroyed the environment.

Mira and Carnelian exchange a look. "We're not supposed to talk about it," Carnelian begins.

"Well, it's not so much that . . ." Mira says.

"More like no one wants to talk about it," Carnelian concludes.

"So we don't. It happened a long time ago."

I wait, and finally, reluctantly, she tells me.

"It was when my parents were about our age. Someone came to Harmonia, someone from Eden."

"We don't know that," Carnelian interjects.

"Where else could he have been from? Anyway, we didn't get notice from EcoPan, so we're guessing he crossed the desert somehow. We found him one morning wandering in a field nearby, and took him in. We fed him, gave him clothes, and then that night . . ." She breaks off, swallowing hard.

"What happened?" I prompt.

"He killed the family he was staying with. The parents,

the grandparents, the three children in the household. He used some kind of gun that dissolved part of their bodies. It was terrible. Only one member of the family was spared, a young man who was out all that night courting his sweetheart. In the morning he found them, and the outsider was gone."

I don't even know what to say. How could someone do something like that? Why would someone cross the desert, find this wonderful place, and then commit such a terrible crime?

"There's something else you should probably know," Mira adds. "The young man who wasn't killed along with his family was Zander's father."

"So Zander grew up with stories about someone from Eden killing his ancestors?" No wonder he hates people from Eden. "Whoever did that was a psychopath, though. Or, maybe they had been reprogrammed? I don't know. But how can he really think people in Eden are all like that?"

"I just know it affects him deeply," Mira says. "He hates everything from Eden, and he hates technology. So watch your back."

I'm silent for a moment, then Mira says brightly, "Enough of this! You need a distraction. I know what we can do."

"What?" both Carnelian and I ask simultaneously.

"Not you, love. You have to work. This is just for Rowan."

Carnelian sighs dramatically and says, "Work! No rest for the wicked."

Mira throws her arms around him and kisses him. "I know you love your job, so don't expect any pity from me! And maybe after the Passage Test I'll make up for it by . . ." She whispers something in his ear that makes him blush.

"On that note, you ladies have fun, and I'll see you tonight." He leaves with a huge grin on his face.

"So," I ask when we're alone. "Where are we going?"

She smiles at me knowingly. "You haven't been here long. There are a few secrets you haven't learned yet."

"Secrets?" I ask eagerly.

"Just wait, you'll see."

I get excited as she changes course and leads me away from Harmonia. Although logic tells me she's not talking about anything that might help my plan, I can't help but feel a sense of anticipation as I'm let into each detail about my new home. Anything could prove to be the clue that will help me achieve my goal of getting back to Eden.

We walk through a trackless forest. A couple of times she stops, checks the angle of the sun, and backtracks before resuming her course. "I don't come here often," she explains. "I don't want to risk anyone else finding out."

"Why?" I asked.

"It's nice to have a place that's just for yourself, isn't it? Ah, here we are."

We're standing in front of a dense tangle of rhododendrons. I know these plants—large shrubs or small trees—tend to grow in a tight, impenetrable thicket. As Elder Night said when teaching Mom and me, if you come across rhododendrons, go around, not through. People have gotten so stuck and disoriented in rhododendron thickets that they've actually had to be rescued.

"Now turn around and close your eyes."

I do, and hear the rustle of foliage, then to my surprise the clink of metal and what sounds like a latch unlocking.

"You can look now."

I turn and see her dark, freckled face peering out from the bushes, a frizz of her hair snagged on a branch.

She beckons me, excited, conspiratorial, and she reminds me of Lark. I feel my throat tighten as I remember the abandoned tower Lark took me to, her special hideout where she could think her own thoughts, dream her own dreams.

Mira holds the branches aside for me as I step through. There's a stone wall with a door fashioned out of some unknown material. I'm tingling with excitement. Can this be some secret that will help me with my plan?

As soon as I'm inside, I forget about my scheming, lost in the wonder of absolute beauty. Mira has taken me to a secret garden.

Hidden behind the double fortress of rhododendrons and walls, the garden is open to the sunlight above, and holds the most miraculous collection I can imagine. Even the nightclubs of Eden, with their fake flowers in neon colors, couldn't compare with this spectacle. I grew up with steel and concrete and symthetics—I am still in awe over a blade of real grass. Imagine how I feel seeing more species of plants in one small space than I've seen so far in all of Harmonia.

"What is this place?" I ask in amazement.

"I'm not sure, but it's old. Really old."

"Pre-fail?"

She shrugs. "Maybe. But look, there are plants growing here that don't grow anywhere in the forest. Things I've never seen in the wild."

It's true. There are exotic, delicate blossoms, fragrant buds that don't look like they'd survive in the forest or the fields. "This garden was made just for pleasure," I say. "Just for the love of plants, of beauty."

Strange as it may seem, this goes against the beliefs of Harmonia. We're supposed to live in harmony with nature as much as possible, not control it. We don't have livestock, even for milk. No domestic bees for honey, only wild ones. No pets. And though we grow vegetables and fruit, we don't have any gardens that aren't specifically useful. They have edible plants or medicinal ones. Growing something just because it is pretty is frowned upon. I find that very strange. Why wouldn't beauty be as important as food? But I'm still learning all the ways of Harmonia.

Mira pulls me in deeper. I see white statues of elegant figures—slim girls, boys with cloven hooves, a timid gazelle. A lizard with a blue tail crawls sinuously across one of the statues. Jewel-colored beetles crawl and buzz from plant to plant.

There's a fountain in the center, with a statue of a man sculpted in marble. He holds one hand out in benediction, but the other is curled in a fist. It looks almost like part of the Sign of the Seed, the gesture we make inside of Eden to remind us about the magic of life, of what we lost. But it also looks like a threat. Or maybe like someone clutching something possessively to their chest. I can't be sure.

The marble man is tall, lean, with the most benevolent eyes that seem to follow me. With a gasp I realize who it is.

"Aaron Al-Baz!"

Mira follows my gaze. "Really? I thought it must be a famous horticulturist, whoever designed this secret garden."

"You've never seen a picture of him?"

She shakes her head. They have a library, with both written and digital records, but most things are taught orally, the wisdom passed down through stories and demonstration. Harmonia kids don't sit in classrooms.

"Well, no wonder his garden is so well taken care of," she says. The fountain is pristine, just like the rest of the garden. The water in the fountain bubbles and gushes in decorative splashes in an algae-free pool. Through some trick of engineering Aaron Al-Baz seems to walk on water, unsupported.

I turn away. Seeing that vile man who killed so many people—and who continues to delude so much of humanity centuries after his death—fills me with disgust, and taints even this beautiful place. Still, it is indeed beautiful, and I look at the flowers instead. "You do all the work?" I ask.

She grins, a gleam in her eye. "Look closer at the bugs."

I peer at the tiny walking and flitting jewels. At first they seem like regular beetles. Then I notice the uniformity of their movements . . . and the fact that they seem to be working. Not just eating, or protecting their territory, or the things that insects normally do. No, these little bugs are tidying up! I watch one prune a dead leaf. When it drifts in a gentle zigzag to the ground, another beetle is waiting to grind it into tiny bits so it can more easily join the soil. Azure water bugs pluck detritus from the fountain and scour the sides.

"They're bots!" I gasp, and she nods. "I didn't think this kind of technology was allowed in Harmonia. The elders are always talking about the need for labor, to appreciate the responsibility of being stewards of the environment. They say that if bots take care of things we'll take them for granted."

I puzzle over it as I walk around the garden, marveling at the beauty around me. "No one else knows about it?" What would the elders do if they knew? Would their beliefs in keeping nature unfettered make them destroy this place? I understand that Harmonia has certain rules for a reason. I mean, we humans messed things up pretty badly before. But how strict are they? What would the elders do to keep their laws intact?

"No one knows, not even Carnelian. My father and I found this place, and this was our special spot. We didn't even tell my older brothers and sisters. I'm the youngest, you see, and Dad knew I always felt a little like the others always got the best of everything. He made sure this was a place just for us, something that made me feel special." She sniffs, and pushes her hair back from her face. I know her father died just a year ago.

"Then why did you tell me now?" I ask, curious.

She takes a deep breath. "Well, part of it is that you're hurting, more than I've ever seen anyone hurt before. People here tend to be happy. Even when my dad died . . . it was the most awful thing in my life, but it was part of the natural order, you know? It tore me apart, but . . . I don't know if I'm explaining it right. We live, we die. We rejoice when a baby is born, and we mourn when someone dies. It is part of nature, the endless cycle, and that makes the pain somehow easier to bear. Like when winter comes—we miss summer, but we understand what is happening. The pain you feel, though . . ."

She breaks off as she struggles to understand what I've been through. I've told her a lot, but not everything.

"I'd think you'd be happy here, being free from Eden. You have nature, your mom . . ."

In a way I am happy. I'd believed that Mom had sacrificed her life to save me. But EcoPan was so impressed at her dedication in keeping me safely hidden for sixteen years, and her determination to give me a real life beyond our courtyard, that it plucked her from near death.

Mom told me how she'd lain bleeding on the street, certain death was only moments away. She remembered a greenshirt kicking her in the ribs with his boot, saying, "She's not going to make it, load her up," while another hauled her up and threw her painfully in the back of a robot transport. *I'm still alive*, she tried to tell them as the bay door shut on her and the transport lumbered toward the morgue. She told me about the shock of having been shot—really shot—in the first place. The greenshirts usually used stun weapons. She couldn't believe they considered her crime of hiding a second child to be worthy of lethal force. Chief Ellena must have issued new orders around then, authorizing deadly force to anyone accused of that crime. She must have just been starting to experiment on the second children.

Then suddenly the vehicle disintegrated, Mom told me, and she was enveloped by a swarm of tiny silver bots that encased her in a sphere. When she woke up, she was laying in grass, and Elder Night and a few others from Harmonia were waiting for her.

"But you aren't happy, even though you keep up such a good front that the elders and even your mom believe you are. And it troubles me deeply to see you like this. When I think of the things you've told me that go on in Eden, it fills me with pain, too. And anger. You left people you loved behind. Will you tell me about them? I know about your brother, but there must be someone else special to make you so heartbroken and bereft."

"There was someone back in Eden," I admit. "Two some-ones, really."

She sits down on a bench in the shape of a giant tortoise. "Tell me."

"I've mentioned them before." I've told her the story of my life, more or less, all the events leading to my escape from Eden. But I left out a few crucial details. They were still too painful—and frankly too confusing—to talk about. But now the combination of this peaceful garden and Mira's friendly interest make me feel more inclined to open up.

"I'm guessing one of them must be Lachlan," she says, and I nod. "He sounds insufferable and irresistible."

"Yeah, that about sums him up. He's the strongest person I've ever met. If there's ever a hard thing to do, he'll do it. He puts everyone else before himself. He would have died to save the second children. Maybe he has." I wipe away a tear that falls down my cheek. "He's stubborn, too, and won't always listen to reason."

"Sounds like a good match for you."

"But in his tender moments, the few times he's opened up . . . I don't know. I see the person he could have been if he'd been born into a peaceful world. An artist. A father. Anything but a fighter. I think he hates all the things he's had to do to survive."

"And you love him?"

"I do," I admit. "But then there's Lark."

Mira's eyebrows go up. "The girl with the lilac hair?" Of course she's featured prominently in my stories, too. "She definitely loves you. From what you've told me, she'd stop at nothing to save you." I've told Mira how Lark infiltrated Oaks to reach me, but I made it sound more like she was helping the Underground than trying to help me. I guess I didn't fool Mira.

"I feel like I've known her all my life. She is Ash's best friend, and when I had to hide all my life, I lived on stories he would tell me about her. When I finally met her in person, the connection was magical, electric. She has this open heart, this . . . goodness about her. She really believes in a better world, and would do anything to achieve it."

Mira is silent for a moment. "There's nothing wrong with loving them both, you know."

"It means someone has to be hurt," I tell her, gently stroking the pale pink petal of an extravagant blossom. "And whatever I choose, I'm going to be hurt, too, because either way I'll be losing one of them. And that would devastate me." I look up at her suddenly. "Listen to me, talking like it matters. I'll never see either of them again."

She looks at me strangely. "And that's why I brought you here today."

"I don't understand."

"I want you to trust me," she says.

"I do, of course."

"I mean with everything. And that's why I brought you to the most special secret place I know, shared with you the one thing I haven't told anyone else, not my mom, not the love of my life, Carnelian. Because I need you to know that I can be trusted."

"With what?"

"Your secret." She waits, but I just look at her, taking care to keep my expression blank. "You're planning something, Rowan. I know it. You're not the kind of person to feel all that pain and anger and not do anything about it."

I don't answer, and she presses me. "Does it involve getting back into Eden?"

I almost slide off the bench. I try to answer, but can't make anything coherent come out.

"Come on, I have eyes, and a brain. I've seen other people who were set free from Eden, and none of them acted quite like you. They had survivor's guilt, maybe. They missed their families and made a big show about wanting to go back for them, but you could see in their eyes that they were relieved to be free, once they realized they had been in a prison. After a while, people learned to forget about the loved ones they left behind. Even your mom, and she was one of the worst. Almost as bad as you at first. But logic prevailed, and she gradually realized that there was no real hope of getting you out. Oh, don't feel mad! She told the elders she was pretty sure you were dead anyway. I mean, a teenager alone with a whole city after her? What chance did you have? Like I said, she and the others gave up. But it's a gradual process. Not with you."

"What do you mean?" I ask, playing for time, trying to figure out my lies.

"You were a wildcat when you first got here—screaming,

crying, running away until they had to sedate you. You begged everyone in Harmonia to help you get back to get your brother and friends and the second children. And then, all of a sudden, like magic, it was like you stopped caring about the people you left inside of Eden. Like all that passion and caring just got switched off. I didn't believe it for a second."

"Maybe I just saw the logic about giving in, like my mom did."

"No way. I haven't known you very long, but I can tell what you're like. You have two people you love in there, plus your brother, and a ton of second children you consider part of your family. I know for a fact you haven't given up going back to Eden and getting them out. You just decided it was better to be sneaky about it."

I study her face. "Are you going to tell anyone?"

Mira doesn't answer my question, but says suddenly, "I wish you had known my father. The things you tell me make me think of him. He was from Eden."

I'm completely stunned. So that's what Zander meant when he called her dead-eye's dughter. I had no idea. "And you never thought to tell me?"

"I couldn't," she says. "I mean . . . you still don't understand about how they feel about Eden here. They just barely acknowledge that it exists. My dad would never even talk about it. I only know because . . ."

She breaks off, and I have to press her to go on.

"No one knows. Just Carnelian, and my brothers and sisters, of course. My dad brought something from Eden."

For a second I hope it might be some kind of technology, something that can help me get back into the city and help my friends. What she tells me is even more surprising.

"He brought amazing fighting skills out of Eden. He wouldn't talk much about it, but I get the impression that my dad was very poor in Eden. That he must have lived in what you call the outer circles. He said people had to fight to survive. His family, in particular, were professional fighters. People would bet on the victor. His fighting kept his family from starving."

I've heard about such things in the outer circles, barbaric bloodsports. But poverty can make people do disgraceful things.

"He wouldn't tell me very much about Eden, no matter how much I asked. But he did teach my siblings and me how to fight. Most of them weren't very interested, but I took it very seriously."

"That seems strange, in a pacifist society," I tell her.

"I know!" she laughs. "But, maybe it was just because he would never tell me about his past, I always kind of felt that there was more to my life than just a quiet existence in Harmonia. That even in this paradise, there would be something to fight for. Now that I finally have some of the answers to my questions about Eden, things he would never tell me, I think I know why I always had that urge to fight."

"I've never seen you fight," I say.

"I know. Who is there to fight? I practice on my own. Sometimes I make Carnelian partner with me. No one else knows. You'll keep it a secret, right?"

"Oh, I'm great at keeping secrets," I assure her.

"The things you've told me about life in Eden also make me think about how my father died."

She tells me how he developed a degenerative nerve disease, so that her once-powerful father slowly diminished before her eyes. The healing herbs of Harmonia could do nothing for him. "Eventually he couldn't walk. Then he lost his ability to speak. But his mind was as keen as ever, and it tormented me to see that brave, intelligent man trapped in his prison of a body." She's weeping silently now, speaking through her tears.

"There was nothing I could do for him. I felt so powerless. I would have climbed any mountain, fought any foe to save him. But there was nothing to fight. When you tell me about the people of Eden, trapped in their prison through no fault of their own, or about people whose entire personalities are taken from them, like yours was, it makes me want to fight. To do for them what I couldn't do for my own father—to break down the prison walls that keep people from being free, their true selves. I couldn't fight a disease. I can fight a government."

She sniffs back her sorrow. "Rowan, I know you want to rescue them, and . . . I'm going to help you."

3

"WHAT ARE YOU talking about?" I ask, astonished at what Mira just said.

"I want to help you," she repeats. "Whatever you're planning, let me be a part of it."

I'm immediately suspicious . . . and I hate myself for it. Mira has been nothing but open and friendly. But I've spent too much time with people who aren't what they appear. What if she's just trying to catch me? What if she secretly thinks like Zander, that the ills of Eden have to be forever contained behind the scorching desert? She's seemed so accepting of me, but what if it is all an act? I search her face for signs of deception, but find none.

"The elders made it clear that it is against the law for me to go back to Eden," I remind her. "We're not even supposed to talk about it. If Elder Night thought we were scheming to go to Eden, she'd . . ." I don't even know what she'd do. There is no jail in this peaceful village, no law enforcement. No law at all beyond the wisdom of the elders. We might be locked in a house for a while, given calming drugged tea like I was when I was first frantic to escape. But nothing truly bad would happen to us. Would it?

"I've been thinking about it ever since you arrived," Mira

said. "There were other people EcoPan set free before you, of course, but none of them had stories like yours. They talked about living good lives, honoring the memory of the fertile Earth. They talked—at first—about the things they missed. The lights, the music, the excitement. And the things they didn't miss, like the crowds, the pressure to succeed, the long workdays, the one-child limit. But it didn't sound too terrible. Even when your mom came, I didn't realize. She was depressed for a while after she arrived. She didn't want to talk much about what happened."

But I told her stories that opened her eyes. "After hearing what you went through, what the people in the Center did to you, to everyone in there, it made me sick. I couldn't imagine someone living in my brain, monitoring me all the time. And bots everywhere, spying. I couldn't believe that Eden actually had slums, that there were people without enough to eat, living on the streets. It started to make me discontented with my own wonderful life here. Like you said: How could I be happy when so many people are suffering not more than fifty miles away?"

"Wait, fifty miles? How do you know that?"

"I overheard the elders talking before you were picked up."

I frown, considering this. Elder Night is strong and healthy for her age, but I can't see her walking fifty miles. And when I first arrived, after they drugged me, they certainly didn't carry me fifty miles back. *How did we travel?* I asked Mom, but she told me she didn't remember. She was only allowed to go to meet me if she agreed to be drugged, too. The elders kept the location of Eden a closely guarded secret.

"I don't know whose fault it all is," Mira goes on. "Is it EcoPan's fault for interfering? Is it the government? The one thing I'm sure of is that it isn't the fault of the everyday citizens of Eden. They deserve better. I can't help thinking that if they were here, out in nature, away from all that concrete and artificiality, they would be peaceful, and equal, and . . . happy!"

She sounds as enthusiastically hopeful as Lark. It makes my heart ache.

"Maybe," I say. "I don't know, though. EcoPan told me that every time people in Eden were left to do what they wanted, they went wrong. They started wars. They allowed social inequality. They messed Eden up, and EcoPan had to interfere to fix everything."

"Yeah, but that's because they're prisoners. How can a prisoner ever behave normally? If they lived out here, there wouldn't be competition, or social pressure. How can anyone hate out here in the wilderness?" Her face is aglow with faith. "If we managed to open up Eden and let everyone out, they could act like the real animals they're supposed to be. Animals don't hate each other, or control each other. If the people of Eden could only be natural, they wouldn't mess up their society."

I'm not sure if I agree with her. I feel a little guilty as I say, "I hadn't really thought about getting *everyone* out. I was mostly thinking of the second children, and Ash, and Lark."

"Well, first things first, I guess. Once we get past the Passage Test we can scheme and plan." She looks absolutely inspired now. "If we can figure out how to get anyone out, it will be a miracle."

"I had an idea that maybe when we get word that EcoPan has chosen someone else to be released to Harmonia, I can go with the elders, like Mom did."

"That was an exception, though, because EcoPan told them you were family. They want you to forget all about Eden. They know letting you that close would just set you off again. They'd never let you go. No, with that one exception, only the elders are allowed to go to meet newcomers. No, your best bet would be to get ranked first in the Passage Test. That's how people become elders."

With some regret we realize it is getting late, and we have to head back to Harmonia. When Mira has locked the garden door behind us, I say, "So if I come in first in the Passage Test, I'll be given access to information I need to get to Eden? Now that you're on my side, our chances of getting access have doubled. One or the other of us has to get first place."

"Er, coming in first place in your group isn't the same as being ranked number one."

"What do you mean?"

She goes on to explain to me that the participants are graded according to their performance in the trials, so that technically someone comes in first, second, third, and so on. But that's not what being placed in the first rank means. "It's like getting a perfect score, versus just getting the top score," she says. "We aren't graded on a curve."

To my surprise, I find out that even if I'm the best of this year's competitors there's very little chance I'll be placed in the first rank and allowed to become an elder.

"It's theoretically possible that several of us could be put in the first rank," she says. "But highly improbable. Most years no one gets in the first rank at all."

"I'd wondered about that," I say. "I just figured all you had to do to be an elder was get old! But not all old people in Harmonia are elders . . . and not all elders are that old."

"The youngest is about forty, I think."

"Wait, so the last person to get the first rank was more than twenty years ago?"

"I told you, it's rare. Carnelian did extremely well on his Passage Test, and he's only in the second rank."

I gulp. My chances at finding out helpful information seem to have dwindled.

"Don't worry," she says as we walk back toward Harmonia. "We'll come up with something. Just do as well as you can on the test, and we'll focus on getting to Eden after that. First things first!"

MIRA AND I part company at the edge of the village. After we change our clothes, we'll reunite for the Wolf Moon ceremony. In the meantime, I seek out our tree.

I call Harmonia a village. It is more like a forest of tree houses, scattered widely through the woods. Only from the top floor can I see the bubble-like structures that surround other people's trees. It is strange after the tight-packed Eden to live in a place where most of the time I can't see my nearest neighbors. Yet, it is familiar, too. In my childhood spent hidden away, I didn't see anyone but my family. It feels comfortable being just with my mom, particularly after our separation. At least now I am free to wander to the other tree houses to visit my friends, or to the more tightly clustered buildings at the center of Harmonia that surround the village green.

I walk on the softly crunching oak leaves, and even though it has been three months I still marvel. I thought I was doomed to a life of concrete beneath my feet. Actually, I thought I was just doomed, period.

Everything about this place is a revelation, a celebration. I walk around in a kind of ecstasy, in awe at the complexities of the natural world.

Here is our house, a clear, glass-like structure built on and surrounding the trunk and high canopy of a stately oak tree. The house is virtually its own biosphere. We give the tree the carbon dioxide we exhale, the nutrients it needs. It in turn bestows on us oxygen and shelter.

Every time I see our oak, I think of the camphor tree in

the Underground, which we once thought was the last surviving tree in the world, now burned to a crisp. Really, there are billions of trees on the planet. The Earth had been healed long ago, or was never as damaged as we were told in Eden. Yet in this green world, I still mourn the destruction of one camphor tree.

Harmonia is about openness, about community, about living as one with the natural world. This is reflected in our dwellings. They are made of glass in part to remind us that none of us is separate from the others, that there is no such thing as secrecy. We are equal, and anyone who glances in any of the houses can see that no one has more than anyone else. A curtain shields our bathing and sanitary facilities from prying eyes, but beyond that our lives are open books.

I look up into our tree house, and see my mother on the second of three stories. I pause in a clearing, and when she sees me she runs down the spiral walkway that connects the levels of our house. The top floor is mine, the middle floor is hers, and the lowest level is for welcoming company. There are no dining or cooking facilities. All our meals are communal, another way in which we're like the people of the Underground, the hidden second children who forged their own secret community.

Mom greets me with a furious scowl. "Rowan, you're late! Where were you? Do you know how worried I . . ."

She can't keep the angry act up for long, and we both break into a laugh at the same time as she pulls me into a hug. Our dynamic has totally changed since I came here. She used to devote all her energy to keeping me sheltered and safe. She was always paranoid that I'd do something to put myself or the family at risk. In her heart, though, all she ever wanted for me was freedom. Now, finally, she says she can give me the wings I need to soar.

After the first few days, she started pushing me to explore my new world. She wanted me to have the experiences I was denied living as a secret member of society, hiding in our house all my life. Now she encourages me to go out, to run through the woods, to climb, to swim . . . No matter how dangerous it is, she doesn't seem to worry. "Life is about risk," she tells me. "Live life to its fullest!"

I love that the worry lines that perpetually marred her face in Eden have been erased. She's so happy here, even with what she's lost. She lives in the moment now, grateful for the things that remain.

We sit together on a low log that has been sanded down to a comfortable perch. "Are you excited about tonight?" she asks.

"More nervous about tomorrow," I answer with a laugh. Mom is taking the test along with me. The test happens only once a year. The natural-born take it when they turn seventeen. Anyone from Eden takes it in the next cycle after they arrive.

"It seems strange to have a celebration the night before a test," I say. "How can any of the new candidates enjoy themselves? I don't want to eat too much, and I really should go to bed with the sun. How else can I rank high enough to become an elder?"

"Oh, sweetie, it doesn't matter what score you get! I know, it's a matter of pride. But it's not really that important as long as you finish. And there isn't really any doubt that you'll do that. Why, someone told me that a few years ago a woman in her seventies took the Passage Test."

"Really?" I ask, amazed. No one will tell me much about it, but it is rumored to be an extremely arduous test. I can't help but be worried. I've asked Carnelian over and over again what the test will involve, but even he, one of my best new friends, won't tell me any details. He won't even tell Mira! All we know is that we go out into the wilderness, and—hopefully—come back. Carnelian says it is the way every citizen proves their devotion to the land, to nature, and fully shows their willingness to be a part of this world.

Then I remember other things I've heard. "But someone told me that people have died during the test."

She swallows before answering. "Yes . . ." she drawls before breaking off and looking past me into the shadowed woods.

"And that it's mostly people who grew up inside Eden."

"But imagine what most of them are like! Soft, coddled people—and you're neither. They may have proven to Eco-Pan that they have the mindset necessary to make a good member of society outside of Eden, but life out here needs a dedicated body and adaptive mind as well as good intentions."

"It feels like just another EcoPan test," I grouse.

She opens her mouth to speak, then presses it closed again.

"We're not going to have this argument again tonight, are we?" I ask wearily. Mom was the one who gave me the journal written by EcoPan's creator, Aaron Al-Baz. We both know that he was a maniac (however good he believed his intentions to be) who all but wiped out humanity to start the world anew. And EcoPan was his creation. Mom is firmly of the opinion that the vast computer program called the EcoPanopticon has transcended its creator. She thinks that humans might be corrupt, but the duty of EcoPan is to save the world, humans included. She's had to struggle a lot with this, I know, but after I told her everything that happened to me since she was gone, and everything I discovered, she was more convinced than ever that EcoPan is benevolent, and it is only humans who ruin things.

But I've been inside the Center, at the mercy of the experiments they conduct in there. I had my identity taken from me. EcoPan allowed that, even if it was a human doing it. We are the computer program's toys and playthings, its test subjects. Its slaves. EcoPan is powerful enough to create a paradise. Instead it made a prison. If it is a god, it is a heartless one.

My mom realizes we shouldn't argue on this stressful, important night, and instead she leans her shoulder against mine reassuringly. "Whatever you feel about EcoPan, here in Harmonia it is no longer an issue for you. Out here, we're free to govern ourselves."

"But your son is still in there! How can you . . . ?"

"Rowan," she cautions. "Do you have to wound me over and over? Don't you think I mourn his loss? But to drive myself insane dreaming of the impossible—I just can't do it, Rowan. He's lost to us."

I sigh. We've had this conversation many times before. I modify my argument and say, "But we still rely on *some* technology to make our homes, modify our crops, irrigate our fields, and dispose of our waste. We have power. It might be clean solar and wind power, but we still use technology."

"Yes, but that's . . ."

"What? If there are computers and circuits and bots, what can it be but EcoPan behind it all? We still haven't fully escaped . . ."

"Hush."

"No, why won't you talk about this?" As much as I've learned about Harmonia, there are still many nagging questions. Most important, "Are we really free out here?"

"Of course we are," she says, then smiles as someone approaches: Elder Night. We don't have a president or king, but rather a council of elders who serenely and logically govern our peaceful village. I've seen Elder Night mediate the most benign disputes. One person wanted to switch tree houses,

another petitioned to keep an orphaned baby squirrel she rescued for a pet. The move was granted after some negotiation
that seemed to please both parties. However, the elder decided the squirrel had to be returned to the wild, although it
might not survive, because our laws forbade keeping domestic
animals. *We cannot risk reviving the old ways where animals
were treated as slaves*, she said.

Frankly, I don't see how keeping an adorable pet squirrel
on your shoulder and feeding it hazelnuts would lead to animal slavery.

We have no implants here—natural-born outsiders never
receive them, and newcomers from Eden have theirs disabled
as soon as they are set free—yet there is always something
or someone controlling us. I still can't decide if that's a good
thing. I know how people messed up the world once. And
EcoPan told me how, generation after generation, people inside Eden created bad governments and hurtful policies that
diminished freedom and peace. EcoPan let them, to a point,
then orchestrated a societal reset, manipulating them through
their implants so the whole city could start over.

Yes, people can be bad. But shouldn't they be given a
chance to be good, too? Don't rules keep people from freedom, and if they are free, maybe they could be even better
than the rigid rule-makers expect them to be?

These are big questions, and I bite them back as Elder
Night approaches.

"Hello, my children," she says, inclining her small, elegant head with its simple steel-gray coif. She must be nearly
eighty, but she is lovely, the few lines on her face signs of
character more than age. She always moves slowly, and at first
I thought she must have some joint pain, but the more I watch
her the more I think she is simply as unruffled as a pond on

a windless day. When she took the newcomers to the mountains to see the wolves, she hiked at a steady, unrelenting pace few could match. She seems like an admirable, formidable woman.

"Elder Night," Mom says, making the Sign of the Seed in front of her: a clenched fist rising, with fingers gradually spreading out like sprouting new tendrils in spring.

"Come now, Rosalba, no need to cling to the old superstitions of Eden."

I startle at the sound of my mother's name. Having spent almost all my life with only my brother, and my father typically absent, I've so rarely heard her called anything other than Mom. But she has such a beautiful name. It means white rose in some long forgotten language of pre-fail Earth.

"Here we don't have to worship the idea of a seed," the elder continues. "Here in nature, we instead devote our energies to actually nurturing those seeds.

"Forgive me, Elder," my mom says meekly. "Old habits die hard."

"But die they must, if you wish to be a full member of Harmonia. What a joy it is to have a mother and daughter join us at the same time, and test together."

"We are honored to be here, and have the chance to prove ourselves."

Elder Night nods again in a friendly way and is turning to go, when I blurt out a question. "Why are we ranked in the test?"

She freezes mid-turn, and I feel my mom stiffen beside me.

"I mean, I completely understand why we take the test," I add, acknowledging that as a newcomer I have to yield to this new way of doing things. "But why will some people be ranked higher than others? I look around at Harmonia, and everyone seems to be equal. There are no circles like in Eden, no rich and poor. Everyone is given an equal amount of food and resources. What does ranking matter?"

Elder Night looks at me with a twinkle in her eyes, and extends her left hand, palm up. "On one hand it doesn't matter at all, my child. We are all animals here, humble and equal parts of the ecosystem. But on the other hand . . ." She holds up her right hand, and points to the glow that emanates from our tree house as dusk is falling. "For Harmonia to survive, some of us have to be a little bit more than animals, if you see what I mean."

"I think I do," I reply. "You mean some people are allowed access to the technology that helps us lead simple lives with minimal impact on the environment."

She nods. "And that allows most of our other citizens to live as much apart from technology as possible. You are quick-witted, Rowan. An asset to the community. But speak of it no more. If you rank high in the test, you will be burdened with certain responsibilities. Nothing onerous, and you can rest easy that you are helping Harmonia survive. If you pass but don't do so well, no matter! Your life will be just as happy here." She spreads her hands wide to encompass the slowly darkening forest we live in. "We are at home in the Earth, where we belong." Her face is blissful. "What more could any of us want?"

She glides away, her lean, elegant body moving with ease over the rough terrain of roots and rocks.

Mom slaps her hands on her thighs and stands up. "Now you better get ready, young lady! The Wolf Moon festival starts in a couple of hours. Your clothes are a dirty mess, and frankly, you could do with a shower." She fans the air in front of her nose and I giggle. "I'm going to go help set up the feast for tonight. I put out the pale green linen tunic for you, the one with the hummingbirds embroidered on it. That will look pretty for tonight." She kisses me, tells me she'll see me at the festival, and heads toward the center of the village.

I take a long shower, relaxing as the hot water soothes my muscles. This exemplifies the strange dichotomy of life in Harmonia. On one hand, this is natural springwater, as pure as can be. The soap is infused with flowers—pale lavender blossoms that remind me of Lark's hair, and darker petals of verbena—so that my shower smells almost as good as Mira's secret garden.

And yet contrasted against all that naturalness is the hot water itself. We're supposed to live as much like animals as possible, but animals don't get hot water. Unobtrusive solar cells give us electricity, hot water, refrigeration. Though we grow some of our own food, we also have things like grain, bread, tea, and olive oil that we don't grow here. They are made somewhere else, and it can't be close or I would have found it on my explorations. Who grows them, who moves them, and how, I don't know. But I have my suspicion. I think there are bots growing our crops, making the extra things we need. And a transportation system to bring the food to us.

It's all so frustrating, because I feel like if I knew more about all this, it might help me get to Eden and free my friends. But there's no way to learn more until I get through the Passage Test. And even then, I might not be deemed worthy of privileged information like that.

I dry off, and slip into the outfit Mom picked out for me. The flowing tunic has two layers—a sheer, gauzy, embroidered pale green over a darker green. Together they flow beautifully, making the ruby-and-emerald-colored hummingbirds stitched into the gauze seem to flit over summer foliage. It's new, and so lovely I'm almost afraid to wear for fear of getting it dirty. Well, it should be safe tonight. Tomorrow morning

I'll put on something old and practical that can withstand the rigors of the test.

The color and embroidery are the kind of thing that Lark would like, and I wish she was here to tell me I look pretty in it, or so I could let her borrow it. I blush at the thought. If the world were different we could live like that, a peaceful, placid world of sharing and laughter. She could have that here.

I smooth down the flowing layers of my tunic and leave the cloistered private area that blocks a small portion of the glass house from the rest of the world. Now I'm out on display, as we all are at almost every moment of the day.

The neighboring houses look like giant crystal confections, brightly reflecting the sinking sun. I can see dim shapes moving in the nearest ones, and I smile as I comb my wet hair, thinking of happy families that never have to worry about being monitored, or having any family member taken away.

Then a movement below my house catches my eye. Is it Mom coming back? No, I realize, peering closer—it's Zander. He lounges against a tree and looks up at me insolently. His stare doesn't waver. Even from up here I can see the malicious smirk on his face.

In that moment all the rage I felt when he insulted me and my mom earlier today surges up in me again. There were people around us before, and they stopped us, but no one is here to stop me now. I don't care what the consequences are. I'm going to confront him. Maybe to yell at him. Maybe to force him to tell me why he hates me so much. Maybe to beat him senseless.

I slam down the comb and run down the stairs after him.

By the time I get down he's gone. I catch a glimpse of him walking into the thicker woods, and sprint after him, my fists clenched in determination. Zander is going to answer for the hateful things he's said and done.

4

I'M SO EAGER to confront Zander that I never see his two brothers. They are younger than him—one sixteen, the other fifteen—but they are close to his height and bulk. One of them tackles me from the side as I run, slamming into me with such force that I smack into the earth. I struggle, but he holds my legs while another one digs his knee in my belly. When I open my mouth to scream, he shoves a ball of moss into my mouth and clamps his hand over it. I try to fight, try to roll to my side, spit it out, bite him . . . but the moss is choking me and the only way I can breathe is to lie still and breathe through my nose. I'm pinned down and helpless.

Then Zander saunters up.

"Well, well, well, what do we have here, my brothers?" he drawls. "A piece of garbage fouling this beautiful Earth. Stinking city scum." He kneels next to me, exchanging an amused look with his siblings. Then he spits in my face.

I close my eyes just in time, but I can feel the disgusting slime sliding down my face. I'm almost glad for it. The rage that comes over me overwhelms everything else. If not for the fury, I'd be terrified.

"I'm going to explain something to you," Zander says.

"I'll use small words, to make sure you understand." His brothers laugh. "Tomorrow, you're going to fail every test."

I think he's insulting me, and I squirm against my captors, shaking my head *no*, and at the same time wiping most of his spittle onto my shoulder. Then he goes on, and I realize what he means. "You're going to fail on purpose. If you don't, very bad things will happen to you."

He leans his face very close to mine. "The elders favor people who EcoPan released. They think you must be something extra special to be picked out of a million people. They always grade the Eden scum easier than the natural-born. I intend to get the first rank, city trash. I'm going to show the elders exactly how superior the natural-born are. When I'm an elder, things will be different around here."

I make an inarticulate grunting sound of rage. "Oh, I know what you're thinking," he says. "You're thinking that just because you fail miserably, it won't necessarily mean I get ranked in the first tier. And you're right." He closes the remaining small distance to whisper in my ear. "Mostly I'm doing this because I don't like you." He chuckles, and I shiver as his hot breath touches my ear.

I slam my head into his nose, and he falls on his backside as a red spray covers half his face. "You stinking little . . ." He calls me the most disgusting names.

My satisfaction is short-lived. The next instant he's pulling my head back by the hair and screaming at me. He cocks back a fist, but his brother stops him, saying something about being too obvious, the elders will know. He manages to get control of himself.

"You're going to fail tomorrow, understand?"

I shake my head no.

He smiles, which I know is a bad sign. "I was hoping you'd

say that." He holds my hand, almost tenderly. Then he gives my pinky a vicious sideways jerk. I hear a sickening crack, feel an agonizing stab of pain that seems to travel up my arm and settle in my belly. The moss muffles my screams.

"Are you going to fail tomorrow?" he asks, taking hold of my next finger.

I shake my head, though tears are streaming down my cheeks.

He looks at his brother. "See, I told you Eden scum is stupid." Without even looking at me, he breaks that finger, too, closing his eyes in bliss at the loud crack of bone snapping. "We can do this ten times. Pretty soon it won't matter whether you agree or not. You won't be able to take the test with all your fingers broken."

I need to take it, to be accepted here, to have access to information I might need to free my friends . . .

Reluctantly, I realize that I have to play along. It might hurt my pride to give in . . . but it will hurt my fingers far worse if I don't. I nod.

"What's that?" he asks, moving on to the middle finger. "I can't understand you."

I nod more frantically, trying to say *yes* through the moss.

"Good girl," he says, patting my head. "I thought you'd listen to reason. I'm just glad it took you a while. Now, I know you're thinking as soon as we let you up you'll run right to Elder Night and tell her what happened. But remember, we can find you anytime, and accidents do happen. A lot can kill you out here. And if you don't care about your own safety, think of your mom. If you tell anyone about this, I'll . . ." He leans in to whisper again, the most filthy things, and this time I don't dare try to retaliate.

The three brothers run off, and when they're gone I spit

out the moss, choking and retching. Then I hug my injured
hand carefully to my belly, rocking, feeling in shock.

This is supposed to be a peaceful paradise.

———

FOR A WHILE I'm too shaken to walk. Finally I drag myself
to my feet and walk in a daze back toward the heart of Harmonia, cradling my injured hand. I can't go to Mom. She'd
know right away that something is wrong. Part of me wants
to scream to the entire village what just happened. They'd
have to believe me, right? My broken fingers, his broken nose,
the dirt and tears . . . there's ample evidence. But I haven't
heard of any kind of punishment system here. It really isn't
needed. What would happen to him, so that I'd be safe? He
wouldn't be imprisoned or banished. He's right—he can find
me, or my mom, anytime he likes. And in a world that's supposed to be without crime, with hardly any laws, what's to
stop him?

I never thought I'd say this but—what I wouldn't give for
a greenshirt and a couple of securitybots right about now.

I realize with a start that too much peace and harmony
can have its own dangers in a civilization. All it would take is
a few more like Zander and his kin to turn this from a placid
egalitarian society into a violent dictatorship where might
makes right. Maybe a society needs prisons and punishment.

For now, though, I need to pretend that everything is
okay. I'll put in an appearance at the Wolf Moon ceremony,
go to bed early, and then do my best on the trials. I'll face
whatever consequences come later.

If I didn't have any intention of telling Mira or anyone
else, I probably should have looked in a mirror before going
back to the village.

At first they don't notice. Mira and Carnelian are sitting

near a bonfire, so I join them. The flickering firelight dances over me, and I try to make normal conversation, holding my throbbing hand in my lap.

"Do you know, there was really no such thing as a fire inside of Eden," I tell them. "We didn't have much that could burn. Everything was man-made—no wood, of course—and it was made to be fire-resistant and safe." I chuckle. "Couldn't risk a big fire in a closed system. It's still so remarkable to me to see real logs burning."

"Oh, they're not real logs, Rowan," Carnelian says.

Mira snorts. "Did you really think we'd sully the Earth with ash and carbon monoxide and all the garbage that comes with burning wood? That we'd chop down trees just to see the pretty fire?"

Abashed, I scowl at not having figured that out myself. I don't take the slightest offense at Mira's directness. That's just her way. She might be a little bit abrasive, but she's already proven herself to be a caring, loyal friend.

"What are they burning, then?" I ask.

"Totally synthetic," Carnelian explains. "They bring them in from . . ." He breaks off, biting his lip.

"From where?" I press.

"I'm not supposed to talk about it," he says, looking away.

I roll my eyes. "You know how I *love* secrets."

Mira nudges me with a laugh, and I manage not to wince as she jars my injured hand. "You don't think I've tried to make him talk? And I have methods you never even dreamed of!"

"You'll find it all out after the Passage Test," Carnelian says with confidence. "I'm sure the two of you will come out in the first or second tier. There are about a dozen participants this year, a bigger than normal group, and you two easily out-class most of them. After you rank, you'll know everything

I know, more or less. Believe me, it isn't that interesting. Just maintenance stuff for me so far."

Mira's a nature lover like me, always wanting to be running in the woods like a deer, studying animals, climbing things. Carnelian, on the other hand, is completely into tech. He always begs for me to tell him about all the innovations in Eden.

Carnelian goes on, "I can't wait until I've progressed far enough they let me get my hands on the coding, or ride the hypertubes to other facilities!"

My heart is thudding hard at what Carnelian just said. Hypertube access! Other facilities? That must be how they get to distant Eden so fast. And I knew there must be places besides Eden and Harmonia, and Carnelian just confirmed it! But I don't dare ask any direct questions. For one, if I do it will remind him that he's said too much and he'll be more careful next time. For another, I don't want to give him a clue to what I am planning. Later I'll ask Mira not to tell him, though I'm guessing she assumes that anyway. I don't think he'd like the idea of her helping me with my foolhardy plan.

The more I learn, the more seems to fall into place. It's nothing like a plan yet, but I feel closer than ever before.

"You look lost in thought," Mira says. "Bet I know what you're thinking about." She shares a conspiratorial wink.

"No, I'm just . . ." I begin, and turn to face her. The firelight illuminates my face fully for a moment, and Mira gasps.

"What happened to you?"

"Nothing. I . . . I fell down."

"Yeah, right. Your tunic is torn. And . . . is that blood?" Carnelian notices, and peers at me, too.

"It's not mine," I say.

"Like that makes it any less of a story!" she says with a snort. But I can tell she's really concerned. "What happened?"

"Your hand is hurt," practical Carnelian says.

I try to hide it, but he takes it carefully in his and starts talking about how to set the bones, the best way to bind the fingers to each other for proper healing, exercises to do to maintain mobility after they mend.

"Yes, Carnelian, that's fascinating," Mira finally interrupts. "But what we should be talking about is exactly how this happened." She glares at me. "And don't you dare tell me again that you fell down!"

"I don't want to talk about it. It's better if I just take care of him myself."

"Him? Who would dare . . . Oh! Zander?"

I don't want to confess, but she reads me perfectly.

"I'll kill that bikking . . . Ugh!" She seethes. "We need to go to the elders." But when I tell her why I'm against the idea, she reluctantly agrees. "Then we need to teach him a lesson ourselves. Between the two of us we can take him on." Her hands are balled into fists.

I don't know about that. He's a big guy, strong from a lifetime of hard outdoor work. He makes the residents of Eden seem soft by comparison.

"Please, just go along with me on this, guys. We can figure out what to do after the Passage Test. I think if I tell anyone I'll just make things worse right now."

She can see things my way, though I can tell she's itching to take action. Even Carnelian argues for telling the elders, but he respects my wishes.

"Just don't let your mom find out," he says. "You know no force on Earth would keep her from telling the elders. Or more likely beating up Zander herself."

"Then help me act normal by having fun tonight!" I say, forcing a smile. "For now, I need to try to put Zander's attack out of my head. Tomorrow, though, I'll be alert for more treachery." Carnelian won't let me go without getting me a cup of herbal tea he swears will lessen the pain. It tastes bitter and strange, but a few minutes later the agony has subsided to a dull ache.

All the lights of Eden's fanciest entertainment circle can't compare with the warm dancing glow of a bonfire out under the stars. The fire crackles, and if the logs aren't made of wood, well, I can't imagine anything more realistic.

Somewhere, a reed pipe is playing a haunting melody. Elsewhere, someone sings. Closer to the fire, a group of people beat drums in a complicated rhythm. Most of the villagers are dancing on the close-cropped grass.

I try to remember the happy crowds I saw on my first night of freedom. Neon colors, garish lights, gaudy clothes, smiles so huge they couldn't be real . . . Everything in Eden was fake. Maybe even the emotions. After all, with EcoPan having its electronic finger in everyone's brain, how could anyone know what they really felt? Maybe all that fun of the elites of Eden was an illusion.

Here, though, I believe that people are truly happy. They don't have half as many possessions as the people in Eden, but what they have is real. Including their emotions.

Mira rises to dance, pulling Carnelian along behind her. He slouches and stomps with no sense of rhythm, and I have a feeling he'd rather be sitting somewhere talking instead of dancing. But I also see the glow in his eyes when he looks at Mira, and I realize that making her happy is what makes him happy.

"Join us?" Mira asks.

"I like watching," I say.

"You're not stuck behind a wall anymore, Rowan. You have the whole world—you might as well be dancing in it!"

She's right, but it's still hard to escape that feeling of isolation and separation imbued into my childhood.

"You need some time alone, without me hanging on," I say.

She looks quickly serious. "Rowan, don't *ever* think that! There's enough love and friendship for everyone." Then her eyes crinkle in laughter. "Besides, we wouldn't be such a good couple if we didn't have other people to distract us from each other." She winks at Carnelian, then looks back at me. "We can't fight in front of you."

I know she's kidding. Different as they are—she active, abrasive, and fiery, he calm and introspective and logical—they still seem to be a perfect match. I like being with them just to watch their happiness, the way they tease each other, the undertones of affection behind every word. They give me hope.

As I watch them dance, subtle memories of Yarrow come to the fore, and I realize that she has memories—false, implanted memories—of a lifetime of dancing and socializing. I let her take over, and she makes me join the other dancers. I show my friends some of the popular dances of Eden, and they laugh at them, but before long I see them being copied by people all over the village green. I don't like to let Yarrow out too often. I lost myself in her for so long that I worry she might take over again. But sometimes she can be a useful ally.

Night deepens, and I pull Mira aside and say, "Shouldn't we call it a day? We have to get up early, and who knows what's in store for us tomorrow."

She shakes her head, and the movement turns into a sway, then a shimmy of her irrepressible body. She can't help dancing, moving. In the woods she runs as fast as me, and is an even better tree climber, though I'm better at rocky walls. Lately she's been teaching me a series of tumbling exercises she's mastered, and though my body still doesn't feel like it's obeying me, I can do basic flips and handsprings now.

"Tonight we live, for tomorrow we may die," she says merrily, but her words make me shiver. I wish I knew what we would face tomorrow. Every year has different tests, so Carnelian couldn't tell us much anyway, but he could give us an idea. If only he wasn't sworn to secrecy . . . or his ethical standards were looser. "Besides, you have to stay for the presentation. Look, it's starting!"

THE REVELRIES HAVE calmed as if by mutual agreement, though I heard no signal. The full moon has risen directly overhead. Drawn by the sudden movement of the villagers, I follow toward a dais at the edge of the village green. Elder Night mounts the stage.

She picks her way carefully, deliberately up the steep stairs, but needs no assistance. With a sense of utter calm she paces to the center of the stage and waits for quiet.

"Another Wolf Moon has come," she intones, and though she doesn't shout, her voice is easily heard even where I am at the back of the crowd. "And we celebrate the benevolence of the Earth that has allowed us to be part of nature, not separate from it. Every year when the full moon rises red in the sky we come together and remember the sins of our ancestors, the crimes of our species, and we renew our solemn vows to never fall into the same trap as they did. May this bloody moon remind us of our blood deeds, so that we may never repeat them. May it remind us of the wounds the Earth has suffered because of us, so that we may heal them."

She flings up one arm, the sleeve of her linen gown falling back to reveal lean muscle and sinew as she points at the huge russet moon. The call it a blood moon, but I have seen blood in its every variety, flowing and freshly spilled crimson, slick and vital, as well as the blood of old wounds, dried and rusty. No, the moon is not quite like blood. It is more like blushing bone, a ghostly, ominous red, a bloodshot eye looking down on us.

Elder Night steps to the side of the stage, and new figures mount. For a moment they look perfectly normal to me, and I can't figure out why a frisson of nervous laughter runs through the gathering. Then I realize they are dressed like people of Eden, in loud colors and synthetic fabrics. The clothes don't flow like our soft linen garments do here in Harmonia. Instead they have odd angles, features without function, stiffness and creases.

The essence of Yarrow that remains in me looks on them with approval. *Last season's fashion*, she murmurs in my head, but she admires the tight boned bodice, the square lampshade skirt, the fairy lights imbued in the fabric that make it seem even more alive than the wearer. Not bad, fashion-conscious Yarrow thinks from her refuge in my head.

I stroke the thin, comfortable wrinkles of my linen tunic, pale green, dyed with lichen, and think how lucky I am not to have to wear plastics against my skin.

Seeing those actors pretending to be in Eden makes my heart ache with a painful mixture of mourning and hope. Realistically, I know that some or all of them are back in prison, or dead.

Or worse.

Which would be worse, really? I know the Chief wants to have second children for her mind-altering experiments. They never felt the interfering touch of lens implants, were never meddled with by EcoPan, and Eden's head of intelligence came up with unique and torturous ways to alter a person's very identity, to give them new memories. Or even, as she did with poor manipulated Pearl, to wipe them completely clean.

I'd almost rather Lark and the others were dead than tied down with wires probing their brains, stripped of their true selves.

And Lachlan, where is he?

I always think about him before I fall asleep. I think about the night I spent in his bed, chaste but so intimate. I think about the way he's saved me, the way I've saved him. We've fought side by side. Every night as I look out through the glass that barely separates my bed from the natural world, I imagine laying in his arms, safe.

But every morning when I wake up, the first person I think of is Lark. The joy of her smile. The wonder of her kiss . . .

And the rest of the day—whenever my mind wanders from agriculture demonstrations, Natural History classes, and the hundred tasks and lessons I have to get through to catch up to the natural-born—I think about Ash. My twin brother, my other half.

Once, my love had been mixed with resentment that he had been firstborn, condemning me to the life of an illegal second child, always hidden, always in danger. But after I found out that I was really the firstborn, that he had taken my place because he could never survive his debilitating lung condition without extensive medical care, I was proud that I had been able to sacrifice myself to save him. Later, I learned that his lung injury had been caused by our own father, when he tried to solve the "problem" of twins by aborting one of us. He chose Ash to live, but accidentally hurt his unborn son, while unwanted I was born healthy and whole.

I told Mom how my dad tried to redeem himself by saving the imprisoned second children. I don't know if she forgives him. I don't even know if I do. What does it matter, though? We'll never see him again. If against all hope I manage to break back into Eden—and even more improbably break out again—it certainly won't be to rescue *him*.

I shake my head and try to focus on the Wolf Moon ceremony. The actors put on a pantomime of high living and excess. One mimes driving a car that belches out acrid fumes, while another has a little device that seems to let her inhale toxic smoke directly into her own lungs. People around me shake their heads at the stupidity of our forebears.

"Look upon what we once were," Elder Night proclaims. "We are still humans now, but we are a different kind of animal than our ancestors. Different, primarily, because they forgot that they were indeed animals. In the pride of their species, thinking that their great brains and opposable thumbs marked them out for a special destiny, they disregarded the natural laws, the proper harmonies that govern nature. They set themselves above the Earth—so high above, that when their fall came, it was catastrophic."

In an instant the mummers rend their bright clothes, tearing them off to reveal sickly gray rags. Some unseen stagehand unveils a red lantern that casts a molten glow over the actors. They pull ashes from their pockets and scatter them high so they rain in a downpour, then swirl with each frantic dancing step the actors take.

"Thinking they had become gods, thinking technology would be their salvation, humans thought they'd found a way to stop the climate change that threatened to destroy the planet—and still be able to burn the fossil fuels they loved so much. They created a self-replicating particle that was supposed to regulate the atmosphere, control greenhouse gases, stop the rapid warming of the globe."

The dancers and actors are frenetic now, tearing at their

skin as if it burns, writhing in a pantomimed agony that is both terrifying and beautiful.

"The fools!" Elder Night shouts. "Selfish, shortsighted fools! They could have changed their lifestyles, destroyed their cars, let the good of the Earth prevail over big businesses and their ravening hunger for money. But no, they wanted to have it all. They sent their particles into the atmosphere, but they had made a terrible error. They had interfered too much with the natural order of the planet, and she had enough. The entire Earth rebelled, destroying itself to save itself."

The actors slow now, holding hands and looking lost as they wander through a wasteland. "Most humans and animals were wiped out. The few survivors would have been doomed, if not for the foresight of our hero, our founder, the creator of the EcoPanopticon: Aaron Al-Baz!"

The villagers go crazy, cheering and shouting and stomping their feet for a man long dead, for the man they believe to be their savior.

The man who voluntarily destroyed human civilization.

I wanted to tell them as soon as I got here. I was astonished they didn't know, that they still believe the myths and lies told inside Eden. They think Aaron Al-Baz is a savior. But really he was a madman, an environmentalist and genius who made a unilateral decision to wipe out humanity for the good of the planet. He created a virus that killed all but a fraction of a percent of humans. More than seven billion people dead in the span of a week! At the same time, he unleashed a program, the EcoPanopticon, that took over every computer system in the world. EcoPan used computers and factories and the defense system—everything with a wire or a chip—to make an army of robots. EcoPan was tasked with two things—save the planet, and preserve humans.

EcoPan, logical as any machine, saved humans by imprisoning them in Eden. It implanted lenses in each survivor to monitor and even alter their thoughts. It made them think they were the lucky few, the chosen, when actually they were the survivors of a mass murder. It kept them in prison and fed them lies so they wouldn't try to escape. It told them the Earth was destroyed, even though EcoPan managed to restore it after only a few generations.

And for all the power it held over the survivors, for all the good an all-powerful program like EcoPan could do, it still allowed inequality and hate and poverty to thrive inside of Eden.

It let humans be their old horrible, selfish, shortsighted selves to each other, as long as they didn't harm the Earth. Its prime directive from its creator was to keep the species alive. It didn't care who suffered or died in the process.

I hate that these people—these supposedly free people—believe that Aaron Al-Baz was a good man.

As for EcoPan, I'm not sure how I feel. It's a machine, subject to the will of its creator. And yet it has grown to such an extent, makes its own decisions . . . I just don't know. I am grateful that it managed to save some of humanity, a million or so out of the billions that used to roam the planet. I'm grateful that I was set free to live in the natural world. But I resent EcoPan because it could do so much better. If we have to rely on technology to survive, shouldn't that technology make the world truly a paradise?

It would be nice if just once EcoPan would ask us our opinion about the way it is running things, Yarrow says inside my head. She's a pain, but she makes me chuckle sometimes.

Mom knows, too. She's the one who gave me Aaron Al-Baz's handwritten journal. When I talked to her about whether we should share our knowledge, she advised against it. "We have no proof. The journal is still back in Eden somewhere." I have no idea where it might even be.

It feels so wrong, though, hiding the truth from people. However upsetting it might be, however much it might shake the foundations of their faith, isn't it better that they have all the information? Then they can decide for themselves. Maybe they want to believe the lie. Maybe it is easier. But they should be free to choose.

I've zoned out as the Wolf Moon pantomime continues. Now Elder Night draws it to a close. "Tomorrow, the newest members of our society, and the youth who have reached the age of seventeen, will prove themselves in the wilderness with a series of three tests. They must understand that we are no more—nor less—important than any other part of nature. Never forget that. We have our place here as much as a bacterium or an ant or a wolf. We evolved to fill a niche. Never believe yourself above any other living thing. And yet, don't let yourself be ashamed of your species either. We have made mistakes, but we fortunate few have learned from them, and our descendants will never forget the lessons we will teach."

She throws back her head and utters an unearthly cry, like a wolf's howl but higher pitched. All around me, the villagers imitate her in long ululations. The noise is overwhelming, and suddenly I can't take it anymore. I shove my way through the press and head for the quiet of home. As I turn away, though, Mom finally finds me.

"Hey you! I saw you across the crowd but didn't want to miss any of the ceremony. Come try the hazlenut cookies I made." She grabs my hand, and I can't help but cry out. Her face becomes instantly serious and she looks at my crooked fingers. "What happened? Did you slam them in a door? Let's get you to the healer, maybe she can . . ."

She notices my dirty, rumpled tunic, peers more closely at my bloodshot eyes. "Rowan, sweetheart, what happened to you?"

I shake my head, but somehow my eyes flicker across the village green, to where Zander is holding court with his two cronies and a few girls, talking in a loud voice. I tear my eyes away from him almost immediately, but Mom notices and follows my gaze.

"That piece of . . ." I blanch at her words, shocked that my gentle, peaceful mother could use such language, even now. Then I remember how she fought to give me a good life, how she sacrificed her life to save mine, and I realize that there is no force on Earth stronger than a mother, whether it is Mother Nature, or my own mom. I'm suddenly afraid of what she might do.

She charges across the green, a terrible light in her eyes, and though I grab her arm I can't seem to slow her down. She's like a mother bear protecting her cub. Zander and his brothers don't notice her until she's almost on them, and though Zander must outweigh her by fifty pounds, and towers a head over her, even he shrinks back under her furious gaze. He gives a little nervous laugh, and Mom tenses, prepared to . . . I don't know what. Scream at him, accuse him before all of Harmonia, lunge for his throat.

Before she can do any of these things, Elder Night appears, serene as ever, seemingly unaware, or perhaps just unconcerned about the drama unfolding.

"It is time for the candidates to toast the Wolf Moon," she says, as behind her come other elders with carved, polished wooden goblets on trays.

A cup is thrust into Mom's hand, another into my own. Mom looks at it, then tries to give it back. "Elder Night, you must know that . . ."

I tug her back by the arm, and she shakes me off so hard that I spill a third of my drink down my tunic. "Mom, please!" I hiss at her. "Not now! Talk to me about it first!"

Her nostrils are flaring, and her teeth are actually bared, but my words break through and she steps back.

"This isn't over," she growls.

Elder Night smiles at her benevolently. "On the contrary, it is just beginning." She addresses all the dozen people participating in the trial, who all now hold cups of a deep reddish-purple liquid that clings stickily to the sides of the goblet. "Now, raise your cups and salute the Wolf Moon, the Blood Moon, the great Eye of the Night." I look up at the pale red orb, and it does seem to look down on me. Does it approve of what it sees? It makes me think of the green faceted dome at the Center, in Eden, that glowing green eye that seemed to keep watch over all of that prison city. We are watched everywhere.

"Now drink!" Elder Night cries. "And may your eyes be clear, your ears sharp, your heart pure, and your mind like that of an animal. Let the Earth guide you home."

I take a sip. It is sweet, sticky, obviously alcoholic. Yarrow thinks it is delicious, if a bit unrefined. I don't like it, but luckily a lot of it spilled, and I don't have to swallow as much as the others to seem polite. Mom seems to like it, gulping it down quickly. The murderous fire drains from her eyes.

I feel strangely relaxed, too, and grin at Elder Night as she is turning to leave. Then I remember something that bothered me about her speech earlier. "You said that humans evolved to fill a niche." My tongue feels thick.

She nods. "We are only animals, like any other." It is a common refrain here in Harmonia.

"Wolves evolved to live together in packs, to respect a leader, to hunt and kill their prey."

"Yes," she says, looking like she wants to get away, like she has more important things to do tonight.

"And that is natural, right? Because the Earth led them

to fill that niche?" I feel like I might lose my train of thought any moment, and hurry to blurt everything out. "And a virus evolved. It might make us sick, wipe out an entire population." I shiver, thinking of a world of piled corpses, of the stench and rot that must have followed Aaron Al-Baz's murderous travesty. "And rats evolved to sneak at night, and birds to fly, and some snakes have venom. Things all evolved their different natures in order to survive. You tell us we cannot hate the rattlesnake for biting, or the nettles for stinging. It is what they are made to do, and it is up to us to learn to understand them."

"Yes, child, we are all part of nature."

Then I shock her. "What if we humans evolved to be destructive? What if that is our purpose? What if our place in nature is to destroy it?"

She gasps, and her mouth gapes for a moment. Finally she tightens her lips into a fine line and says only, "Finish your wine, child."

I look into the depths of my cup where the liquid swirls, fascinated by the movement, the sheen of moonlight on the wine. For a while I'm lost. Did I just say something? Was it important? I can't remember. A hand touches mine, tilting the cup to my lips, and I drink deeply, down to the slightly bitter dregs.

After that, I know nothing . . .

TOO MANY TIMES in my life have I woken up having no idea where I am. At least this time, I have a pretty good idea *who* I am.

My eyes are grainy, like they're filled with nanosand, and there's a strange sour taste on my tongue. The remnants of Yarrow that still lurk in my brain recognize this as the aftereffects from some drug. *And not the fun kind*, she adds sarcastically. Lately, she's taken to having her own narration inside my head, sounding like an annoying, more experienced sister.

It's dark, but a gray sort of darkness that I know my eyes will adjust to in a few minutes. Right now I can only see nebulous shapes around me that could be rocks or boxes or bears, for all I know. But I can't hear anything beyond a muffled echoing sound, like a great and peaceful creature breathing.

The floor beneath me is hard, and I can feel that my body is stiff and cramped. Then I moan in agony when I try to roll to my side and forget about my broken fingers, almost squashing them. I reach out carefully with the other hand and find that the floor is cool and uneven: stone. Natural stone.

The faint light is coming from some distance away, a pinhole window giving enough light that I can just now tell that

I'm in a cave. The echoing sound is the flow of air coming in from the cave mouth, snaking past me into tunnels of untold depth.

"Mom?" I ask, against hope. My voice bounces weakly off the walls. More loudly I call out, "Hello?"

Hello . . . hello . . . hello. My voice returns mockingly to me from deep within the cave.

Light from the entrance glints off something nearby. I reach out my good hand, and touch a perfectly smooth metal ball. The second my fingers meet it, it seems to explode into blinding light that, as my pupils contract, resolves into a projected image of Elder Night.

"Good morning, and good luck as you begin the first of three tasks that will usher you into full membership in the community of Harmonia."

Her image in the hologram looks so serene and composed. Obviously *she* isn't hungover from being drugged. It must have been in the wine, I realize. No wonder she was so adamant that we all drink it. I try to piece the likely events together. We were drugged unconscious and transported to separate locations. But where? And how?

The hologram of Elder Night goes on. "You have been given no supplies to aid you in your missions. Remember, we are only animals, and as such we must be suited to survive like animals in the wilderness, without any food or weapons or tools except for those you can gather yourself. You must weigh the benefit of pausing to fashion tools, or gather medicinal plants or food, against the necessity of speed. For you will be ranked in order of completing your task. But remember, this is not just a race but a test of judgment, and of your inner qualities."

The hologram seems to fix me with bright birdlike eyes, and though I know this is prerecorded and the same thing is being seen by every competitor, it feels like she is talking to me

directly. "Some of you believe you have an advantage because
you have spent all your life in Harmonia, living in the forest,
comfortable in the forest, with seventeen years of knowledge
about wilderness survival. But the native-born should not be
arrogant or complacent. Remember, those who were freed
from Eden are here because of all the population of that prison
city, they were deemed the best of the best—most compas-
sionate, bravest, respecting and protecting the Earth. Whatever your origins, I wish every one of you the best of luck."

Zander must be seething when he hears those words! I
wonder if he's listening right now. I wonder if some of the
competitors will miss out on first rank because they slept in.
Or did I sleep in? I have no idea how late in the day it might
be. In a panic at losing time, I roll to my feet, anxious to get
started. Then I force myself to sit again. Elder Night hasn't
even told me what my first task is! My legs bounce nervously
as I wait for her to continue.

"Living in a community, as part of the land, requires sacrifice. Will you put yourself in danger to help a member of
your tribe? In the Trial of Earth, we will find out."

Her image vanishes, replaced by a schematic showing a
long, broad valley. Stylized stars mark seven places along the
rim, equidistant apart. A pulsing star flashes in the middle. I
take in a confusion of topographical information, showing
elevation and waterways, but can't really decipher the details.
"Here you will find a member of Harmonia who has been
gravely injured. You must reach them, and give them as much
medical aid as you can. If you do not reach them by midday,
they will die. The Trial of Earth begins now!"

For just an instant the image remains, showing the geo-
graphic obstacles between me and the person I have to rescue.
I try to memorize it, but the next second it is gone. All I'm
left with is an impression of some extremely difficult terrain.

I tap the metal sphere, but it stays stubbornly unresponsive. I guess I'm not going to be given any more information.

I'm night-blind again from the aftereffects of the hologram. Lights pulse against my eyes in the darkness of the cave. But even though I can barely see, I stumble and trip as fast as I can toward the entrance. The contest has started, and I have to go as fast as I can!

But the contest isn't the most important thing. There's someone hurt out there, a member of my community. I have to help them. So what if others are also en route to them. What if they don't make it, and the person is lying in the forest hurt and alone?

I stub my toe on an unseen rock, and that forces me to stop and think. This is a test. There's no one actually hurt, just someone pretending. It might not even be a real villager, just a target. Maybe it is another hologram ball, projecting a simulation, and we have to say how we'd treat a real person.

The realization that no one is really in peril calms me a bit, and I pick my way more carefully toward the blinding glare of the cave mouth. It's full daylight. I might be hours behind everyone else. I can't take the time to think and worry and ponder anymore. If I want to win, thinking isn't a luxury I can afford. I'll just run out of the cave at my top speed and . . .

I skitter to a halt at the edge of a chasm. Rocks break loose under my feet and tumble over the edge. I watch them as they fall . . . a long, long way down.

The cave opens up onto a huge valley, miles across, heavily forested in the interior. I'm looking down over a vast expanse of green treetops. I can see the rocky cliff walls in a broad, almost circular section of valley. Dark spots hint at other caves. From the schematic I guess that some of them might hold the other candidates.

Or did. They might be at the target site by now!

I can't think like that. That's a defeatist attitude. Just focus on yourself, and do this to the best of your abilities. Don't worry about the other people in the test.

I'm a little reassured when I remember how Mom knocked a lot of my wine out of my cup. I probably got a smaller dose than anyone else. I hope that means I woke up sooner. I have a good chance of being the first one to start this test. If only I can finish it.

Taking a deep breath, I look more closely at the cliff face below me. It is steep, almost perfectly straight, but I can see plenty of handholds, and the rocks don't look too crumbly or sharp. I should be able to make it down without too much problem.

My mood begins to brighten. It is almost as if this challenge was designed for me. I've loved climbing since I was little. Though my only wall was the one surrounding the courtyard of my house, where I spent the first sixteen years of my life hidden, that wall was a challenge. Natural stone, with the narrowest of hand- and footholds, it taught me a great deal despite its limitations. Once I was out in Eden, I found my aptitude for climbing served me well.

This won't be exactly easy, but it won't be impossible for someone like me.

Mira should have a pretty easy time of it, too. The kids in Harmonia learn to climb with ropes and pitons, but she's strong and gutsy enough to figure out free climbing pretty fast.

I worry about my mom, though. She's not as young as she used to be, and though she's fit, she spends most of her time on low-energy activities, like gathering herbs or studying birds. Still, she's smart and careful. She should make it down.

Stop thinking, I tell myself. Stop worrying. Be like an animal and just do this.

Then I remember my broken fingers.

Easy as I tell myself it would be, the truth is any climb on an unfamiliar face is dangerous. You have to be in top form to minimize risk. With my hand crippled, I don't know if I can do it.

But I have to.

I look down at the ruin of my beautifully embroidered tunic, and sigh. The hummingbirds are spattered with dirt and blood and the dark mulberry splotch of wine. I wish someone had warned me to wear something more practical to the Wolf Moon festival. I never dreamed I wouldn't be able to change. Oh well, I might as well accept that it is ruined, I think, as I tear a strip from the bottom.

I'd like to have a stick to use as a brace, but there's nothing suitable in the cave. I make do with just binding my two broken fingers together, as straight as I can manage. While I'm doing it, it hurts so much that tears spring to my eyes. After my fingers are immobile, though, it subsides to a dull ache. At least Zander didn't break my first or middle finger. Without the use of those, I wouldn't have a chance. This way, though, I might be able to keep those broken fingers out of the way. It will be hard, but my only other choice is to admit defeat. That's something I'll never do.

Without another thought I lower my legs over the edge and turn to face the wall. I keep my body neutral against the rock, neither hugging it nor pushing off. At the first good toehold I start to relax. I'm like a squirrel, or a mountain goat—a natural climber.

Before I know it the cave entrance is ten feet above my head. The injured fingers aren't as much of a hindrance as I'd feared. *How do you like that, Zander?* I think smugly. The treetops are still fifty feet below me, and the ground who knows how much farther. But this is comfortable. This is where I belong.

I settle almost into a trance as I descend. My muscles are like instruments, and this climb like improvisational jazz. There's some predictability, some patterns, but the details keep changing. It's beautiful, really like an art form, and my body sinks comfortably into the effort, happy to be straining and sweating. A fall from this height could kill me, but I'm not afraid. I feel free.

This is what life should be like—a natural life. *This* exact moment exemplifies everything that was missing inside of Eden. Here it is me—muscle, breath, hands, and brain—against the rocks and trees and wind and wilds. No, not against. The wilderness might be something I seem to struggle against, but it is more like a partner in a wild dance. I try to choose the steps, the direction, but sometimes I have no choice and nature takes the lead.

I breathe deeply of the cool, mossy scent of the rocks, the sharper smell of the forest canopy that is just now even with me. Only another thirty feet or so to go, and I'll be on the ground. From there I'll do the other thing I do best—run. I'll run like a deer, like a wolf, swift and strong through the forest.

I've never felt so alive!

Here, down lower, the rocks have vines growing on them. In the determined, tenacious manner of all life, the roots have wedged themselves into the tiniest fissures and grown, anchoring into cracks that have slowly widened over the years. The rocks are looser here, but no matter. The vines have taken hold firmly, so I use them, too.

The thick, flexible vines feel like they were made for my hand. I lower myself another ten feet using mostly the foliage. It's thrilling, like using Mira's climbing ropes—so much faster than feeling for each handhold, testing it, searching for another. I swing sideways from one to another, the wind swooshing my hair away from my sweaty face. It doesn't feel like a contest anymore. It just feels like fun!

I shouldn't have let myself relax into the fun. The vines gave me too much freedom. That last swing took me too far from the other vines, and there are no good holds in the rock anywhere within reach. Bik! I'll have to swing pretty far back.

Holding onto the vine with one hand, I push a bit off the rock face and swing myself sideways, reaching with the other hand. I can't quite reach.

I push again, harder this time, and see the nearest hold is just an inch away. The next one ought to do it.

I've already committed to the hardest swing of all when I feel the vine's roots start to give way.

I scream as the handhold I'm straining for slips out of reach and I'm in freefall. I drop almost a dozen feet before the vine unfurls down to a secondary set of roots. Somehow I manage to hang on as the sudden stop jerks my arm violently. I judder and smack hard against the cliff face, smacking my forehead hard.

For a few seconds I hang there, stunned. I don't move until blood starts to drip into my eye. Luckily it is my blind eye, so it doesn't affect my functioning, but it is intensely annoying.

Though the wound is minor, it forces me to take things a little more seriously. Anything can happen to me out here. I could be hurt and trapped in the wilderness for days, slowly dying, with no one ever coming to help. I wipe away the blood, acutely conscious of my own vulnerability.

Blinking away drips of blood that are more annoying than worrying, I make my careful way down the last stretch of cliff face until with absolute relief my feet touch the flat earth. When I think of lying crippled on the rocky earth, my broken body prey to any passing predator . . .

It is all I can do not to kiss the ground.

I press the wound for a few moments, and luckily the bleeding stops. But it also makes me think about the victim I'm supposed to be rescuing. I know it isn't real—it will just be someone pretending to be hurt—but I have no doubt my treatment will be graded in great detail, as if a life really depended on it.

I remember Elder Night's holographic advice, and think maybe I should try to find some of the healing herbs I've been taught about. When I first started exploring the forests and fields all of the plants looked the same to me. Mostly, I was so overjoyed at actually seeing real live plants that the fine details were lost on me. Now, I can recognize some of them. Not nearly as many as most residents of Harmonia, though. Mira, or even Zander, could probably heal anything with plants they could find within arm's reach.

I set out as best I can figure in the direction marked by the holographic map. There were lines indicating a stream, I think. If I can find that, it looked like it flowed past the target point. I should be able to follow that easily enough. If only I can get there before the others.

Before I've gone very far I hear a twig snap. I whirl, but see nothing, and though I hold my breath, there is no sound beyond the breeze and the rustling trees. Zander, I think at first. But no, he emerged from one of the other caves ringing this valley and would be to eager to complete his first trial to stalk me.

What if some predator has picked up the scent of my blood? There are wolves out here, cougars, bears . . . Elder Night might say that wild animals seldom attack humans. But seldom feels a lot less like never when you're alone in the woods covered in blood.

I start walking again, and for a while all is well. Then I

hear another branch shift just out of sight. It sounds for all the world like it was crunched under a paw, or foot. This time I don't stop, but try to vary my pace so if whatever is making the noise is matching my stride to stay hidden, I'll throw it off the pattern. I think I hear something . . . maybe. I can't be sure.

"Hello?" I say softly. Of course no one answers.

It is just my imagination. Or a hungry bear. Either way, I didn't really expect an answer.

When I quicken my pace, though, the faint almost-sound speeds up, too.

If it is indeed my imagination, I have a better—and bigger— imagination than I thought. I break into a run, expecting to be pounced on any second . . .

7

I THINK SOMETIMES the fear of seeming stupid is all that makes me brave. Like now, I'm running through the forest at top speed being chased by . . . probably nothing? I mean, I definitely heard something, but as someone who spent their whole life without hearing so much as a chirping sparrow, frankly all the noises out here sound kind of threatening. The first time I heard all the ruckus a squirrel can make, I was sure a bear was going to pop out of the shrubbery. Mira had a good laugh about that one. I'd practically climbed onto her shoulders!

Now I'm sprinting terrified from a cracking branch. Come on, Rowan! It's far more likely it was a deer or a raccoon than a predator. Herbivores outnumber carnivores. Anyway, humans aren't natural prey for any predators. Any sounds I hear now are probably nothing more than chipmunks fleeing in terror from the giant biped crashing through their home!

This makes me laugh, and I slow, and finally stop.

Nothing reaches my ears but the sound of breeze and birdsong, the faint buzzing of insects, and the sound of my own thudding heart.

Whatever it was, or wasn't, it's gone now. I resume a quick

hiking pace toward where I guess the center of the valley lies. The underbrush is too thick to run right here, anyway.

Slowing down a bit gives me a chance to look at my surroundings more closely. It also gives a fly a chance to settle on the blood that's dried to a crust over my eyebrow. I pluck a few leaves of things I recognize, but I don't think any of it is really going to help me. There's a plant called boneset, but I can't remember how it is supposed to help mend bones. Do I feed it to them, or just slap it on their broken leg? If I can find the stream, there might be a willow tree growing near it. Mira once told me that willow bark is good for headaches and fevers. But I think she said it had to be made into a tea, and when I find the victim there won't be fire nearby, or water, or a pot, or a cup . . .

This is useless, I decide. I don't know enough to compete with the natural-born. I know to hold a broken bone still, apply pressure to a wound . . . and that's about it.

Abandoning my hunt for herbs, I move more swiftly now, getting used to the tangled forest floor. The trees are huge, far bigger than the camphor tree in the Underground. Some have broad, dark green leaves, and I recognize them as oaks. Others, standing alone with little clearings around them, are the kings of the forests, the mighty redwoods. Elder Night told us that to the north of us, many days' journey, are a kind of redwood that gets even taller. But these already seem impossibly huge. Just looking up at them makes me dizzy.

I find that the ground is more clear under the redwoods than under the other trees, so I chart a zigzagging path that takes me from giant to giant. It might be a little bit longer in absolute distance, but I feel like I'm moving more efficiently. At least I'm not getting snagged on brambles at every step.

From the lightning-fast view of the schematic, it looked

like it would only be a couple of miles to the center of the valley, but after an hour I still haven't found my goal. The foliage is so dense that it could be twenty feet away from me and I might never know, if the supposedly injured person didn't cry out.

Did I pass the center? I'm disoriented, and I have to take a quiet moment to calm myself and reorient my thoughts. I stand with my eyes closed, my hands at my side, listening, feeling, sensing the way Elder Night taught me. Become one with the forest, and it will tell you its secrets. I open my eyes, and take in the world around me.

Details come to me that were lost in my earlier rush. I remember gradations of color in the foliage. In some places the trees seem a slightly richer green. Of course, trees growing closest to the stream are going to be just a little bit greener and healthier. I can't see the water, but I can tell where it is.

In that moment of stillness I hear a step. Though a little part within me flinches, I have a new connection to the wilderness around me and I can tell at once that it isn't a human step. I'm not afraid. Very carefully, I turn my head and see a deer step clear of a bramble patch.

She sniffs the air, but I've lost whatever civilized smell I once carried from Eden and I smell like her world now. She's not afraid either, but accepts me as another animal, not a predator but a peaceful creature like herself.

I remember the first moment I caught a glimpse of the outside world, when the earthquake shut down the man-made desert and I reached the edge where I could see a flower-filled meadow and a forest. A deer had stepped into the clearing, the most magical thing I'd ever seen. Even after months in the wilderness, it's lost none of its magic.

She looks behind her, makes a gentle sound, and a dappled

fawn trots into view. Less dignified than its mother, it dances on impossibly elegant legs until it trips and stumbles near me. When it gets its spindly legs back under itself, it sniffs my leg.

Tentatively, I reach out a hand and stroke its white-spotted coat. I'm mesmerized. Never have I felt such a part of nature.

Then another sound interrupts us, this one unmistakably human. With wide, startled eyes the doe bounds away, her white tail a beacon for her fawn to follow. In an instant they are gone.

I turn, and see Zander.

Then, before he can even threaten me, Mira comes into the clearing.

"What a nice surprise," Zander says. "I can take out two Eden scum at the same time. After this I'll just find your mother and . . ."

My fists ball up, but Mira is much faster. She makes it look like a beautiful dance as she steps nonchalantly up to him and without apparent effort throws him over her shoulder and slams him on the ground.

"It's all in the hip," she notes to me as she keeps hold of Zander's wrist. She twists it when he tries to stand, and puts her foot elegantly on his throat. "Move again, and I break it. I go for bigger bones than fingers."

Fury and fear vie on Zander's face. He wants to fight, but he won't risk being disabled for the tests.

"Now, when I let you go, you're going to scurry along like a good little bunny, and you're going to leave my friend alone. You saw how easy it was for me to do this, right?" She tweaks his wrist, making him wince. "What do you think will happen if you try to retaliate? I'll just leave that to your imagination."

She lets him up and steps back. He stands unsteadily, rubbing his wrist, obviously yearning to retaliate. Wisdom prevails this time, though, and with a foul curse he runs off into the forest.

"That was the most amazing thing I've ever seen!" I gush.

"Admit it, when I told you I could fight you had your doubts."

"Er, maybe. I certainly never imagined anything like this. It was . . . beautiful." I never thought I could see fighting as beautiful.

"You won't have to worry about him for a while." She hugs me tightly. "Great Earth, am I glad to see you!" she says. "I feel like I've been wandering through the woods forever. What happened to your face? Don't tell me it's nothing. That's going to leave an awesome scar! Lucky! Do you know where . . . no, never mind. I forgot we're competitors! But I know it has to be around here somewhere."

"I know where to go. Come with me."

"No," she says firmly. "I'm not a cheat."

"We can use any resources we find in the wilderness," I point out. "Well, you found me!"

I want to get the top rank, of course, but there's no way I'm going to abandon Mira. She still refuses, but I have an idea. "Here, I'll draw you a map. Then we can race each other there. We're so close you'd find it in a few minutes anyway. This makes it more friendly, and fun."

"But I know you really, really want to win."

"So do you. But I've learned to never turn your back on your friends, no matter what. Anyway, it's not just about getting there. We still have to treat whoever is there. And I won't help you with that!"

Mostly because I probably can't. Mira's pockets are stuffed with an assortment of herbs I can't begin to recognize. She'll probably know exactly what to do for the patient.

She nods, then hands me a stick and clears away leaves from a patch of forest floor. "Draw away!"

I sketch the way to the target and show her the right angle to keep the sun over her shoulder, and when she has it down, I scribble out the map with my toe.

"Be careful," Mira says. "Zander is out here, too, and if he catches you alone . . ."

I grin at her. "He has to catch me first. And so do you. Go!" And I take off at top speed toward the rendezvous.

8

FOR A WHILE we run companionably side by side. But this is a race, not friendly exercise. The river has to be just ahead, and I think the site will be to the right once I cross. So I veer away and in a moment she's out of sight. The foliage changes gradually, and I know that any moment I'll reach the stream.

Ah, here it is! I hear the melodious sound of water, and part a wall of ferns to find a broad but shallow stream. Tumbled rocks line the bed, and bigger boulders lay scattered across the waterway. My face lights up. I can jump from stone to stone and cross without even getting my feet wet! I'm over within a minute, scaring silvery trout with my shadow.

Upstream, where Mira must be crossing, it looks like the stream narrows. It is probably deeper there, with a swifter current. She won't have such an easy crossing. She can swim very well, of course, but when she comes out wet on the other side it will slow her down. Not much, but maybe enough to give me an advantage.

For just a moment I pause, listening. I don't hear her. For a moment longer I wait, picking up one of the smooth oval river rocks and tossing it restlessly from hand to hand. Well, this is a competition, and I'm sure she made it safely across.

I jog off in the direction where I'm sure my first trial awaits, squeezing the smooth stone in time with my pace.

I notice a change in foliage again, then the woods seem brighter. The trees are more slender, farther apart. Soon I have to shade my eyes when I step out of the shadowy forest into a bright meadow.

In the middle is a slab of stone. On that stone is a woman dressed in a white dress, lying with her arms folded over her chest like a sleeping princess in a story. There's no one else in the meadow.

I start to walk up to her . . . then break into a run. I can see a huge red stain spreading across her white dress. I know it isn't real, but something takes over in me.

"What happened?" I ask, but of course it doesn't matter. I do this first thing, the most important thing—I press the heel of my hand hard into the deep crimson stain that is blossoming from her abdomen. She makes a low moan, but doesn't speak. The blood is warm beneath my palm. It feels so real!

I check the rest of her body while I keep applying pressure, but this seems to be the only wound. What could it be from? There are no guns here. A knife? Was she gored by a boar? I have to shake my head to make myself focus. It's just a sponge or bag of blood hidden beneath her dress, to simulate bleeding.

"Don't worry," I can't help but tell her. "It will be okay. I'm here to help you."

Only then do I finally look at her face.

It is the face of a stranger.

In my astonishment, I accidentally let up pressure on her abdominal wound, and I feel hot blood seep against my palm. Harmonia is small, with only about three hundred people. I don't know them all well, but I thought after a few months here I was at least familiar with everyone.

But I've never seen this woman before in my life.

Her eyelids flutter, and her lips move as if to speak. "It hurts. Cold . . . so cold." With my free hand I feel her forehead. It is cool and clammy with sweat. "What happened to me?"

"I don't know." Whoever this woman is, she is an excellent actor. I completely believe that she is disoriented and in pain.

"There was a knife . . ."

"Hush," I tell her gently. "It's going to be fine." Of course it is. When I'm finished with this test, the next person will come and do the same thing. I look at the white dress, the bloodstain, and realize that there are no other fingerprints on the white linen fabric. The blood has welled from what appears to be a fresh wound. That must mean I'm the first one here!

But that is only half the battle. I still have to save her.

I press down for a while longer, but when at last I dare to take my hand away and check, the blood wells up again.

"Bik! This isn't working!" I want to ask her what to do. After all, Elder Night said we can use any resources, and this unknown woman, probably a natural-born, surely knows more than me. But as soon as I look into her startlingly blue eyes, they roll back in her head and she passes out. I need to do something else, and soon.

I look over my shoulder, feeling frantic. She's dying! I press two fingers to the side of her neck and feel her pulse growing slower as her life ebbs away. How is she doing that? Did they give her some drug?

There has to be some herb I can use. At least if I try I might get some credit. Even if whatever I do wouldn't save her in real life, I was first here, and if I can just make a good show of trying, I should be graded well. Is anyone even watching? Is my patient the one grading me?

Think, Rowan! Remember your lessons from Elder Night, or your walks with Mira. She'd babble on and on about this plant and that, and I'm ashamed to say I tuned out the details sometimes.

I know there are plants that can help stop bleeding and keep wounds from getting infections. One of the best, Elder Night said, is cobwebs. Yet somehow it doesn't seem that a bundle of stuff that came from a spider's rear end would be too sanitary, and I don't see any spiders right away, so I skip that. The only other thing that comes immediately to mind is honey, and that isn't any help either.

"Why couldn't you have had a broken bone?" I ask the woman, who appears to be unconscious.

I turn as far as I can while maintaining pressure, scanning the sunny meadow. There has to be something here. I recognize chamomile, and even remember what it is used for . . . but this woman doesn't need a tea to help her sleep. I see at least twenty other kinds of plants in the field, but my brain won't latch onto any of them. Some look vaguely familiar, though. I remember a couple of names, but not a single thing about their medicinal qualities.

Yarrow, says a stealthy voice inside my head.

"Quiet," I say out loud. Am I going totally crazy? My implanted alter ego is having way too active a role in my life.

Yarrow, she says again, and I can't believe the fabricated version of myself is actually trying to have a conversation with me.

"Yeah, I know who you are, now be quiet!" I hiss as I think. Great, now my patient will report that I'm a crazy girl who talks to herself.

Then, with a little gasp, I realize what she means. What *I* mean.

Here and there, scattered amid the grasses and daisies

and thistles, I see plants with tightly bunched clusters of tiny white flowers and feathery leaves. The plant is called yarrow, and now I remember Mira pointing it out. It's one of the best herbs for staunching blood flow, she told me on one almost-forgotten walk. I noted that I could have used some multiple times in the last year . . . and promptly forgot that tidbit of information. Luckily, the other person living in my brain didn't.

Sheepishly, I say, "Thanks, er, Yarrow."

I can *feel* her roll her eyes inside my skull.

Oh, great Earth, is this the new normal for me? I truly hate to admit it, but I might almost be getting used to her. She can be helpful, and it's nice having someone who understands me. For all our differences, we have the same core.

Finally, I have something helpful I can do. But then I realize it's no use because I can't just walk away to pluck them. Even if I run, she might bleed to death while the pressure is off. I sigh. Do they have to make this so hard? Since all this is fake, why don't they just have one of the elders here so we can just tell them what we'd do in a real-life situation.

I guess that wouldn't achieve the super-high stress level I'm feeling now. That's part of the test, too, I'm sure.

I turn, gauging the distance, the time it would take me to run there and back, and realize the risk is too big. I better just apply pressure and say reassuring things until the test is over. I switch hands, wiping the very realistic blood onto my pants. My hand brushes something hard. It is the river rock I absently picked up earlier. I'd slipped it in my pocket when I found my target. Suddenly, I see what I need to do.

My linen shirt is finely woven, and once I worry a frayed piece with my teeth the hem tears in a long strip. Carefully, using the three functional fingers of one hand and any other body parts I can to brace and angle the fabric, I shift the angle and keep tearing until I have a long strip. Shifting quickly, I move my hand and put the stone over the place where the supposed wound is, where the blood is flowing under the ruined white dress. Then I carefully wind the strip of cloth around the woman's abdomen. The first strip goes around twice, and I tie it over the rock so that the pressure is concentrated on the injury. That buys me enough time to tear off another long, narrow strip and reinforce the first.

There, that should hold enough pressure to give me time to gather some yarrow plants. The woman lets out a low moan. "I hope I didn't make it too tight." It must be uncomfortable having a rock pressing into your gut. She doesn't break character, though, and her eyes stay closed. Okay then.

I run to the edge of the meadow where the yarrow is growing, pluck a few of the feathery fronds and crush them until my fingers feel moist from the juices. The leaves smell bitter, but good, too. I grab up another handful. Elder Night says that to be a good steward of the Earth you should only take a little bit from each plant. Never pick so much that the plant dies. Now I grab at them so eagerly that I pull up the roots, too. Well, maybe I'll be deducted a few points, whatever the grading system is. I'm just proud that I came up with yarrow in the first place.

I jog back and unwind the bandage just enough to reach the wound. Looking closely for the first time, I see a rent in the fabric. Will she change to a fresh dress for the next person? I wonder. If this was real, I'd have to get the herb right on the wound, so I hook my fingers in each side of the hole in her dress and tear.

Her pale bare skin is marred by a gaping hole. I can see a thin layer of yellow beneath the skin, then the dark red of muscle tissue. With a gasp, I recoil. No makeup or sponge soaked in red dye can give that kind of realism. That looks like a real wound.

But . . . that's not possible.

Feeling sick, my hands trembling, I pack the crushed leaves the deep gash and bind the wound up again. I watch the wound anxiously. Soon the blood flow ceases.

I did it.

The woman opens her startling sky blue eyes and sits up, perfectly at ease.

I realize I'm breathing hard. This was as strenuous as running, as fighting. Having someone's life in your hands is completely draining. Even if it is fake. As it must be.

"Well done, Yarrow," the woman says serenely.

For a second it doesn't register. Then I blink hard and say, "I'm Rowan."

She frowns for a moment, seeming to look inward. Then her face breaks into a broad smile. "Of course, how silly of me."

"Are you . . . okay?"

"Of course," she replies.

"Who are you? I've never seen you in Harmonia, have I?" I don't want to seem rude, but I'm sure I'd remember her.

"Of course," she says again, absently, and reaches out for my arm. At first I think she's patting me, thanking me, congratulating me. Then I feel a sharp sting and the world goes blurry.

"Not again," I say in exasperation as I slip from consciousness . . .

9

THE AIR IS cooler, crisper here. When I open my eyes, the blue of the sky seems somehow translucent. For a moment I lie here, knowing another test awaits, but enjoying the clarity and simplicity of the moment.

I hear a moan beside me. "What now?" someone says. I roll over and see one of the other candidates, an apple-cheeked girl named Lotte. There's someone else lying just beyond her, still unconscious.

Looking around, I find we're all here, in various stages of waking up. I count, glad to see that all twelve of us made it this far. Well, I'm glad about eleven of us . . .

"Mom!" I cry, and jump to my feet. She rubs her eyes and gives me a sleepy smile.

"How did you do on the first test?" she asks.

"I don't know. I found the injured girl, and treated her, but . . ."

"A girl? I had an old man with a broken leg."

That's strange. I thought we'd all headed to the same person and place. "Did you know him?"

"I . . . I'm not sure. I think it must have been one of the elders in disguise. He didn't look familiar, but I mostly focused on the leg. I was so glad I managed to cross that huge river."

"What? The place I crossed wasn't deep or wide at all. I was worried about you climbing down the cliff, though. I'm glad you made it."

"Cliff? I didn't have to climb."

I realize we must have had slightly different tests. I wonder if we were all directed to different locations, if we were even all in that valley.

"Wow!" I hear Mira say behind me. She's on her knees, looking out over a vast blue body of water that stretches as far as the eye can see. There's not even a breath of wind, and the water's surface is like a mirror, reflecting the pellucid blue of the sky.

"Is it the ocean?" I ask in wonder.

Mom strides to the edge and dips her fingers in, smelling and then tasting the droplets. "Fresh," she announces to everyone. "It's a lake."

"Shut up, City," Zander says. He's sitting a little bit away from the rest of us, hands on his knees as he looks over the lake. "Of course it's not the ocean, and we don't need a sub-human like you to tell us that."

I clench my fists, but the pain in my two broken fingers convinces me that this might not be the best time to challenge him. *Get through this*, I counsel myself. *There are more important things to think of, like your friends in Eden.*

"What do we do?" Lotte asks. "Are we supposed to work together on this one?" Her knees and knuckles are scraped bloody. Whatever her first challenge was, she had a hard time of it. I bet she's hoping for a little help now.

"Tests are always individual," Mira says, coming to stand beside me. "But there are *some* of you I'd be willing to help." She glares at Zander. At least I have people on my side this time. I decide to ignore him.

We're interrupted by a gentle hum that draws our attention

to another silvery ball. I watch an image of Elder Night form, the hologram strange and ghostly in this clear bright light.

"Good afternoon, my children," she says in her soothing, serene voice. "You have completed the Trial of Earth, and now you come to the next trial. Your task is to go to the ancient city and therein recover an artifact that symbolizes a reason our old civilization fell. You must complete this task by nightfall. You will be judged not only by your speed in reaching the city, but also by your choice of artifact. In this trial you must learn to know without seeing, to look beneath the surface of things. You must also trust that the wisdom of the elders will not allow you to come to harm. My only further advice is this: when you find the city, go beneath the domes and your path will be easier. Good luck, and may the Earth bless you, my children."

For a moment we are silent as the image flickers and is replaced by a scoreboard showing our respective ranks. We're divided into two clusters. Mira, Mom, and I are in the highest ranking so far, along with Zander and several others.

"That just shows our relative positions in two general sets," Mira says. "The top competitors, and the bottom tier. We're doing well, but there's no way of knowing if we have any hope of getting ranked in the first category at the end." The display fades and vanishes.

"No map this time?" Mom asks.

"Great," Lotte says. "The city could be anywhere."

I look around. Before us, the lake spreads uninterrupted. Behind us, curving around us, are mountains. The tallest ones are farthest away, with snowy white caps.

"We're a long way from home," I say in an undertone so only Mom and Mira can hear. "Have you seen mountains like this before?" Mira shakes her head, and I try to calculate the distance. I've been on daylong excursions from Harmonia, and when I tried to run away I was gone for two days. If we were within fifty miles of this place I'd surely have seen the tops of these mighty peaks. "We must have taken one of the hypertubes," I realize. "Here, and to the first site. We could be hundreds of miles away from Harmonia."

"I just hope they let us be conscious for the ride home," Mira says. "Think how fast those things must go! We're missing all the fun."

A network of hypertubes! There must be some way to take advantage of such a huge system. If I can find an access point . . .

"They should have given us a map," Lotte whines, and most of the others seem to agree. "How do they expect us to find a city out here without any hints?"

"They don't expect *you* to find it," Zander says as he stands up and scans the mountains. "But I know I can. Ancient cities were scars on the Earth. A city will leave signs for hundreds of years if you know what to look for. Don't any of you even think about following me," he adds as he starts off away from the river.

"Forget him," Mom says. "If we have a system and work together, we can cover a lot more ground. I bet that's part of the test—to know when to cooperate. Quinn, Lotte, if you take the south then Rowan and I can scout north, and the others can branch off in between. When we find any traces, we let everyone know. That way we start on equal footing, and we can work independently to find our own artifact."

It's a good idea, and I applaud Mom for her ability to organize people. Only, I think Lotte's wrong. I think Elder Night did give us clues. There's a nagging feeling in my head that the answer is more simple than anyone thinks, if only I could see it. If only I could—what was it Elder Night said? Learn to see beneath the surface of things. It is a lesson everyone should learn. If the Center officials had been able to look past the letter of the one-child law and see the second children as valuable people, things inside of Eden would be different.

Of course, I think wryly, if they had been able to look beneath the surface, literally, they would have found the Underground, the second children's hidden shelter, and then the illegal residents of Eden wouldn't have had a chance.

As Mom is organizing the expedition, and I'm thinking about the Underground, I suddenly break into a laugh.

"Beneath the surface!" I say. "Know without seeing. I know where the city is!"

"Where?" Mira asks, excited.

I spread my arms to the vast lake before us. "Right here."

They look at me like I'm crazy.

I don't have any idea how it got there, but I know for a fact that the city is under the lake. But there's only one way to prove it.

Rather than trying to explain my crazy hunch, I kick off my shoes and wade in.

For the first few steps it is shallow. Minnows shimmer as they flee my feet. Then the bottom drops out from under me abruptly, and I sink with a sputter all the way under. I bob up, shocked fully awake by my sudden dunking, and turn to give the other competitors a thumbs-up before striking out with a smooth stroke. Every once in a while I pause to look down under the water, but all I can see is a pale sandy bottom.

The water is cold, and I'm getting tired. Maybe this wasn't the best idea. Zander probably found an old highway and is following it to the city right now, while I waste all this time on a foolish idea. He'll be ranked first, and I'll be ranked . . . I don't even know what the lowest level is.

But I can't bear to go back and climb out onto the bank in defeat, a wet, shivering, bedraggled failure. That thought pushes me farther out into the lake until I try one more look. I swim out for another few strokes, then dip my head under the water.

At first I only see a blur, and my heart sinks. I'm still over the flat, featureless bottom, same as ever. Then the ripples from my swimming dissipate, leaving the surface clear enough for the sun to shine strongly through. There, far beneath me, I can make out a grid of uniform lines.

I have to come up for a breath. "It's here!" I shout, but duck down before they can yell anything back. I have to wait again for the wavelets to clear, but when they do I can see not only what must be city streets, but also the roofs of buildings, all laid out beneath me. It's hard to make out details through the water, but there's no doubt that it's a city trapped under the chilly lake waters.

My head pops up again, and I gulp a few deep breaths. On the last one I hold it, and tuck down in a dive, kicking hard, striving for the rooftops. The pressure builds as I swim down ten, twenty feet, until my ears pop and equalize. I shake my head, and work my jaw until my ears feel normal. I could go down a little farther, but my lungs are starting to cry out for air. Reluctantly, I kick back to the surface.

"The city is down there!" I shout to my mom and friends waiting for me on shore, but it is too far away for them to hear me clearly, so I start the long swim back. Their shouted questions become clearer as I near the shore, but I save my breath for swimming.

Part of me wishes I'd kept my revelation to myself. This is a competition, after all. Maybe we're mostly proving that we personally have what it takes, but there's also an element of showing that we're better than the other people in the trial. Having grown up in Eden, Mom and I are at a disadvantage. These people have been swimming their whole lives, and I know they can swim farther, dive deeper, hold their breath longer than I can. Now that I've showed them the secret city, they'll easily surpass me. Maybe I should have gone off with them to search the mountains, then doubled back to investigate the lake on my own, or just with Mira and Mom.

No, I decide—that's exactly the kind of thing that Zander would do. But these people are my friends, my neighbors. I'll be living with them for the rest of my life, and what good is a community whose members don't look out for each other? I wouldn't be happy with myself if I didn't help my friends.

I made the right choice. I can only hope that the elders look at it that way when they judge.

I stagger out of the lake, shivering, and Mom rubs my arms to warm me up as I tell them what I found. Some are skeptical, thinking it was just rocks, that my mind saw what it wanted to see. "No," I assure them. "I've had too much experience doubting my reality to be easily fooled. That's a city down there."

We waste no time in heading out, agreeing to swim out together then once we're over the city to explore on our own as we search for an artifact to present for the trial. As we're about to go in, I hear an unwelcome voice.

"What are you doing, going for a swim? That's no way to win." It's Zander, strolling back to see what we're up to.

"Oh, did you find the city already?" I ask with mock sweetness. "Well done."

He looks at my sopping wet body, then his eyes widen as he understands. "Beneath the surface, eh?" I expect him to be mad that he didn't figure it out first, but he just takes off his boots and shirt and starts toward the water's edge. "Don't start feeling smug, city scum. You might have found it, but I'm the best swimmer in Harmonia. You don't stand a chance. I bet your patient died on the last test."

He laughs, and steps confidently into the water.

Lotte, everyone's friend, calls, "Look out, it drops off!" just a moment too late, and I have the gratification of seeing Zander plunge down just like I did.

Then we're all in the water, striking out for the deep. It feels almost like a game now, all of us swimming together. Almost like the capture-the-flag game I won yesterday morning. Part of me is enjoying the easy camaraderie of people my same age. But part of me remembers how yesterday's game could have turned out. So I take care to stick to Mom and Mira, and we all stay away from Zander. He's right, he's much more confident than any of us in the water. I'm just glad he's so focused on getting the best artifact and being ranked first that it doesn't occur to him to try to drown me.

As soon as we're over the flooded city, they start to dive down. I wait, watching, to see what they come up with, taking advantage of the opportunity to rest as I tread water. They are down longer than I can hold my breath, but one after another they come up empty-handed.

"The bottom is too far," Lotte says as she gasps for breath. "I can almost get to the rooftops, but not any farther."

Everyone else has the same report. Though he doesn't deign to say anything, Zander hasn't retrieved anything either. I can see his scowl as he takes three deep breaths in rapid succession and dives down for another try.

I make a few attempts, but I can get no farther than the others, not even reaching the top of the tallest roofs. There aren't any artifacts up there that I can see, even if I could reach it. I start to consider whether I can pry off a piece of a building . . .

Mom, as usual, has some good ideas that rely on teamwork.

"If we weighted ourselves, we could sink faster," she muses. "That way we could get to the bottom before we ran out of air and got exhausted. Maybe if we held rocks."

"But how would we get them here?" someone asks. "We can't swim with rocks."

"We could build a boat, or no, a raft. Something just strong enough to carry the rocks, and we could push it out here and take turns going down."

They like the idea, but the sun is sinking lower in the sky. We might only have a couple of hours until sunset. Could we build a viable raft in time?

"Or we could fish for things," Mom offers a little desperately. "The way ancient people used to catch fish for food. Make a line with vines, weigh it down, fashion a hook for the end. If we drag the streets we might snag something."

They are good ideas if we had plenty of time. I still felt like there must be a clue in Elder Night's message. "What did she say about a dome?"

"Go beneath a dome," Mira quotes. "I didn't see any domes, but if we can't reach street level, I don't see how we're going to get below a dome even if we find one in the first place." Her shoulders heave in an exasperated sigh, making the water around her ripple.

Some of the other testers are talking about heading back to shore, either to construct something, or in hopes that over the generations an artifact might have washed up on shore. It wouldn't be following the letter of the elder's instructions, but it might be better than nothing, they're saying. Mira looks undecided.

"I'm not ready to give up," I tell her. "There's more to the city than this little bit we've seen. I'm going to look for a dome."

"What's the use if you can't even . . ." she begins, but if I hear any more protests I might give up. I start swimming farther out. Mom and Mira follow reluctantly. The few who are staying in the water float and watch.

The water is surprisingly clear and still, but despite that I can only see things more or less clearly straight below me. Beyond that everything fades into a bluish blur. It is impossible to scan ahead, to search for anything resembling a dome. It will be a matter of luck if I find anything. I swim for a long time before I see directly beneath me a roundish golden smudge that looks different from the square and rectangular building tops.

I don't want to announce it yet. Everyone would come over, and they'd be disappointed if I'm wrong. And maybe there's a part of me that wants to succeed all on my own first, before I help out anyone else, even if I will share my information eventually. So without a word even to Mira and my mom, I dive down to investigate.

Once I'm down about ten feet, I can see that I was right—it is a burnished half sphere, with lines in the same color radiating out from it. From above, it looks like a resting octopus. I kick as hard as I can, pull with my arms, and still my lungs are burning long before I reach the golden dome.

Maybe, if I gave it everything I got, I could reach the dome. But I don't believe I'd be able to get back to the surface afterward. At least, not conscious. I've read that in the salty oceans people float easily, buoyed up by the water. If this was salt water, I would probably rise back to the top with minimal effort. But in this fresh water it is almost as much of a struggle to rise as it is to swim down. Even if I could make it to the dome, I'd have to save something for the return trip.

"It's no good," I tell Mom and Mira as they swim over. "It's there, but I can't make it."

Mira tries several times, resting between each attempt, warning me about the dangers of blacking out if she doesn't give her body enough time to get rid of excess carbon dioxide. We float together, despondent. My only consolation is that no one else has figured out a way to get town to the sunken city.

Mom never runs out of hopeful ideas. "We could get hollow reeds and build a long breathing tube. We could fill gourds with air and weigh them down with rocks at intervals of ten feet. It might be enough for one breath . . ."

Mira shakes her head. "We only have another couple of hours." Already the sun's low angle makes it a little harder to see under the water. It would be a lot easier if it was directly overhead.

"Well, if we fail, at least we all fail together," I say. "Maybe that is part of the test, to accept that some things aren't possible. Or she wants us to come up with something clever, like the artifact that caused the most damage to the environment isn't in the drowned city—it's us!"

"Clever," Mira says, floating lazily.

I run through Elder Night's words again. She clearly said to go beneath the dome, that it would make it easier. What else did she say? Oh yeah, trust that the wisdom of the elders wouldn't allow us to come to harm.

I sit up suddenly—or would have sat up if I wasn't floating on my back. As it is, I mostly make a big splash as I curl myself upright. "I'm going to try one more time," I say, trying to keep the excitement out of my voice. This might not work, and if it doesn't . . .

If I tell them, they might try to talk me out of it. Or Mira might volunteer, being the better swimmer. Which does make sense, but since I thought of it, I should be the one to take the risk. I won't put either of them in danger.

I slow my breathing, slow my heart, force myself to be calm. Five very long deep breaths, then three very quick shallow ones with strong exhales. Then, finally, one last deep full breath.

Quite possibly my *very* last breath.

10

I WISH I had been swimming all my life. Even in this stressful trial, the utter peace that seems to come over me as soon as my head is submerged is astounding. My pulse slows automatically, my thoughts become somehow both more calm and more focused. I feel as if I've been welcomed into a different world, a weightless dimension with no sharp edges, where everything flows smoothly, even my thoughts.

I pull myself deeper beneath the surface with strong, slow strokes, kicking my feet with a rhythm like an easy jog. The golden dome looms closer with each stroke. This time I make it farther than I have before, so close that I can make out de signs embossed on the dome. In the center there's what looks like a starburst. Around the outside I can see letters, but I'm not close enough to make out what they say.

My lungs are aching, and every part of my body is telling me to kick to the surface. Every part except my brain. Elder Night says we are animals, but I wonder if this little difference is what actually sets us apart from our wild brethren— that we can put aside our survival instincts in search of a higher purpose. Any animal would know that if it kept swimming down right now, it might die. I'm animal enough to know that, too . . . but human enough to ignore it and keep going.

A few more strokes, a few more kicks, and my limbs start to tingle from lack of oxygen. Now I can make out the words on the dome: "Supernova Systems." Another kick, and I can press my hand on the dome, smooth and metallic, untouched by corruption after all this time under the water.

My diaphragm is convulsing now, my body desperate to breathe. It takes every ounce of self-control to force my lungs not to take a suicidal breath. I've committed this far, trusting to Elder Night's words. I have to go on.

Using the very last of my strength, I kick as I slide along the outer edge of the dome, using the raised designs and letters to pull myself to the lower edge. Under the dome, Elder Night said. I can feel the darkness creeping along the edge of my vision as with one last pull I glide under the dome and look up . . .

To the shimmering ripples of the surface. A surface just a few feet above me.

My trust was not misplaced. There's a pocket of air trapped beneath the golden dome!

I rocket up into the air, the beautiful, blessed air, and take the sweetest breath of my life. It tastes a little stale on my tongue, but I don't care. I made it! My faith paid off!

It takes a moment for my vision to clear as my brain relishes the oxygen and my bloodstream flushes out excess carbon dioxide. When I look around, I'm amazed. This isn't just a little air pocket. The dome is the size of a large building. The entire testing group can easily breathe in here for hours while we make scouting trips down to street level. I duck my head and look below. The streets are still far below, but maybe some of us can make it, as long as we have this way station.

I swim around the inside of the dome. It is like a covered

swimming pool, and it is hard to remember that I'm in an air bubble deep under water. The inner dome is the same burnished gold as the outside, darkly shining. Wait, it shouldn't be this light in here. I realize that the dome itself is illuminated, casting a sort of sunset glow over the interior. So there's a power source?

The dome is held above the street by stout underwater columns. I see the remnants of what might have once been elevator tubes that would have brought people up from street level, but for what purpose? And why is this dome still filled with air when the rest of the city is flooded?

Then, about ten feet above the waterline, I notice openings all around the dome. Those are the things that looked like octopus arms radiating from the center. Tunnels, all branching out from the dome! It looks like the elevator system once brought people directly to the tunnels, but now all that is gone, except for crumbling ruins. However, there is a ladder carved directly into the side of the dome leading to each tunnel opening.

It feels strange to be at the mercy of gravity after the weightless water, I think as I climb the ladder. Every sound echoes in this chamber. The ladder was probably used for maintenance crews, and is a bit awkward to navigate, but luckily the curve of the dome here isn't too extreme. Water drips off me, plinking into the water below.

The tunnel is clear, air-filled like the dome, and stretches as far as I can see. And like the dome, the tunnel walls themselves are lit up with a golden glow. From here I can see straight into some of the other tunnels. They are clear, too.

I think I know what it is: an elevated transportation system. It must have ferried people all around long ago when this was a thriving city. Now the people are gone, but somehow the system that kept air flowing and the lights on persists.

Maybe it was solar-powered and enough sun filters through the lake to power parts of the city. That's simply amazing! Or maybe the elders devised a way to reactivate part of the city just for our test. Either way, it gives us a chance to explore the way life used to be before most of humanity perished.

I'm a little baffled, though. Even with advanced technology, is it possible that the city has been preserved so well throughout the thousand or so years since the Ecofail? Some of the city, made of materials that required maintenance and upkeep, has indeed crumbled away, but so much of it remains intact that it makes me suspicious.

For a while I poke down one of the tunnels. It's fascinating, almost empty but not quite. It looks like it was just been shut down for maintenance today. There's a food wrapper of some sort on the ground, and a stray piece of clear plastic wrap. Near the entrance is a poster made of a material I don't recognize, showing a happy family sitting on a checkered cloth by a riverbank. The mother and father are holding glasses of a pale pink bubbly liquid, and the detail is so fresh, so perfect, that it makes me thirsty. The five children in the image are playing a game with a large colorful ball.

Children! More than one, to the same parents! Even though that is commonplace in Harmonia, seeing it here, so naturally, makes me feel an emotional little catch in my throat. I wonder what life was like in this city. Above the happy family it says "Welcome to Three Rivers." It seems like such a pleasant place. Sure, it was flawed, as all civilization was before the fail. It had waste and garbage I'm sure. But it sickens me that the cheerful family in the picture must have been wiped out along with almost all of humanity.

"Oh bik!" I say aloud. I just realized how long I've been down here. I want to explore more, but my mom and Mira must be frantic, thinking I've drowned!

As I hurry back to the dome, I see a clear panel that gives me a view of the city below. The glass is a bit grimy, so I rub it with my sleeve and peer down at the remnants of a great city. There are boulevards where people would have strolled with their friends; shops and offices—all the trappings of bustling, comfortable life.

There's an open area right below me, what looks like a kind of town square. Maybe there was a park where children once played. What happened to this place, I wonder? What happened to the people? I climb back down the ladder and lower myself into the water, taking deep, calming breaths before my long ascent. As I do, I take one last look around. There's another poster made of that strange, enduring material. This one is an exaggerated map showing the city's attractions. Here is a place for river rafting expeditions, there a place for hot air balloon rides across the mountains. Restaurants, hotels, an amusement park, playgrounds, sports fields . . . this place must have been bustling in its heyday.

The map shows domes like this one scattered throughout the town of Three Rivers, all connected by that tube system. I bet that the entire closed system has air and power in it. We can explore to our hearts' content, at least until the sunset deadline. I better get back and tell everyone.

Just as I'm taking my last preparatory breath, I see an inset in the main city map, showing the surrounding landscape. The city sits on the easternmost of three rivers that flow south until they almost converge. A star on the map says "You Are Here."

For a moment I stare at that map, wondering how on Earth the city went from a riverside town to a city beneath a lake. I leave before I come to any conclusions, but it nags at me as I swim up to the bright surface.

Mom meets me halfway up, her face going from terrified

to relieved the moment she sees me. She intercepts me in an embrace that is half hug, half clawing rescue as she drags me up to the sunlight.

Panting, her eyes wide, she says with exasperation, "I want you to have freedom and adventures, Rowan, but there *are* some limits!"

I can't help but laugh, even as I sincerely apologize for the worry I caused.

"Glad you're not dead," Mira says blandly as her own face relaxes into a relief she tries to hide under flippancy.

"Me, too," I say. "I had my doubts there for a minute, but Elder Night said to trust her words, and it worked."

Mom shakes her head. "I'm surprised you were able to trust the words of any authority at this point."

"Believe me, it wasn't easy," I tell her. People in charge have a reputation for lying, I've found.

I tell them what I discovered, and after a brief consultation Mira swims off to tell the others. A while later most of us are under the dome, except for Lotte, who swore she didn't have an ounce of energy left to keep going. I think it's just as much fear as exhaustion, though. There was a haunted look in her eyes. Even if we all went first, she'd never commit her faith to such a risk. I understood, and I didn't think any worse of her. Most normal people prefer a safe, comfortable life, and will embrace security even if it means giving up the possibility of something better.

For just a second when he first emerges in the air bubble under the dome, Zander catches my eye. I'm not sure what I see there. Maybe a grudging respect, combined with (and probably overwhelmed by) irritation that he owes this to me. Still, it is enough to make me think that maybe, after I've proven myself for the next twenty years or so, he might be brought to admit that everything from Eden isn't corrupt.

For now, though, the best I think I can hope for is that if he catches me alone he'll only break another finger, not my whole arm. Baby steps.

We branch off into the tunnel system to search for artifacts. As the group separates, Mom shouts out a warning to remember the way back. Mom, Mira, and I stick together of course, choosing the same tunnel section. There's a little dance as we figure out who is going to walk ahead—the first person will naturally see any interesting detritus of society first, and maybe thus win the challenge.

"You should go first," Mira says. "After all, you're the one who found this place."

"How about we take turns," I suggest. "Mom, the oldest, should go first, for the first twenty steps. Then you, then me, each for twenty steps."

Right away, Mom finds an electronics panel. Its small door is open, revealing wires and fuses. Mom pulls one of the fuses out. "Maybe this," she says. "It represents mankind's reliance on technology, which led them to neglect the environment."

It's a good choice, I think.

The next stretch seems empty, and I have the idea that the farther we get from the station, the more meager the pickings will be. These tubes were made for a sealed vehicle to move through. People would only be out in the stations, so it would only be there that they would leave their personal effects behind. I'm sorry about this, because it would have been nice to learn a little more about how they lived. I can see from the poster they were really no different than us. People of the past are painted as monsters hell-bent on their own destruction. But in the poster they just look like people doing their best to be happy.

Everything seems so peaceful and normal down here, as if the tunnel has just been shut down for maintenance and isn't buried under thirty feet of water. I wonder how this happened. I know from Eco-History classes that climate change melted the polar glaciers, made the water levels rise, but that would flood the coast, not an inland city.

For a while it looks like we might not find anything else interesting. Then, while Mira is in the lead, she gasps and bends down quickly, coming up with a small, shining thing. "What is it?" she asks excitedly. "Is it jewelry?"

Mom and I both recognize it. In school they showed us pictures of old pre-fail currency. We explain it to Mira as she turns the pretty silver coin over and over, letting the golden light emanating from the tube shine on the head embossed on one side, the angry-looking bird on the other.

"So, the metal itself isn't worth anything?" Mira asks, puzzled. "But you can exchange it for things like food and clothes?" In a world where everything is provided, where people work for the community not for reward, the concept of money is alien. She tosses up the coin and catches it neatly. "It only has value because everyone agrees it has value?"

I nod, and tell her how people would compete to have more money than their neighbors, how they would fight and kill for coins like this one, destroy the environment, start wars, let children suffer, all for the sake of getting more money.

Mira shudders. "I've definitely found my artifact," she says, pocketing the coin.

When it's my turn to take the lead again, we hit a roadblock—literally. The tunnel is blocked by what must have been the vehicle that once ran through it. All we can see is its bulbous back end. It blocks the entire path except for a few inches all around. We have to turn back.

Mom rubs my shoulder. "It's okay, you can have my artifact." When I refuse, she says, "Or pull something else out from that panel, a wire or something."

"No, I can't just copy you." I try to look hopeful, but as we retrace our steps I'm feeling more and more glum. There isn't time to try another tunnel. It must be near sunset.

The tunnel is completely bare; we missed nothing. Only at the last moment do I see something on the ground, something small and forgotten, by both the original inhabitants of Three Rivers City and by these people in the test. I scoop it up and shove it in my pocket.

When we get back to the dome, I see that everyone has something. Zander keeps his find hidden in his cupped hands, so I'm guessing it must be good. Quinn has the biggest thing, a monitor as big as his chest, wires dangling from where he ripped it out of the wall. One person has what looks like a toy, a small figure of a curvy woman. Others have objects I don't immediately recognize, things that must have been useful so long ago but are irrelevant and forgotten now.

We return to the surface with our prizes . . . all except Quinn. Elated about his fabulous find, he doesn't stop to take physics into consideration. After a deep breath he jumps from the ladder to duck under the dome and return to the surface . . . but he isn't strong enough to kick up with that extra weight dragging him down. I can see his panic as he tries to decide what to do as he sinks slowly, wasting air and energy fighting the pull. He tries to get back to the dome, to take a breath and try again, to buy time to think of a way. But the heavy monitor pulls him past the rim of the dome. His only choice is to drop it, and I watch it disappear into the depths of the sunset lake as Quinn goes back into the dome. I know he'll search for something else, but he'll either come up empty-handed, or too late.

At least he's alive.

The competitors shiver on the beach, comparing their finds. Not me. I keep mine tucked away.

Zander struts up. "What did you find, City?" he asks with derision.

I don't want to show him, and cover my pocket with my hand. He sees the protective gesture and grabs my hand away, and since it is my injured one I can't fight him. I jerk my hand away before he hurts my fingers any more, and he pulls my artifact from my pocket. "Look at that!" he crows, holding it up for everyone to see. "Garbage! That's all she can find, because that's all she is!" He throws my scrap of plastic wrap on the ground, where a breeze catches it. I have to chase it before it blows away, all dignity lost. I catch it at the feet of Elder Night, and stand up slowly, holding out my offering.

"Tell me why you chose that," she commands in her serene voice.

I gulp, not wanting to admit that it was the only thing I could find at the last minute. "It . . . it shows the endurance of the temporary." I'm pleased with that phrase, and go on more enthusiastically. "It is plastic wrap, used to cover one leftover piece of food, for maybe a day, and then thrown away. The next time someone wanted to cover food they didn't reuse this one—they tore off another piece. It was easy, convenient . . . and deadly. Used for just a moment, this plastic is still here after all this time, as perfect as it was the day some mother tore it to wrap her child's sandwich. It will live longer than our species, probably. This artificial thing will get in oceans, in the bellies of whales, in our very bloodstream before it is gone. And when they used it, the people of long ago didn't care at all, as long as it made their lives easier. That was the attitude that brought about our destruction."

Elder Night closes my hand around my terrible treasure and gives me one simple nod.

Then she addresses the others. "You have completed the Trial of Water . . . and I think you all understand why I did not name the test to you beforehand." She chuckles. Yes, that would have made it too easy.

Then, as the sun is sinking low on the horizon in a red-and-pink glow, she questions each person about their find. After a while Quinn emerges, weary and empty-handed. I have no idea how mine compares to the other artifacts . . . but in the end, as Elder Night passes by me again, she gives me a smile that buoys my spirits.

When she has finished, she says, "I'm sure you know the routine by now, no need for sneakery or surprises. I have a meal laid out for you just beyond the trees. After you refresh yourselves, you'll be given a pill that will render you unconscious. When you wake, the next test will begin. I am proud of all of you. Some of you have surprised me, for good or for ill, but you are all showing your true natures, your strengths and weaknesses, and the community of Harmonia embraces all of you. Enjoy your respite, and may you show your best selves in the third and final test."

She points us to the feast, then drifts away into the forest.

I sit with Mom and Mira and a couple of others, talking about the first two tests, and when the feast is over, when I've drunk my fill of honeyed tea, I reach along with the others to take one of the pale little pills on a dish at the center of the table.

11

SLOWLY, I DRIFT toward consciousness. The first two trials have been pretty extreme, so I can only imagine that they must have something almost impossible for us on the third and final test. Just like the other times, I have no memory of being transported. I could be anywhere—the ocean, a desert. As I lay in a semiconscious haze, letting the tranquilizer wear off, I try to prepare for every possibility. By the time I manage to open my eyes, I'm ready for anything.

Air or fire, Yarrow says.

Maybe both, I think sleepily.

What, then, falling off a cliff . . . into a volcano?

The one thing I'm not prepared for is waking up in a soft, comfortable bed.

With Zander.

I scramble off the bed, literally brushing my arms with my hands in revulsion as if something disgusting was crawling on them. What the bik is going on?

Zander snores away.

This has to be a test.

What, a test of your patience? A test to see if you'll murder him in his sleep?

I have to admit to Yarrow that the idea has some attraction.

Then I have to pull myself together and take stock of the situation. This looked at first like one of our traditional bubble houses, high up in a tree, but there are differences. This is a one-room structure, a simple sphere situated just under the canopy. I don't know what kind of tree we're in. It is some kind of conifer, maybe a relative of redwoods but not as massive. Still, we're pretty high up, at least fifty feet, and there are no branches on the trunk below us. We're surrounded by the same kinds of trees. I see other one-room bubbles just like this one, in other trees, none too close. Are there other candidates in there?

Then I notice other differences about this structure, and the others I can see. While most bubble houses are wrapped around the trunk, integrating the tree into their architecture, this one is hanging suspended from a limb like an ornament. Also, more troubling, there are no stairs. The only access is a hole in the bottom.

In the room there's only a bed, and a coil of rope. And Zander.

So, you strangle him maybe?

I wish. Fire. Air.

Even with that guess, I do not immediately notice anything odd when the light around me seems to flicker. It is morning, and at first I think it is just the light filtering unevenly through the overhead limbs and the rest of the forest as the wind blows through them. Then something about the character of the light makes me take a second look.

Fire!

I've never seen a wildfire, but I envisioned it creeping insidiously along the ground, with flames licking up tree trunks as they climbed skyward. I never imagined that a forest fire could come from above.

Maybe it was sparked by lightning. Maybe there was a

fire on the ground far away that sent up a shower of embers to rain down on the nearby trees. Whatever the cause, the ground is clear but suddenly a raging fire is spreading with incredible swiftness through the tree canopy. Before my eyes I see it jump from tree to tree, and take hold until each tree looks like a giant matchstick.

The fire is still some distance away, but it is coming closer. I have to get out of here!

We, Yarrow reminds me. *We have to get out of here.*

I might grumble a little, but there's no doubt about what I'm going to do. I shake Zander and shout, "Wake up!"

No response.

Inside my head, I can actually feel Yarrow grin wickedly.

I shout at him again, but he lies insensible. Did they drug him more deeply than me? *What other choice do you have?* Yarrow asks with glee as I slap his face. The sound echoes in the bubble, but he doesn't respond. I hit him again, harder this time. Nothing. He's breathing, he has a pulse, but he's dead to the world.

I run to the glass to check the fire's progress. In disbelief I watch it reach one of the most distant bubble rooms. Is there anyone inside? Frantic, I press my nose to the glass and look for motion inside. I can't see anyone. Did they already escape?

Or are they drugged, too?

The fire rages in the branches above the bubble. Suddenly, the bubble bursts, sending crystals of glass showering through the flames. The fire got so hot that it exploded!

I flinch back, shielding my eyes even though it is still far away. And still the fire comes closer, leaping to the next tree. In only a few minutes it will be here.

Okay, calm down Rowan, Yarrow cautions. *This is a test. First of all, you're probably not in any real danger, right?*

I wouldn't be so sure about that. I could have fallen off the cliff, or drowned. Maybe the elders take precautions, but there's risk of death in each of these tests.

And second, you've been given the tools to pass each test, if you know what to look for. Here's it's easy. A climb, and a rope. Just lower yourself down and escape the fire.

She's right, of course. But what about the unconscious Zander?

Leave him, Yarrow says, but I know she doesn't quite mean it.

But if I can't wake him, what choice do I have? All I can do is climb down, and hope that he wakes up in time. Or look for help. Yes, that's what I'll do.

I tie the rope up to the only possible anchor, the bed, and tug against it, testing its strength. Yes, the counterweight is enough to hold me. I try one more time to wake Zander, then give up. I'll have to figure out how to help him later.

Then, just as I'm about to lower myself down with the rope, I see movement in the nearest of the bubble rooms. I run to the glass and peer through, expecting to see Mira or Mom or the other competitors.

Instead I see a bubble full of children.

There are a dozen of them at least, and I'm just close enough to make out their faces. They aren't children I know from Harmonia, but they remind me of them. One resembles Lillibet, all of three years old, a precocious girl who follows the elders everywhere, begging for stories. Another is reminiscent of Ianni, a shy boy of ten with a passion for insects. He told me all kinds of interesting things about ants. I've gotten to know all the children of Harmonia in my time here. I don't know these children, but there's no doubt I have the same urge to protect them.

And now many of them are trapped, and in terrible danger.

I wave my arms, signaling to them frantically. One sees me, and they all rush over to that side. I point to the approaching fire, and mime climbing down a rope. But when the kids part, I can see that they have no bed, no rope, nothing in their bubble except their own sweet selves.

Every instinct tells me to run to them, to reach them quickly, and then I'll find a way to help. But there's no way I can climb that tree. It's straight up, without branches, and the bark is too crumbly to offer any handholds.

To climb it I'd need to use the technique they use here to climb the redwoods to reach beehives. They loop a length of rope around the trunk and their own hips, also holding the rope in each hand, and brace their feet against the bark. Then in slow increments that require incredible strength, they fling the rope up the trunk a few inches, pull themselves up, and repeat the process over and over. Sometimes they wear special shoes with spikes to help brace against the tree, though the purists don't do that.

I tried it once, and the results were laughable. I made it about five feet up and fell on my backside.

But I've seen Zander do it. He and his brothers are masters at honey-gathering, and they can zoom up the tallest redwoods tirelessly.

I can't save those kids, but Zander can.

I have to get him down. Somehow, even though he in unconscious, I have to lower him and hope he wakes up in time to save those kids. If I get him down, and follow him, we can . . .

You can't follow him, Yarrow points out.

Oh, bik, she's right. Zander can climb the redwood, but the kids can't get down that way. They're too small and weak. He'll have to climb up, with our extra rope tied to him. Then he'll have to maneuver onto the branch holding their bubble, tie the rope to that, and swing around the bubble to the access point on the bottom. From there he'll have to brace the rope with his own weight and strength while one by one the kids climb down.

He needs the rope. If I climb down after him, the rope is still attached up here. There will be no way to release it.

I have to lower him down, then untie the rope and drop it down to him.

I have to trap myself up here so that he can save the kids.

Bikking wonderful.

If only Zander were awake, so he could get himself down. As it is, I don't know if I'm going to be able to do it. But I have to.

And what if he doesn't regain consciousness once he's down? I'm operating on the assumption that he just received a higher dose and will be out longer than I was. But what if I lower him down and he doesn't wake up?

I pace the bubble for a moment, trying to come up with any other option. I can lower myself and go for help, but this isn't Harmonia. I have no idea where we might be. There's no guarantee I'll find any help. As crazy, as risky and uncertain as my plan is, it is the only thing I can think of.

My surroundings take on an orange glow as the fire comes closer, passing from treetop to treetop where the boughs touch. I try again to wake Zander up, pinching him, slapping him. I'm tempted to break one of his fingers, but I don't quite go that far. At last, I give in and try to pick him up.

Well, that's not going to work. He outweighs me by almost a hundred pounds. I'm strong, but not that strong.

Instead I roll him out of bed, ignoring Yarrow's satisfaction when he hits the ground with a thump. I roll him to the access hole, which is hard enough. Then I try to figure out how to attach the rope to Zander. Even though I can't lift him, I think if I loop the line around the bed and around my body I can belay him down. Mira showed me a technique that a smaller person can use to support a much bigger person's weight. It won't be easy, but I have to do it.

I roll him back and forth, trying to tie the rope around his hips and legs in a harness that won't slip off even as he hangs unconscious.

I run back to the glass to try to signal to the children that help is on the way.

Oh, great Earth, no! I thought we had more time!

The fire isn't traveling in the path I'd predicted. As it scorches the dry needles and makes the sap spark, the terrible inferno has changed course. It is only one tree away from the children.

I can see their terrified, frantic faces. They are pounding on the glass, begging me to help them. But I'm doing the only thing I can do.

I check the knots one last time on Zander's improvised harness. As I'm reaching around his waist to check the last knot, I feel his hand clamp down on my wrist. "What the . . ." he begins groggily. His mind may be confused, but his body is perfectly awake, and holds me in a vise-like grip.

Suddenly his eyes fly open. He takes in my face, the rope, the hole, the long drop . . . and shoves me backward. Off guard, I go down easily, and in a second he's on top of me.

"What were you trying to do, city scum? Hang me?" Before I can stop him, he's looped the end of the rope around my neck. I manage to get my hands up between it, but he's pulling it tight and I can only keep a little slack to breathe. And talk.

"Wake up, Zander!" He still looks bleary. "It's a test! You have to get down . . . the children!"

But he picks up the rope and uses it to shake me. "Shut

up, I've had enough of you. I don't know what's going on, but this is the last time you cross me." He shakes me until my head lolls, tightening the rope each time as I buck beneath him.

"Save them!" I gasp, and slip out one of the hands that is protecting my throat. As the noose tightens more, I use that hand to point to the children in peril. "Trust me. Let me lower you down."

He still doesn't completely understand what is going on. I know how I felt when I first came out of the drug-induced stupor—hazy and disoriented. I couldn't latch onto more than one idea at a time. That's what Zander is doing now. He sees his enemy, he sees rope, and he comes to the worst conclusion.

Finally, he follows my finger and sees the kids. He releases me instantly, and I scramble up, rubbing my throat. "No! You doomed them!" I cry. The fire has taken hold on the children's treetop. It eats through the branches like a living thing, growing, devouring. I can see the children screaming. One of them takes a desperate risk and jumps out of the access door, dropping fifty feet.

She falls into a crumpled heap, unmoving.

The next instant the glass bubble shatters from the heat. I turn away, hiding my face in my hands.

"You could have saved them!" I cry accusingly. "If you hadn't fought me, you could have saved them."

I feel the heat growing around us, and through my fingers I see a flickering orange glow as the fire consumes our tree, too. I don't care anymore. I hear the sound of our bubble exploding, but I feel no pain, and the world goes black . . .

12

I WAKE UP.

A stretch, a sigh that turns into a dramatic, jaw-popping yawn. Great, another day in paradise. A paradise without a single boutique, or beauty salon, or nightclub. A paradise without a single pill or bikking swig of alcohol!

I scowl, then smooth my face. I think about the frown lines on Mom's face. I know full well that a sour expression can age a person way beyond their years. Of course, she had a lot of responsibilities as chief of intelligence for all of Eden, but . . .

I sit up, my heart racing. I'm not that person! In the first hazy awakening of my brain I was convinced I was Yarrow. For a moment, Rowan didn't exist.

It's a terrifying sensation, to think you're losing yourself. It is something I face every moment of my life now.

I force myself to take deep breaths, to calm down, to think about who I am, where I am, what is happening. I am Rowan. I am in Harmonia, freed from Eden by EcoPan. My mother is Rosalba, not Ellena.

Stupid girl, Yarrow says. *You need me.*

I shake my head, trying to bury her, and continue the litany that will fix my real identity in my head. Rowan. I am

Rowan, a second child. I am seventeen. I just completed my Passage Test.

The Passage Test. I know I competed, but somehow the details are fuzzy. I was running through the woods. Someone was hurt. There were goose bumps on my arms, cold water . . . Beyond that, I can't remember. Yarrow pushes insistently against my consciousness, but I shove her aside. She is determined this morning.

But I have more important things to do than listen to her whine about the lack of coffee and parties and pills. I need to find out how I ranked on the test.

"Mom!" I bellow. There's no answer. What time is it? Light is shining strongly through the clear walls of our tree house, but I can't tell the direction. It could be mid-morning or mid-afternoon.

I stand and stretch, balanced on the balls of my feet, hands high above my head. My hummingbird-embroidered tunic lies in a crumple on the floor. Its former beauty is marred by mud and sweat and blood. It reminds me of something.

Of course it does, you fool, Yarrow says. *Don't you remember . . .*

I shut her up as fast as I can and head downstairs to the communal room. I'm not in the mood for her griping today. "Mom!" I call again, but there's no one else here.

I guess I'll have to wait a bit for my results. I head back upstairs to shower and dress. When I'm done, I stand on a chair to get a better view, and look toward the village green. From just the right angle I can see a sliver of the center of town through the trees. I'm hoping I can catch a glimpse of Mom, or Mira. I'd rather find Mom first, though. I'm not at all confident about my results, and if I didn't do well it will be easier to take it in her comforting presence. If only I could remember how I did. It should seem more strange to me, but somehow I don't feel the need to dwell on it. Perhaps I am learning serenity.

No, you bikking idiot! Yarrow screams in my head. *You were given too many drugs to remember, and your head is muddled. But I'm separate from the rest of your brain, and I remember perfectly. Just listen to me!*

She forces my Rowan-self to yield, and suddenly I'm flooded with memories from the previous day. Each test comes back to me in perfect detail. Especially the last one. The terrible choice of saving Zander and sacrificing myself. The failure of my plan thanks to Zander's unthinking hate. The children dying . . .

It wasn't real, Yarrow reassures me. *None of it. You were unconscious, but the part of me in your head isn't as easily controlled, and I was conscious when the whole bubble turned into a screen. The fire, the trees, the children—it was all a sophisticated vid projected inside the sphere.*

The children are safe? I ask hopefully.

There never were any children. It was all a test.

Was Zander really there?

Yes, Yarrow says in my head. Then she chuckles. *And for the rest f your life I can remind you that you slept with Zander!*

Shut up, I say, but I'm not angry. I'm just happy that this is finally over.

But I still don't quite get how Yarrow can know things I don't.

I am a part of you—and also apart from you. You've compartmentalized me so well that what happens to the Rowan aspect of you doesn't touch me. Your brain has rewired itself. Might prove useful to have a backup personality if Mom tries to mess with yours again.

"Don't call that horrible woman Mom!" I shout.

Sorry. Old habits Now, let's go find out how you did on the test. Hmm, looks like a lot of activity going on in the village. Something's up.

She's right. There's more bustle than I'd expect in the sliver I can see of the village green. This is such a well-ordered place that people seldom need to hurry. But now I see people in the distance running in and out of my field of vision. Something is definitely up.

It must be that the results are in. I can't wait for Mom to come home. I have to know now!

I hurry to the village green, where I find a lot of people clustered. There are two or three others from the test, but not Mom, or Mira.

"Congratulations," Quinn says. "You really deserve it!"

I thank him, my hopes rising as I press forward to where at least two dozen people are looking at a projection with a list of names.

"Good job, Rowan," someone says, but I don't even notice who as I strain to see. If they're congratulating me, I must have been ranked first, right?

But when someone finally passes me the paper and I scan it for my name, my heart sinks.

Second tier. It's Zander's fault. I know I would have ranked first tier if I hadn't been partnered with him for the Fire Trial.

Second tier is very respectable, and that's why I'm getting so many congratulations. But it's not high enough to become an elder, to be trusted with the highest technology, the secrets of Harmonia that I know must exist. I'll have access to some, just like Carnelian. But I'm worried it won't be enough to help me in my quest to save my friends.

It's okay, I tell myself. It was just an idea, a nebulous notion that might have helped. It's not like I had a concrete plan that was ruined. Still, it makes my goal seem even more like an impossible dream.

I was so eager to see my results that I didn't even look at the rest of them. What I see makes me feel a little better about my achievement. Only three of us managed to get the second rank: me, Mira . . . and Zander. That gives me some satisfaction. At least he wasn't rated first. That must be burning him up. Quinn and most of the others were put in the third tier. Lotte, to no one's surprise, is in the fourth.

Then I check my mom's rank.

I can't believe it.

Suddenly there is a commotion at the far end of the green, near the Hall of Elders. Two of the younger, stronger elders are carrying something between them. It takes me a moment to realize it is a stretcher. Whoever is on it is covered.

Dead? Why else would they cover someone.

"Who is it?" people call as they hurry to help. "What happened?" Is it one of the testers? With a sick suspicion I think it might be my mom, and I run to the fore of the crowd. With that rank I just saw . . .

But we're shooed away by the elders, who assure us that its nothing to worry about, everything is under control and an announcement will be made shortly. "None of our friends or family are hurt, rest assured," Elder Night says. I hear sighs of relief all around me. Mine is among them.

We mill for a moment. The people of Harmonia have been conditioned to help. We're a community, and when something is wrong we all feel like we have to pitch in. I can tell they feel awkward not having any task to do in what is so obviously some kind of crisis. We all watch the Hall of Elders without seeming to do so, waiting to be needed.

Suddenly, to my immense relief despite what Elder Night said, my mom comes out of the hall. She ignores the villagers' questions and heads straight to me.

She's flushed and out of breath. "Hey," she says with a brightness I can tell is forced. "You were ranked in the second tier. Well done!" She sounds excited, but I still feel crushed, and it shows. "Oh, sweetheart, it's still an amazing achievement! Very few people get ranked first."

"You did," I say flatly.

For a moment she doesn't speak, but watches me anxiously for signs of tears or anger. Then I throw my arms around her. "Oh, Mom, I'm so proud of you! You deserve it!" And she does. She's a better person than me, with straightforward priorities. She knows exactly how a human should act to be part of the natural world. She might have been born in Eden, but she belongs here. She doesn't question everything. She is like an animal in the ecosystem—she has a place, and she fits it perfectly.

"I'm sorry," she tries to say, but I shush her immediately, telling her over and over how proud and happy I am for her. To myself, I'm thinking that this might be even better. The elders already suspect me. I tried so hard to get back to Eden, to solicit their help when I first came here, that even with a top ranking they probably wouldn't trust me with all the information I'd need. Mom, on the other hand, is so perfectly adapted to Harmonia that they won't keep anything from her. She'll be an elder, with all the secrets and responsibilities that go along with it. And of course she'll be able to use that knowledge to help me get back to Eden.

Won't she? For a moment I have doubts. No, she loves Ash. For his sake, if not for the sake of my friends or the other second children, she'd risk it.

"Let's celebrate!" I say. "Who knows, maybe I'll even congratulate Zander. I just won't shake his hand!" I flex my fingers, which I just now notice feel almost completely better. Did someone heal me while I was unconscious after the last test? Tentatively, I ask Yarrow, but she can't remember that either.

"Rowan, listen, I want you to stay inside today, okay?" My mom's voice is strained, and I can see twin lines of tension between her eyebrows.

"Why?"

"You . . . you had a hard day yesterday," she stammers as she draws me away from the village green.

"So did you, and you're outside," I point out. "What's wrong?" She hesitates. "Tell me!"

"There's some trouble in the village."

"About me?"

"No. Well . . . no, not really. But it will be better if you stay away. Easier."

"Easier for who?"

"Oh, sweetheart, it will just upset you." She's maneuvered me halfway back to our house now. "Trust me, and stay home for today. I'll do my best to take care of it. I'll have a say now that I'm an elder."

"Take care of what?" I just barely manage not to shout. "You can't hide things from me, Mom. You can't protect me. After all I've been through, I deserve better. What is going on?"

She draws a deep breath, and lets it out with a sigh. "When we get in the house I'll tell you." Dutifully, I follow her inside. She gets a glass of water and takes a long drink before saying, "There's a stranger in the village. Someone from Eden."

"What!" I stare at her with wide eyes, my mouth agape, as she tells me what happened that morning as I slept.

Early that morning, as Mom was getting her first instruction on the responsibilities and privileges of being an elder, a signal came in. She explained to me that there are monitors all around Eden that scan for human activity, so that when Eco-Pan releases someone the elders of Harmonia can go to meet them. Normally, they would receive a communication from EcoPan beforehand. That someone would appear without warning was unusual, and troubling.

"Usually only the elders can go on the hypertubes," Mom said, "but they made an exception for me when you arrived, since it was the first time any two people from the same family were chosen. They didn't know why, they just got word to include me that day. We only found out once I saw who EcoPan had sent out."

Mom was chosen to go with Elder Night and a few others to investigate. It was a good way to begin her training, see how she handled herself in a real crisis.

"When we got there, we found a man, half-dead of thirst and heatstroke. He was just beyond the desert, staggering, gasping out incoherent things about war, and hope. When he saw us he passed out almost immediately."

My heart feels raw. I know it can't be anyone I know. There are a million people in Eden. And yet . . .

"We weren't sure what to do. We had no instructions from EcoPan. The elders wanted to follow protocol, but didn't want to act hastily. So we took him back and waited for word from EcoPan. We thought maybe it had forgotten to tell us. I mean, it has a lot on its mind! Er, on its chips? Processors?"

"Did EcoPan contact you?" I ask, breathless.

"No. We think he's an escapee." She shakes her head. "The elders are debating about what to do."

"What do you mean, what to do? What *is* there to do? You give him food, water, medical care, shelter. You welcome him!"

"It's not that simple," she says sadly. "He hasn't been

chosen. He is a corrupt member of Eden. He doesn't belong here."

I look at her, aghast. "You sound like Zander."

"I don't hate people from Eden like he does! But I don't trust them, either. You know what they're like as well as I do. Most of them, anyway. They can't be trusted here in the natural world."

"This isn't you talking, Mom."

"I'm an elder now. My first responsibility is to keep Harmonia safe. I argued in his favor, Rowan. I spoke for him. But it wasn't any use. I don't agree with the elders' decision, but I understand why they made it."

"What decision? You can't send him back!"

"No," she says gently. "They aren't going to do that."

I sigh with relief. "Well, that's good. So, what? He has to live in isolation? Under guard?" That's understandable. It will take time for him to learn about our ways."

"No, sweetheart. They decided . . ." She swallows hard. "They decided it's too dangerous to let him live."

13

"THIS IS SUPPOSED to be a paradise?" I ask as I pace back and forth in our common room. "A place where we all live in peace and harmony? And the elders—supposedly the most wise, calm people here—have decided to kill a refugee?"

"Rowan, it's not that simple," Mom soothes.

"It is exactly that simple!" I rant. "This man has escaped from a terrible place, a prison he was sentenced to before he was born. You know as well as I do what it is like."

"Calm down for a minute," she says. Which she should know is exactly the thing that will *not* calm someone down. Especially me. "This is why I wanted you to stay home. I know this is upsetting, to you in particular. And it is to me, too. But this is a matter for the elders to decide. We have laws here."

"Laws that apparently make murder legal," I snap. "Mom, I don't understand why you're not up in arms against this . . . this crime against humanity. This poor man managed to escape, looking for a sanctuary. We need to help him, not kill him. Why, it could be a second child. It could be Ash."

"It's not," Mom says.

"Who is it? What's his name?"

She shakes her head. "He hasn't regained consciousness since we put him in the hypertube. He's not old, twenties I'd say, but he could be younger or older. He has a beard, and he's pretty dirty and blistered from the desert so it's hard to tell. We will talk to him before the final decision is made, but right now the elders seem set on it."

"It's so wrong."

"I agree. But they are weighing one man's life against the future of humanity, and the Earth itself."

"That's a little extreme, don't you think?"

She takes my hands and pulls me onto a long cushion on the ground that serves as our sofa. "You're right—one man doesn't matter. He could live with us, and everything would probably be okay. But what about the next man? And the one after that?"

"He is the only one to ever succeed."

"Not true. You did it once," Mom points out. "Maybe things are changing in Eden. New technology could let people cross the desert. A hacker could shut it down. A new government, or rebel group, could put so much pressure on the society in Eden that escape is the only option. This man is like . . . a bacteria. Most of the time people don't get sick from just one bacteria. But if there are more bacteria, and they start to spread, before you know it you have a disease. This man is the first symptom of a disease that could wipe out Harmonia."

"Then keep him prisoner," I say desperately. "Take a month, a year, and see if anyone else comes."

Mom shakes her head. "This place succeeds because only certain kinds of people are allowed to live here."

"Give this man a chance to prove that he is like us! If he escaped he is resourceful, he hates Eden. He longs for the real natural world. I'm sure of it."

"You're still very young, Rowan. An idealist. What if he is a murderer, fleeing persecution? What if he was sent by the Center to infiltrate us?"

I admit that it is entirely possible. "But three hundred people can keep one person under control, watched and guarded, no matter what his story is," I insist.

"But he was not chosen. He is not pure. What if he speaks his poison to the young people of Harmonia? Why walk when you could drive? he might say. Why not use plastic—what harm could just a little do, and it is so convenient? Then, before you know it, it would be why eat nuts when you could slaughter an animal for its flesh? I know people inside Eden claim to respect the Earth, but that is because they have no choice. Turned loose, there is no knowing what any of them would do."

Part of me can see what she is saying. But in my heart I know it is wrong. Everyone needs to be given a chance. No one is inherently criminal because of where they were born.

I want to yell at her, to argue. I want to storm to the Hall of Elders and demand to see this man from Eden, fight them with words or fists until he is released. But I know I have to be clever about this.

So I nod, still frowning, and say, "I get it, Mom. What we have here is too precious to risk. But what if he is worthy? What if in escaping he passed EcoPan's tests? Couldn't Eco-Pan have stopped him from escaping if it wanted to? Who are we to judge him?"

This gives her pause, and I press on. "I knew a lot of the rebels of Eden after you left. People who love the Earth, and humanity, and were fighting for a better world. The second children know about community. They were exactly like the people of Harmonia." With their leaders sometimes wearing blinders, their humanity taking second place to the good of their tribe, I think but don't add. "If it is one of the second children, or someone who has been helping them, maybe the elders will give them a chance."

"Well, anyone could say they were a rebel, just to get on our good side."

"I know all of the second children," I remind her. "As well as a lot of the people who helped them. If I can take a look at this man, if I know he's one of the good and trust-worthy ones, it will give you ammunition to help save his life. You *do* want to save him, don't you?"

"Of course," she says. "As long as there is no threat to Harmonia."

"Then let me see him. Just a quick look. If I know him, I'll vouch for him. If not, then I'll have to accept whatever the elders decide." I force a resigned look on my face.

Mom buys it. "They might not agree, but I'll try."

Together we go to the Hall of Elders, and at the heart of its warm wooden interior I present my case for seeing the es-capee. It is all I can do not to rant, to beg, to try to assert my will over theirs. But I make myself speak calmly, rationally, as if I don't have a real stake in the matter. Inside, I feel like I'm falling apart.

The elders listen as I speak, with my mom standing be-side me.

"You are full of compassion, child," Elder Night says. "That is an admirable quality, a most humane quality. But it must be tempered with hard, cold practicality. I know you don't remember, but during the third test you showed that you will let compassion override your duty to the Earth, and your guilt as a human. Guilt you, and I, and everyone here must constantly work to expiate, even unto the cost of our lives."

She comes nearer and takes me by the shoulders. "What

good will it do you to see him when his fate is sealed?" Her voice is so gentle, yet her words are deadly. "Nothing either you or he can say will alter the unpleasant necessity. The kindest thing would be to . . ." I can tell she's weighing the next word carefully, "euthanize him while he is still unconscious."

She could have said murder. That's what it is, really. Or assassinate. After all, he is being killed for political reasons. Euthanize, though, sounds clinical and humane. Once Mira, in tears, ran back from the fields with a little grass snake in her hands. She had accidentally wounded it with her spade while she was weeding. The elders said it couldn't be saved, and killed it as mercifully as possible. This Eden escapee is like that to them—unsalvageable, so he has to be put down.

"I understand," I say, bowing my head. "It is for the good of Harmonia. No matter how hard it is, I know you will always do what is right. I hope I always do likewise."

Elder Night nods in approval, but before she can turn to go I add, "Still, I think you should wait until he awakes. If he is the first of a wave of escapees, you should know. If there is even the slightest chance that more people might follow him, you should be prepared."

The elders mutter in alarm. "Its not very likely—" Elder Night begins, but I interrupt.

"It would be more humane to kill him right away. But it would be more practical to question him first. For the safety of Harmonia. And I think it might be helpful if I could at least see him, just a glance to know if he is a second child. Knowing that will help you decide if whatever he tells you is the truth."

Elder Night ponders a moment. "Very well. Just for a moment."

As calmly as if I'm conducting a mere business transaction, I follow her deeper into the Hall of Elders. This is the first time I've ever been inside this building. The burnished wood has a gentle glow, and feels more like home than the tree house bubble. I'm used to walls, and this is the only structure in Harmonia that isn't all or in part see-through. The only place where secrets can be properly kept. I wonder if they're letting the rest of the village know what has happened, what they plan to do.

Two elders, robust women in their forties, stand guard outside an unmarked wooden door. They greet Elder Night, and look in some surprise at me, but one of them pushes open the door and lets us inside. An elder in his sixties stands by a bedside, a heavy, knobby staff in his hand.

In the bed is an unconscious young man, his face red and blistered beneath the dirt. And blood.

"No," I say. "I don't know him."

I walk out again, as Elder Night thanks and praises me. Mom puts an arm around my shoulder. "I know it's hard, sweetheart," she says. "At least you didn't know him."

"What if it had been Ash?" I ask her softly.

She catches her breath in a quiet sob, quickly suppressed. "I can't even think about that."

She walks me home, then tells me she has to get back to the other elders.

"When will it happen?" I ask.

"Not until tomorrow morning, I'm sure," she tells me. "He's in bad shape. It will be a while before he revives enough to answer questions. If he ever does. If not, well, I guess that would be for the best."

I nod, calm and accepting, and walk up the stairs. When I turn around, Mom is still watching me. I school my face until it is perfectly appropriate—melancholy over harsh necessity, serene knowledge of acting for the greater good—and raise my hand in farewell before I walk steadily up the rest of the way.

Even when the door closes I stay calm. Anyone could be watching. I look as normal as can be . . . until I reach the bathroom, the place most closed off from the rest of Harmonia.

Then I fall to my knees, pulling at my hair, screaming and sobbing uncontrollably.

It was Lachlan.

Lachlan, injured and helpless and alone. One glance was enough to tell me how much he has suffered, not just in his desert crossing but the whole time since the Underground was destroyed. There's a new scar above his eyebrow, and his knuckles are split and scabbed. He's lost weight, too, and though his body is still well-muscled, there is a wasted look to his face. No wonder Mom couldn't tell how old he is. Hardship has aged him in my absence.

Oh, great Earth! How did I have the strength to stay calm when I saw him? How could I not fly to his side, kiss his sweet, suffering face, cut his bonds . . . tear a them with my teeth if I had to? Why didn't I fight the elders, or all of Harmonia, to save him?

Because like Elder Night said, I can't let my compassion get in the way of hard, cold practicality.

I'm already a little suspect because I come from Eden. If I show excess concern for the escapee, or even the slightest resistance to their plans, I know that they'll guard me as long as he is alive. Once they realize I know him, they'll assume I'll try to save him.

And if any of them have heard my stories, ones I've only really told to Mira and Carnelian but which might have spread, as stories do . . . if they know I love him . . .

The only way to help Lachlan is to entirely deflect their suspicion. So I made myself be cold and heartless. I pretended to agree with them.

Now, with a last shuddering sob, I straighten up and

clench my jaw in firm resolution. I only have until tomorrow morning to save the man I love from certain death.

Then, if I do, maybe he can help me save the woman I love, too.

I have no idea how I'm going to rescue him, but I know I have to look as normal as possible to the rest of Harmonia until I make my move.

Unfortunately, I look anything but normal when I open the bathroom door and find Mira standing just outside with her hand poised to knock.

"Sorry, I let myself in to talk about . . . Are you okay? No, stupid question. Obviously you're not. Is it because you were ranked second tier? Well, at least I'm in the second-tier club along with you. It will be okay. I know you'd hoped to . . ." She stares at me more intensely. "No," she says. "I know you. I know what you've been through. You're not going to break down like this over what is essentially a bad grade. Come on, Rowan, you can tell me."

I have misgivings. If the wise elders see nothing wrong with murder for the greater good, if even my mom is ready to accept it, however reluctantly, how can I expect Mira to understand. But she has already agreed to help me get back to Eden to save my friends, and this is part and parcel of that quest.

I tell her, and watch her face shift from amazement to angry disbelief. "No one out there even knows someone escaped from Eden," she says indignantly. "I heard there was someone being carried on a stretcher, but they said it was Elder Jacques, who twisted his ankle. Can you believe the elders were going to keep this from us?"

She's even more surprised when I tell her who it is. She jumps up and down, hugging me. "It's like a legend, a fairy tale!" she says excitedly. "True love, coincidence, adventure . . ."

"And danger," I add. "They're going to kill him tomorrow morning."

She stares at me in dumbfounded disbelief. "No," she says slowly. "You must have made a mistake. All life is precious. Animal and human. The elders would never kill someone. Not even someone from Eden. It doesn't make sense." I tell her the reasons the elders gave, but she's still shaking her head. "No. That's the kind of logic that *sounds* right if you don't pay close attention, but it isn't. Not really. There are so many other alternatives! Listen, we have to tell everyone else. The rest of Harmonia won't stand for this. We're not murderers. The elders think they're protecting the people, but if the people know, they'll put a stop to it. I'm sure of it!"

I think of the people I've come to know in Harmonia. Placid, timid Lotte at one end of the spectrum, and Zander with all his vitriol at the other. In the middle, the others are pleasant, kind, earnest people. But are they leaders, or followers? Will they think for themselves if it is easier to let the elders do their thinking for them?

And even if they do think it is wrong to kill a stranger who stumbles into their midst, how many of them are willing to act? There is a world of difference between having a private opinion and taking a public stand. They are part of a community, and while there is strength in numbers, there is also weakness. A break in the unity reduces the strength, so everyone is conditioned to go along, not to make waves.

That probably works most of the time out here. There's so rarely any source of conflict. I don't agree with Mira. We might get a little help, but the majority will side with the elders. It is a sad case, they'll tell themselves, but it is for the greater good. Then when it is over, the community will still be whole.

I tell Mira my thoughts, and she comes to agree with me.

"We have to break him out," I say after she swears to help me.

"But how? You said he's guarded. We can't *fight* our neighbors!"

"Of course not," I say, privately thinking that a few unconscious elders, hit on the head with a rock, would be a small price to pay for Lachlan's life. "But we have to get in somehow, and then get him out."

"And not just out of the hall—out of Harmonia." Something strikes Mira. "Wait, if you get him out, what are you going to do?"

I haven't had time to think that far ahead.

"Are you going to live in the woods? Wait, what am I going to do if they find out I helped?" She looks for a moment like she's having misgivings. She just realized there are huge consequences to what she's contemplating. It is treason to Harmonia. She could be facing exile from all she has known all her life.

Then a huge grin spreads out over her face. "It's just what Carnelian and I always talked about! Oh, great Earth, this is perfect! I have to tell him! He'll be on our side. He'll help."

"Wait, you're not worried?"

"Rowan, we always fantasized about striking out on our own! Harmonia is great, but can you imagine really living in nature, in a cave or a hut you built yourself? Bathing in a spring, drinking from a birchbark cup, making your own tools from stone?" Some people would find it ghastly, but she's talking about it like it is heaven. "But people aren't allowed to leave Harmonia. Carnelian and I talked about it— living as close to nature as possible—but we might never be brave enough to do it. But if we save Lachlan, if we flee into the forest . . ." She's laughing now. "Oh, Rowan, I knew as soon as I met you that you were going to be exciting."

She's going on about her dream, expanding it to include people we can rescue from Eden. "All your friends, your brother, the second children . . . If Harmonia won't take them, we'll make a place for them. We'll live as we were intended to live, and we won't control or exclude anyone!"

I'm not so sure people were intended to live that way. If we had time, I'd argue that humans have evolved to make things, to change their surroundings, to provide comforts for themselves, and that intelligence comes from learning moderation in the things we make and change. But this is not the time or place, and I'm just glad that Mira is so eager to help me now. We can work out our entire futures later, once we save Lachlan's life.

"But how do we get in? And how do we get him out again?" Mira asks.

"Maybe we don't," I say. "Maybe we make them come out, and bring Lachlan with them."

I have an idea. Only, Mira isn't going to like it.

FIRST I HAVE to make it through the rest
of the day. While my brain is awhirl with dreadful thoughts,
I have to smile with my neighbors, accept their congratulations. I'm an adult now, and they have officially accepted me
as a member of Harmonia. The change is even more notice-
able for me than for the other test-takers. The natural-borns
had less to prove. Now the villagers know that EcoPan was
right to pick me.

It shows that no system is perfect. People have faith in
systems all the time, and yet those systems fail them. The
system should have weeded out anyone who would defy the
community, question the laws, put people at risk. Yet here
I am.

The day is endless. With infinite slowness the sun creeps
toward the horizon, and I smile, and simper, and chat. I look
sincere when the older members of Harmonia talk about the
responsibility that awaits me. I nod earnestly as they tell me
of the need to be a role model for the younger generation.

As I socialize I pick up things here and there—bits of
dried moss, the white gauzy fluff of seed heads, curls of bark.
I play with them absently as I talk, slipping them into my
pockets when no one is looking. Even if they saw, they prob-

ably wouldn't remark on it. Soon my pockets are stuffed with soft, dry bits of plant matter.

Kids swarm over me, asking about the test. They never wonder why I hug them all extra tight. Such precious lives. I think about the children of the Underground. What good is any society that lets children suffer?

The festivities aren't quite as exuberant as the Wolf Moon festival, but there is an air of celebration at painful odds with my internal state. The honey cakes are dry in my mouth, the pure spring water tastes stale. And still the sun creeps slowly toward night.

Mira comes up to me near evening. "I talked to Carnelian. He needed some . . . convincing." She gives me a wry look. "You know how he feels about adventure. He is totally on board with the rescue *in theory*. It just took me a while to persuade him that the risk is worth the reward, and that the risk isn't that great in the first place."

"But it is," I tell her. "I'm feeling guilty that I've gotten you involved. What if . . ."

She puts her fists on her hips. "As of this morning, I'm an adult, just like you. You haven't gotten me involved. I choose to be involved, because it's the right thing to do."

"But the consequences are suddenly greater," I say. "Before this morning, I would have said the worst that could happen to us if we defied the elders is, I don't know, a strict talking-to. It never occurred to me that they'd consider executing someone. Now that's on the table, not just for him, but maybe for you and Carnelian if we get caught."

"We're citizens of Harmonia," she says. "I'm sure they wouldn't do that to us. And that's *if* we get caught. We won't."

"You're so sure?" I ask.

"It's a good plan."

It took me a while to talk her around to it. On the surface

it seemed to contradict the teachings she was raised with. Now, though, she's entirely on board.

Later, Carnelian brings me a strange bouquet. It is made of clusters of dried cattails, the brown sausage-like seed clusters near the top of flexible reeds. He has made it pretty with curlicues of dried grasses and ribbons dyed purple and pink. "Congratulations," he says and kisses me awkwardly on the cheek before giving me a wink that could be seen a mile away and shambling off. He's not the best co-conspirator, but I'm glad of his help.

Night falls, and still we wait. Everyone believes I am happy. As it gets later, everyone believes I am tired. I fake a yawn and get sympathetic jokes about resting while I can— adult responsibilities begin in the morning.

I say good night to a few people, ostentatiously so they will remember later. To Morgan the potter I say, "It's funny how some nights when I'm extra tired it's even harder to fall asleep. I just stare at the ceiling. It's like I'm too tired to fall asleep. Does that ever happen to you?"

I cock my head, waiting for him to dole out the words of wisdom he loves to share. In this case, I happen to know how he deals with sleepless nights.

"Moonlit walks," Morgan says. "That's the ticket! Just get out under the night sky, all alone with your own thoughts and nothing but the frogs and the breeze for company. It puts things in perspective. After I walk by my lonesome under the moonlight, I sleep like a baby."

I thank him for his advice, and promise I'll try it if I have trouble falling asleep.

There, I've done it. No one, not even the watchful elders, thinks anything in particular is on my mind. I'm a good, obedient little member of society, following the rules unthinkingly. I've even set up my cover story in case I'm caught late at night when the village is in bed. I'm just following Morgan's recommendations. He'll vouch for me if I'm caught wandering before I can put my plan into action.

Fooling my mom is going to be harder.

She's waiting for me at home, deep consternation on her face. "There you are. I thought you'd be home sooner."

I yawn—not faked this time—and tell her that a lot of people wanted to talk to the newest official members of society. "In fact, they were asking about you."

"I was too upset to socialize," she says. "I'm surprised you were able to . . ." She bites her lip. She doesn't want to accuse me of being heartless enough to enjoy myself while an innocent man was condemned.

"Life goes on," I say with a shrug. "I don't like it, but . . ." I break off. I can't push indifference too far with her. She knows me too well.

"Rowan, I was thinking. Tomorrow morning I'm going to approach the other elders again. After they've had the night to sleep on it they might see things differently. If I appeal to their conscience, their humanity, they might spare him. At least for a while, so they can think things through more carefully."

She waits for my happy response. "That's great, Mom," I say. "I'm sure you'll be able to convince them." I start to head upstairs to my bedroom.

"Rowan," my mom begins, and I stop on the steps.

"What?"

"Oh . . . never mind honey. Sleep tight."

"You too, Mom."

I go up three more steps before I stop, then whirl and run back down to her.

"Oh Mom, I love you so much! These last months with you, after I thought you were dead . . . I've been so lucky to have them. To have just a little more time with you."

"Rowan, what's gotten into you?" she asks as she hugs me back, half-suffocated by the fierceness of my embrace.

"I just don't know if I tell you often enough how much I love you. You are the most amazing woman, and I hope every day I can make you proud of me."

"Sweetheart," she says as she strokes my hair, "I am always proud of you. I'm always on your side."

For a second I study her face, wanting so much to tell her what I'm planning. She might help me. But I think of those two warring urges within her: to keep me *safe*, and make me *happy*. The first sixteen years of my life were governed by the former. She made so many sacrifices to keep me safely hidden behind our house's walls. Happiness was part of that sacrifice, hers and mine. Now, though she has loosened up so much, urging me to have adventures, I still think deep down that yearning for safety prevails.

I want to think she'd help me save Lachlan. But I think her first thought would be to save me.

So I say nothing, but let her go and head to my bed without another backward look.

Even thought I know it might be the last time I ever see her.

Every time I try to think about that, pragmatic Yarrow stops me. *You're not going to let Lachlan be killed,* she points out correctly. *So don't think too much about the consequences. None of them are going to sway you. When you rescue Lachlan you'll have to leave. That's the only option. Don't think beyond that. Anything can happen.*

"Sure," I whisper to her, "that's exactly the kind of attitude a party girl like you would have. Don't worry about what's going to happen once the sun comes up if the party is still raging through the night."

Still, her philosophy helps me get through the next hour without going crazy.

I lie on my bed, under covers but fully clothed, and wait for the house to grow quiet. I spend my time thinking about Lachlan, wondering if he is awake, in pain. It is torment. When I'm sure Mom is in bed and everything is perfectly still, I count very slowly to a hundred. Then I do it again, a deep breath for each count. Finally I roll out of bed and feel in the darkness until I find my shoes. Holding them in one hand, I pick up the pack I've prepared and throw it over the other shoulder.

The broken lower stems of Carnelian's bouquet litter my bedroom floor.

There are no lights outside, and the nightly bonfire in the village green has been doused. Those artificial logs are designed to burn without pollutants and extinguish themselves after a set time. Environmentally conscious people living in the heart of a forest are very careful with fire.

With painstaking caution I creep downstairs and let myself out. The night is still. Even the owls are quiet tonight. My footsteps sound loud to me in the heavy hush, but I tell myself that no one is awake to hear me.

Carefully, avoiding the houses and sticking to the shadows beneath the trees, I make my way toward the Hall of Elders. I don't go directly to it, but skirt around in the deep woods until I come to its rear. I know that some of the elders live there. Elder Night is one of them. Others have their own homes, and only go to the hall for official business. On this night I'm sure there will be more elders there than usual, guarding the prisoner.

But there is no one in the back. If this were Eden there would be security cameras and bots around any important building. I wouldn't have a chance. Here, though, they only guard the obvious points—the front (and only) door, and the prisoner himself.

Certain that I have the back to myself, I retreat into the woods for a moment, gathering what I need. Near my hiding place I separate it into piles according to size.

For a long time I crouch in the branches of a rhododendron, watching the back of the wooden hall like a cougar watching its prey. I know that Mira is watching the building from her house, which is nearby. Carnelian is with her. She's waiting for the very obvious signal that will tell her it is time to play her part.

Finally, when a half hour has passed without any sign of a sentry, I take what I've brought and what I've gathered to the back of the building.

I've stolen a paring knife from the communal kitchen, a small, wickedly sharp blade mostly used to peel and slice root vegetables. I tell myself I won't put it to any more deadly use tonight. This is a tool, not a weapon. I won't let anyone get hurt tonight.

I cut a long slice into one of the dried cattails Carnelian gave me, taking care not to cut all the way through to my fingers. Though it looked solid on the outside, the size and shape of an ear of corn, it explodes into chaotic fluff under my knife. Tightly packed in the cattail are the plant's seeds. Millions of them. Freed from their compression they make a mass of cloudy whiteness ten times the size of the original cattail. I open all of them the same way, patting the fluff into a ball. Bits float around my head, tickling my nose, and I have to stifle a sneeze.

I put the fluff into a tent of twigs propped up against the wall of the Hall of Elders. The dried branches like slender fingers trap the white cloud. Heftier branches fortify the structure. Larger logs, as thick as my arm, lay ready nearby.

Then, with a deep breath, I pull out a piece of flint from my pack.

The elders taught me how to make fire as part of our survival training. However, they frown upon its use except in the most dire emergencies. Cooking fires, hearths for heat were never a problem when human populations were low. After all, fires are a natural phenomenon. Started by lightning in tinder-dry forests, some trees and ecosystems actually depend on fires to survive. But fires also make pollutants, the elder taught me. One person, one village using fire won't hurt the Earth. But the symbology is as important as the reality, and to use fire (real fire, not our artificial logs) indiscriminately is to show a disregard for the Earth. So though we learn to make fire in case we are trapped away from Harmonia in the dead of winter, we aren't supposed to make a fire with real wood, ever.

What I'm doing now feels like a sacrilege.

It also feels indescribably thrilling, as I strike the piece of flint against the metal blade and see a spark fly to the intensely combustible cattail tinder. It ignites in an audible *whoosh*, and I jerk back as the heat hits my face.

The fire burns through the cattails quickly, leaving ash behind, but the twigs catch too, their dried bark singeing and crumbling as the wood burns. I blow on it gently, and like a living thing the fire feeds and grows. When it is well established I lay the larger logs on it, propped up in a triangle against the building.

After a while, they start to burn, too. And so do the wooden planks of the Hall of Elders.

The smolder is slow, creeping into the wood. The fire has to be encouraged, given just enough wood but not too much, enough air to give it the oxygen it needs to combust, but not so much that it is blown out. A new fire is a fragile thing.

But I help it grow strong.

There is something so primal about this real fire, a smell, a feel that the fake fire just can't match. The dancing red and orange flames are hypnotic. The first human to tame fire must have felt like a god.

Then I feel ashamed. The elders are right. We are just weak humans who would descend into destructive behavior within a generation if we weren't kept in control. I can feel the urges in myself.

You're only human, Yarrow says mockingly from inside my head. Or is she trying to be reassuring?

This fire is for a purpose—to save a life. This is an exception, I tell myself. I'm not someone who would harm the Earth.

The flames are leaping high now, higher than me, embracing the wall. What's on the other side? Lachlan's cell is on the opposite end, but someone might be sleeping right here. Any moment now the fire will burn through the walls and smoke will start to fill the Hall of Elders. I can only hope that no one will be hurt.

You don't really care, Yarrow whispers to me. *As long as you save Lachlan.*

"That's not true!" I snap back at her.

I want her to be wrong. But I've already shown that I can kill for what I believe in. And if the elders are advocating executing someone who has committed no crime, who only wants the freedom it is every human's right to pursue . . .

No, I fervently hope that no one gets hurt. But if they do, it is worth it in the battle against what I know in my heart is wrong.

Sure, Yarrow says infuriatingly. *But would you do all this if it was a stranger from Eden, and not Lachlan?*

"I hope I would always do the right thing," I tell her.

Funny how the right thing with you always seems to involve doing a lot of wrong-ish things along the way, she points out.

I hide in the woods again, far from the angry fire, positioning myself now so that I can see the front of the hall. Is it taking too long? What if the place is filling with smoke so fast that the elders inside just pass out, dying in their beds before anyone can spread the alarm? Have I just doomed not only Lachlan but the elders, too, to a terrible death?

Clenching my jaw, I watch and wait. Somewhere out there Mira and Carnelian are watching too. Long moments tick by.

Then, finally: "Fire!" someone gasps, barely audible. An elder runs out of the hall, trying to shout a warning, but mostly just choking. Almost immediately Mira and Carnelian rush up to him. Too fast! Will he be suspicious? No, the elder is too distraught to notice that they just happened to be nearby, to respond so quickly. He must know all the people here will take decisive, swift action. He's not surprised that two responsible young people are on hand to help.

I see the three of them confer briefly. The elder looks like he is going to run for more help, which would be disastrous. We need as few people here as possible. Carnelian catches his arm and points inside. I know he's saying that any delay might doom those who remain in the building. Together, the three of them run in, and the general alarm isn't sounded. The rest of Harmonia sleeps soundly.

How I wish I could be with them! But though I've defrayed most suspicion, it would all return if the elders saw me there now. It makes sense that Mira and Carnelian are on hand. A happy couple kissing under her family's tree house, running to help at the first sign of danger? Only coincidence. But if the girl from Eden showed up at a suspicious fire where an Eden prisoner was held, all their suspicion would come flooding back. They'd try to restrain me.

Then you'd have to use that knife for something other than vegetables, Yarrow jibes.

At last, the elder and Mira come out supporting a coughing woman. Mira runs back in, and she and Carnelian come out with another man. In and out they go, bringing five more people out, until at last Elder Night emerges, walking unassisted with a cloth pressed to her face. But where is Lachlan? Are they going to leave him to die?

No! There he is! Carnelian comes out at the head of a stretcher, with one of the guards behind. Oh no, Lachlan is still unconscious. This is going to make things a lot harder. Running tends to help in an escape.

I see lights come on in nearby tree houses. Any moment, half the village will be thronged around us. There is only the smallest window of opportunity. Come on, Mira! Do it now!

I see her run out of the building one last time, her face smeared with soot. She staggers to the elders and gasps out the story we decided on. I can't hear her from my hiding place, but I know what she's saying.

"There's someone trapped in one of the rooms. A beam fell across the door, and I can't move it. Quick, the fire is almost there! I need everyone, or he'll burn to death!" The elders all follow her. Inside, in the smoky darkness, I know Mira will loose them and run back out again.

Now is my moment.

Breaking from cover, I dash to Lachlan's side. I can't waste time looking at him, but the glimpse I get of his haggard, unconscious face makes me fear the worst.

"Stop!" Elder Night cries, coming at me as though she could physically stop me. She must have been just inside, in the shadows where I couldn't see her. "How dare you? Help! Help!"

I clench my fist around the hilt of my knife. Part of me wants to strike her. Stupid old woman, so bound by rules that she can't even protect a helpless, desperate, harmless young man! What good is wisdom if you put it to this use? I don't know if it is Yarrow or me thinking these thoughts.

I don't know what I would have done if I was alone. Luckily, this is part of the plan. Carnelian comes up behind her with a big hemp sack, the kind we usually use for storing apples, and slips it over her head. While she struggles, he winds a cord around her arms and legs. Her shouts are muffled as he carries her just past the edge of the woods and lays her down gently. Someone will find her eventually.

Mira runs out, a look of fierce glee on her face.

"Let's go!" she says, and joins me at the front of the stretcher. We each take half, while Carnelian picks up the back. Before the elders can realize they've been tricked, before any more villagers come to help with the fire, we've carried Lachlan into the woods.

In the confusion of the fire, it will be a while before anyone realizes what happened. When the elders come out to see Elder Night gone, they'll think she commandeered some villagers to take Lachlan somewhere safe. With her voice muffled in the sack and the cacophony of rescue efforts, no one might find Elder Night and learn the truth until daybreak, a few hours from now.

We did it. Everything went perfectly. I can't believe it. So many things could have gone wrong, but here we are, with Lachlan safe!

WE'RE FREE.

Or, as free as we can be carrying a heavy, unconscious man, with an entire village about to come after us, maybe in minutes, maybe in hours. Him being unconscious for very long wasn't part of the plan. Feeling a sense of déjà vu, I try to wake him, but he remains completely out of it. We were counting on him being mobile. Having to carry him will slow us down so much we might be caught.

"We have to find a place to hide until he wakes up," I say.

"But where?" Carnelian asks. "This close to the village, there's no place that they don't know about. There's nowhere to hide."

Mira and I exchange a look, both thinking the same thing.

"And it could be hours until he wakes up," Carnelian continues. "We don't know what they gave him and . . ."

"There's one place," she says. "It's a bit of a hike, but not too far. We can hole up there and then when he's awake make a break for it. If we're careful about tracks, and if they don't come for us until morning, and if he wakes up relatively soon, we should be okay."

That's a lot of ifs, Yarrow comments.

"If only there was a way to wake him up faster," I muse.

"The place we're going might be able to help with that, too. I'm just not sure . . ." She bites her lower lip. "I wish I had paid more attention!"

She won't tell us any more now, though, but leads us onward as we laboriously hike with our heavy burden. We clamber over roots, through tangles of vines and thorns, and all the while I just want to take Lachlan in my arms, cover him with kisses, weep just to see him again.

"How come I never knew about this place?" Carnelian asks when we finally make it. "It seems like it would be a perfect place to be alone with your boyfriend and . . ."

"That's why I never showed you!" she quips. She parts the thick tangle of rhododendron branches in exactly the right spot and unlatches the well-hidden door.

We set him down near the fountain of the strange half-man, half-fish creature. Lachlan looks like death, so limp and helpless, his cheeks gaunt, still covered in the dry dust of his desert crossing.

Mira is busying herself with some of the plants. This is so

not the time for gardening, Yarrow quips, but I pay attention when Mira comes back with an assortment of leaves, blossoms, and a narrow yellowish root. She kneels down by Lachlan, next to me, holding the collection of plants in her lap.

"We all learn about the healing power of plants," she says. True, that has been part of my training these last three months, but after a lifetime without any living, growing things beyond a few hardy kinds of algae and moss, I'm afraid that plants mostly look alike to me. Marvelously beautiful, of course, but I think I'm too overwhelmed simply by the fact that plants exist to pay attention to how many lobes a leaf has, or the number of petals on a flower. I'm making progress, but it is slow.

"My father was fascinated by medicinal plants. After he got sick . . ." She gulps, and it is a moment before she can go on. "He tried every remedy the Elders could suggest, but nothing worked. So as he got worse, and had less to lose, he started trying the plants in this garden. They don't grow anywhere else, you see, so he hoped there might be something that could work, something we'd never find in the woods.

One thing he tried put him to sleep, another made him have visions. He tried different combinations. One mixture helped the cramping that came with his wasting disease. Another made his mind feel like it was floating, so he didn't worry about the future. Other herbs and combinations had less beneficial results. One made him vomit for days. Another slowed his heartbeat so much I thought he was going to die then and there. But this combination," she says as she holds up the plant material, "made him exceptionally alert. His pulse increased, he couldn't sit still, and he didn't sleep for two days. So I was thinking, maybe if we give that combination to Lachlan, it will wake him up."

"It's worth a shot," I say. "The longer we stay near the

village, the greater our chances that someone will track us and try to stop us."

"There's only one problem," Mira says.

Of course there is, Yarrow gripes. *Although, it's nice to have only one for a change. Usually there are a dozen problems at least.*

"When my father tried his different medicines, he took them home and made them into tea. We don't have any way of doing that here."

"We have water," Carnelian says, gesturing to the fountain.

"And we have fire," I say, taking out the flint.

"But we don't have anything to boil it in," Mira says.

My shoulders slump in defeat.

"Of course, he was only in the beginning of his experiments. Maybe the plants don't need heat to bring out their properties, I don't know. But the bottom line is we can't just shove the plants into his mouth. He can't chew them if he is unconscious. So one of us is going to have to chew up the leaves, flowers and the root, and then . . ."

There's nothing I wouldn't do for Lachlan. Even chewing up nasty, bitter plants that make my tongue go numb and spitting the resulting juice into his mouth.

We will never speak of this again, Yarrow says.

For a while, nothing happens to Lachlan. If what I'm feeling is any indication, though, this should definitely do the trick. I did my best to spit everything out after I'd chewed it, but I must have swallowed some because I feel my heart racing as if I'd chugged three supercaffeinated drinks. My heart is racing, and I can feel my fingers and toes begin to twitch, itching for activity.

For a long moment, Lachlan just lies there, same as before, his face slack. Then I see his eyes start to move beneath closed eyelids, back and forth, like he's following some frenetic game. Soon his eyes flutter open. He moans, and instantly I'm pushing his hair away from his brow. He blinks blearily, but then his golden second-child eyes manage to focus on me.

I stroke the cold sweat of his cheek. "Lachlan, you're safe." With the entire village coming in search of us within a few hours at best, safe is a bit of a stretch, but it's what he needs at this moment.

"Are you real?" he gasps. Slowly, as if I might dissolve at any moment, he reaches up to touch my face. "You're alive? I thought I would never see you again. The explosion . . ."

"I'm as real as you are," I say, and chuckle, because I can hardly believe that myself.

He smiles back, then winces, but smiles through the pain. "That smile. I dreamed of that smile. The memory of it kept me going, even when knowing I'd never see it again made me almost despair."

A troubled look crosses his face. "Wait, is this real? Am I . . ."

I can tell exactly what is going through his head. As someone who has woken up in one too many bad situations, I know he is thinking this is too good to be true. He thinks he might be a prisoner in the Center, that everything he sees is the result of a drug or a mind implant. I hasten to reassure him.

"EcoPan set me free. It saved me from the explosion in the Underground, sent me here."

"And where is here, exactly?" he asks with a touch of lingering suspicion.

"The natural world. You made it out of Eden. But the people of Harmonia—the place we live—wanted to kill you."

"What?" He looks confused, aghast.

"An outsider came before, and killed people. They don't trust anyone from Eden, really, but they have to accept the people EcoPan chose. Don't worry, you're safe now."

He makes a choking sound of relief, and suddenly I'm in his arms. He's holding me like he never wants to let me go.

"These are my friends, Mira and Carnelian."

I help him sit up, and he looks around. His jaw drops in amazement. "Did I make it out? Did I cross the desert? I feel like I've been dreaming for days."

"Harmonian drugs are pretty strong," I say, making Yarrow chuckle inside of me. "I've experienced them quite a bit myself lately. Don't worry, things will become clearer soon."

"Where am I?" he asks.

"You made it to Harmonia, a city not too far from Eden. It's a village that exists close to nature, and sometimes EcoPan selects people from Eden to be set free, to live in Harmonia."

He's gazing in wonder at the garden around him. Although it is night, there's a bright moon overhead. That light is enhanced by the gardening bots disguised as beetles. Every jewel-like carapace is glowing as they scurry about their chores. They illuminate the exotic flowers and foliage with a mystical glow.

Lachlan is entranced. "The living world," he breaths. "I believed you when you told me—I really did. But even then, I never imagined it could be like this." He spreads his arms to the orchids, the vines full of white flowers like stars, the heady floral scent that fills the air. He pulls me into his arms, whispering fiercely into my hair, "Oh, Rowan, do you know what this means? It means the people of Eden have hope!"

I feel deliriously, deliciously happy nestled in his arms. I want to stay here forever, in this magical garden with my loved ones all around me. But we're not safe here. And some of my loved ones are missing.

"Can you walk?" I ask him, breaking the spell. "We have to go."

Suddenly it hits me exactly what I've dragged Mira and Carnelian into. This isn't just an adventure. This is something that is changing their whole lives, making them leave behind everything they've known since they were born. "Not you two," I add suddenly to Mira and Carnelian. "We can't let you become involved in this. It's . . . it's an Eden matter. You have your own lives here."

"Nonsense," Mira says adamantly. "We're adults who made our own decisions. We want to help Lachlan. We want to help everyone in Eden. I was already planning to get back into Eden to help your brother and friends."

"Really?" Carnelian asks, surprised. He just got roped into this at the last minute. I think despite what Mira said about his enthusiasm, and his willingness to risk himself and leave the life he knew in Harmonia behind, he hasn't really thought this through.

"We were raised to help people, to prevent suffering, to bring peace to all living things," Mira says. "The elders might have forgotten what that means, but we haven't. We can't be happy in Harmonia while thousands of people are suffering in Eden."

"So," Lachlan says, "what's your plan?"

"Er . . ."

Lachlan struggles unsteadily to his feet, standing with his shoulders squared, breathing deeply of the nectar-scented night air. He looks at me with that maddening, mocking expression I've missed so much. "Let me guess—no plan?"

"Well, not exactly." I admit. "I hadn't really gotten that far yet. See, there was this test, and then you showed up . . ."

"Sorry I ruined your complete and total lack of plan," he says dryly . . . and winks at Mira! I suppress a giggle. The two of them are bonding already.

"Whatever the plan for Eden is, right now we have to get Lachlan far away from Harmonia," Mira says. "Can you run?" He nods.

"Mira, Carnelian, are you sure about this?" I ask. "No one saw us tie up Elder Night. You can come up with a story to cover yourselves. You ran after us, and lost us in the forest. They'll believe that. Go back to your peaceful lives.

"No way," Mira says, and Carnelian echoes her.

"There's a difference between a peaceful life and a useless life," he says with sincerity. "We're blips in time, a few pounds in a biomass of billions. I want my existence to count for something."

"Well said," Lachlan says, clapping him on the shoulder.

But I'm not ready to go yet. "Tell me what's been happening inside of Eden," I beg. "Lark, Ash, what happened to them?"

"Ash is alive. I don't know where, not exactly. I haven't seen him, but word got passed to me that he escaped. He told everyone what you did, how you blew up the Underground to disrupt the power system, so all the captive second children could be set free. I . . . I thought you had died that day. I mourned you. Oh, Rowan!"

I'm in his arms again, and I can feel him shaking against me.

"Where is he now?" I ask.

"Somewhere in the outer circles, I think. There's so much chaos inside of Eden right now. All I know is that he escaped the first attack on the Underground, and was found after the explosion. After that, I haven't heard anything about him. I've been operating in the inner circles, and communication between circles has been hard."

"What about Lark," I ask.

I feel him go rigid. "Lark?" he asks, looking completely confused, but then Mira interrupts.

"I know you want to ask him more, but all that won't do us any good if we're captured. We have to move!"

"And, if you don't mind me butting in to your lack of

a coherent plan," Carnelian says with a wry wink, "I know exactly where we should go."

"Where?"

"Well, I am ranked in the second tier, and we seconds have access to the hypertube codes. Mostly so we can perform maintenance. Not like we're actually allowed to go anywhere in them. But I can open the doors and activate the motors and programming, so I'm pretty sure I can actually make one go where I want it to go."

"You mean, you can get us away? Far away?"

"I think so, as long as we get there before anyone thinks to disable my codes."

Before we leave the enchanted garden, Lachlan plucks a flower, a pink-purple blossom with golden pollen in its heart He tucks it inside his shirt and gives a lingering glance over his shoulder at the magical bower.

"Just wait till you see the rest," I whisper to him, and lead him out into the woods. He stands stunned, looking up at the trees all around him. Bats soar and dip overhead, searching for insects with chirps and whistles. An owl hoots softly in a nearby pine. "It's not like I thought," Lachlan says. "It's bigger. It's realer!"

We run through the forest, away from Harmonia, that paradise I thought was my reward. Carnelian pauses now and then to check his heading against the stars that peek through the treetops, and corrects our course.

The terrain is growing more hilly. Stones threaten to twist our feet in the dark. Another hour of jogging through the woods and we come to a rocky outcrop.

"Here it is," Carnelian says. "They made sure it is far enough from the village that no one will stumble on it accidentally."

"I don't see it."

"Look, right there," he says, pointing to a high but narrow cleft in the rocks. The depth of blackness behind hints that there might be a cave, but the opening is far too narrow for anyone to get through.

Carnelian leads the way. Then, seemingly at random, he moves one rock to pile it on top of another. He frowns, cocking his head. "It's hard to remember, but I think that's right." Then he very deliberately leans against the skinny trunk of an almost leafless sapling right by the fissure in the rock.

"Carnelian, be careful!" I cry, because it looks like he's knocked the young tree over. It tilts about fifteen degrees, and I hear a creaking sound.

To my amazement, the crack in the rock grows wider. With a grinding of seldom used gears, the cave is opening up to reveal a small room inside. Lights come on automatically, revealing metal walls, and elevator doors. From the outside I can see there's only one large button, with an illuminated arrow pointing *down*.

"That's amazing!" Mira says, looking closer. "I can't see any mechanism in the rock. It's so cleverly hidden."

The first and only warning I get is a single snap of a twig. Then suddenly it's like there's a bear in our midst. Zander springs from the forest seemingly out of nowhere, swinging a huge club studded with spiky knobs. It's so shocking that we just scatter, diving out of the way of his weapon. He swings wildly, with full force. If it hit us it would break our bones, smash our skulls.

The attack is so fierce and so fast that before we know it he's gotten between us and the door to the hypertube. We stand ringed around him, out of reach of his swinging club as he easily holds us at bay. Mira wants to fight, I can tell, but even with her considerable skills the club is a serious threat.

"Stay back!" he shouts. "Do you really think I'm going to let you destroy all we've worked for in Harmonia?"

I glance at Lachlan. At least Zander doesn't have a gun. There's no such thing in Harmonia. But this club he's fashioned out of wood is almost as lethal. We could probably subdue him if we worked together, but not without at least one of us getting hurt.

"Zander, stay out of this," I shout at him. "We're no threat to Harmonia. In fact, we're leaving. You'll never have to deal with us again."

"I don't believe you," he growls, swinging his club as Lachlan makes a feint toward him. "You want to open up the prison and let all the scum spill out, bring their abhorrent technology and destructive ways to our paradise."

"Zander, people from Eden aren't scum," I say in my most reasonable voice. "They're just people. Just like you."

I have to hand it to him, he's brave. Sure he's bigger than any of us, and armed. But there are four of us against one.

Not bad odds. But five against one is even better.

I see a shadow come from around the rocks, and then quiet as a panther, a hooded woman slips around from behind the rocky outcrop and tackles Zander from behind. It catches him totally off guard and he sprawls, rolling to kick her off him. But it's all we need. Mira springs, wresting away his club, and the rest of us pile on top of him. Mira raises the club over her head . . . but she just holds it there, threateningly.

The hooded woman takes a case from her bag, snaps it open, and pulls out a needle and a vial of clear liquid. While Zander struggles, she slides the needle into his arm, and a few seconds later his eyes roll back in his head and he flops limply.

The woman stands, holding up the needle. A glint of moonlight catches a liquid drop on the tip. The plunger is still half-full. She shakes her head, letting her hood fall back.

It's Mom.

WHILE MOM STANDS threateningly near us, I dash between Mom and Lachlan.

"Mom, don't put me in this position," I say, my voice dangerously low. "You know what I'm doing is right. Don't make me choose between you."

"Rowan, you're not thinking straight," she begins, taking a step closer.

"Don't!" I warn, and slip my hand into my pocket where I can feel the knife hilt. I never would. Of course I never would.

But I can't let them take Lachlan back. I can't let him be executed.

"I'm not your enemy, sweetheart," she says, advancing slowly.

I don't know what to do. I can't fight my mother. My hand comes out of my pocket, empty.

"Please, Mom, just go back to Harmonia and pretend you never found us. He won't be a threat to your way of life, I swear. I'll take him far away, and no one in Harmonia will ever see him again."

There are tears in my eyes as I say this. I always knew that saving Lachlan would strip me away from Harmonia forever, and that meant losing my mom. I almost managed not to think about this inevitability. There's no sacrifice I wouldn't make for Lachlan. But that doesn't mean my heart isn't torn in two.

"It's not going to work," my mom says. "They'll find you and bring you back." She takes another step and I stand frozen between two people I love. Then she smiles. "At least, they will if you're using second-rank codes. Carnelian, don't you know they'll shut down the hypertube and lock it if you attempt to actually ride in one. You'd be held there until the whole village arrived." She grins at me. "And what would happen to Lachlan then?"

"You know this is Lachlan?" I ask, amazed.

"Sweetie, I've known you all your life. Do you think I can't tell when you're lying? I remembered your description of him and put two and two together. And of course I knew you were going to rescue him. So I pretended to go to sleep, and waited for you to make your move. Which was a spectacular one, by the way."

I tell Mom how we used the plants to wake him.

"He's still pretty wired," I say.

"But otherwise in good shape," Mom says after looking him over. "They gave him intravenous hydration and nutrients so he's actually in pretty good shape."

"Heal him so they can kill him?" I ask wryly.

"They're wrong. So completely wrong. I always knew it, but I was so concerned about protecting Harmonia. They are, too. The elders aren't evil people. They're just blinded by their beliefs. So blind they've forgotten how to think. I had been planning to tell everyone in Harmonia the truth, force them to weight their conscience against the elders' decision. Even if most people agreed, there might have been enough dissent to save him. At the very least, the elders couldn't hide their actions." She stands up, so straight, so strong. "I refuse to live in a city of secrets again."

"You only just got your first tier ranking," Carnelian says. "How do you know how to run the hypertubes already?"

"I don't, not really. I'll be relying on you for the details. But they gave me the codes as soon as I got my results after the test," Mom adds, puling a little notebook from her pocket. "I was supposed to be studying the codes and procedures, memorizing them precisely so I didn't have to carry around a written record that might fall into the wrong hands." She giggles. "Looks like *mine* are the wrong hands!"

"I can't believe my mom is actually having fun on this adventure," I say in an aside to Lachlan.

"Like mother like daughter," he answers. "I remember seeing just that look in your eyes when we were running away from trouble."

"And running into it," I add. Somehow my hand has found his.

"We should hurry," Mom says. "If Zander is here, the others must know, and can't be far behind."

But there's no other sign of pursuit. "Maybe not," I suggest. "Zander seems like the kind of guy who would just come after us by himself. If he saw what happened he would have sounded the alarm, but if he came up later he might have decided to try to track us on his own."

"I hate to admit it, but he's a good tracker," Mira says. "*Almost* as good as me."

So we might not be in any more immediate danger.

The others head to the door, but I hang back. "You . . . you're going to leave him?"

"What else are we supposed to do?" Mira asks, looking at Zander's unconscious form with disdain. "He tried to kill us."

"I don't think he would have . . ." I begin, but Mira interrupts.

"I know you always want to think the best of people, but

he would have bashed our skulls in or dragged us back to the elders if he could. He's like . . . a rabid animal. It might be part of nature, but it's not a part you want around you."

"He's doing what he believes in" I say. "We should try to change his mind."

"And if we had time, I'd agree with you," Mom interjects. "But now we have to go, while my codes still work."

They enter the building, but I linger behind. There are panthers out here, and bears. Wolves, too. While he's unconscious he's at the mercy of any predator that wanders by.

Seriously, Yarrow asks with an exaggerated sigh inside my head as I grab Zander under the armpits and try to drag him into the room. *Do you forget that he broke our fingers! Maybe a bear will gnaw off a few of his.*

Shut up, I tell her. If you can't help . . .

I am helping. I'm amazed you managed to keep us alive for so long, Rowan. You have awful survival instincts.

"Oh, no, Rowan," Carnelian groans as he sees what I'm doing.

"Rowan, come on," Mira says. "You can't . . ." She breaks off when she sees the determined expression I throw over my shoulder. I can only budge Zander's bulk an inch at a time, but bik it, I'm not going to leave him out here. I wouldn't do that to anyone.

"We can keep him sedated, and leave him here in the station. He'll be able to get himself back to Harmonia. It's not like they won't be able to track us themselves once the sun comes up. They'll figure out where we've gone. We just have to have a good head start. But I won't leave him unconscious alone in the woods. I can't."

With a sigh them help me drag him inside, and the rock doors slide closed behind us.

It feels cramped with all of us in this little room. Mom

consults her book and enters a code. The elevator doors soundlessly open, and we step inside, leaving Zander on the floor.

I can barely feel the movement of the descent, just a faint sort of tremor beneath my feet. But we go down for a long time. Finally the doors open.

"Wow," Mira breathes. "I mean, I'd heard about the hypertubes. You can keep a lot of secrets, but you can't keep *everything* secret. But I had no idea!"

We're gazing over a huge, illuminated room. The air is cool and dry. The cavernous room is starkly empty except for a giant metal pipe that looks like a mutant worm, silver and segmented. It bisects the echoing space. I can see clear access doors on the side.

Mom punches in another code. "Looks like my codes still work."

The clear door opens to reveal a capsule inside the tube. The curving walls are a shimmering mother-of-pearl, and the sides are lined with plush seats upholstered in bright turquoise.

"Where are we going?" I ask, watching with some amusement as Mira and Carnelian dare each other to cross into the threshold first. They look as apprehensive as I was the first time I tried to swim across the river. I guess the world is full of currents that push us out of our comfort zones.

"We want to get far from Harmonia. My initiation study book lists places the hypertube links with hundreds of miles away. I don't know anything about any of them, but there are basic descriptions. What do you think of this one?"

She flips a page and shows me a map with a neon blue tracing leading south, then west: the path of one of the hypertubes. I study the topographic lines, figure out the mileage, then realize what the change of elevation and other indications are hinting at. "Is that one by the ocean?" I ask with excitement.

She nods, grinning.

"The ocean!" I say with a sigh, turning to Lachlan. "Can you imagine it?" I've forgotten all danger at the prospect. For someone who grew up in a world with nothing but city and humans, any aspect of nature is still a boon. But the sea! I never dreamed I'd see it, swim in it. I can picture the majestic beauty of the crashing waves, the endless bounty of life hidden in its depths. Yes, I can imagine a home by the sea with Lachlan . . .

"But what about Ash?" I ask. And then I realize that in the excitement I didn't even tell her. "Ash is alive! Or, he was, after the explosion." I told Mom what happened when I blew up the Underground, but I had no idea what happened to my brother. "We can find him, get him out of Eden . . ."

Mom sighs. "You can't just go charging into Eden, Rowan. How would you cross the desert? And even if you made it, there's a price on your head, and mine. And how would we get him out again? Oh, Rowan, I know you want to save him. So do I. And we will!" She sounds brightly enthusiastic, and for a second I wonder if she's humoring me. "But we have no idea how. Right now we have to get away from Harmonia. You know what will happen to Lachlan if they catch him."

I gulp. "Okay," I concede. "We get far away first." I don't like that my mission has changed so dramatically. I'm happy beyond belief that I have Lachlan, but I can't give up on everyone else.

Can I?

What if Lachlan is enough?

What if the idea of breaking into Eden is a foolish, suicidal dream?

Maybe I should be happy with what I have. It is so much more than I ever thought possible. Mom. Lachlan. My two dear friends. Freedom. The ocean, and a whole world to explore. Realistically I know that will most likely all slip from my grasp if I try to get back into Eden. I'll loose it all.

"How long will it take to get there?" Lachlan asks.

"Um, I'm not sure," Mom says. "We can't get directly there anyway."

"Why not?"

She studies the maps a moment longer. "Looks like this is a direct hypertube, just to one destination: the central terminal. We have to go to that main station. It's the place where all the tubes branch out. From there, we can take a direct line to the ocean."

"Okay," I say. "How far away is the main station?"

Mom presses her lips together in a thin line before she answers reluctantly, "It's not far. In fact, it's directly outside of Eden."

A SHIVER RUNS through me, head to toe, and when it reaches my feet I actually stand, poised as if I'm going to run away. But there's nowhere to go.

Eden.

For the last three months, since my miraculous release, I've told myself I'm going back. But it was all hypothetical, a future I'd face when the time came. Now I'm zooming underground toward my old prison home and I'm terrified.

Against all conceivable odds you escaped, Yarrow says, *and now you want to go back?*

No, I don't, I tell her in my head. *I want to run away from here as fast as I can.* With Yarrow, my other self, I can be honest, even if I'd never confess the shameful depth of my fear to anyone else.

That's the trouble with you, Rowan, Yarrow grumbles to me. *You know the best way to keep us alive. You just never actually do it.*

It doesn't matter now, I think as the hypertube builds up speed. We're not going to Eden. We'll just be stopping near the outskirts. We probably don't even have to leave these subterranean depths. We just change tubes and take off.

Still, it is far too close for comfort. I feel like the power and authority of the Center can reach out across the divide and snatch away my freedom if I even get close.

I make myself settle down, and I can finally talk about what's most important to me. "Lachlan, what's been happening in Eden?"

The tale he tells turns my selfish dread inside out, replacing it with incredulous fury.

Eden had a civil war.

And in a way, it was my fault.

"My brother Rook helped me escape when they stormed the Underground. It's good to have a greenshirt on your side. But an explosion had gone off right near me, and it was weeks before the dizziness passed, or I could hear again. By the time I was ready to fight, a lot had happened."

The more prosperous middle and inner circles had often been largely spared from interference in their memories and neurons. The wealthy and educated were always more easy to control by traditional methods. Financial incentives, comfort, and a feeling of superiority were usually enough to keep them in line.

"Not so now," Lachlan says. "Everyone, rich and poor, knew there was something deeply wrong in Eden. Chief Ellena feared she was losing control, and that made her even more ruthless. There was unrest everywhere. But no one could agree on the exact nature of the problem, or the solution. Rebel factions were springing up in every circle."

Tales started to spread of a prophet who the Center had tried to imprison but who slipped through their clutches. "The prophet spoke of a green land beyond the desert, a world of plenty just waiting for humans to take over."

A sick feeling settles in my belly.

"She was a prisoner of the Chief, but many, many people in the Center heard her prophetic ravings. An orderly, a menial worker, recorded her words. He was a member of the Dominion sect."

I gasp. The Dominion is a very secret organization that believes humans should have dominion over the Earth and all living things. It is the exact opposite of everything Eden is supposed to stand for. They think animals are made to be eaten, that the Earth is vast enough to be abused and still recover, still give humans her blessing.

"He spread that recording among the Dominion followers, and that attracted more. Suddenly there were thousands of people who were convinced that there is a living world beyond Eden, that it is their manifest destiny to find it and fill it, to use it and exploit it."

"But they can't . . ." I choke out. "You mean, as soon as they hear about all this wonder out here, they want to lay waste to it?"

"They think it is their right. The Dominion was in open war with the Center, trying to find a way out of Eden. Guards were posted everywhere, and the outer circle turned into a militarized zone."

I was only trying to tell the truth, to let people know there was a way to live with space, with freedom, without government control. The survival of the natural world was supposed to be happy news. But there are always some people who will corrupt anything.

"But the factions couldn't work together, and no single group could achieve dominance. Still, they caused a lot of trouble for the Center."

"Things sound pretty bad," I say.

"You have to be hopeful, Rowan," Lachlan urges. "Yes, things are terrible now, but great things can come out of chaos."

"But now it sounds like all that's coming from it is death," I say miserably.

"Chaos is better than blindness and apathy. They were fighting. If they could have come together, the Center might have been overthrown."

But they didn't, he tells us, and then Chief Ellena implemented her new plan.

"The Center looked like it was in trouble for a while. So many people were mobilizing against it. But then the Center came up with a new way to control the people."

Usually, the lens implants that every legal citizen of Eden has can only control them in minor, basic ways. Through the lenses, EcoPan subtly turns their attention away from things it doesn't want them to see, keeps them from getting too curious. And the lenses can be used to monitor their actions and, in a rough way, their thoughts. But most of that came from EcoPan. At times when the Center wanted to really mess up someone's perceptions, they had to do it through surgery, going directly into the brain to access the connections already initially forged by the lenses.

Changing people completely, like the Chief did with me or Pearl, was a slow and complicated process. Until just a couple of weeks ago.

Chief Ellena came up with a way to broadcast complicated mind control directly to anyone with an implant.

"This can do far more than they'd ever done before," Lachlan tells me. "Overnight, almost the entire population was as calm and happy as if they were drugged. In a way, they are. We think the signal stimulates the centers of the brain that identify pleasure and contentment. Suddenly everyone, even the most passionate of the rebels, stopped worrying."

It almost sounds nice, doesn't it? Yarrow says.

"They're like happy zombies now. They've forgotten about the rebellion, forgotten about the fighting. I mean, there are still bullet casings in the street! People's wives, children, friends are missing! And no one cares. They do their jobs, eat their synthetic food, go to school, play games, gossip . . . and look almost like they did before. Almost normal. But nothing bothers anyone anymore."

I know what we're all thinking—the same thing that Yarrow thought. In a way, it sounds like a Utopian society, right? Everyone content, no one complaining. A happy, peaceful population where everyone knows their place, and accepts it.

I shudder with a deep, terrible chill.

"The worst thing in the world is to be forced to feel something," I say softly. "Even if it is happiness. We have to stop them."

"The second children aren't affected," he says. "Only people with the eye implants."

"*Everyone* with implants is affected?" I ask.

"Almost. There are some . . . glitches. Some people seem to break out of it, at least for a while. Some go almost numb, uninterested in anything around them, even eating. But for the most part, everyone is under the Chief's control. But . . . you remember Flame, right?"

Of course. She's the intense, red-haired neurocybersurgeon who deactivated my lenses. She could only remove one, though, so I'm left with mismatched eyes. "Flame has been deactivating as many people as she can, severing the connection with the Center. She learned a lot from your surgery. We basically have to kidnap our old allies and do the procedure. Once it's done, though, they remember what they were fighting for and rejoin us."

"Do you know how to stop it completely?" I ask.

"Flame and the others are working on it. I haven't seen her since the raid on the Underground, though. I've been working near the Center, sabotaging security, trying to cut Center communications. The main rebel holdout is in the outer circle.

She's there, I think. I only get bits and pieces of what is going on. Communication has been difficult, as you might imagine."

Flame is focusing on a way to stop the mind control. Meanwhile, Lachlan embarked on a mission of his own.

"It might not work," he admitted. "There might be no way to stop the Center. But maybe we can escape it. That's why I had to reach the outside. I thought if I could cross over, if I could prove that there was an outside world, it would give people hope and purpose. They would unify. We could stop fighting the Center directly, and focus instead of finding a way to open up Eden. We all have to leave."

"Even the Dominion faction?"

"Who knows how many of their members are true fanatics?" Lachlan says as he holds my hand and leans close. "I think many of them are just desperate for something to believe in. Anything, other than the city, which is all they've ever known. If a starving child dreams of a candy store, do they fantasize about eating just one sweet? Or do they dream about going crazy, devouring everything in sight with no thought of the consequences? I think if the Dominion knew there was actually an outside world, if they could see it as I have, they would never want to risk destroying it."

I stare out the window at the flickering blur of the tube walls flying past. Am I the only cynical one? Everyone else seems to believe wholeheartedly that if humans had a chance in the natural world they wouldn't mess it up. I'd like to think that . . . but I'm still not sure.

The hypertube comes to a stop. I have no idea how far we've traveled. Its speed is impossible to calculate. We'd been traveling no more than twenty minutes, but we could have gone fifty miles or two hundred.

"Uh-oh," Mom says as she flips through her guidebook. "I made a mistake. Don't worry, not a major one. I hope." She gives a nervous laugh. "The main terminal is just outside of Eden. It's just in a separate facility than this one. We have to leave this station, go to the surface, and walk . . ." She squints at a diagram. "Oh, not far at all. A few hundred yards. No problem."

I let everyone else go ahead of me. I hear Mira's exclamation of disappointment. "I can't see anything! Just desert."

"You were hoping for smog and grime and factory turrets?" Carnelian asks. "The wails of tormented souls?"

"Well, you hear about hell for so long, you kind of hope it is going to look a little more impressive," she says.

I have to take a deep breath before I step into the open. The sun, just risen above the horizon, glows molten in the east as I look toward my old home.

Mira is right—it doesn't look very impressive. The pale gold desert shimmers with blistering heat. Beyond that, I know, is the line of the towering bean trees, but they are camouflaged, and hide any trace of the city beyond a sort of fog, the haze of the particulate dome that arcs over the whole city. We were once told it protected us from the harmful effects of the sun's interaction with the atmospheric particles that supposedly destroyed the Earth (the supposed reason everyone in Eden had to get lenses). But we know that was all a lie. The lenses were for monitoring and mind control. What is the hazy dome for? Some other way to keep humanity trapped and controlled?

Still, I know that there are more than a million people just a few miles away. A million people at war, suffering, struggling.

Finally, I ask the question that has been struggling to come out. The question I have been so deeply afraid to ask. Until I ask, until I know, anything is possible, and I can pretend that the best-case scenario is true. When I asked

Lachlan about Lark earlier, he reacted in an odd way. More than I could attribute to jealousy. Does that mean he doesn't know . . . or knows, but doesn't want to say?

And Lachlan hasn't volunteered anything. That can't be a good sign, can it? If she were alive, he would have told me straightaway, right?

"Do you know what happened to the second children?" I ask in a trembling voice. "To everyone?" I'm afraid to say Lark's name. Afraid to hear bad news.

"I wish I could tell you more about your brother. I'm sorry. It has been hard to coordinate communications, and we've tried to divide the resistance cells so that if someone is captured and interrogated—or mind-probed—they can't give away too much. I know most of the second children made it out of the Center, thanks to you, and your father, but what their fate is now, I don't know."

"You don't know about Lark?"

He gives me a puzzled look. "Lark? She . . ." He swallows hard. "Did they wipe your memory again?" He takes my hand and says very gently, "Rowan, Lark died. Don't you remember? The nanosand took her when we tried to cross the desert."

"Oh, you don't know!" I beam at him. "She's alive! The nanosand doesn't kill. It's just another lie we've been told. It swallows people down to an underground holding station, and they're sent to the Center, imprisoned or reeducated or experimented on, or whatever evil thing the Center wants to do. I saw her! She was in prison, alive!"

"Did she get out with the others? I know everyone from the Underground escaped."

"I don't know," I say. "I was hoping you knew."

He shakes his head. "I'm so sorry, Rowan. I haven't seen her or heard about her. But you have to remember, there's been a lot of chaos. I've only had contact with a couple of the second children. None of them have mentioned her, and of course I wouldn't think to ask."

Strangely, I feel almost elated. I was braced for the worst news. To still not know means that all possibilities are still open. If he doesn't know Lark and Ash are dead, they might still be alive! I feel a surge of hope . . .

"The station is this way," Mom calls, interrupting my reverie. "Come on, Rowan. We'll come back soon, once we have a plan. I promise."

But so many things can go wrong between promise and fulfillment. Just a few miles away, a computer program and a madwoman are controlling people's minds. Somewhere in there, Ash might be alive. And Lark.

Lachlan is looking at his lifelong home, too. "I used to think we had to fix Eden," he says, choosing his words carefully. "Now I know that it is irrevocably broken. EcoPan, the Center . . . there's no way Eden can be saved. Humanity needs a new beginning."

"We'll be back, Rowan," Mira says, taking Carnelian's arm and following my mom.

But we're here now. If we leave, who knows what might happen? Once we're at the distant sea, Mom's access codes might be revoked. We might be stuck there.

We don't have a plan. I know it would be suicide to go into Eden without a foolproof scheme, an army of allies. And even if we had that, how could we get in? Even with an exposure suit, the desert almost killed Lachlan. If only the hyper-tube had a conduit that ran underneath the desert, I think, as with heavy feet I turn away to follow the others.

If only there was a way across the desert, through, or over, or under . . .

Quick as lightning, I make my impulsive decision and take off running.

"Rowan, come back!" Mom screams, but I hardly hear her. I'm racing into the brutal, scorching desert sands.

The heat smacks me like a stone wall, making me stagger as my skin instantly flushes red.

"Rowan, are you crazy?" Mira shouts. "We have to go! You can't get across that now. You'll die."

I stop and turn around. "I can't leave them inside. I can't leave them without hope!"

"The desert will kill you, Rowan," Lachlan says, stepping tentatively onto the sand. "You can't cross without protection. Even with it. You know that. We tried before. I don't know how I made it across this time. I was sure I was going to die."

"You risked your life for what you believe in," I shout across the blistering sands. "You don't expect me to do the same?"

"It's not the same," he argues, coming closer. "I had a chance. You have no chance of getting across."

"I have no intention of crossing the desert," I say, and I can see the relief wash over him. He holds out a hopeful hand. "I'm going to go under it." His hand falls and he stares at me in confusion.

I turn and scan the horizon. Any moment now . . .

He sees it before I do. "Nanosand!" he cries in warning, and I run.

But I don't run away from the mobile, hungry threat.

"Rowan, look out!"

And Mom shouts, "What are you doing?"

"The nanosand will take me to the Center," I yell back to her. "It's a way into Eden!"

"Don't be crazy!" Lachlan fumes. "Even if that's true, you'll just be delivering yourself to the Center. The Chief will experiment on you again. You'll forget everything." I can see the anguish on his face. "Please, no. Not after I only just found you again."

I can feel my heart breaking. But it is also breaking for the people imprisoned in Eden. I walk toward the nanosand. It in turn is stalking me, creeping closer, expecting me to flee.

"It's suicide! You'll be caught, and never escape from the Center."

"Maybe," I say. "If I don't have help." Then I stand still and let the nanosand take me.

"Oh, great Earth, no!" Lachlan is running to me. Mira and Mom and Carnelian, too, braving the heat in an attempt to save me.

My skin crawls as if with a thousand ants when the nanosand envelops my feet. It brings back terrifying memories of my other encounters with it. Watching Lark being swallowed up, certain I'd lost her forever. And the time the nanosand caught me, dragging me inexorably down until it choked me, blinded me . . .

Lachlan saved me then. I won't let him save me now. When the dragging sand makes my feet lurch, I don't try to keep my balance, don't try to escape. I let myself fall backward, out of Lachlan's reach.

He skids to a halt, despair naked on his face. "What have you done?"

"I'm going back. And you're right, I'll definitely be captured if I go alone." *Do it*, Yarrow screams at me inside my head. *I know it doesn't feel fair, but do it, or we'll die!*

"But you, Lachlan—you're the best fighter I know." The nanosand drags me slowly down, but I fight my fear. "And Mom, you used to work for the Center. You know their buildings, their procedures." *That's right*, Yarrow says in her selfish, practical voice. *Convince them. You need them.*

Lachlan is pacing the edge of the nanosand like a thwarted

panther, desperate to reach me, but powerless. I hate that I'm doing this to them, but Yarrow is right. "Carnelian, you know enough about tech to bypass any security system they've got. And Mira, you can run as fast as me, climb as high, you're braver than I ever was." The nanosand trickles into my ears, and their protesting shouts grow muffled. "With your help, we have a chance to save people. To save all of Eden."

"Follow me!" I shout as the nanosand brushes my eyes. I squeeze them shut, then struggle to free a hand to pinch my nose closed. "Follow me, or let humanity down. Follow me, or lose me forever."

The billion tiny particles pulling at me seem to redouble their effort, and the sun disappears as the suffocating sand closes around my face . . .

FOR A MOMENT I can still see the sun's reassuring glow through the sand, through my closed eyelids. Then I sink deeper and I'm encased in black silence.

Be calm, Yarrow tells me. *This is part of your plan. It will all work out. You'll sink through the nanosand and in just a moment you'll end up in a holding pen beneath the desert.*

My plan? This was your idea! And it wasn't a plan, you idiot, I tell her. It was an impulse. I couldn't be so close to my friends stuck in Eden without trying to help them.

It seemed like a good idea at the time. Now, not so much.

I'm sinking into the most terrible danger. And I'm alone.

I feel so guilty for trying to manipulate them like that. I'm glad—almost glad—no one made the rash decision to join me. If I'm doomed (and I surely am), at least I'm doomed by myself. I put myself in a position where they couldn't rescue me, where the only possible way to save me was to join me. I was wrong to expect them to cast their lot in with my crazy idea.

As the seconds tick by and I sink slowly, despair begins to clutch at me. Despair, and a frantic, maddening urge to breathe. How long will it take to make it through to the holding cell? I was thinking no more than a minute, but that has to have passed by now. The second initiation test showed me exactly how long I can hold my breath. That time is rapidly coming to an end.

Don't panic, I chant to myself as my diaphragm clenches and my mouth tries to open against my will. *You're not an unthinking animal—you're a reasoning human. Yes, this is unpleasant, terrifying. But you know, logically that it has an end.*

When did logic ever win against biology? Panic creeps up on me, and suddenly pounces. No amount of lecturing can help me. My brain isn't even working well enough to form coherent thoughts. I squeeze everything shut—my mouth, my eyes, my pinched nose—and curl up into a ball, screaming in my head. For just a second I hold the terror in check. Then my body, my animal nature, takes over and I'm flailing in the nanosand, reaching out for anything to grab onto, desperate to save myself. I can't help it. The threat of death, the will to live, overrides all reason.

All my struggling only uses up oxygen. By the time the second minute has come and gone, my mind is a red haze, my chest is convulsing. And then, I can't help myself. I open my mouth, gasping desperately for a breath that isn't there, screaming soundlessly into the powdery sand.

Nanosand, almost-microscopic bots in a hive-mind swarm, fills my mouth, creeping insidiously into my lungs . . . and I go limp.

I'm dying. I'm alone.

A vibration shakes the nanosand, and it thuds against me in waves like slow-moving water.

The next instant a hand finds mine—a big, callused hand. A tender hand that tucks mine within its fingers, pulls my whole body closer and curls protectively around me as I slip from consciousness . . .

I WAKE CHOKING and gasping. I can feel each tiny particle of nanosand crawling up from my lungs, spilling onto the floor, where it coalesces before marching off like a line of ants. I take a deep, grateful breath, and look around. I'm in a bare room with other people, strangers. Before I can take stock of the situation I see a tube descend from the ceiling. Like some strange creature giving birth, it deposits Lachlan, then Mom, and Mira, and Carnelian, too. They fall in a sandy heap and choke up the sand.

They followed me! Relief and guilt are so mixed I don't even know what to feel.

Mom gets shakily to her feet and turns on me with mixed feelings of her own: relief and fury. "Don't you ever *dare* do that to me again! I *won't* lose you!"

Besides the five of us, there are a few other people in this perfectly square, perfectly white room. One of them has a survival suit on, similar to the one we used when we first tried to cross the desert. Two blond men have makeshift protection—masks that shade their eyes and face, loose clothing that covers their skin, thick-soled shoes. They obviously tried to prepare for the journey, to no avail. A trio of green- and gold-coiffed women who are obviously from the inner circles are wearing some kind of skin with veins running through it. The veins pulse as liquid runs through them—a cooling system, I think. I wonder if it would have worked if the nanosand hadn't caught them.

In one corner sits an old man with no protection whatsoever. His clothes are rags, his skin scorched. He rocks forward and back, staring into space, muttering to himself.

"Who are these people?" I ask.

"Some are rebels, I'm sure," Lachlan says. "Others are

glitches, people who for whatever reason aren't completely affected by the mind control, or who it affects in unpredictable ways. Random people who either through luck or strength of character managed to resist the Center."

"You all tried to cross the desert?" I ask as I brush the last of the nanosand off my skin. Everyone in the room watches the final grains skitter across the room of their own volition and disappear down a grate where the floor meets the wall.

There are nods and murmurs of assent. "It's out there," a green-haired woman says. "The wild world. I know it is! The prophet said so. She saw it!"

I didn't think it was the right time to tell her that I was the supposed prophet.

"Whoa, second children? All of you?" The blond men peer into our eyes. Mom's are still flat-colored with the lenses, even though they are deactivated, but Lachlan, Mira, and Carnelian all have natural eyes. I have one natural, one with a lens. They clap us on the back, murmuring slogans of rebellion.

But the three elite women curl their lips at us. "The only thing worse than prison is a mixed prison," one says with a sneer.

They get dirty looks from the blond prisoners, who obviously come from some of the outer circles. "When we are free, we'll be equal," one says.

"We'll never be free if we don't find a way to cross the desert," grumbles his companion.

"You didn't prepare," the man in the survival suit tells us. "It's amazing you didn't die before the nanosand got you."

"We weren't exactly planning to go into the desert," Mom says.

"Ah, you were on the run. Rebels then?"

"Don't be stupid," one of the people in makeshift protection says. "We're all rebels."

"Outer-circle idiot," mutters the green-haired elite.

"Bikking inner-circle weakling."

"There's no point in dealing with them," Lachlan murmurs to our group. "I told you there were many factions, all at odds with each other. Many people want to cross the desert."

"We need to focus on getting out of here," I say, turning to Carnelian. "Do you see any way?"

He frowns as he looks around. "There's an access panel by the door, and maybe a way to get at the wires and controls inside the ventilation system."

"There's only one way out of here," comes a voice from the ground. It's the ragged man covered in dust and burns. "Death, and rebirth."

"There he goes again," one of the elites says. "That's Old Leo. We've been in here for two days, and that's all he talks about. If you'd died, old man, this wouldn't be your fourth time in here."

"Oh, that lunatic is lying," says the man in the survival suit. "We all know we're going to prison for trying to get out. They're not going to let him go to try again. We're all doomed."

The elite rolls her eyes. "So dramatic! We'll pay a fine and be on our merry way. I know the first magistrate." She examines her nails and yawns dramatically.

"Death came," Old Leo says. "Did you know that Death is a woman? She stuck needles in my eyes. She tried to erase me. But I came back to life." The ragged man gives me a maniacal grin. "I remembered everything. I remembered this place. The desert speaks to me. The Earth speaks to me. A bird flew overhead and dropped the answer in my hand."

He fishes in his mouth, his fingers probing between his lip and gum where he is hiding something. Finally he pulls the object out, a trail of slime making a bridge from mouth to fingers. I catch a glimpse of what looks like a pebble, but don't pay much attention. He's obviously not in his right mind.

"It doesn't matter if I never make it out of Eden," the old man says, not sad, but resigned. "If a million ants try to cross the river, most of them will drown. But a few will make it, and the ants will go on. I'm fine with being an ant carrying a seed. As long as I know that somewhere out there there's a world with ants and seeds in it."

How quickly I've taken it for granted, that living world outside of Eden. I can hardly remember that all this man has known is a sterile city, like this cold white room, where the only living things are other people. I want to kneel by his side, to whisper there *is* a living world beyond the desert, that I will get him there if I can.

But he doesn't seem to need any more hope. He has all he needs, in his quiet way.

Instead I ask Lachlan, "If he's been captured and had his memory altered, how is it he can remember being in the desert, being here four times?"

"Because there's no such thing as perfect mind control," Lachlan tells us as we separate ourselves from the other prisoners. We cluster by Carnelian, who has taken out a set of small tools rolled in fabric and is probing the control panel, ferreting out its secrets. "We've been learning a lot about what Chief Ellena is trying to do to the population since you left, and the Center just isn't as skilled as it thinks it is. That guy, for example, looks like his mind wasn't in the best shape to begin with. If you try to alter someone unstable, the results are unpredictable. Also, the more often they meddle with someone's mind, the more likely people are to start having memories and flashbacks, no matter how much they try to erase them."

"Beyond that," Lachlan goes on, "I know that Flame

came up with a way to locally block the mind control transmissions. She managed to create 'dead zones' where the signal is blocked. The outermost circle is blanketed with them, so they are all protected. And though I haven't been in contact with the outer circle rebels directly, they've managed to smuggle disruptors out to some of us. We've set up interference points all around Eden. Every time someone steps in one, they become their real selves. It might only last for a moment, but every time someone is free, every time they question what they think, it helps them break away from the Center's control. The Center keeps finding the dead zones, and shutting them down, but we keep installing them. But it's a stopgap measure. We need to figure out how the Center is broadcasting the control signals. Maybe we could set up larger-scale interference. Maybe we could stop it entirely."

We check on Carnelian's progress. Some of the other captives are watching with interest, but the elite trio are openly dismissive. "Don't you think we've tried everything by now? We've been here for hours. There's no way out."

Carnelian gives them a wry look. "No way out, huh? So you're saying that even if I get this open you're just going to stay right here?"

"Like I said, it's impossi—"

She breaks off in amazement as the control panel sparks and the door slides halfway open.

"You were saying?" Carnelian asks with a raised eyebrow.

Mira laughs and hugs him. "Let's go!"

"But go where, exactly?" he asks.

It's a good question.

The door opens on a maze of corridors that branch out from an octagonal room.

"Are we under the city, or out in the desert?" I ask.

"Probably under the outer circles," one of the captives

says. "I didn't make it far before the nanosand swallowed me, and I didn't lose consciousness when I went down. I landed in a capsule that snapped shut around me, and a bot rolled me here. It didn't take more than a minute or two, so we're not far from the desert."

"We just have to find our way to the surface," Lachlan says. "Once I get my bearings I can get us to a safe house in the outer circles. If any of the old ones still exist."

"Ew," says one of the elites. "I am *not* slumming it in the outer circles. Bad enough crossing through to get to the desert." She turns accusingly to her friend. "Birdy, I can't believe I went along with your dumb idea. Who wants dominion over dumb old nature? Bugs and dirt are probably gross anyway!"

"You're Dominion?" I ask her.

"Well, *yeah*. They throw the *best* parties."

I can't help but laugh. Between fanatics and the bored rich looking for the latest trend, I don't know which is worse.

"Though lately none of the old gang seems to care about it," she goes on. "We planned this escapade weeks ago, twenty of us, and now only the three of us still wanted to try." Of course, I think. They were the only ones of their old Dominion group who escaped the Center control for whatever reason. A trio of glitches.

"Which corridor do we take?" I ask.

Mira examines the branching hallways. "Look at the floors. See how shiny this one is, but there are little grooves, like something mechanical and heavy has rolled over the exact same path a lot of times."

"Bots must go this way, transporting prisoners to the Center," I say.

"And here, this one is more scuffed. People walk on this one."

"Maybe it's part of the water or sewer maintenance system?" I guess. Lark, Lachlan, and I used the wastewater system to infiltrate the Center once. I bite back a pang of pain. Where is she now? The last I saw of her was her blank face behind the prison door, staring at me without recognition. My father freed the prisoners, but in that state would Lark have even known to run?

"Could be," Mom agrees, snapping me back to the present. "What about that corridor?" Mira examines it, her woodland skills translating smoothly to this artificial environment. "No marks on the floor." She bends and swipes with her finger, showing the faintest layer of dust. Then she walks a few steps in, sniffing. "The air is staler. They don't keep any circulation system going, so it must not be used regularly."

"Which could mean it is unfinished, or leads to a dead end," Lachlan says.

"But it is also the path on which we're less likely to run into angry bots or people with guns," I say.

We agree to go down that corridor, and I wonder again: have I doomed my friends and family in my eagerness to save other friends and family?

Do I ever make the right choice?

18

I WORRY THAT we're going to be saddled with all of the other prisoners. Is it selfish of me that I don't really want to save everybody right now?

You do *want to save everyone*, Yarrow clarifies in my head. *Big-picture everyone. Just not these people, at the moment anyway. Ash and Lark first, and then all of humanity. Anything in between is too hard right now.*

See, she gets me.

The only one who doesn't come with us is Old Leo. We leave him still sitting in his corner, gently rocking, rolling his tongue around the secret seed he has hidden. I try to talk him into escaping with us. "They'll torture you again, try to erase your memory, change who you are."

He just looks at me serenely and says, "How can they change who I am? I'm me. Who else could I ever be? Even if I die, I'm still me."

The rest come with us. Everyone wants to get back to wherever they came from. No one more than the green-haired inner circle elites. I think they realize now how real their little adventure has gotten. Heedless of danger in their haste to get home, they take the lead down the corridor.

"Sweet eye effect," the nicest of the three elites tells me

as she scurries after her friends. "Two colors: half citizen, half second child. I think I might try that. Birdy! Wait for me!" She flutters her little white hand in farewell as she and her high society friends look for a way home. If we are in the outer circles, I wonder how long they'll last out here.

After many twists, turns, and dead ends, the long, unused corridor has led us to the surface—to a war zone.

A war zone full of smiling people.

It is the craziest thing I've ever seen. We come out onto the street in a narrow alleyway that is shrouded from the slanting, dim morning sun. From the shadows I look out at a broad outer circle street where the windows are either smashed or boarded up. Glass and building plaster litters the street. There are no bots scurrying to clean the mess.

"This is the next-to-outermost ring," Lachlan says after a quick reconnaissance peek. "It was heavily involved in the rebel fighting, but the Center got it under its thumb once the Eden-wide mind control was upgraded."

I can see evidence of the battles all over the street. Amid remnants of destruction people walk with absolute calm, like they are strolling through a flower-filled meadow on a sunny day. They are smiling. When they cross paths with another person, they nod. Their faces are relaxed; even the middle-aged people look strangely young, without the slightest tinge of worry clouding their faces.

Mira and Carnelian come up behind me. At first they are staring open-mouthed at the tall buildings. "It's all so bare, and angled, and hard!" Mira shivers as she clutches Carnelian's hand as if for protection. "It's awful."

And she hasn't even seen the worst of it yet.

We see a small group of children pass by. Two of them are holding hands and skipping in a strange, methodical way. There's a look of abstract joy in their eyes as they pass before a wall painted in an abstract rust-red design, freckled with a random scattering of dots.

"I guess I could get used to it," Mira begins . . . Then her fist flies to her mouth to stifle a cry. I follow her intense gaze.

"Oh, great Earth!"

"It's blood," she breathes in disbelief. "And bullet holes."

Mira, an expert tracker, can read the whole story as if it is happening now. She pushes her way forward. "They lined people up there, against the wall." There are tears in her eyes. "They lined them up and shot them." She takes a tentative step toward the scene of horror. "More than once. The blood is at different stages of . . ."

"The fighting was brutal for a while," Lachlan says.

"Chief Ellena authorized lethal force?" I ask. "Against her own people?" Bad enough to single out people she thought were a threat, but to kill citizens on the street? She's completely lost control.

Which is worse, I wonder—fighting and dying for a cause, or living in peace indifferent to injustice? A tiny part of me appreciates that these people are at least safe, even if their happiness is an illusion.

"And nobody cares," Carnelian says. "Those little kids are just walking by as if . . ." The horror is robbing us of the power of speech.

"They *can't* care," Lachlan says grimly. "They're under Center control. They've been working from the middle outward to totally brainwash the people into complacency."

A couple of the outer circle people from the holding cell sidle up to us, introducing themselves as Cedar and Cliff. "This ring is still in the reclamation process," Cedar says. "Once the population is completely under the Center's sway, they'll send in bots to clean up all traces of the fighting."

"The people have already forgotten," Cliff adds. "Or just don't care."

"The outermost ring is holding strong, though," Cedar says. "We're blocking most of the Center's signals for now, and the resistance is strong enough that they don't dare send in troops . . . yet."

My friends are looking at the scene in abject horror. It is completely outside of anything they've experienced. Again I feel the crush of guilt. Mira, Carnelian—they've never even saw a gun! They only know what one is in theory. They've spent a life removed from blood, from violence. And I bring them to *this*?

I have a moment of existential confusion. Was that really me who rashly decided to jump back into Eden and lure people I love after me? I hardly know what came over me, to make me do that. I feel like I can't save anyone without risking anyone. I'm happy to risk myself, but was it fair to let them come, too? But . . . I'd never succeed without their help.

For just a second, I hear, or maybe feel . . . something in my head. It isn't me—either one of me. It isn't a voice, exactly. It is a presence. A sort of nudge. It aligns me, settles me, almost as if I'd taken one of Yarrow's pills that made me stop analyzing my past actions and focus on the task at hand.

I shake my head, feeling a little better, and ask Lachlan, "What do we do now?"

He has been conferring with Cliff and Cedar. They are outer-circle men, rebels.

"We can take you someplace safe," Cedar says. "For you second children there's always someone willing to help." He smiles at us. "You started it all. You're the original rebels. And it helps that you're immune to Center control."

The man in the sophisticated survival suit bids us farewell with a curt nod. He is on some mission of his own, allied with no one. The three elites strike out confidently in the opposite direction.

We see a few other people, but they are all lost in their happy inner worlds and hardly seem to notice us. We duck down an alley, and make our way as unobtrusively as possible. Finally we reach the outermost circle. We slip in through an underground tunnel connecting a factory with a warehouse, and are met by an armed man and woman. After a hasty conference the woman takes charge of the three elites and leads them away.

"There aren't any securitybots out here?" I ask Cedar as we move on. "Surveillance?"

"Between the legitimate rebels and the criminals who wanted their deeds to go undetected, the outer circles had been pretty much cleared of security cameras. Once we learned to hack the bots and use them ourselves, the Center stopped sending them out here. They rebuilt and repopulated farther in, but the outermost circle is holding out. So far. For now, we mostly come and go as we want. And for the last few weeks, anyway, the Greenshirts and the Center haven't made any incursions out here."

"We made them pay a heavy price last time they tried," Cliff adds.

"It won't last, though," Cedar says darkly. "The mind control signal is getting stronger. We can block it for now, but there are other problems."

"They're drawing all their resources to the Center, diverting power from the outer circles to the inner ones," Cliff says. "Cut off food shipments, too."

"It's a siege," I say.

"And if they capture the outermost circle, the resistance will die. They'll control all of Eden."

"Luckily we won't starve, at least for now," Cedar says

more cheerfully. "Most of the algae used for food is grown in the outer circles. Speaking of which . . ."

We've come to one of the algae spires, the twisting, beautiful spirals of growing algae that people of Eden believed were one of the few forms of life to survive the Ecofail. The highly nutritious algae is harvested and converted into various forms that more or less resemble real foods. At least, that's what I believed before I tasted real foods. My first wild blueberry dispelled that notion entirely.

"This one was damaged during one of the early skirmishes," Cedar tells us. "It's no longer operational, so no one will come here to steal food, and the Center won't waste resources trying to destroy it any further."

"So it makes a perfect hideout," says Cliff. He leans near the door, mutters what must be a password, though I can't hear what he says, and someone inside pushes the door open.

"Hi, Angel," Cliff says, drawing the person into a hug. Over his shoulder I can tell it's a woman with a kerchief tied over what looks like gray hair. Her face is smudged, her body is gaunt, but she's smiling in benevolent welcome.

"I see you've brought us some new friends," she says, straightening out of the hug to beckon us in. I'm in the lead, and she smiles directly at me, open and warm.

I see that her hair isn't gray, it's silver, made dull with dust, unwashed, unstyled.

I see that perfect face, greasy and dirty, still lovely. All the pride and arrogance are gone. Instead she looks caring, competent, almost maternal despite her youth.

She holds out a work-roughened hand to me. A hand that a three short months ago was moisturized and manicured, the nails buffed and painted the most fashionable color.

"Hello," she says. "My name is Angel."

"No it's not," I whisper. "It's Pearl."

19

SHE LOOKS AT me in sweet sympathy, as
if she's used to dealing with people who are deluded or confused. "Come in," she says. "Are you hungry? We don't have
much, but there's always enough for guests. Oh, what pretty
hair," she says to the elites behind me. "It reminds me of . . ."
She breaks off with a quizzical expression. "Isn't that funny?
I can't remember what it reminds me of!" She gives a little
laugh and ushers us all inside.

"It's Pearl!" I hiss in an aside to Lachlan. He peers at her,
but he only saw her for a little while in the Underground. I,
on the other hand, worshiped and admired and feared her as
Yarrow. For a while, Pearl was the most important person in
my life.

Wow, Yarrow says smugly in my head. *She looks rough.*

Stop gloating, I chastise her. This isn't a beauty contest.

Maybe not, but if it is, I definitely win.

"This is our Angel," Cedar says. "She came to us a while
back, and just took over—in the best possible way. We were
a ragtag bunch out here. Bad communications, never had
enough to eat. We found her wandering the street where there
had been some heavy fighting about three months ago. She
must have been disoriented by an explosion. Couldn't re-

member her own name. We call her Angel because, well, she is one!"

"We took her in to feed her," Cliff says, "and she wound up taking care of us. I've never met anyone who can organize a group of people like Angel. She finds us food, healers, weapons. She goes out and chats with a few people, and comes back with more information than our best spies could get in a week. She's turned this movement around."

"Yeah," Cedar confirms. "When I look at Angel, I feel like we actually have a chance against the Center."

Pearl demurs. "I'm just a cog in the machine. Just because I have good organizational skills . . ."

"You found out who the spy in our ranks was. You moved us into this place. Since you came, none of our children have starved to death. The movement continues because of you, Angel."

"Uh, Angel, can I talk to you alone?" She nods, and I beckon Lachlan to join us. The others are brought upstairs to rest.

"You're not Angel," I tell her when we're alone.

"Oh, I know," she says lightly.

"You do?"

"You heard them—they found me alone and hurt after a battle, with no idea who I was. But I had bruises on my wrists, my face. Signs of terrible abuse. Whatever life I came from, I'm not sorry to leave it behind. Whatever else I was, I was a victim. Now I'm doing some good."

I open my mouth . . . then snap it shut again, exchanging a look with Lachlan.

I remember the haughty, prideful, cruel Pearl, the one who ruled the Oaks school absolutely, crushing any opposition. She could tear apart a reputation, destroy anyone's self-worth. Once, she even drove a girl to attempt suicide. And yet she was no more the real Pearl than Yarrow was the real me.

I am now, Yarrow interjects. *Part of you, anyway. You can't escape that.*

But then there was the other Pearl, a victim of Chief Ellena's wicked machinations just like me. The Chief had taken a kind girl and transformed her into a monster, a tool to do her bidding. Pearl was threatened, coerced, and finally neurologically altered to turn her into the person Yarrow had both feared and admired. I only had a glimpse of the real Pearl. I think she was a kind person, but too weak to stand up to the Chief's bullying and manipulation—and surgery.

Then, after Pearl helped save my life, after the Chief decided she was no longer of any use to her, Pearl had her memories wiped. She could recall all the basic human things she'd learned, the functional things—how to dress herself, how to eat—but she had no memory of her personal identity or history. She was a clean slate.

The Chief told me that she'd send Pearl to the outermost circle, the slums where the dregs of society live. She meant it to be a punishment. Pearl came from an elite family (now probably programmed to forget they'd ever had a daughter) and had grown even more prideful of her elevated position after being turned into the queen of Oaks. Naturally, the Chief thought that would be what Pearl would hate the most.

And it might have been what the Oaks Pearl, the manipulated Pearl, would have despised. But as it turned out, the qualities that made Pearl the ruler of the school—controlling all the students, inducing terror or worship whenever she chose, planning exquisite parties down to the last detail—all translated perfectly to being the guiding force behind a rebel cell. She might have forgotten who she was, but she still had the social skills to bend people to her will. Now, though, she used it benevolently.

Left without the experiences that shaped her, her core self remained. For all her efforts, Chief Ellena couldn't erase that. Pearl was her true self, and the best of her was coming out to meet this difficult challenge.

I can't get over how happy Pearl looks. How . . . fulfilled. She is messy and gaunt and tired, with an oily nose and greasy hair. But I can tell she's found a place where she feels comfortable. She likes feeling useful. She likes putting her talents to use. I can tell from Cedar and Cliff that she's loved and respected.

She's found all that for herself.

Would she really want to know about her past? The way she was manipulated and tortured, her very brain changed as she was forged into a new and not very nice person? Would she be happy with the Pearl who ruled Oaks with a dainty manicured fist?

There was pain in her past, and no doubt there would be shame at her actions. I don't think knowing who she was would make her happy.

So I make the decision not to tell her. At least, not yet. Maybe when all this is over. If this is *ever* over.

"Did . . . did you know me? Before, I mean?" Her brow crinkles.

"Um, no. At least, you look like someone I used to know."

She smiles in apparent relief. "What did you want to talk to me about, then?"

"You're in charge here?" Lachlan asks.

"Well, no one is really in charge."

"But you're the one who gets things done," I say, and she nods. "We need to tell you a few things. And they're . . . unbelievable."

"Try me," she says, pushing a stray silver hair back under her kerchief. "I find life goes more easily here in the outer circles if I believe just about everything. Especially the unbelievable." Her eyes unfocus briefly. "Of course, most of the time it is something unbelievably bad. But sometimes people can be unbelievably good."

I am loving this new Pearl. Er, I mean Angel.

And so, we tell her not who she is, but who we are. And where we've come from. I don't fill in every detail, but I give her the bones of the story.

She listens with rapt attention, her hands clasped, leaning forward to catch every last word. "It's like a story! Heroes from another world come to save us."

"We're not heroes," Lachlan says.

"I've heard of you," Pearl/Angel tells him. "The rebels tell stories of your escapades. No one here has heard of you in a while, since the explosion of the Underground, and the prison break."

"Now I'm back to save my brother Ash—my twin," I conclude. "And to get Lark out, if she's still alive."

Angel's mouth drops open, and she gapes at me in a way Pearl never would have. "Rowan, I can't believe it!" Angel says.

"Wait . . . I never told you my name. You *do* remember me!"

"No, but . . ." She gives me a sly smile. In the old Pearl, this would have been terrifying. I would have known she was up to something, and dreaded finding out what it was. But now her secrecy seems only to contain a surprise. "Wait here, I'll be right back." She runs out of the room, then almost immediately dashes back. "I'll be gone awhile. I'll send someone with food. Oh, you just wait!" She looks giddy as she dashes off again.

The others join us, sitting around a table while we wait

for food. One of the rebels comes in to serve us a meal. At first I don't recognize her, but when she sets down the tureen of soup I jump up and hug her.

"Mom, it's Iris, the matron from the Underground!"

Mom greets her happily. She's heard a lot about the motherly woman who provided some comfort to me when my own mother couldn't be there. As they start to talk, there's a clatter from the door, and spoons scatter across the floor.

"Bik it!" a little voice says. "I know, I know, Iris, now I have to write an essay on why I shouldn't swear, but swearing seems to make everything better."

A little figure staggers in, overladen with plates and napkins piled so high in her arms that they cover her face. When she squats down to try to pick up the fallen spoons, the top plates almost slide out. I spring over to catch them . . . and then catch Rainbow in my arms.

"Stop, or you'll . . ." she begins, then sees who I am, and more importantly who is behind me. She shrugs out of my hug and charges for Lachlan. "Lach!" she screams. "You found us! Buttercup said she heard her dad say you were in the inner circles blowing things up, but no one would tell me anything. Why did you go away for so long?"

"Well, I'm back now, little one."

"Will you stay?" she asks, looking up at him with hopeful eyes.

Lachlan glances at me, and I know what he's thinking. The same as me. I came for Ash and Lark, but can I really live with myself if I don't save Rainbow, and Iris, and all the people like them—the other second children?

And if I save them, what about the rebels? And the people being brainwashed. It feels overwhelming.

"You better eat something," Iris says, ladling out a big bowl for Lachlan. "You're skin and bones."

"That's what happens when you live in a sewer for months, and then cross a desert," he says with an indulgent smile at the woman's motherly ways.

"You crossed the desert?" Rainbow asks in awe. "You mean *the* desert?"

"Don't know any other desert," Lachlan says, and Rainbow clambers onto his lap while he tells her the story.

It sounds like a fable, and she has probably heard similar tales her whole life—fantasies about an outside world, a future free of walls and prisons and government control. She listens, rapt, but it doesn't seem to strike home that this is any different until Lachlan takes out the flower.

It is crumpled, a little wilted, but its beauty is remarkable in this artificial world. Rainbow's eyes are huge as she tentatively reaches out one finger to stroke a creamy petal. She has seen the camphor tree, but never has she witnessed anything as beautiful as this.

"It's real?" Iris asks, arrested in the middle of her bustling. "You mean, it's not just a story? Or not just another city outside of this one, another ring behind another wall?"

"It's as real as the sun, Iris," Lachlan says with a laugh. "And you'll see it someday." He places the flower in his water glass, where it floats like a water nymph.

"Will I see it, too, Lach?" Rainbow asks.

"Hmm . . . no, I don't think so. The outside isn't for little girls who curse."

"Not fair! I promise I won't bikking curse ever again!" She claps her hands to her mouth, her eyes aghast. "I mean, starting now."

"Oh, I guess you have to come. If we left you all alone in Eden you'd just get into too much trouble."

She nods sincerely. "Yeah, I'd probably blow something up." Making things go boom has been her lifelong dream.

As soon as I can squeeze it in, I ask Iris if she knows anything about Ash. She draws in her breath, and I'm sure she's going to tell me something terrible. But in the end she only says, "Let's just wait a bit, and I'll ask around for him." Which gives me no satisfaction, but is far better than bad news.

Iris, practical, starts to talk with me about what this means for the second children, for the rebels, for all of Eden. I've never seen anyone look so happy. "This changes everything!" she gushes. "We won't have to fight against something. We'll be fighting for something. I can't believe it! That I should live to see the day . . ."

I want to tell her not to get too excited, that there's a lot to do before anyone can leave Eden, that—selfishly—it isn't even my main reason for being here. Rescuing Ash and Lark is my top priority. But it would be cruel to crush her with pesky realities like that, and I let her go on, while Rainbow assaults Lachlan with a thousand questions.

"Are there snakes? Do you wear them like necklaces? What about the ground? Does it just go on forever? How far can you dig? Is there really such things as birds, or did someone just make that up? Really? And they fly? Can I fly out there? Can I have a pet? I want a lion! I want three lions! And I'll hug them and brush them and ride them . . ."

When I can, I ask Iris about what happened to the second children. She tells me that my father not only opened the prison cells that held her, Rainbow, and most of the other second children. He actually conducted most of them to safe houses or to the outer circles, where the Center influence was weaker.

"He never went back to the Center," Iris says. "The government has a huge price on his head. He's as hunted as the rest of us."

"So you all made it?" I ask with tears of joy in my eyes.

She nods. "There are a few unaccounted for. Some, like Lachlan, disappeared in the initial fighting. Others went their separate ways after we escaped from the Center."

I name as many as I can, and she tells me where they are, if she knows—here in the outermost circle, in other hideouts, or staying with sympathetic families in the inner circles, or living fringe existences in the alleys and sewers. Most of the second children are out here. I wish I could see them all, but they are scattered throughout this huge outer circle.

"You need your strength, too, girl," Iris says with authority, and makes me dig into the soup while we wait for Angel to return.

As I take a bite, I ask her the most important question. "Do you know what happened to Lark?"

Iris shakes her head sadly. "She was there in the prison, I know. I saw her when they marched me to my cell. But I never saw her in the escape. I don't know what happened to her. I'm sorry."

I bow my head. The darkness in my mind grows, and I think she must be dead. But by sheer force of will I make myself cling to hope. Chief Ellena said she was going to use her as a test subject. As horrible as that is, it gives Lark value in the Chief's eyes. She might be tortured, but that means she might be alive—she's strong, a survivor—and if she is, I'll come for her.

If the situation wasn't so dire, it would be funny watching Carnelian and Mira being introduced to synthetic Eden foods.

Mira makes a face when she sips a hot-pink blended algae drink flavored with artificial strawberry and vanilla essence . . . then she immediately dips her head for another sip. "It's awful, and I want more!" she says as she licks the pink foam from her upper lip. "It's like they took a strawberry and, I don't know, squeezed out its soul."

"We're drinking strawberry souls?" Carnelian asks.

"Tortured souls!" she sputters as she tries a savory, salty stick of fried starch. They make a similar concoction in Harmonia, out of sliced potatoes and other tubers, cooked in oil. "Delicious, tortured souls." She crams three of the tasty sticks in her mouth.

Carnelian takes a tentative bite of one. "They're scientifically designed to be enjoyed," he says. "It's like they pinpointed the places on the tongue that would react, programmed the exact amount of salt and fat that would make a person happiest." He looks across the table at me. "I understand why people want this." He puts the fried snack down and pushes his dish away. "Machines, computers, science can give you everything you want, all the things you are programmed by nature to crave."

"It's what humans worked for since the earliest days of civilization," I say. "Crafting a world to suit them."

I eat to maintain my strength, but the food tastes too artificial to me. It is too perfect. When you eat a wild berry, you take your chances. Some are sweet, delightful. Some are bland. For every perfect berry there's a tart under-ripe one, or a too-ripe fruit just starting to ferment. There's a little bit of an adventure to every bite. Here, each bite is predictably perfect.

Beauty lies in imperfections, I think.

In about an hour we hear a soft tap on the door. Iris goes to the door and opens it a crack, talking to someone there I can't see. Then with a nod she excuses herself, calling the reluctant Rainbow after her. After she goes out, the door opens fully and Pearl walks in. There are three people behind her wearing deep hoods that must have shaded their faces from any scanning securitybots or cameras. Two tall figures, one smaller and slender. One of the taller ones carries a pack that looks familiar. But my attention is on the smaller one. Could it be Lark? My hopes rise, my heart leaps, despite my more pessimistic brain calculating the odds and telling me to brace myself for disappointment.

The smaller one pulls back her hood to reveal a disarray of bright red hair.

"Flame," I say, unable to completely keep the disappointment from my voice.

"My first success story," she says wryly. "Well, partly successful. Any trouble with the lens I couldn't remove?"

"You mean, besides being blind in that eye?"

"Touché," she replies with a cocked eyebrow, and accepts Lachlan's welcome, and a quick introduction. Then she steps back, leaving the other two front and center.

I glance at Pearl and see her look of expectation. She nods to them, and as one they pull back their hoods.

Ash.

I'm in his arms so fast I don't even see who the third person is. Oh, great Earth, my second self! My brother! I babble incoherently, feeling his tears—or are they mine—on my cheek.

"You're alive," we both say simultaneously, then laugh at that harmony, and at the joy of finding it to be true. I give Iris an accusatory look over his shoulders, and she shrugs, mouthing the word, "Surprise!"

Then Mom has wrapped her arms around both of us and we rock in the middle of the room, crying, laughing, not able to believe the astounding good fortune that has brought us together again. Lachlan, Mom, Ash . . . my circle is almost complete. Almost.

"Here," he says, thrusting the pack into my hands. "When

they attacked the Underground I looked for you. When I couldn't find you I grabbed your pack and managed to escape. I never thought I'd be able to give it back to you!"

He hands me that old familiar satchel, worn and now with a few scorch marks.

"I thought you'd want that notebook back in particular," he says.

"You read it?" I ask.

"We all did," Flame says. "As little faith as I have in humanity I can't say I'm surprised that our hero Aaron turned out to be murderous scum. It was a shock at first, but it really served to unite the rebel factions in the end."

I'm glad they know the truth. I start to ask Ash more about how he escaped, and what happened after, forgetting about the third hooded figure.

"I followed you that day," Ash says. "I was running to the Underground when it exploded. The rubble half buried me. I never dreamed you'd make it out alive. Where have you been?"

"You don't remember?" EcoPan must have wiped his memory.

I draw breath to tell him, but notice that Mom's gaze has traveled over Ash's shoulder to the third newcomer, who has finally pulled back his hood. Instinctively I put myself between him and Ash, an angry, protective wall.

Mom looks at the husband she never thought she'd see again.

I look at the man who tried to kill me while I was still inside of my mother's womb.

"What are you doing here, Dad?"

FOR A MOMENT the three of us stand together, touching, connected, a unified force against him. This man hurt us, hurt our family. He was the physician general for the Center government. When Mom was pregnant with twins, he tried to terminate one of the fetuses—me. Without her knowledge, under guise of giving her a checkup (she couldn't go to an outside doctor, who would report the illegal twins) he sent a focused sound wave into her womb that was supposed to end me. But it went wrong, and ended up damaging Ash's lungs instead of harming me. It left him weak and left me a prisoner in my home for the first sixteen years of my life.

Then later, he betrayed me to the government in exchange for power, for a cushy position. He betrayed Ash, sending him to jail for his role in hiding me. And his actions led to Mom getting shot and, as far as any of us knew at the time, killed.

He always resented me, maybe hated me, though I know it was at least partly because of the deep and crushing guilt he felt at what he'd tried to do to me, and what he wound up doing to Ash.

And now here he is, standing in front of us at the rebel hideout.

"Is he a prisoner?" I ask, forcing my voice not to shake. My shoulder is touching Mom's, and I can feel her tremble beside me.

Ash separates himself from us and goes to stand beside his father. Our father. "He's one of the leading members of the rebellion, Rowan."

I shake my head. "No. You can't trust him."

"He let everyone go," Pearl points out. "All the second children trapped in the Center cells. He saved dozens of lives."

"And he knows everything there is to know about the inner workings of the Center," Ash continues. "Not to mention about their mind control system."

"That's because he was one of the people who stuck needles into my brain and stripped away my identity!" I shout, balling up my fists. "Maybe he did save the second children, but in his heart he only thinks of himself. You can't trust him. He'll betray you."

Then Mom, too, leaves my side, and when she and Dad embrace I have to look away.

I don't know what to feel, what to believe. I spent most of my life feeling my father's distance, his animosity, and having no idea why. Then I learned about everything he did, and hated him. Can a person change? Can one generous, noble act make up for past wrongs?

"I've missed you, my love," Mom says.

My father is weeping, blubbering, and I want to be disgusted, accuse him of hypocrisy, but when I look at them together I see something so tender, so true, it seems to transcend all past, all future, existing only in this moment with crystal clarity.

She loves him. She forgives him.

I wonder if I ever can.

"He told me everything, Rowan," Ash says. "I can't hate

him. People do bad things sometimes because they are scared, because they see nothing but a world of bad choices before them and tell themselves they have no option but to pick the best of all the bad choices. That's what Dad thought he was doing." Ash takes my hand. "Not everyone can be a revolutionary like you, Rowan." He gives me a crooked little smile.

I don't forgive my dad, not in my inmost heart. But I have to respect Mom's decision, and my brother's. So I won't say any more now.

I push him from my mind, focusing on being happy at my reunion with Ash. (*Why isn't anything just unmixed happiness with you, huh?* Yarrow asks me. *We never get something good without something bad tagging right along.*) I introduce him to my Harmonia friends. Mira seems giddy to meet him, ridiculously optimistic about our chances on our mission here. Like the luck that brought us all together is a sign for future success. I want to tell her that this isn't a storybook, or a romantic vid, with coincidences and simple happy endings. But it won't do any good to bring her down.

"Enough with the happy reunions," the efficient Flame says briskly. "Lots of love and resentments, all tangled together—we get it. But now we have to get to the matter at hand. Angel filled me in on your story. So, the tales of the outside world are true?"

Lachlan shows her the flower. Dad and Ash and Angel are as enraptured as Iris and Rainbow were, and immediately start chattering about plans for the future.

"Interesting, yes," Flame says dryly. "It could prove useful in the future. But it doesn't really matter much to us now. No point in dwelling on step twenty when we haven't even taken step one."

"No," Lachlan says. "We *have* to think about the outside world. It is our future, our beacon of hope."

"It's a pipe dream," Flame says, blowing the floating flower so it spins in the glass of water. "Oh, I believe that it is there, but we can't give the people that kind of wild hope. It's too big. We rebels have to have manageable goals. We need a fight we can win. I don't see how we can get more people past the desert, but I do know one way to fight the Center, and from that, greater things may come.

"Rowan, Lachlan," Flame goes on, "you couldn't have come at a better time. And with allies no less." Flame examines the capable-looking Mira and Carnelian.

"What's been going on?" Lachlan asks.

She reiterates what Lachlan and our rebel guides told us—after a war that involved many rebel factions, the Center has finally gained the upper hand with an all-encompassing mind control device that goes far beyond the original intent of the lenses. The majority of the population has been forced into an eerie contentedness, ignoring all remnants of the war as the Center rebuilds. The only holdout is the outermost circle.

"I learned a lot from my surgery on you, Rowan," Flame explains. "Sorry you had to be my less-than-successful test subject, but thanks to you I've been able to disconnect people's lens implants with about a 95 percent success rate."

Don't ask about that other 5 percent, Yarrow advises me.

"And more than that, now that I have a better idea how the mind control signals are transmitted, I found a way to block them. But only in a limited space. We have blockers throughout the outermost circle, so that almost everyone out here is immune to the mind control. And Lachlan has been busy setting them up here and there in the inner circles."

"I thought that might be you that invented them," Lachlan says. "Rook got the devices through his contact, but the way things were set up, no one knew anyone else's name."

"A wise precaution," Flame says. "Some of our other

agents weren't as careful, and when one got captured and tortured, he named names and the entire cell was captured. Did the devices work as well as I hoped?"

"I've been focusing on the security points, forcing the Greenshirts to see things clearly, at least for a while. There has been some rebellion among the ranks. Not nearly enough, but I hope it made some difference."

"You're doing good work out there," my father says. "Now we have a new assignment for you."

"What is it?" I ask, bristling. The others might trust my father, but I still half think he might be sending us into a trap. Or he might actually mean well now, but if he gets captured, he'll sell us out for a chance at personal safety.

"We're just barely holding out here," Flame says as she starts to pace. Her restless energy needs an outlet. "All it will take is a concerted push from the Center to take down our defenses and overwhelm us."

"Why haven't they done that already?" I ask.

"We don't know. Maybe they need all their resources in the inner circles now. Maybe they figure we're not going anywhere, so there's no hurry to crush us. We need to take advantage of the time we have, and stop them once and for all. And now, finally, I know how to get control of the signal. Once I do, I can cut the link and get the Center out of our heads forever."

She goes on to explain in great technical detail how the signal interacts with the lenses, then notices our blank looks. "Never mind that. You don't need to know how I take it down. The important thing is . . ."

To her surprise, Carnelian breaks in with a question. "Okay, but if you just destroy the transmitter while the signal is active, won't it send out such a blast of power that every brain connected to it will be fried?"

She looks at him in amazement. "How did you . . . ?"

Carnelian shrugs. "We use principles of crystal resonance in our farming techniques. The soil is infused with microcrystals, and when a low signal is broadcast through the soil it resonates in the crystals at a frequency that repels insects and grubs. We don't have to use any pesticides. It seems like the idea behind this is more or less the same."

"I'm impressed," she confesses. "We'll talk more later. I can use your help when I break into the Center. But yes, first the signal has to be disconnected from everyone's brain. We can't just blow the place up!"

"Wait, you want to break into the Center?" I ask. "That's suicide."

"You did it once," she points out.

"Yeah, but they weren't expecting an attack. Now they're at war, they're ready."

"Leave that to me," Flame says. "And your friend is right. We can't just destroy the crystal dome. We'd turn most of the population into vegetables at that rate."

"You know," Carnelian interjects, "we've found that vegetables can actually communicate chemically for long distances . . ."

Flame gives him a withering look. "I already said I was impressed. Now stop showing off. When we get into the center, it is a pretty basic hacking and reprogramming job to change the frequency so it no longer resonates with human brain activity. That will shut down the mind control. But we also need fighters."

"I know which one I'll be," Lachlan says.

"There's only one problem," Flame adds.

"Oh, only one?" I say with a hysterical chuckle. "Break into the most tightly guarded facility on the planet, reprogram a complex bunch of code, figure out what to destroy, and then how to do it . . . and there's only one problem?"

"EcoPan set up the original system," Flame says after one of her elaborate eye rolls. "From what I can tell from all the lens connections I've examined, its original purpose was pretty benign. Monitoring, that kind of thing. I don't like it, but I guess EcoPan needed to know what was going on with the people it was protecting."

"It was a little more insidious than that," I begin, but Flame dismisses me with a wave.

"Now isn't the time for philosophy, or history, or whatever you were going to lecture me on. We can all agree: Mind control bad, freedom good. Death bad, life good. Right? So pay attention!"

She sighs, and resumes her pacing. "EcoPan didn't want anything to be changed without its permission or knowledge. So it set up a system that could not be broken by any casual hacker. The system doesn't need a password to access. There's no code, no cheat, no retina scan or thumbprint that will let someone access the system. Many lives were lost getting the truth about how to access and change the mind-control program. A dear friend of mine, a spy in the Center, discovered it and relayed the information with her dying act."

Flame swallows hard, fighting back emotion. "At the heart of the Center, the hardware access point, there is a small dish perched under a scanner. Only when a certain thing is placed in that dish will the system be unlocked. Only then can I change it."

"What thing?" I ask. "What is it?"

She pauses—she sure has a sense of the dramatic—and then says softly, "A seed."

"But that's easy," Mira says with a laugh. "We can just . . ." She breaks off, remembering where she is.

"No seeds, my dear," Flame tells her. "Not a single bikking seed in this sterile place."

Lachlan and I exchange a look with sinking hearts.

"I could have taken a seed," he says numbly. "I plucked a flower, and I could just as easily have taken a seed . . ."

"If only we'd known!" I say. It doesn't seem fair. The one thing we need to save Eden is found in abundance just a few miles away.

"We could cross the desert again," Carnelian suggests.

"Lachlan just barely survived," I say. "What are the odds any of us would survive a round trip?"

Then I have a thought. "The camphor tree! It must have made seeds, right?"

"We thought of that," Flame says. "We managed to get a team into the wreckage, but there was absolutely nothing organic left."

"None of the second children who lived in the Underground preserved a seed?"

"We tracked down everyone we could. No one has one."

"It was considered disrespectful to keep a seed," Lachlan explained. "We didn't have the resources to propagate another tree, so any seeds it made were destroyed."

"Then it's hopeless," Mom says.

We're all silent for a moment, envisioning the likely future. In time, the Center will send its forces against the holdouts in the outermost circle. The rebels will put up a brave fight, but the Center has the numbers, the firepower. They might try to preserve life at first, but when that becomes too costly they'll simply bomb or gas the outermost circle and rebuild later. Or they'll find a way to shut down Flame's dead zones, so anyone who hasn't gotten surgery to remove the lenses will revert to being a placid, indifferent zombie.

It's a grim future, but I don't see any realistic alternative.

WE BRAINSTORM ABOUT plausible solutions, but come up with nothing.

"I feel so powerless," I murmur to Lachlan. *So stupid, you mean,* Yarrow interjects. "I rushed in here without really thinking, just charging forward, and somehow I thought that if I just acted decisively everything would somehow fall into place. That once I made the choice to do this, to be brave instead of safe and comfortable, I'd find an opportunity to help everyone here."

Like I said, stupid. And you dragged everyone else into your stupidity. So you better get on the ball and start doing a better job. Why don't you stop feeling sorry for yourself and think for a minute. I could tell you . . .

I shut her up as well as I can, focusing on Lachlan instead of the other me in my head.

"You found your brother," Lachlan points out.

I look lovingly at Ash across the room, where he's leaning close to Angel, arguing quietly about something. "I know, and that's amazing. But there's always something more to do. I have to find out what happened to Lark." I see a fleeting look of discomfort cross his face. "And even if she is alive, even if I save her, how can I say I've done enough? The second children are still in danger. All of Eden is virtually under a spell. I'm just one person, but there has to be something more I can do!"

"Until we can find a seed, there's not much we can do," Lachlan says.

"Except hold our territory, and be ready to fight," my dad says as he walks over to us. "Young man," he says to Lachlan, clapping a hand on his shoulder with this weird paternalism I've never seen before. "If you can spare my lovely daughter for a while, I'd like to take her on a tour of our rebel circle."

I stare at him. He's acting just like a real dad, which is a completely new thing to me. It's kind of embarrassing. What's next, is he going to ask Lachlan whether his intentions toward his daughter are honorable?

"Of course . . . sir," Lachlan says, and I giggle when his voice squeaks a little on the *sir*. He and I exchange amused looks to suddenly be in these conventional roles of protective father, pursued daughter, and suitor.

"We'll meet for dinner tonight," Flame says as we leave. "Before sundown. We eat before dark to conserve power."

"Yeah," Ash says. "If there's a choice between a night-light, and having enough power to keep Flame's disruptors going so we can all think straight, I know which one I'm choosing!"

"Are you coming with us, Ash?" I ask eagerly. Now that I've found him, I don't want to let him out of my sight.

To my surprise, though, he declines. "I have some . . . things . . . I need to talk about with Angel. Er, provisioning matters. Anyway, I'm sure you and Dad have a lot to talk about."

A little hurt, I say, "Okay, I'll see you at dinner then," and set off into the outermost circle with my dad, to see the rebel stronghold. Mom gives me an encouraging thumbs-up as I leave. Does she really think we can have a normal family?

I can tell Dad is uncomfortable as he walks by my side through the streets. He keeps up a steady stream of descriptive, one-sided conversation, telling me about the rebels.

"The outermost circle always did its own thing more than the rest of Eden," he says, "and it only made sense to be as far as possible from the Center if we were fighting its policies. So as the rebellion grew, everyone who was sympathetic wound up here. First, they came from other circles to meet and organize. But later, when it became an open rebellion, many relocated permanently here. We have a mix of people from all circles. When the fighting started, we evacuated even more people out here, noncombatants and children. Even when the fighting was heaviest, we managed to keep the Greenshirts out of this circle. We kept our people safe."

"Sounds like you've done a good job," I say, reluctant to praise him.

"I had a lot of help. Flint—you know him, of course, leader of the Underground—was the liaison of the second children, and since I'd had more contact with the inner circles, I represented the rebels who originated there. After Flint was killed in the fighting, I took over some of his roles, too."

"Flint died?" I ask, with truly mixed emotions. He tortured me, tortured Lark. But it was all in the name of protecting the second children he loved so loyally. I disagreed with his methods, but is intentions were good. "I'm sorry to hear that," I say sincerely.

"We didn't always see eye to eye, but he was a good man, in his way," my father says. "In the early days of conflict, we fought among ourselves as much as we fought the Center. But since we moved out here, we've gotten along pretty well." He chuckles. "I never would have dreamed that a rebellion is as much about diplomacy as it is about fighting."

"And now the fighting has stopped?" I ask him as he takes

me to one of the armories scattered around this circle. It is filled with weapons so that in case of attack, every citizen can arm themselves quickly.

"For now. As soon as Chief Ellena mastered the widespread enhanced mind control, there was no need. We lost a lot of our best fighters then. But strangely the people who came from the outer circles proved to be more resilient to the mind control than the inner circle elites. No one quite knows why."

"Maybe it is because out here, in a circle of poverty and crime, they always have to be on guard. Someone is always trying to cheat them, or take something from them, or hurt them. So when the attack came from their own heads, they were more braced for it. They wouldn't fall for things as easily as the soft inner-circle people."

"We were soft," Dad says. "Soft, and blind, and selfish. I knew, in theory, that there had been poverty out here. It was shameful in a society like ours, and it could have been corrected so easily. But like every other elite, I had my own concerns, and didn't really care. Same with Chief Ellena getting increasingly out of control. We all saw it, but it didn't really affect us, so we ignored it. I'm ashamed, Rowan."

He gulps, and stops walking. "I'm so ashamed of everything I did. I'm going to spend my life trying to make up for it all. I know I never will. But I'd give my life if it helped make amends for the person I used to be. It's just—and I don't mean this as an excuse, just an analysis of human nature—it's so easy to do the easy thing, you know what I mean? To go along, to let your money and power count for everything, and not really care about anyone but yourself. I fell into that trap. Now I know better."

He takes me by the hands. "I'm not going to ask you to forgive me, Rowan. I just want you to know that I'm trying to make things better."

"You got the second children out of the Center," I say, letting my hands stay in his, but limply. Part of me wants to cry, to forgive him and hug him and be happy that I finally have the kind of dad I always wished I had. Another part, though, thinks it is too late for that. "That goes a long way."

"I couldn't get everyone out, though. Your friend . . . Ash's friend. The girl with the pale purple hair. She was in one of the cells. When I got the doors open, everyone else streamed out, and I directed them where to go. I didn't notice she wasn't with the others until we were almost out of the Center. I tried to get back, but I was carrying two kids who were too weak to run, and by the time I got someone else to take them for me, the guards had been alerted and there was no way to get back inside. I'm sorry, Rowan. I think she'd been drugged. I think that's why she didn't run out with the others."

That matches with what I saw the last time I saw Lark— sitting in her cell with an utterly blank expression on her face. What if they wiped away her old memories? What if she has no idea who I am?

What if she's dead? Because I know that Lark would have resisted the Chief's attempts at control with her last breath.

"Do you know what happened to her?" I ask.

He shakes his head sadly. "My first task had to be getting all of the second children to safety. And I was hunted myself. I only survived by hiding in the outer circle. They don't like out-siders, but the second children told them how I'd helped them, and they decided to trust me, and gradually, the other few elites who have joined our cause. Once the fighting started, commu-nication between the circles was difficult. We would smuggle out Flame's disruptors, but had no idea who was getting them. Evidently, it was your boyfr—um, friend Lachlan. I've heard all about him, you know, and I have to say I approve."

Not that I need your approval, and I don't even know ex-

actly what Lachlan and I are in the first place to be approved of, but . . . "How did you hear about him?"

"From Flame, and the girl who wants to marry him."

My eyebrows shoot up.

"I mean Rainbow!" my dad says with a laugh. "Don't worry, it's good to have a little competition. And of course his brother told me all about him. He sounds like an incredibly brave, resourceful, dedicated young man."

"Wait, Rook is here?" I ask excitedly. "Where is he? Can I see him?" I love that big lug of a guy who joined the Green-shirts just so he could get inside the system and protect his second-child brother. It's nice to have a man who is so big and strong and well armed on your side. He must be a real asset to the rebels. I'm guessing he's probably stationed on the border between circles, with a giant gun, ready to fight off any attackers.

Dad leads me to a big building painted in pale spring-green, decorated with multicolored flowers made from little handprints dipped in paint. When he opens the door, I see Rook on all fours, a bunch of yellow yarn on his head, roaring and batting at giggling children with his "paws."

"Rook fit in immediately as Iris's second in command in the nursery," Dad says with a wry grin.

"I can see where Lachlan gets it," I mutter as I walk in, remembering the way the children of the Underground used to swarm over Lachlan.

Rook breaks off mid-roar when he sees me. He stands up, his woolly mane ridiculously skewed, and gapes at me before bellowing "You're alive!" and sweeping me off my feet to whirl me around in a dizzying hug. "I can't believe it! Does Lachlan know?"

"Ow, easy on the ribs!" I say breathlessly. He puts me down with an embarrassed grin, and the kids who are gathering around us start to giggle. "He knows—and he's here! He made it across the desert."

Rook looks amazed. "And he came back? Did he find a way to get other people out? We've lost many people in the attempt, but if he managed it . . ."

I shake my head. "He just barely made it, and almost died when he reached the other side. I don't think anyone else could have done it, but you know him. When I saw him there he was so dehydrated . . ."

"Wait, you were there, too? In the outside?"

I tell him a quick version of everything that happened. I'm not sure if the children should be listening. Some are second children I remember from the Underground, some are strangers, but all are too young to shoulder adult worries. But then I think, even if we fail, maybe my story will plant a seed in them. Maybe it will be the next generation that breaks free.

Rainbow has come in from her chores, and lords our friendship over the other children like a little queen. She commandeers my hand, then my lap, and as more children come in and demand to hear the story from the beginning, she takes over the narration.

After a while, Iris comes over to chase them away. "Enough chitchat, it's time for play. Life can't be all serious, even out here." They obey her instantly, and I see that her matronly role hasn't changed much from the Underground, just expanded. She cares for more kids, and feeds more people.

"They've been playing what Rainbow calls 'Fire and Boom.' They reenact the attack on the Underground. At first she made all of the inner circle refugee kids be the Greenshirts, but I eventually convinced her that wasn't fair. And they play 'Escape,' which is like tag, but they call the person who is *it* the Chief, and if she tags them they have to do what she says, and help her hunt the others. But look at that!"

It takes me a while to figure out what the children are playing now. After a moment, though, I realize that they are playing out my story. Rainbow is me, of course. She pantomimes
waking up in the outside, living world. Her look of amazement
is heartrendingly realistic. Then the kids jump to Lachlan's
desert crossing, with all of the boys vying to be Lachlan. Rainbow wants to play this part, too, but then realizes that another
little girl will then take over as me, so she grudgingly consents
to let a gangly red-haired boy take the role of Lachlan. The
boy staggers dramatically, and when he gets across the make-
believe desert, there's a scene of romantic reunion such as only
a nine-year-old can create.

I laugh at their antics, but make sure they don't hear. They
are taking it very seriously, and I don't want Rainbow to be
offended.

"I'm glad you gave them another story," Iris tells me.
Meanwhile, Rook has gone in to play the part of the nanosand. He grabs them by their ankles and slides them backward across the slippery floor, while they squeal in mock
terror. "I know reenactment is a way that kids deal with
trauma, but frankly it was getting a little rough on me to have
to see the attack over and over again in miniature form. This
is at least hopeful."

I watch them until late afternoon, then I'm shown to a
small private room where I can wash up and relax a bit before
the communal dinner.

I splash cold water on my face, marveling that even the
water here is different. Water is water, some might say, but in
the wilderness it is more complex, flowing from deep underground, bubbling up in clear springs. This Eden water has the
same molecules, but it tastes different somehow. Too pure—
artificial and flat just like everything else here.

There's no bed, but a cushion on the floor provides a

comfortable resting spot as I look through my backpack. I cuddle my childhood toy, Benjamin Bananas, a chimpanzee rubbed almost bare with years of love. There are a few articles of clothing, a hairclip, and some, but not all of my art supplies. There's paper, ink, erasers . . . but my sketch pencils, charcoals, and chalk are gone. I imagine Ash might have given them to the children. It must be hard to keep them occupied in a rebel zone. I'm glad if my art supplies can keep their minds off the troubles for a while.

Then, in the few moments of respite before I rejoin the others, I flip through the slim, small notebook my mother once found hidden in the walls of our unique stone house — the house that had once belonged to Aaron Al-Baz. I read through his confession. He makes no apology for his actions. Despising and distrusting humanity, despairing of its ability to stop its headlong rush to self-destruction, he decided the best course of action was to wipe out most of it and start anew. He created EcoPan to run things after his death, to control mankind and continue the work of restoring and protecting the environment.

He saved the Earth from humanity, but at what terrible cost.

I come to the end, which is actually halfway through what had once been the original notebook. I can tell that the last pages had been torn out. Aaron affixed his signature to the last remaining page. I wonder what those missing pages might have said. He confessed to mass murder without shame — what else could he have written that was so bad he couldn't risk letting future generations read it.

Looking closer, I notice for the first time that there are faint etchings in the back cover. This manuscript was hand-written. Turning the inside back cover at different angles to the light, I realize that these barely perceptible indentations must be the marks of whatever he wrote on the last page. The lines are too faint to read, but what if . . .

I dig through my art supplies, in case I missed something. But no, every pencil, chalk, and charcoal that might have helped is gone. I want to dust the last page to bring the etchings into sharper relief. But all I can find is a miniscule crumb of red chalk dust, neglected by whoever took my things.

Curious, I crumble that bit over a tiny section of the back cover, pat it lightly down, and then blow it away. I still have to angle the page, and squint to make anything out, but when I do I'm no less curious.

The Heart of EcoPan, it reads.

Then someone knocks at my door, calling me to dinner, and I decide this is a mystery to solve later. Tonight or in the morning I'll ask Rainbow if she has any chalks. Then maybe I'll find out if EcoPan is less heartless than I believe.

"They're having a little party in your honor," Iris tells me as we walk in together. "Nothing fancy—we don't have much. But there will be some musicians, and an acrobat, and . . ."

Yawn!

Be quiet, Yarrow, I tell her in no uncertain terms.

Oh wow, an acrobat. Now that's what I call a party.

I won't have you disparage my friends, I tell her.

Oh, I love your friends. I just hate their parties. I miss the good old days.

Can't you think about anything else? Something helpful, maybe?

Seriously, why do I have to be stuck in the brain of such an idiot?

This isn't the time, Yarrow, I hiss to her in my mind. *Your party-girl ways won't help the rebels out of this mess.*

Oh no? Like I helped the time we snuck out to that killer party at Tidal?

I remember—or I know from Yarrow's memories—how we partied at that exotic water-themed club. I remember the water slide, nearly drowning, the escape from the Green-shirts . . .

There's nothing at that party that will help us, I tell her.

She sighs, and I feel her exasperation with me. *Before the party, you dolt. How did we escape from Oaks in the first place?*

My eyes light up and I say excitedly, "The Chambers of Mysteries!"

22

"THE TEMPLE CONNECTS to Oaks," I explain once I've gathered everyone together. I tell Lachlan, Ash, Mom, Dad, Flame, and Angel. I don't want to get anyone else's hopes up yet. Dinner, and the party, are on hold.

"The Sisters and Brothers are some of our teachers," I go on, "and the school has a close relationship with the Temple. The main part of the Temple is guarded. Just by the Brothers, of course, and they couldn't put up much of a fight, but they would be enough to cry a warning. If you approach from the school, though, the way should be clear. At most, there might be one sleepy attendant."

Flame looks impatient. "But why would we want to go to the Temple?"

I tell them how, what feels like a lifetime ago, my Oaks friends and I broke into the Temple as a way to sneak out of Oaks and go to a fabulous party. It seems so shallow now, and thinking of the girl I was, I blush.

"We passed through the Skyhall, and I found the Chambers of Mysteries." I describe to them the honeycomb of rooms, dozens of connected hexagons, each room with six doors, each leading to another exactly like it. Most were empty, but one held something very interesting.

"Bunch of superstitious nonsense," Flame grumbles.

Until I tell her what I found in one of the rooms. "I was separated from the others, and in one of the six-sided chambers I found a bowl of dirt. Real, fertile dirt!"

"Were there any seeds?" Flame asks tersely.

"No," I say, hesitantly. "But there were a lot of rooms, and I only saw a few of them. If there is dirt from the outside, living world, held as a relic, mightn't there be seeds, too?"

"It is possible," Flame admits. "But the odds are pretty slim."

"Think about it, though," Lachlan says. "Someone in the Center had to have access to a seed in order to access the system in the first place, to change the programming, right? So there has to be a collection of seeds somewhere. If we know that there are relics from the outside, guarded by the Temple Sisters and Brothers, it is reasonable to think there might be seeds there."

"Sure," Flame agrees. "Or there might have been one seed. Just one. And Chief Ellena already used it to reset the programming."

I cross my arms. "Do you have any other ideas?"

"Well, no," she admits. "But how would we get inside? As you say, the Brothers might not be fighters, but there are surely enough of them in the main Temple to raise an alarm. We can't go through the street entrance. And Oaks is a closed school, with security. It's not like we can just walk on the grounds and start poking around."

My father concurs. "We don't have the forces to make a large-scale attack. Whatever we do, it has to be a precision maneuver, in and out with no one the wiser."

"And ideally, without loss of life," Angel adds. "They might be Greenshirts and Center officials and inner circle elites, but they are also our neighbors. It's not their fault they're being controlled."

We're all silent for a moment. Then, "There is one way." I bite my lower lip. "Maybe."

"You can't pose as a student," Lachlan says. "They'll know who you are in a second."

"If I tried to pass as an Oaks student, they would. But not necessarily if I came from a different school. Flame, you can still do fake, temporary lenses, right? Give me an identity that can stand up for a few hours?"

"Sure, but Center elites pay top dollar to have their precious princesses protected. You can't just saunter into the school."

"One day of the month I can. And so can the rest of us. One evening a month there is a party on the grounds for alumnae, parents, and for kids from other schools who are hoping to transfer to Oaks. Security is light."

"It's possible," my mom says. "But only one day of the month? We might not be able to hold out that long. When is the next one?"

"Er. I've been living by moon cycles and seasons for the last few months. I have no idea what the date is today. But I know the open party is always on the same day of the month." I tell them when that is.

Flame sighs. "Figures."

"What?" I ask. "Is it almost a month away?"

"Even worse," she says. "It's tonight."

We debate for a furious few moments, with the end result being that there is no way we can possibly get an equipped team together in time. But they're just as certain we can't wait another month. By then, the Center will have made their final attack and the outermost circle will be overrun.

"It's impossible," Flame says at last as she gathers up her things and heads for the door. "Absolutely impossible, and completely bikking insane." She tosses her final words over her shoulder as she leaves. "I'll have my part ready in two hours. You all better do the same, because I'm going to be seriously annoyed if I pull a miracle out of my pocket and you guys don't come through, too."

Mom and I look at each other and, despite the seriousness of the situation, can't quite stifle a laugh.

"Now we just have to form the team."

"I think we have them right here," Lachlan says.

"No!" Mom and I say simultaneously.

"Mira and Carnelian got dragged into this. They don't know the city, the security, anything about our ways. We can't let them put themselves in danger."

"Rowan," Mira says, very seriously, "how can you insult me like that? And Carnelian, too. We weren't dragged—we jumped! We know the risks, and we both think the reward is worth any danger we might face. We had plenty of chances to back out, to go home, and we didn't take them."

"Much as I hate putting anyone at risk . . ." Lachlan begins.

"Besides yourself," I say in a low aside.

". . . it might be our best bet to have them along. Angel, you said there was a spy in your group recently, right?"

She nods. "Someone we trusted a great deal."

"And I know all of the rebel groups are organized in separate cells so that if one person is captured or compromised, the whole organization can't be brought down. This is very risky, and if the Center finds out what we're after, they'll keep it under closer guard. We only have a chance now because they have no idea we know that we need a seed to access the system. The people in this room are trustworthy."

I can't help meeting my father's eyes. I see lingering shame there, and determination not to let his family down again.

"So I think the mission to get the seed should only involve the people in this room. It will be a quick infiltration—Rowan for knowledge of the school grounds and procedures, some to go into the Temple, some to serve as a distraction. And all of us to fight our way out if necessary. But if all goes according to plan, we'll be in and out with no one having any idea we're not prospective students and their families."

My father agrees. "Then we can take more time to plan the attack on the Center itself. That *would* be absolutely impossible to do with a few hours' notice. That will require our most elite forces, our best weapons, days of scenario training and drills. It will be the most dangerous, and most important, thing we've ever done. We'll be lucky if we're ready for that part of the operation in two weeks."

AFTER FRANTIC PREPARATIONS we have our fake lenses that, when scanned, identify Mira, Carnelian, Angel, Lachlan, Ash, and I as students in a second circle school who hope to get accepted to Oaks for their final year of school. Mom, Dad, and Flame are posing as parents. The identities won't withstand intense scrutiny, but if we can avoid detection on the way there, they won't have to. Oaks prides itself on being for a special, elite kind of person, and as long as we carry ourselves like we belong—in fact, like we are better than everyone else—we will probably be admitted without much inspection.

I question the wisdom of bringing Pearl along. As one of the most notorious students Oaks ever had, there's a definite risk of her being recognized. I don't want to spoil her new life here by revealing her identity, but she is determined to come with us. After talking it over with Lachlan, we decide she should come. Her retinal scans within the school should still show her as Pearl, even if her identity in the rest of Eden has been changed. The school has its own security system. It might be useful to have a set of eyes that can magically open any door in the school. Though I'm nervous about the situation, I make sure her outfit includes a heavy veil, which seems to be fashionable at the moment. With her face hidden, that should be enough.

At the last moment, I slip Aaron's notebook underneath my clothes. That phrase, Heart of EcoPan, echoes in my head with a low-key buzzing. Somehow, I can't leave the notebook behind.

We move along underground tunnels, alleys, and secret passages through buildings and basements. The journey takes until nightfall.

"The party starts in the afternoon," I tell them. "That's mostly for the older alumnae. They have a few caffeinated cocktails and talk about old times. Then once night falls the younger set takes over with a special themed party. I wonder what it will be this year. They can be pretty strict at Oaks, but the students have found plenty of ways of circumventing that. On alumnae nights, it's a lot easier. There's so much coming and going that the teachers can't keep track of the students. And they don't want to make the school look bad by criticizing or punishing their own students in front of parents or prospective applicants. So as long as the kids keep out of sight, it can be the most wild night of the month."

"So they won't even notice us?" Mira asks. "Good. I don't want anyone looking at me."

Somehow I get the feeling she isn't just talking about the success of our mission, and I ask her about it.

"Are you kidding?" she says. "Look at me! I look like a freak!"

She's wearing a dress of incredibly bright yellow and orange faux feathers that contrasts beautifully with her dark skin. It is short in the front, but trails down longer in the back. Her hair has been tamed beneath a chic little cap that looks like a bird in flight. Tendrils of fluffy marabou twine around her arms, suggesting the new feathers of a fledgling.

"You look absolutely adorable!" I gush. "There are going to be girls copying your outfit in the next few weeks."

"I look like I just tumbled out of a nest," she grumbles. "People are going to go blind looking at me."

"I know colors aren't very loud in Harmonia," I tell her. "But here, people really like to stand out."

"Yeah, Mira," Carnelian says. "You'll blend in by standing out."

Still, she looks down at her garish clothes in disdain, and I know she is longing for the moss-dyed linens of home. Carnelian is pulling at the high, stiff collar of his pin-striped ensemble, rubbing his wrists where the material scratches. I've taken wild animals and lured them into a cage.

We don't meet with any trouble on the way, which my dad says is surprising in itself. "I half thought we wouldn't make it this far."

"The eternal pessimist," Mom says with grumbling affection. It is so strange to see them together. It is like tragedy and hardship have somehow wiped out all past mistakes and grievances and let them get a fresh start. Like Pearl with her wiped brain, they have a clean slate.

"It is strange, though," Lachlan muses as we reach the inner circles, the place where he has been operating for the past three months. "Usually there is a checkpoint right there, across the bridge. I worried it might be tricky to evade, but it is unmanned."

I feel a strange buzzing in my head as we pass through.

"I guess this is just our lucky day," Angel says. She seems to be the most hopeful of all of us, and gives a little twirl as we sneak along. The rebels keep a storehouse of disguises for the times they have to move in other circles, and from the choices Angel selected an ethereal cream-colored dress in a princess cut, so simple in style, unadorned except for a single artificial rose in her décolletage. The rose, too, is cream, with the faintest hint of pink in the center spreading out like a blush. A silver headband holds a gauzy half veil that she has pushed back over her hair now. Later, when we get to Oaks, she'll put it down. I made sure of this. It would be bad on so many levels if she got recognized. Still, I don't want to tell her why.

Such a difference between the old Pearl and this new Angel. It is almost impossible to believe that the cruel girl who dominated the school and this sweet resourceful person are one and the same.

It is at that moment, when I've paused to admire the new Pearl, that I see her hand slip into my brother's. Not just for a moment, not just in temporary reassurance. There is a kind of possession there. A permanence.

I can't help but gasp. "You two! You're . . ."

They see me staring at their linked hands. Ash and Angel exchange looks. "Well," Ash begins, and flushes. "We're kind of . . . I mean . . ."

My brother was never the most eloquent at bravely expressing his emotions for women, but his flustered face tells me everything.

Angel confirms it, more succinctly. "When I joined this rebel cell and met him, he seemed so familiar. Like I knew his face well. I thought maybe we'd known each other before I lost my memory, but he says no, we never met. Still, when I look at his face I feel . . ."

She breaks off, and I wonder how she was going to finish the sentence. Instead she just smiles at him, her eyes full of love. "We started dating a while ago, and so far, so good."

It is a bright moment of joy in the middle of incredible tension, and I hug first Ash, then Angel.

A little later, when she and I are walking a bit apart from the others, Angel confides in me, "Before, when I stopped my-self, I was going to say something I know Ash wouldn't like. But I know you would understand. When I first saw his face, I felt the strangest sensation, like I had something to make up for. An obligation to make him happy. Like I had hurt him and had to make it better. Isn't that silly? And of course no guy wants to know that your feelings for him started out as some kind of guilty sense of obligation. Not very romantic, right? But after I got to know him the sensation faded, and now I just love him, purely and completely. You look so much like him, I felt a flash of it when I first saw you. Are you sure we haven't met? You acted odd when you first saw me."

Part of me still feels like I should tell her. But now, when everyone has to be highly focused, is not the time to distract her with the story of her life.

"After we finish this, there are some things I want to talk about," I tell her vaguely.

We come to the point where we have to leave the protec-tive hiding places and proceed the rest of the way in the open city streets of the inner circles.

"Just be confident, a little arrogant," I advise the ones posing as students. "Laugh with us, and look scornfully at everything and everyone who isn't part of your group."

"I know you'll want to duck your head," Lachlan says, "or slink near the wall so no one will notice you, but that's the worst thing you can do. Keep your head high, and look like you own the world. Or at least the city."

I remember how to turn on the act.

No, that's me, Yarrow chimes in. *You're still the timid girl who is more comfortable behind walls.*

Whatever, as long as it gets the job done.

Ash is his old schoolboy persona, a bit nerdy, not extro-verted, but he'll obviously look like he belongs. Lachlan of course is used to masquerading as everything from a blind outer-circle beggar to an inner-circle elite, so he looks fine. Mom and Dad look just like old times, when I'd see them getting ready to go out to one of his hospital dinners, or her Center functions—conservatively well dressed, comfortable with their place in the universe.

Mira is putting on a bold face that I think will carry her through the night. I have confidence that she can do anything. Carnelian looks uncomfortable, but I remind him that people will mostly be looking at the girls anyway.

"In a party like this we'll circle each other, judge each other, vie for dominance," I explain.

"Like a wolf pack," Carnelian says.

"Exactly!" I tell him. "You've studied wolves, so you'll do fine. So, ears forward, tail up, and let's be the alpha wolves at this party!"

"WE DID IT!" Angel squeals, and I shush her.

"Don't look glad—look bored and superior," I remind her. Our group, split up to be less conspicuous, has made it into Oaks.

Instantly Angel seems to transform. She seems taller, more elegant, her neck angling to show off the most lovely contours of her face as she looks with well-bred disdain on the partygoers. I gulp in amazement. She has become Pearl.

Then the illusion shatters as the corners of her mouth tremble with the threat of a giggle. "Like that?" she asks. "I never knew I was that good of an actress."

"It is perfect," I say. Too perfect. Frighteningly perfect. For a moment, every part of me yearns to defer to her as I used to back when she was the queen of this school. I adjust her veil, making sure it covers everything but her lips. It doesn't completely hide her, but it is dark now, the party illuminated by fairy lights and fake fire torches, and I don't think anyone will look at her that closely. If all goes well, we shouldn't be here more than a half hour.

Ash, Mom, Mira, and Carnelian will head to the outer, public portion of the Temple. They will be acting as sentries, ready to tackle anyone who tries to enter. Low-key, trustworthy-looking Ash will be their point man, ready to convince anyone who comes that they have an innocent reason to be there, and that no one should go any deeper into the Temple. They are to engage as a last resort, and are mostly there to let the four in the vanguard know if anyone is coming for them.

The rest of us are going into the inner sanctum of the Temple, the roofless Skyhall and the sacred honeycomb of rooms that is the Chambers of Mysteries. Even though I've been there before, that won't be much help. I can only clearly recall the way through the outer area of the Skyhall. Once I got to the hexagonal rooms, it all looked the same, and I have no memory of the route I took. We'll have to rely on trial and error. With so many people searching, though, it shouldn't take long.

Only some of us are armed, though. We weren't sure about security at the entrance to Oaks, and figured that if the armed members were caught, at least the rest of us could get through and try to continue the mission.

Angel (who more and more I want to call Pearl, now that we are back in our old haunts) and I are, out of the group, the ones best able to look like arrogant inner circle elites. We mingle with the crowd, checking for any overt signs of danger while the others make their way into position. We can't all go that way at once. It would be too obvious. We'll join them in a moment.

If our lenses have set off a silent alarm, or if any Center officials or security show up for a random check, Angel and I will be the first to spot them. We all have tiny, hidden earbuds to communicate with each other. They're so sensitive they can pick up our speech as well as transmit the signal, so we don't need a separate microphone. At the first sign of trouble I'll sound the alarm.

Or, I think grimly, take care of it myself.

After a few moments, we judge it is time to head into the Temple with the others. But I'm anxious. What if I'm wrong, and there are no seeds here? Was it foolish to put all of us at so much risk over what is essentially a hunch? It would make sense if they had seeds in the Chambers of Mysteries, and other relics from the Earth they all thought had perished. But I know it is by no means a sure thing. I have to admit that the most likely scenario is that we will come out of the Temple shaking our heads, and we'll have made this dangerous journey for nothing.

"I can't believe people live like this," Angel says. "So much waste, so much effort put into things that don't matter, like clothes, appearance. I know they're forced into complacency by the Chief's mind control, but they were like this before, weren't they?"

I nod, thinking I was right not to tell her. She'd be aghast at the person she used to be, even if it wasn't her fault.

"I don't even know how heavily these people are being controlled," I say. "Lachlan told me that they focus most of the signal from the mid circles outward. In here, people are controlled by other means. Money, comfort, striving to be more fashionable and popular than your neighbors." I look at the elaborate shallowness all around me. "The inner circle elites do a good job of controlling themselves, numbing themselves to the problems around them."

"It's disgusting," she says, and her lip curls into a sneer as we walk toward the temple.

That one small expression is our undoing. Most of Angel's face is hidden, but that sneer is telltale.

Two girls are walking by, their elaborate floppy hats drooping over half their faces, barely sparing us a glance. Then one of them stops, and grabs the other by the arm, jerking her to a halt, too.

"Hello," Angel says affably.

"Pearl?" says an incredulous voice. It's Lynx.

Then the other pushes back the brim of her hat and squeaks, "No bikking way! It is her!" It's Copper.

Oh, bik! Now that we've been spotted, it will be too dangerous for us to follow the others into the Temple. We'll have to stay out here.

No one else has recognized us before now. Pearl is so unlike her usual self, and I'm more or less in disguise, too. They knew me with bleached hair, and now it is back to its true, lustrous dark hue. I'm wearing a snakeskin bodysuit, and the hologlasses that are fashionable at the moment. The projection is a scaled pattern in glittering black and gold that makes it look like I have a serpent's slit eyes. I can see clearly out, but no one can see my eyes.

Now Copper and Lynx barely look at me. They appear uncertain, almost cringing, their eyes darting around the room warily, and at first I think they're planning to turn us in. In a moment, though, I realize it is their old fear of Pearl returning, that nervous deference and desire to stay in her good graces. I silently will Pearl to speak.

"We didn't think we'd ever see you again," Copper says uneasily. "You're still registered as a student, but the faculty won't say . . ."

"We heard your family lost all its money," Lynx interjects.

"I'm sorry. We really didn't think you'd be back." Copper looks miserable and unsure. "She took your room, threw out half of your stuff."

"We told her to wait and see, but . . ."

"She said you'd never be back. She said you were finished."

"She said you had a baby."

"That you were a synthmesc addict."

They are talking in lightning-fast patter, as if getting in a certain number of words would make everything okay. Beside me, Angel is looking confused, but has wisely decided not to say anything yet.

"Look, we didn't have anything to do with it. If you're really back, you better talk to her."

Finally Angel speaks. "Talk to who?"

"Why, the one who took your place. Lark, of course."

It feels like the deafened silence after an explosion. Voices around me grow indistinct and then fade away entirely. The edges of the room blur. She's here?

"Did I hear my name?" I hear the sweetest voice in the world say.

I turn, and see a lilac-haired goddess. A goddess who resembles Lark. But it can't be. This girl is all the things Lark despised. Her hair looks like a team spent all afternoon coloring and styling it, like each single strand was dyed a unique color so that when she moved, her hair looked like a cascade of wildflowers blowing in the breeze on a sunny day. Her clothes are exquisite. Not overdone and overblown like so many people's here. Deep, low-cut violet velvet hugs her curves—curves which are decidedly more exaggerated than they were a scant three months ago. The dress is all that single color, with no sparkles or embellishments. Sleeveless, with a high slit to the thigh, it leaves a lot of skin exposed. She doesn't wear a single piece of jewelry.

All of her ornaments are on her skin.

They aren't tattoos, as I thought at first glance. It's not a hologram either, because it seems to be not just on but *in* her skin. Maybe it is some kind of paint, but it isn't something anyone was using when I left. In any case, designs seem to flow across her skin as if they were alive. Fish swim sinuously across—and apparently through—her flesh as if she were a

living aquarium. Stunning reef creatures in jewel tones dance
playfully over her exposed skin, while a sinuous eel wraps
itself around her leg, starting at her ankle, disappearing between her thighs. She is a living work of art, a masterpiece.

But her face! It is that which makes me question whether
this is really my own Lark. Her face is different. Not just her
expression, but the contours, altered in subtle ways. Objec-
tively, it makes her more beautiful. Her face is perfectly sym-
metrical now, her eyes a little bigger, her nose just a fraction
smaller. Her mouth, naturally full and curvy, is now positively
lush. The planes of her face, the angles of her cheekbones and
jaw have all changed in subtle ways.

It's like someone tried to make a perfect copy of Lark.
Not an exact copy, but to make her perfect.

It is horrible.

But after the quickest glance I know without a doubt that
it is truly Lark. Despite those changes, I can tell from more
subtle clues—the way she moves her hands, the fresh-cut-
flower smell of her skin—that this is really her.

She's looking at Pearl, obviously recognizing her, but I am
the one who breathes her name.

"Lark."

Her eyes dart instantly from Pearl to me, and for one
unguarded instant I see her perfect composure falter. Then it
is back, and she says my name, gasps it with surprise and apparent joy, and suddenly her arms are around me, my face is
in her hair.

For a moment I stand immobile. I don't know what to
think. How can she be here? The last I saw her she was a
prisoner, sitting unresponsive in a cell. I didn't know if she
was drugged or if she'd had her brain wiped clean. I suspected
the worst—that she was left to a horrible fate of experimen-
tation, resisting all she could, being cruelly conquered, and

when there was nothing left of her, tossed aside to a gutter or a grave.

Frantically, I try to think of an optimistic explanation. Maybe without me around, Chief Ellena had no reason to keep Lark. Maybe it was mostly to torture me, and with me presumably blown up, Lark just wasn't any fun anymore. The Chief could have returned Lark to her parents, perhaps with selective parts of her memory wiped, and they just kept her enrolled in Oaks.

But no, I make myself realize even as Lark rests warm against my body—it can never be that easy. If Chief Ellena let Lark live, it has to be for some malicious purpose. With me, and with Pearl, she wanted to create the perfect citizens in the intense crucible of an elite private school. And she wanted to see how far she could alter someone's mind before they went insane.

Lark has to be another victim of her sick experiments.

I tell myself to be ready for anything. Lark could have been reprogrammed in any way. When I was Yarrow, I had no real memory of my past. I acted in ways I now find abhorrent. Lark might be like that.

At least she knows who I am. I'm surprised the Chief didn't wipe all memory of me. But then, I know that Lark's brain chemistry makes her hard to program. She has epilepsy, and every time she has a seizure, the electrical activity in her brain resets at least some of whatever mind control is being used on her. I remember that her lenses malfunctioned, and most of the time she couldn't be tracked. Maybe she managed to fight the Chief's mind manipulation.

Only one thing is for certain—as of this moment, my mission has changed. Let the others focus on getting the seed, I think as I finally let my arms twine around her. My main objective right now is to rescue Lark.

"Did you come for me?" she whispers into my ear, her breath warm and ticklish.

Without the slightest hesitation I say, "Did you imagine I'd let you go?" I can't trust her with the truth until I know more about what happened to her. Maybe she's free, under no control, and ready to be an ally. Maybe she's a mind-slave and I'll have to rescue her against her will, and she won't be her old self until Flame surgically disconnects her lenses and whatever else the Center might have in her head.

She disengages from my hug, looking smugly satisfied. Then she turns her attention to Pearl. "I'm surprised you have the nerve to show your face here." She turns and whispers something into Copper's ear, and the girls giggle together, while Pearl blushes.

"Do you know me?" she asks innocently.

This makes Lark, Copper, and Lynx break into more uproarious laughter.

"What's the joke, Lark?" I ask with an edge to my voice.

Lark stands in her most arrogant pose, looking for all the world like Pearl, like the old Pearl, but amped up. "Well, we heard a lot of rumors about what happened to dear old Pearl. Frankly, I believed the story that she had a baby with a school janitor. But I'm so relieved to know another tale was true—that she went crazy, and had to have a lobotomy. Ha! Look at her empty eyes. Poor thing." She puts on a mocking tone of sympathy, then laughs.

"Rowan, what's going on?" Pearl asks in an undertone. "How do they know me?"

"Yeah, *Rowan*," Lark says, emphasizing my real name, to the confusion of the other girls, who know me as Yarrow. "What is going on?"

"What's wrong with you, Lark?" I ask. "This isn't you."

"Isn't it?" Instantly her entire demeanor shifts and she

laughs it off. "I was just teasing. You know how it is in this school. Come on, we have a lot to talk about. Let's go to my room."

I glance at Pearl.

"Oh, Copper and Lynx can keep her company," Lark says. "Right now the two of us have a lot to catch up on. And maybe some plans to make."

It is everything I can do not to look toward the Temple. I don't want to risk doing anything to jeopardize our plan to get the seed, but I have to at least get Lark alone, where we can talk openly and honestly.

"It's okay," Pearl says. "I'll get something to drink, and *talk to our friends.*" Her emphasis makes me sure she's going to use the earbud transmitters to let the rest of our group know what is going on. I hope they're okay. I think we would have heard by now if there was trouble. I just hope I have time to figure things out with Lark before we have to flee.

I automatically head toward Lark's old room, but she leads me instead to my old room, which apparently is now hers. It has been completely redecorated, except for the lights I had on the walls, the ones that reminded me of the crystal cave in the Underground.

"So," she says lightly, still not turning around. "What's new?"

"What's *new?*" I ask, aghast. War and death, miracles and tragedy. She's talking like none of it ever happened. "Lark, what's wrong with you?"

"What's wrong with *me?*" she asks, whirling on me with a fierce and frightening light in her eyes. Have her lenses been enhanced? Her irises seem to glow the same lilac as her hair. "There's absolutely nothing wrong with me. Are you kidding? I have it all—everything I always wanted."

"Lark, this doesn't sound like you. I think the Chief . . ."

Lark throws back her head and laughs. "Oh, so just because you were a victim you think I'd be one, too? No, Rowan. I wasn't altered. I just grew up. A little time away from you and I began to realize what I actually want in this life, and how to get it. Look at me now!"

I do, and see the most beautiful and the most disappointing thing I can imagine.

"It was you—you and your weakling brother—who held me back. I was soft then, looking for a cause, someone to take care of. Poor sickly Ash! Poor endangered Rowan. You were so interesting then . . . for about five minutes. Now I've found real meaning in my life."

"I don't believe you. Those things mattered."

She comes close enough that I can feel her breath on my face. I'm mesmerized by those perfect lips, but horrified at what she's saying. "I rule this place, and one day I'll rule all of Eden. Pearl was nothing compared to me—a joke. The queen is dead, long live the queen! Now *I'm* the center of attention. It's not all about Rowan, the interesting second child with all of her *troubles*, and all of her *needs*."

"It was never like that," I protest.

"Selfish Rowan, who always put herself first and expected the world to bow and scrape to serve her."

I reach for her and she turns away from me, but not so quickly that I can't see that the peculiar glint in her eyes is unshed tears. When she speaks again, her voice is ragged.

"I did spend a little time in the Center. Call it . . . a retreat. It gave me time to think about where my best interests lie—and who my true friends are. I was *loyal* to my friends!" She smashes her fist against her thigh, and I see her shoulders shaking. "And what did it get me?"

She whirls around. "You abandoned me!" I step toward her, but she shrinks back, holding her hands out defensively.

"I loved you, and you left me in a cage to rot!" she shouts at me. "I didn't matter, as long as you and your precious Lachlan survived. I was swallowed by nanosand. I could have died, and what did you care, as long as you and Lachlan got to run off and find your romantic happily ever after!"

I don't see Center control in her tear-filled eyes. I see deep hurt, a sense of betrayal, and heartbreaking loneliness. I see the barriers she constructed to combat them, to keep herself from breaking. The brittle cruelty, the change to her appearance, her blatant ambition.

The way she is blaming me for all her pain.

"Lark," I say gently. "When I lost you in the desert, I thought I would never be whole again. When I found out you were alive, imprisoned by the Chief, not a day went by when I didn't think about you, scheme for some way to save you. For three months I tried to get back into Eden to save you, fearing all the time that Chief Ellena might have killed you, or . . . changed you."

"The outside?" she asks. "What do you mean?"

"It's real," I tell her. "I made it there. And I want to take you there. Oh Lark, you should see it! It's better than we ever could have dreamed!"

"You're lying," she says, but I can see her grief start to break, her hard heart soften.

"I came for you, Lark. This isn't you, this isn't what you want. Come with me to the living world outside of Eden."

"I . . . Do you mean it?" She sniffs, looking suddenly younger, more innocent despite her enhancements. "You didn't abandon me?"

"How could I?" I ask her. "I love you, Lark. I've loved you from the first moment I saw you."

She takes a deep breath and lets it out with a shuddering sigh. "I've missed you," she says in a small voice.

"Let's go. We can escape here, find our way to the outermost circle and escape Eden for good." It isn't the time to mention all of the things we have to do in between—stop the Center mind control, maybe free the rest of Eden, too. Lark seems too unstable for that. I need her to understand how much I care about her, help her heal from her sorrow and sense of abandonment.

"I want to, but . . . I can't. Not yet."

"Why not? What's keeping you here?"

"Well, there is the rain festival coming up, and I have the perfect dress . . ." She stops short at my incredulous face and bursts into laughter. Not mocking, superior laughter, but the real old Lark chuckle, full of real, irrepressible mirth. "I know, I've been acting just like that kind of person for months. Acting. Oh, great Earth, Rowan, how miserable I've been! How much I've despised myself!"

"Then let's go," I urge her.

"Soon, very soon. Tonight. It's just . . . after your escapades the school locked down on the students a bit. All the Oaks students have an implant that notifies the staff if we leave the grounds without authorization."

"Oh no!"

"Don't worry, I have a friend who can deactivate it. Do you think Oaks students aren't going to find a way to sneak off campus? Some things never change. He's at the secret party. You remember those? Oh, I really don't want to miss it. It has a wolf pack theme. Oh, but this is so much better!" She sounds excited and giddy now, a remarkable change. I can't help but feel a deep sense of satisfaction that I'm the one who saved her from her shell of sadness.

"Meet me at the party in ten minutes. You remember where to go, right? I should be ready to go." She hugs me, then all but dances to the door. "Thank you for coming to save

me, Rowan. You have no idea how much this means to me."
She flashes me the brightest smile, and as she leaves I think, *I'll get used to her new and improved face if she keeps smiling at me like that.*

For a moment I sit on her bed, overcome with surprise and joy. I never really had hope of finding Lark. I'd assumed she met her end in a prison cell. And even if she had escaped or been released, how would I have found her in a city of more than a million people?

Now, almost magically, things seem to be coming together. Everyone I love is near me. Defeating Chief Ellena seems possible. We will save Eden, and return to the outside world, and one day we can relax. One day we can be happy . . .

24

I TOUCH MY ear, activating the hidden communicator, and tell the others that I've found Lark.

"She's coming with us!" I say, unable to keep the giddiness from my tone.

Immediately the frequency is jammed with garbled answers from everyone at once. As they all speak over each other, I catch more tones of concern and even dismay than happiness. When they finally settle down and let one person speak at a time, it is Ash who says, "Rowan, are you sure that's a good idea?"

I'm stunned. "Ash, you of all people!"

"Why is she here?" Mom breaks in.

"She's a student at Oaks," I start to explain.

"No, *why* is she here?" Mom repeats with greater emphasis. "The Center must have a plan for her."

"And why is she here now, right when we're on a mission of ultimate importance for the survival of the rebellion?" Lachlan wants to know.

"It's a coincidence," I say. "She knows me, she wants to come. She doesn't seem like she's under any kind of control."

"Doesn't *seem*," Mom says. "How would you know?"

"I'd know!" I say adamantly. "I've been there myself."

"And you didn't know then," Mom says gently.

"I'm meeting her at the secret party in a few minutes," I tell them. "She has to come with us. I can't abandon her again!"

"I don't like it," Mom says. "I'm coming with you."

"I'm already there," Mira whispers into her communicator, and I hear the sounds of partying in the background. "So is Angel. We came with those two girls, but they abandoned us by something they called the punch bowl. It tasted like fruit juice, but after a glass I think I know why they call it punch—I feel as dizzy as if I've been punched in the head!" She giggles. Uh-oh. The Oaks punch is notoriously strong. For a girl who has never had alcohol other than the drugged wine at the Passage Test, a single glass could send her reeling.

"Mira, what are you doing?" Carnelian breaks in. "Don't put yourself in danger. I'm on my way."

"But you three have to watch the Temple."

It is only then that I realize that the only ones who haven't chimed in are Lachlan, Flame, and my father—the ones doing the most dangerous part of the assignment in the Chambers of Mysteries.

They're fine, Yarrow assures me. *If there was trouble, you'd have heard. If you want Lark, go get her. I admit I didn't used to understand what you saw in her, but with a couple of surgeries and the right clothes—wow!*

You know it's about far more than that, I think, chiding the other person in my head.

Yeah, but before she was just a scruffy outer-circle kid. Now she's spectacular.

You're so shallow.

I'm you. Now, come on, I want to see this party. I'm dying to know what theme they chose. I left them so many great ideas! I had this inspiration for a wolf-themed party. If we manage to escape Eden again, this might be my last chance for fun. My kind of fun. I'll spend the rest of my life mucking around in the dirt being a stupid farmer or something.

I can't help but laugh at my alter ego. She's covering it with sarcasm, but she's as excited about Lark as I am. I check myself in the mirror—for Yarrow's benefit—and head to the secret party hall. As I leave, I give one last look over my shoulder at the room that used to be mine. I had good times here. Yarrow did, anyway. When will things be simple and safe again?

Yes! Yarrow exults in my head. *They* did *use one of my ideas. See, my mark on this school will last!*

⸺⸺⸺

WHEN WE CROSS the threshold we're in a cave. Strange animals are painted on the walls—shaggy elephant-like monsters, huge cats with daggers for teeth. A mock-fire flickers, and shadows of people dressed in furs crouch nearby, striking stone against stone. We're in the primitive cave-home of our ancestors. They hide behind stonewalls from the terrible wild beasts that roam outside.

Then we pass beyond the cavemen into the party hall, to be greeted with a wild primeval wilderness.

A boreal forest scene is projected on the walls, spruce and larch trees amid gently falling snow. Shadows slink among the trees, their eyes menacingly watching the dancers. There are synthetic trees. The old Rowan would have been amazed, because they look almost exactly like real trees. But now I can tell the difference at a glance. These trees have no soul.

It's impressive, though, and I am truly stunned when I see huge, shaggy timber wolves stalking through the partiers. In varying shades of gray and black and white, the wolves pace and snarl right next to the students. I see one of the Oaks kids reach out a hand to one and it sniffs, then snaps at his extended fingers. The boy pulls his hand back with a startled laugh.

A wolf-pack theme, Yarrow says. *Perfect.*

I'm impressed by the technology of the holograms. They're smart, reactive projections that can interact with people. But they're acting like wolves, more or less, and want nothing to do with the people. The wolves interact with each other, but they scorn humans. It's amazing.

The rest of the party is just like I remember it—or how Yarrow remembers it. Instantly my body is swept away by the pulsing, multicolored strobe lights and the pounding rhythm of the music. It's a song I've never heard, sung by a girl with a sultry voice, with the line *I want to live in your skin* repeated over and over to an intricate baseline.

I scan the room for my lilac princess. Over by the crystal punch bowl Mira is watchful, but swaying slightly. Pearl is near her, being propositioned by an Oaks freshman she would have scorned before. Now, though she's clearly not interested, I can tell from her body language across the room that she's being polite.

I have to fight the urge to indulge in this scene. The music, the lights . . . all I need is a drink and I'll be dancing and looking for trouble, trying to pat the surly wolves. Some visceral part of me longs for that, and I have to remind myself that everything depends on this night going without a hitch. I've already thrown a wrench in our perfect plan by finding Lark. Now I have to make sure everything works smoothly despite that. I can't lose my focus.

I make my way to Mira and Angel, and we speak in low voices while I wait.

Suddenly the strobe lights stop flashing, and the room is just illuminated by a multihued glow. For a moment I see afterimages of the lights flashing on my inner lids, still pulsing in time with the beat.

I hear a girl next to me say, "You know what that means."

"Yeah, Her Royal Highness is here," another answers. "Why does she have to be such a buzzkill, shutting down the flashing lights every time she comes to a party?"

"It's a power thing," the first girl says.

A secret smile touches my face. I know why the flashing lights were killed. I know who is here.

I turn, and see the crowd part near the door. It is like a vacuum, an empty space I feel compelled to fill. Slowly I walk toward that lilac-haired goddess. I'm getting used to her enhancements. They seem more natural on second viewing. It doesn't matter what she looks like. She's my Lark.

But oh, great Earth, she is lovely ...

"You came," she says as I glide up to her.

"I told you I would," I say, leaning close to be heard over the loud music. "I'll never let you down, Lark."

For a moment a peculiar expression crosses her face, but she shakes it off with a smile. "Just like old times, isn't it?" she says. "Do you remember when we first met? Under those dim lights in the Rain Forest Club, I thought you were Ash."

"How could I forget?" I ask, feeling mesmerized by the past. That was the most perfect night of my life, my first taste of freedom. But the taste of that forbidden fruit had terrible consequences. Would it all come out right in the end? The suffering and loss would be worth it if I could end future suffering, not just for me but for all the people of Eden.

"So much has changed," Lark says dreamily.

"No," I say. "So much has *happened*. But I haven't changed. Neither have you, I think."

"Maybe I've changed," she says with a sly, seductive smile. "For the better, I hope?"

"You are always my own Lark. The same girl I met in the shadows. My first friend." I stroke a strand of her lilac hair. "There's so much I need to tell you."

"Me, too," Lark says. "But not yet."

"You're right. We have to go." I take her hand to pull her to the exit, at the same time looking over the crowd to catch Angel's eye. With a jerk of my head I tell her it is time to go.

I see Lark's hand flutter to her lips, then, instead of coming with me, she resists and pulls me to her. "Dance with me," she says, laughing.

"We don't have time . . ." I begin. Then she is kissing me, her mouth so soft and warm, parting my lips. I melt into her. Then I feel something slip past my tongue—a little pill that effervesces the second it hits my mouth.

"Lark, what did you do?"

Then, suddenly, I don't care. All I can see is her. The colors, the sounds, the other people fade into a blur, and the only thing in the universe is Lark—her lips, her hands, her brilliant eyes locking mine in an embrace of souls.

We're dancing, more slowly than the music's beat, creating our own rhythm. I see Mom and Ash and Carnelian enter the party, and that makes me vaguely happy. More love in the room, I think. Ash and Pearl. Mira and Carnelian. The more love, the better. My body feels both energized and ultimately relaxed. Why am I here? Oh yes, for Lark. Everything is for Lark.

Time slips away. All I know is the sinuous movement of our bodies against each other. Until . . .

An explosion! Screams! An acrid smell fills the room and students are running for the doors . . . which are blocked. In utter confusion I whirl around and see Greenshirts blocking the exits.

I feel something echoing in my brain. I don't know how else to describe it. A pulse goes through the room like something at a frequency I can almost but not quite hear. Then all at once the screams stop, the panic subsides. All the Oaks students are standing like calm and barely mobile statues, vague smiles on all of their faces. Someone shuts off the music, and the only sounds are from Mira shouting a warning before a Greenshirt grabs her from behind and clamps a hand over her mouth.

They have Ash, and Pearl. Carnelian puts up a good struggle, but a gun to Mira's head makes him stop fighting. I count five Greenshirts.

And one trim woman with short blond hair, wearing an impeccably tailored suit in dove gray, with a gun strapped to her thigh. Chief Ellena. She has an arm looped around Mom's throat, a gun pointed at her head.

I turn to Lark, and in my initial confusion I still trust her completely. I try to get between her and the danger, to protect her. Instead, she bypasses me to stand near Chief Ellena.

I'm forced to admit the painful truth. "You betrayed me!"

She regards me, her face looking unnaturally perfect, supremely cruel. "It hurts, doesn't it?"

No, it can't be true, I think, my head clearing. We were so close. I was so sure . . .

"How could you do this to me, Lark?"

"You left me to rot!" she hisses.

Two Greenshirts move behind me, but don't grab me. Chief Ellena calmly speaks over Mom's shoulder. "Your friend Lark was a much more promising student than you ever were, Rowan. Or is it Yarrow? I could put another personality in there for you if you like. Oh, but with Lark I tried a new technique. Deleting one persona and layering another on top of it turned out to be too traumatic for the brain. As your case proved. The two selves were always fighting. With Lark I kept her core personality and went delving for all the parts she kept hidden. The secret jealousies, the ambition, the vanity. It was all there in her, just buried under all that nobility."

Chief Ellena makes a noise of derision. "We learned a valuable lesson from you, Rowan. Why change a person completely when you can just bring their fundamental human nature to the fore? Every human has those greedy, grasping animal instincts in them. With Lark, I just played them up. So she isn't a new person like you were with Yarrow. She is still Lark. She remembers everything that happened to her. I just helped her see what is truly important in life."

"You took away everything good in her!" I scream.

"Who needs goodness, when you can have power and control?" Lark chimes in. "I'll never be helpless again. I'll never depend on you or anyone else for my happiness."

"Oh, Lark," I say miserably.

"This is the real Lark," Chief Ellena goes on. "The one that was hidden behind petty morality and fear of what society thinks. Her core self. Isn't it beautiful? I did the same thing with the populace of Eden, but I went deeper into the heart of what it means to be a human. Do you know what people want more than anything? What they long for, what they work so hard to achieve, though they never realize it?"

She pauses dramatically. "*People don't want to think*," she says, pronouncing each word distinctly and slowly. "That is the blessing I gave to the people of Eden. Most of them, anyway. And soon, all of them. Very soon."

I look around for any hope of escape. With only five Greenshirts plus the Chief it should be possible. But they are heavily armed, and the other Oaks kids are just milling around, unconcerned, unaware. If we try anything, how many might be caught in the cross fire?

And with a gun at her temple, my mom would be the first to die.

"I am truly surprised to see you again," Chief Ellena goes on. "And on such a noble cause. Rescuing your friend? A friend who despises you? And for that misguided heroism you sacrifice so many of your other friends and allies. No wonder you were such a disappointment to me."

She shakes her head as she looks at Mira, Carnelian, Ash. She doesn't seem to recognize Pearl in her veil. "That was a splendid stunt you pulled, blowing up the Underground," she goes on. "It caused no end of aggravation for us." She caresses Mom's cheek with the muzzle of her gun. "The only bright spot to that event was the satisfying thought that you were dead. Tell me, how did you survive the blast?"

I can't tell her about Harmonia and the outside world. She's heard rumors, but if she ever knew they were true, what would she do? I want to end her control, give the people of Eden freedom. I still don't know if they should be turned loose on the world, or if a million people in the environment will just set about destroying the planet again.

One thing I know for sure is that the Eden that is under Chief Ellena's control can't be allowed anywhere near Harmonia and the peaceful wilderness. If she knew what was out there, she'd want to control it, too. I envision all the people of Harmonia overrun by Greenshirts, forcibly implanted with lenses, turned into robots by this evil woman . . .

"I was lucky," I say stubbornly.

She chuckles cruelly as she squeezes my mom's neck tighter. Mom winces, but grits her teeth. "Not so lucky if you are my prisoner again. Oh, the fun we'll have on the operating table, my dear former daughter! Now tell me!" she growls. "Is there another layer to the Underground that we didn't discover? Do the rebels have some technology that will protect them from a blast of that size?"

"Do you think I'd tell you anything?" I ask defiantly.

She smiles. "Oh, I think you'll tell me everything . . . eventually. Your brain is mine to explore at my leisure, my child."

"She's not your child!" Mom screams, struggling to break free of Ellena's clutches.

"How interesting to find you alive, Rosalba. For the moment. This night is full of surprises."

My mom fumes at her, twisting futilely. "Put down the gun and fight me, Ellena!"

"How . . . touching. What a primal force maternal love is. That is why I never had children. I don't like anything to control me."

"You unnatural woman!" Mom shouts. "Can't you see you're destroying your own species? If you control their brains they're not even people anymore. EcoPan will stop you. Its directive is to save humanity, and when it realizes what you are doing . . ."

"EcoPan has had every opportunity to intervene," she answers smoothly. "It obviously agrees with what I'm doing. For the benefit of all mankind."

One of the Greenshirts checks his watch and whispers something into her ear.

"Already?" she asks him, and he nods. "Well, aren't my troops a model of efficiency? Oh, very well." She backs toward the door, dragging Mom with her. "It appears I don't have very much leisure after all. You and I will have some mother-daughter time later, my dear. And your mother and I have so much to catch up on. The rest of these people are unnecessary. Guards! Kill them all!"

I hear weapons being racked, and I scream, "Wait! I'll tell you anything you want to know!"

She holds up a hand to stop the Greenshirts, and they stand poised with their weapons pointed at the head of everyone I love. Except for Lark. I can't believe she's doing this of her own free will. She might be lost to me, but I still love her — the real Lark, who I know is hidden underneath.

To save her, to save my mom and friends, I tell Chief Ellena all about Harmonia, about the beautiful, living world beyond the desert of Eden. Maybe my words will move her, I think. Maybe it will make her realize that war, that controlling people, is futile.

She doesn't believe me. "Are you still spouting the same deluded nonsense you did before? I suppose I broke you even more than I realized. Ah well, we'll find out when we dissect your brain. If you won't tell me what I want to know, then we have no use for any of you."

"It's true!" Mira chimes in. "There is a world beyond Eden. I live there! I was born there!"

The Chief whirls on her. "Hold her head!" Deftly, the Chief pops out Mira's fake lenses. "Another second child, I see. Is the world overrun with the vermin?" She waves her hand. "Kill her, and round up the others."

"No!" I scream, as without hesitation the Greenshirt puts a gun to the back of Mira's head. I close my eyes at the sound, but when I open them the Greenshirt is on the ground, Mira's foot on his throat. Chief Ellena and the other Greenshirts all have their weapons pointed at Mira, but the Chief laughs and waves them away. "Your wild paradise must be quite dangerous to produce a fighter like you. You're too interesting to kill quickly. Let's see, who shall it be, then?"

The Oaks students standing near her look on with blank faces, oblivious to the threats and violence.

For a moment we do nothing. I feel too paralyzed to act. But Carnelian, seeing Mira in danger, suddenly breaks free of the Greenshirt holding him, elbowing him in the head and surging toward his love. Two of the Greenshirts break from guarding the door to tackle him. One hits him in the head with the butt of his gun, and Carnelian lays on the floor, groaning and insensible. I hear Chief Ellena say in a bored voice, "This is getting out of hand. Luckily, I can delegate." I see Chief Ellena take out a small device and tap in a command. All at once every one of the students seems to come unnaturally alert. Then chaos erupts. The students are fighting—us, everyone. It's like someone flipped a switch in their brains that turned on unthinking aggression.

I realize that's exactly what happened. She's turned on a localized tweak of her enhanced mind control. It probably wasn't even that hard. Just code the brain to signal the body to release adrenaline, testosterone, and all the other hormones associated with violence and aggression. She can't control them with enough finesse to tell them who to fight, but she can turn them into mindless killers and let them loose. With their overwhelming numbers, they'll take care of us as easily as the Greenshirts.

One of the students takes a swing at me, another kicks for my shins. Someone pulls my hair from behind. Luckily none of these people are fighters, but I don't want to hurt any of them, so for now there's a limit to how much I can fight back.

I hear gunshots. The Greenshirts aren't leaving all the fighting to the brainwashed students. I try to reach Mom, my fists clenched, ready to fight, to kill, no matter what the consequences. There's no going back now. This is a final stand for all of us. We're doomed, I know it. Now the only thing we can hope for is to take the Chief down with us. Without her, maybe all this will end.

My murderous charge is halted when a slender arm snakes around my neck, pulling me back and off my feet. Gasping for breath, I pull Lark's forearm off my trachea and roll to my back, but immediately she's on top of me. There's nothing of my sweet Lark in her contorted face, and I know she'll kill me if she can.

I'm stronger than she is, and roll her over so that I'm on

top, but I have no wish to hurt her, and she uses that to her advantage, throwing a punch from the bottom that makes me rear back to avoid it. She uses this momentum to flip me again and we roll, over and over, fighting for dominance, until we hit the wall. We end up with Lark on top, and in the confusion of zombie-like Oaks students someone kicks me in the head, someone else steps on my hand, so that Lark manages to get her hands around my throat.

Her grip is like steel, like an eagle's talons. With the wall on one side, oblivious Oaks students in their stupor on the other, I can't roll her. I can't even get my hands up to fend her off.

This all happens in seconds. I hear gunfire, and wonder why the Greenshirts haven't shot me yet. It doesn't matter. Lark is doing their job for them. My pulse pounds against her squeezing hands, slower, slower . . .

"Lark, please," I beg as my consciousness dims.

For a second she falters and her grip loosens enough to let a little more blood to my brain. "No! You won't trap me again! I'm better alone!" She squeezes, but I've managed to get one hand free, the hand closest to the wall. I claw at her choking fingers, but I'm too weak to get purchase. I wonder what is going on around me. So much confusion, so many gunshots . . .

My flailing hand brushes something on the wall. It is a panel of switches. With the last of my conscious mind I realize what it is, what it means. It's the control panel for the lights and speakers. I flail at the switches, hitting them all, and suddenly the room explodes in flashing light and booming music. The strobes are dizzyingly fast. Lark's eyes grow wide, and she stiffens, which for a moment makes her hands clench even tighter around my throat. Then she topples like a tree, convulsing as the flashing lights trigger an epileptic seizure.

Gasping, I roll to my knees and look at the chaos around me.

Chaos . . . and carnage.

At least a dozen Oaks students lay bloody and wounded. Two Greenshirts lay sprawled on the ground, too.

Then suddenly everything changes. The students stop, looking confused, and start to mill around, averting their eyes from blood and anything else disturbing. "What's happening?" Chief Ellena shouts. "Why aren't they fighting?"

I see a slim figure with hair like fire, furiously typing with her thumbs at some kind of device. It is one of the localized disruptors that blocks mind control! With the students out of the equation, we have a chance to fight our way out of here.

Oh, and there is Lachlan, his face illuminated by muzzle flash as he grimly takes down another Greenshirt.

I hear Chief Ellena shout at her remaining Greenshirts to retreat, and the gunfire stops. There is a scramble near the door, and all I can see is one Greenshirt, with Chief Ellena hidden behind him, dragging my Mom, trying to edge to the exit. He has his gun out, but can't pick a target. At best he'll get one shot before being mowed down. Lachlan and Flame both point guns at him.

"Sorry we were late," Lachlan says as I struggle to my feet.

"Better late than never," I choke out.

My father rushes forward, taking me in his arms. "Are you okay?" he asks, touching my face, looking into my eyes with deep concern. I nod, but point to Mom, held hostage.

"You!" Chief Ellena says, staring at my father. "The biggest traitor of them all. My chief physician, turned rebel. Did you really think you would get away with letting all my little test subjects go? And now this deluded attempt to rescue Lark? All very heroic, but soon you'll realize exactly how little it matters. After tonight, Eden is mine." She laughs wickedly. "But know this: I never suffer traitors to live!" Before any of us can react, she aims her gun around the Greenshirt's bulk and shoots my dad in the chest. Then she ducks out of the door and the Greenshirt slams it closed. I rattle the door, but it is locked from the outside. Mom is gone. While Flame tries to get the door unlocked, I run to my father's side. Oh, great Earth, not now! Not when I've just started to forgive him, when for the first time in my life I have a chance at having a real father . . .

I press at the wound in his chest, but the damage is too great. Dad's eyelids flutter, and he clutches at my hand.

"So . . . proud. So . . . sorry . . ." Then he presses something in my hand, his eyes roll back in his head, and he is gone.

I grind my teeth, clench my fists, and look at the bloodshed around me.

"It better be worth it," Ash says in angry despair.

"Death is never worth it," I say grimly, then hold up the thing my father just gave me. "But . . . we got the seed."

WITH CHIEF ELLENA gone, the Oaks kids are free of their mind control. I don't know if they even remember what just happened, but they are completely freaked out and are fighting to get out of the door. My eyes turn away from my father's corpse. Carnelian is hugging Mira, so relieved his warrior woman is still alive when he thought for sure she was doomed. There are Lachlan, and Ash, and Flame. Lark is in the corner, unconscious. Angel stands panting with a bruised cheek and disheveled hair. She's shaken, but it looks like she acquitted herself well.

"We have to go after Mom!" Ash says, starting for the door, which Flame has just managed to get open. Lachlan catches him by the shoulder.

"That would be suicidally stupid," he tells my brother. Ash gives him a furious look and jerks away, looking to me for support.

"I can't lose her again!" I cry. "You know what will happen to her."

"If we can catch them before they take her off campus . . ." Angel suggests, but Lachlan shakes his head.

I want to go after Mom, but I know it is no use right now. "Chief Ellena didn't bring many people with her because she had to move fast when she got word from Lark that I was here. She got as many Greenshirts as she could, but her objective was speed, not numbers. She thought it was just me and Angel and Mira. She didn't think she'd have to fight all of you. But now that she knows, she's calling in reinforcements."

"Right," Lachlan says. "Your mom will be in a Center prison in moments, and this place will be swarming with troops. We have to get out of here now, or we'll be captured ourselves."

"And then getting the seed will be for nothing," Flame says. "The sacrifices, for nothing." She looks at my father's body. "He might have made some mistakes in his life, but once he saw the right course he was a fearless, selfless leader. The rebellion would not have come this far without him."

I can't have a true relationship with him, but at least I can remember him as an honorable man, at the end anyway.

"With the seed, and time to plan, and more people, we can get into the Center, and not only shut down the mind control, but rescue your mom, too," Lachlan promises us.

Ash shakes his head. "She would come for us. If we were captured, she'd go charging right into the Center . . ."

"And she'd die," Lachlan says harshly. "Come on, we have to leave before more Greenshirts come. Rowan! Do you think the Chief knows what we came here for?"

"No," I tell him. "I'm sure they don't know anything about the Temple, or the seed."

He looks at me questioningly.

"Lark thinks I came for her. Didn't you hear the Chief? She thinks I brought all of you here simply to rescue Lark." *Would I have?* I wonder. *Would I have put my friends, my family in jeopardy to save her?* "I think she still sees us as a bunch of kids on a sentimental mission, not rebels bent on saving Eden. So she might not go all out to catch us. At least, not as much as if she knew the truth."

"Then we have a chance," Lachlan says. "School staff will be here any minute to sort this out and help the wounded. We can slip out in the confusion."

I nod as I kneel to check on Lark. She's still completely unconscious. I hook my hands under her armpits and look around, waiting for one of my friends to help me carry her.

"You're not serious," Flame says.

"What do you mean?" I ask, uncomprehending.

Lachlan answers for her, very gently. "Rowan, she's under direct control of Chief Ellena. It's too dangerous to bring her along."

"She'll lead the Chief directly to us, wherever we are," Flame says, her voice so businesslike. "It might be against her will, but she's the enemy now."

"I know, but this is Lark!" I insist.

"I don't want to leave her either," Ash says, and comes nearer to me so that I assume he's going to help me carry her. It turns out he's not on my side either. "But this is more important than one person."

"Would you leave me behind for the sake of the mission?" I ask hotly. "I wouldn't leave you!"

"Maybe not," Ash says. "But you would try to make us leave you behind, if you were hurt, if helping you threatened the mission. You know you would."

I bow my head to the truth of that, but I can't leave her here. I thought I'd never see her again. She thinks I betrayed her, abandoned her, already. I don't care if half of that was Chief Ellena's manipulation. Part of it is real, and to think that Lark feels that about me, even a little bit, is utterly heartbreaking. I don't ever want to see that look in her face again.

"I won't leave her," I declare adamantly. "But I can't carry her by myself, not for long. Ash?"

He shakes his head.

"Lachlan?"

"That's not even Lark anymore. I'm sorry, but I won't let her be the reason we fail. I won't let anyone be the reason." I can see the effort it costs him to say this, though. He knows the right thing to do—the humane thing. And I know his decision makes perfect sense, and yet . . .

I look from face to face, begging for help. "Mira?" I ask desperately.

For a moment she looks at me. Then, making a sudden decision, she leaves Carnelian's side, even when he tries to hold her back. "From this big lug over here, I learned about love. And from you, Rowan, I learned about true friendship. I know you feel both things for this poor girl here. She betrayed you. It's her fault your father is dead. But if you think there's a chance for redemption, I'll help you to the ends of the Earth."

I'm overwhelmed by her strength of character. She helps me pick up Lark, but neither of us can carry her easily by ourselves. I hear Carnelian give a reluctant sigh. "Here, allow me," he says, and scoops up Lark with ease.

"Everyone deserves to be saved," he says with stolid certainty. "Her now, all people soon."

With a nod of gratitude I follow him out into the dark campus. Our group slips off the grounds and into the street, prepared for anything.

We've made it through the first circle when Ash says, "Bik! Look out!"

There are a couple of party girls, a little too old for the clothes and makeup they're wearing, out for a night of trying to recapture their youth. At first they look like they're going to pass us, just like everyone else has so far. But this time it is different. As they pass us, their lively, shrill conversation ceases and they stare at us.

"They look suspicious," one says.

"Yeah, very suspicious," her friend replies. "We should tell someone."

"They're disruptive," the first woman says with her lip curled in derision.

"Different."

We hurry on, but they follow us, slowly, methodically, robotically.

"We can't be on the streets anymore," Flame says.

"What's going on?" I ask.

"You've seen how the mind control works—people have been programmed to basically ignore anything outside of themselves that is unpleasant, like civil war or injustice or inequality. They're just comfortable, insular in their own lives. Well, with a little bit of a tweak, the Center can activate another aspect of that program that makes people look for anything a little off—sneaky behavior, the wrong clothes, someone out of place—that might clue them in that something is about to be unpleasant. It makes them want to put a stop to it before it tries to disrupt their lives."

I consider this as we hurry away from the women, who are still steadily following us, whispering to each other and eyeing us with suspicion. "So it's another way they make people ignore unpleasantness? Basically by nipping it in the bud?"

"Yes," Flame confirms. "It is an insidiously subtle piece of programming. All of it plays on different aspects of people's natural complacency. Most people will give up all kinds of freedom for comfort. All she has to do is send out a signal, and suddenly every citizen of Eden is a spy."

I gasp as I realize the implications of this. "So those women . . ."

She nods. "Along with anyone else who sees us tonight.

To the average unaffected citizen, we would pass muster. Now every person is asking themselves who we are, why they haven't seen us before, where we're going, are we behaving perfectly normally—or too normally. Every person who sees us tonight is analyzing us . . . and reporting us to the Center. We have to get off the street now!"

"We won't be able to take the sneaky alleys and basement routes until we get farther away from the center," Ash says. He knows the secret rebel routes well now. "Where can we go?"

"I have no idea," Lachlan admits. "We have to be on the streets for a while."

At once, Ash and I look at each other. We know this area well, and simultaneously realize exactly where we should go. "This way!" I say, and we run away from the slowly following women. They've met a man, and as we run they point us out, stopping to confer. Any moment now they'll contact the authorities.

It's a gamble. A big property in the inner circles is rare, and it is entirely possible that a new family is living in our home. But I figure that it is also very likely that the uncertainty of our family status means it couldn't be sold fast. Mom is legally dead, and I don't officially exist, but my father is still the legal owner. The property probably hangs in legal limbo.

So when we turn the next corner, we make a run for it, evading the women and the man, and luckily not meeting anyone else until we reach my old family home.

And so it proves, for we find it looking unkempt and apparently unoccupied.

"Locked, of course," Ash says.

"I can get in through the back door in the courtyard, or one of the windows there," I say, and without further thought start scanning the wall of the back courtyard for handholds.

I've climbed this wall thousands of times—from the inside. I've only rarely scaled it from the outside, and with the smoother, more decorative stone face it is a much trickier proposition. Luckily, we lived in the only house in Eden to be made from real stone. It was Aaron Al-Baz's house almost a thousand years ago, after the Ecofail. All other buildings are made of synthetic material or solar power panels, almost impossible to climb.

I realize how much I've changed in the three months of living in the wilderness. Once, these straight, artificial lines were all I knew, and my mind and body had adapted to dealing with them. Now, after having lived in nature for even a little while, I rebel against all this regularity. Though it was harder at first, my body longs now to climb a tree, with its organic curves, its living skin, the hundreds of bugs and lichens living on its surface. Already, the city seems an alien place.

For a second I turn, my fingers curled around the first handhold, to make a joke to Mira about having a climbing competition. She always beat me up trees. Maybe this time I'd beat her up this wall. But when I look for her, she's already six feet up the wall. There's a huge grin on her face.

"I get to compete on your territory now," she whispers, and with a low laugh I follow her . . . then pass her. This is a lot different from the trees and natural rock formations she's used to.

"Rowan," I hear a weak voice say below me when I've just passed Mira. It can be a climber's doom to look down, but I can't help it. Lark is coming awake . . . just barely. I see her large gray eyes looking up at me from Carnelian's arms. "Aren't you even going to say goodbye?"

My fingertips grip the cracks in the stone impossibly tight, and I have to close my eyes. A tear squeezes from each one. That was what Lark said to me on our first night out together, when she walked me home and was watching in amazement as I climbed the wall.

I didn't say goodbye then. I said, *Until tomorrow*. Now I don't say anything at all. I can't even begin to guess what the future may hold for any of us. But my heart aches with longing for everything to work out.

I return my focus to the wall and manage to climb quickly, beating Mira, who curses at the unaccustomed method of climbing. For a moment we perch on the wall. I look toward the Center, where the green eye of the crystal dome glitters balefully in the night.

Much more quickly than the ascent, I scramble down into the courtyard and then hurry through the house to let everyone else in. As far as I can tell, no one has seen us go inside. We should be safe here until we figure out what to do.

It feels supremely strange having everyone here. I've never played hostess in my own home before, yet I find myself fussing, urging everyone to sit, get comfortable, apologizing for the mess and dust.

Carnelian lays Lark down on a sofa, and then everyone unconsciously moves away from her. They don't know what to think about her. Even Ash and Lachlan, who know her well, are unsure.

Is it stupid that, with fresh bruises from her fingers around my throat, I still want to trust her?

Yes, says Yarrow. *But I would expect nothing less from you.*

The house has obviously been searched. Drawers are open, papers strewn in a haphazard way. They found my hidden room connecting with Ash's. My clothes are pulled out, my mattress askew. I never had many possessions. In a pinch, it had to look like this room was a guest bedroom or storage area. So there couldn't exactly be frilly skirts in the closet or feminine decorations on the walls. No one ever came here—with such a big secret, we naturally discouraged guests—but if they had, they would never have known a girl, a second child, lived here.

Still, it feels strange to be looking at my clothes, my small possessions. There is a scrap of paper on the floor, a pencil drawing. It is supposed to be a self-portrait, but I remember when my dad saw it he got mad and told me to tear it up. What would someone say if they found a portrait of a teenage girl, obviously Ash's twin? I remember instead of destroying it I rubbed out the lines of long, dark hair and redrew it with Ash's short hairstyle. I can still see shadows on the page where my hair used to be.

I was erased. Only Ash could live, publicly anyway.

I shove the drawing into my pocket and help get some food for everyone. The power is off, and when I open the refrigerator there is a terrible rotting stench. But there is still canned and powdered and dehydrated food on the shelf, and the water is running, so Ash and I throw together a meal.

I don't have any appetite, though. So while the others gather around the dark dining table, I wander outside.

The courtyard is the place where I spent most of my life, my one small taste of freedom in my prison. I hate thinking of my loving home as a prison, but it is the truth of it. I was locked up for the best of reasons—for my survival and Ash's—but I was still a prisoner for sixteen years.

I hear footsteps behind me, and turn to find Ash, my second self.

Finally, I voice the thought that has been hovering on the edges of my consciousness for months, ever since this all began.

"Maybe I should never have left that night," I say. "All of this, because one girl thought a courtyard was too small to contain her life. If only I'd known what my need for freedom would be, I'd have—"

Ash interrupts me. "Stayed trapped? I don't believe that."

"But look at what has happened! All the death and suffering. Lark brainwashed. Mom captured. And poor Dad!"

"I never thought I'd hear you say that," Ash admits.

"He was flawed, but . . . he was trying," I say. "Now he's dead because of me. The Underground is gone, the second children exposed. All because of me."

"You're absolutely right," Ash says, and I can't suppress a sound that's half snort, half laugh.

"No, you're supposed to tell me it isn't my fault, that all this would have happened anyway, that I'm just . . . what did Pearl, I mean Angel, say? a cog in the machine?"

"You just want to be told lies and feel better, like everyone else?" he asks. "I don't think so. I know you better than that."

"So it is my fault," I say miserably.

"Yes, but think about what that means. Yes, bad things have happened—but bad things were already happening. At least now a few people are fighting them. Yes, the government is controlling the citizens—but now that we know that, we know how to end it. And the outside, the living world beyond the desert! We wouldn't know anything about that if it wasn't for you. Would you give up all that—not just for you, but for all of humanity—to stay safe in your courtyard?"

"But the rebels might lose. We might be captured. Mom might be executed, or turned into someone who hates me, like Lark."

"Might is a powerful word. There is a lot of hope in might. Before you, we were all weak people in an unjust world, doing nothing about it. Now we have truth, reality. We know how bad things are. Because of you."

He puts his arms around me. "Because of you, sister dear, we have a chance." Then he whispers in my ear. "And incidentally, because of you, I've fallen in love!" He chuckles. "I mean, I'm not the rare and seductive Rowan with two people in love with her. But I'm happy."

I smile and ruffle his hair, which he hates. Which is why I do it. The things people in Eden are missing out on by not having siblings!

"Then what are you doing out here with me? Go inside, back to her. But . . . maybe take Mom and Dad's room? I want to nap in my own bed one last time, and I don't want to have to walk past you and your girlfriend doing . . . whatever!"

He's made me feel a little better, but the grief and the guilt still threaten to overwhelms me. I don't let him see that, though. He wants to believe he's thoroughly cheered me up. He pulls a lock of my hair—which I hate—and heads inside.

I go back to looking at the stars, so much dimmer here in Eden, but that's how I remember them, the faint stars of my childhood. I trace out patterns, remembering the constellations I invented for myself, and the ones Lark told me about that night high on the rooftop. I think of nights in the woods with Mira as she taught me how to navigate by the stars. The North Star, the Big Dipper . . .

Someone is coming, and I turn, thinking it is Ash come back. I wipe my tears away and try to force my voice to be light, saying, "What, need some sisterly relationship advice?"

It's Lachlan.

When I see him, I can no longer hold back the tears. A moment later I'm in his arms, weeping against his chest for what I have done, for what I have lost.

26

"IS SHE AWAKE?" I ask once I get control of myself, and see his face fall just a bit when he hears that my first thought is about Lark. But that's only natural, right? I know Lachlan is okay. It's Lark who might be another person, lost to me.

"Not yet," he says. "Flame is examining her with her handheld scanner, trying to see what she'll be like when she wakes up. She said this is a different kind of brainwashing, as much psychological as just mechanically changing thoughts and memories. She has one of the localized disruptors that can usually interfere with the Center's signal within a small space, but Flame says she really doesn't know what to predict from Lark." He gives me a wry smile. "Predictability—not exactly something either of you is good at."

"And look what it gets us," I say.

"I know what you're feeling right now," Lachlan says gently.

"How can you?" I ask.

"Remember, I've been part of an underground resistance nearly all of my life. We've never been this bold, and the stakes have never been this high, but we've had to take terrible risks before, just to survive. Don't you think I've made my share of bad decisions? Or decisions that led to victory, but also had losses? I've lost people, Rowan. People I cared about, who died because of my leadership. I know you blame yourself for everything that has happened. You blame yourself for your father's death, for your mom's capture."

He takes me by the shoulders and looks into my mismatched eyes. "Rowan, you are not at fault for the evil of the world, for the cruelties of people."

"I know," I answer miserably. "But if you had heard the things that Lark said to me. That I abandoned her! I saw her locked in the Center prison, and I didn't get her out."

"How could you?" Lachlan asks reasonably. "You got everyone else out, though."

"She turned against me because she thinks I chose you, left her there so I could be with you."

"If she really thinks that, she doesn't know you very well," Lachlan says. Before I can object, he adds, "And she does know you well. As do I. I know how you love. It is a powerful, protective love—and it has no limits. It rankled me at first, that you love her, too. Now I know it's just another part of what makes you beautiful and unique. You can love Lark. You can love anyone you want, and I don't mind. Because I know you love me, too."

He's been near to me all this time, but now he closes the last few inches and our bodies are pressed together. His kiss is amazing, like coming home. Not here, not Harmonia, but some home of the soul, the place where I can find peace and rest.

"I love you, Rowan," he whispers to me, and I want this moment to last forever.

Of course, that is when Flame comes out into the courtyard and says, "Unlock your lips and get in here. Lark is awake."

The guilt hits again, as if she's been watching us. Lachlan

might be okay with me caring for both of them, but I know Lark isn't.

We head inside, and I hurry ahead so it doesn't look like we're coming in together. With all the things to worry about, all the tragedy, I know it is silly to be so worried about relationships and feelings, but when all is said and done (if all this ever is done) that's what will remain—the connections between human beings.

Lark is propped up on the sofa, still looking weak and a little disoriented. I feel an ache in my throat when I look at her, and think it is emotion.

No, you idiot, Yarrow says. *Your throat aches because that crazy girl tried to kill you an hour ago. Stay away from her. The last thing you need is more crazy in your life right now.*

She has a point, and I consider leaving the room, if only to buy myself more time to feel calmer. But I steel myself, reminding myself of the Lark that was, not the Lark that is, and tentatively approach.

"How do you feel?" I ask her gently.

"Confused," she whispers. She looks so lost. My compassion breaks through my apprehension, and I scoot her feet over and sit on the far end of the couch.

Could be an act, Yarrow reminds me.

"About what?" I ask Lark.

"Everything!" she says, with a little sound that might almost be a laugh, though she chokes it back with a moan of misery.

"Well," I say, "let's see if we can narrow it down. What part is most confusing?"

I can tell she's mentally going through what must be a pretty long list. "You," she says at last. "Do I hate you or love you?"

I can feel Lachlan watching, listening from nearby, an

amused smile on his face. How can I answer that? The short answer of course is yes, but I think she needs more than a short answer, and with everyone's eyes on me, this isn't the time. I'm desperately afraid of hurting her more than she already thinks I have.

Blushing, I bow my head, but Lachlan answers. "You love her. There's no doubt about that. Almost as much as I do." He winks at her.

"Yeah, there's one thing I'm not confused about at all," Lark tells him with narrowed eyes. "I don't like you very much." She turns back to me. "Could you sit over there?" She points to a chair across the room. "This isn't very comfortable."

I try to tell myself she means physically comfortable—that she wants to stretch out. But I know that's not what she means. What does she feel when she looks at me? Is all of Chief Ellena's implanted hate still in there?

Crushed, I relocate, and Lark speaks mostly to Flame. It appears she's on our side, for now.

"No idea how long it will last," Flame admits. "The algorithms the Chief used are a bit fuzzy to me. Maybe to her, too. This is all still experimental. Lark's epileptic episode reset her brain, for now. And I think—think, mind you—that my disruptors will keep her head clear for now. But for all I know she could revert back to the mind control any moment."

I can tell Flame is supremely frustrated to not have concrete answers. She's used to being well informed, and right.

Lark won't look at me. She appears as nervous and uncomfortable as I feel.

"Whatever your plan is, you have to act soon. Now. The Chief is getting ready to attack the rebels."

"We know," Lachlan interjects. "And we're ready for them. We have fighters ready to . . ."

Flame shushes him. "We think she's mostly her old self, but don't trust her with too much information," she cautions.

"No," Lark says. "I don't mean eventually, someday. I mean now. Tomorrow. As soon as the sun comes up she's sending almost every one of the Greenshirts and securitybots to the border of the outermost circle. They'll be in position by noon. She said . . ."

Lark breaks off, and finally glances at me before saying, "She said they're not to take prisoners."

"You mean . . . ?" I ask.

Lark nods. "She's going to kill them all."

"Would she really do that?" Ash asks. "All this time, she's claimed she's controlling people to preserve humanity—same as EcoPan."

"Power has gone to her head," Lark says. "She just wants control, and will take out any opposition. At this point she doesn't care if she kills thousands if it means no one gets in the way of her controlling the rest of Eden."

"She's insane!" I say. Exactly like Aaron Al-Baz.

"We have to warn them," Ash says.

"If she's attacking in the morning, I doubt we could get through," Flame points out. "There will be patrols, increased security."

"They wouldn't do it," Angel says quietly from her corner. She might not be the domineering Pearl anymore, but her soft voice still commands attention. "Even if they are police and soldiers, even if they follow her command, they wouldn't kill their own people. Life is sacred. We all believe that. They may attack, may capture the outer circle, the people, but they won't kill them all."

Ash nods in agreement. "Most of the rebels aren't fighters. They're everyday people. Families, old people, children. Some of the rebel fighters might die in the battle—we're all prepared for that—but even if the worse comes to the worst, the children and families will be spared."

Rainbow is out there, and the other kids from the Underground. I can't believe anyone would kill them deliberately.

But then, I never could have believed that the peace-loving people of Harmonia could kill Lachlan just because he was from Eden. Once someone is labeled a threat, I guess it is easier for some people to look at them as less than human. That makes them easier to exterminate.

"You don't understand Chief Ellena," Lark says urgently. "Even you, Rowan. You've been under her control, but she's become so much worse now. I've heard her talking about the rebels like they're vermin. She plans to exterminate them. She says they're a negligible fraction of the Eden population, and that human genetic diversity won't suffer for wiping them out. In fact, she says, it will make the surviving humans stronger."

"Easier to control, you mean," Flame says. "The ones she's manipulating are the ones with the most susceptible brains. The rebels are the ones genetically better at resisting mind manipulation. Wipe them out, and there may never be another uprising again."

"Exactly," Lark says. "Which is why you have to stop her. Too many people have died. You can't let more die."

"The Greenshirts are under mind control, too," I remind them. "They might be soldiers, but they are still people, citizens of Eden. They have to believe that Eden is about preserving human life. I bet if we shut down her mind control, the soldiers themselves would rebel. If they had the capacity to realize what she's making them do, there'd be a mutiny."

"That means we have to attack tonight," Lachlan says grimly.

"Yes!" I say. "If we can shut down the mind control broadcast, who knows? The Greenshirts might join the rebels. We can save them!"

"That sounds awfully pretty, Rowan," Flame says. "But it's impossible. We got the seed so that a team of a hundred people could plan and train for weeks to launch an attack that was already suicidal, and probably doomed to failure anyway. It's the bikking Center! This little ragtag group can't just march in and . . ."

"Maybe we can," Lachlan says, halting his pacing abruptly, a light of hope illuminating his face. "In fact right now, and only now, may be the one time we actually can."

"Explain," Flame says.

I understand what he means, and jump in excitedly. "This is the one time the Center will be lightly guarded. The only way she can hope to take the outermost circle completely is if she commits all of her forces."

"Exactly," Lachlan says. "It won't be easy, but with most of the forces elsewhere, it might just be possible. Getting in will still be a problem, though."

"I can get you inside," Lark says.

"How?" I ask her. I remember when she helped us break into the Center before, through the sewers, and I can tell she's thinking of those days, so dangerous but somehow more simple. Her eyes shift away again. "Do you have access codes?"

"Some, but the easiest way is if I just walk you right in. I go to see Chief Ellena or one of the psychologists or doctors once a week, sometimes more often. She's had me bring some of my friends from school. Well, *people* from school. I don't think I have any friends. I'm kind of a terrible person, I think."

"Does she experiment on them, too?" I shudder, as Yarrow remembers her ordeals at the Chief's hands.

"Not really. She gives them psychological tests, I think to

see if they'd make good candidates. Like me. Or you. Or you, Pearl."

For a moment Pearl doesn't react. Then she sees that Lark means her, and she says, "Sorry, my name is Angel."

"No one told her?" Lark asks.

"Told me what?"

"We knew you. Rowan and me. You're another victim of Chief Ellena."

"This isn't the way I wanted her to find out," I say hurriedly. "Pearl, I mean Angel, I'm sorry I didn't tell you about your past. I will, I promise. As soon as we have time."

She gives me a look I don't expect—one of calm acceptance. "Thank you, Rowan, but I don't want to know."

"What?"

"I like who I am. I'm happy with what I'm doing. I think . . . I don't remember my past, but I don't think I was happy then. I feel like this is who I'm supposed to be." She looks at my brother, who gazes back with loving eyes. "And who I'm supposed to be with." She gives a little laugh. "Anyway, when would you ever have time? We have an invasion to thwart, and a government to topple!" She turns back to Lark. "Now, you say you can walk us right in the front door?"

"Well, not the front. I use the staff entrance, but . . ."

"She can't come with us!" Flame says. "Are you crazy? She's okay now, but for how long? Look, Lark, when this is over I'll try to fix you. Permanently. But for now, with the Center on the attack, we just can't have someone who might randomly turn into an enemy spy at any moment."

"But I want to help. I need to help you, to make up for the way I betrayed you. Rowan, I'm so sorry I hurt you. And oh, your dad! I remember when I'd visit Ash. I didn't come over very often—of course they were hiding you from guests—but whenever I did he was so nice to me."

"She needs to come with us," I tell the others. "She's our best chance of getting into the Center and putting a stop to the woman who killed my dad. It's the only way we can set every one of the people free. I want that to be my father's legacy."

"I agree," Mira says. "We need some advantage against these forces, and she's our best chance."

Lachlan glares at Lark. "She comes, she helps us . . . and at the first sign of treachery I snap her neck."

I see a shiver travel through Lark's body, but she nods. "If I betray you, that's exactly what you should do. But understand I won't betray you voluntarily. If she takes over my mind again, if I become a danger to you, then I want you to kill me." She locks eyes with me. "In fact, I beg you to kill me if that happens. I don't want to live like that."

"We go at dawn," Lachlan decides. "That will give us time to plan—and rest—before the troops move away from the Center. We can keep watch from the wall. As soon as they pass, we head in the opposite direction, toward the Center. Flame, Carnelian, I want you to go over exactly how you plan to disable the mind control. Carnelian has the skills to be a good tech backup. Are you sure you know how to disable it, Flame?"

"I'm not sure of anything," Flame says. "But the seed will unlock it, and I can reprogram or disable it for a while anyway. Once I'm inside I hope to be able to find the resonator that is broadcasting the signal. If I can, I can stop it for good."

Lachlan nods. "Lark, Rowan, you both know the inside of the Center better than anyone. We need to plan exactly how we'll make entry, the route to the control station, and what kind of resistance we're likely to encounter. And as soon as we shut it down, we can go to the prison wing for your mom."

We plan fast, Yarrow helping me recall things about the Center I'd rather not remember. We draw a map, and go over and over our plan. It is a simple one, relying on Lark bringing us in unopposed, and then surprise and brute force. People will die in our plan. But more people will die if we don't succeed.

The whole time, Lark talks to Lachlan. Or I talk to Lachlan. If at all possible, Lark and I don't ever address each other. The tension of our avoidance is almost as bad as the tension of planning for battle.

When it is only a couple of hours before dawn, Lachlan says, "Everyone should try to get some sleep. It will be a challenging morning."

Ash and Angel go to our parents' room. Mira and Carnelian cuddle on a chaise. Lachlan stretches out on the floor, while Flame paces.

I go to my room and flop down on my old familiar bed, burying my head in the pillow that smells like my childhood. How strange it is to see my old things. It feels like so long ago that I left.

I see more of my art supplies in the corner, and even though I'm dead tired my curiosity gets the better of me. I pull Aaron's journal from where it is pressed against my skin under my clothes and paw through my supplies until I find a piece of ocher-colored chalk. With the lightest touch I brush it over the inside back cover, gradually revealing the imprint of words written more than a century ago.

I can't read every word, but by shifting the page at all different angles I can decipher most of it:

My end is near, and when my body is no more I join . . .
I will be buried with my child . . .
Where the feet of the colossus tread on the sea amid flowers of every land, there lies the Heart of EcoPan.

There my child was born, there his cradle, there, one day, his grave.

There the very language of his existence is stored, the code of his creation and his destruction. When my child is no longer needed in this world, it is there that he will die.

I don't immediately understand it. Aaron had a child? But I'm too impossibly sleepy to puzzle it all out, and a moment later my heavy eyes close . . .

I WAKE UP with a hand over my mouth, a pressure on my body. My eyes fly open. Lark is straddling me, and I can just dimly see her finger pressed to her lips. Has she come here to finish the job she started earlier? Is she going to try to kill me?

She takes her hand from my mouth and leans so close I can feel the warmth of her breath on my lips. So close . . .

She dismounts from my bed and holds out her hand. When I don't take it right away, she beckons wordlessly.

We slip silently out of the house into the courtyard. Now that I've been in the living world, it seems so strange to be outside at night without the sounds of crickets and nightjars, owls and cicadas. The silence is unnatural.

I guess she's not planning on killing me, but why are we out here when we should be resting for the coming mission?

I have my answer when Lark suddenly shoves me against the courtyard wall, cradling the back of my head with her hand to protect it from the stone. Again I brace for an attack, but her body is soft against mine, and then she's kissing me. Suddenly everything is simpler, and I'm back to that happy moment of our first kiss. It was confusing and delirious and blissful, but pure and easy, too.

"Oh, Rowan, I've missed you so much," she says breathlessly a moment later. "I'm sorry. I'm so sorry." She releases me to clutch her own head, and I notice that she's crying. "Ahh, I can feel thoughts in my head that aren't mine. Or like some wicked version of me. I know you still have parts of Yarrow in you. How do you stand it without going insane?"

"You remember me, and us, and . . ." I prompt.

"I remember meeting you, everything we did together. I remember getting eaten by the nanosand, and then . . . There's a gap. Somewhere in there, everything got turned around. Everything that mattered to me changed. When Chief Ellena was talking to me, everything suddenly seemed so clear. I hated you, hated the second children, wanted to do everything I could to keep Eden safe."

"You always wanted that," I point out.

"But it came to mean something different. I was . . . not a good person. And now, I'm still not. I think. Or I feel like I'm the old Lark and the new one. Both at the same time. But I'm scared. It's like the new Lark is sleeping for a while." She sits up and clutches at my hands in a panic. "I don't want the new Lark to wake up! She's a terrible person!"

"The Chief changed you," I say as I hold her hands.

"Like she did to you? But I remember who I am."

"Flame said she used a different method on you," I tell her. "She said can probably undo it, with a little time in her lab. But right now, she thinks your epileptic seizure reset your brain. Your old self came to the fore again."

"Will she stay?"

"We don't know."

"I don't want to be that person!" Lark says miserably. "She's not me."

"The Chief said she just massaged parts of your own thoughts, your own psyche," I tell her. "She didn't add anything."

"How do you know?" Lark asks. "I don't really know

what she did to me, and Chief Ellena isn't exactly known for her honesty."

"She would be likely to tell me the thing that would hurt me most—that you decided to turn against me of your own free will, that the hate was within you all the time."

"It wasn't," she says. "I swear it wasn't. I hate that even now, in the back of my head, all those disgusting thoughts are lingering." She clutches her head like she can hold it all in, never let me see it again.

"We'll fix you, Lark. If you can just hold on to yourself for a little while longer, Flame will make you like you were, permanently, and we can go to the outside world, and . . ."

I break off, thinking of my love for her, and Lachlan, how I must be doomed to make them unhappy, unable to choose—or else make myself unhappy.

"I talked to Lachlan while you slept," Lark says, reading my thoughts. "We talked about you, how we feel about you. He's an okay guy, you know." It looks like it almost hurts her to admit this.

"Will you do something for me, Rowan?" she whispers in my ear. "Will you tell me about the outside? In case I never see it."

"You'll see the living world!" I vow adamantly. "And I'll be with you. I promise!"

Then, nestling close to her, I tell her about the wonders of a butterfly, the beauty of a flower. I tell her about the cheerful, melodious little birds that are her namesake.

She interrupts me a moment later. "I need to tell you something. Now, while I'm still myself. I don't know how long it will last, and I couldn't bear it if I became that horrible other version of me without you knowing. Rowan, I love you. From the night we met, and every night in between. Ellena might take away my memory, or implant some new personality, but she can never change the truth of my heart. I need you to remember that, in case I ever change. In case I turn against you."

I feel a warmth, joy deep in my heart. It's a feeling that makes the world look rosy in spite of everything that has happened.

"Oh Lark, I love you too," I breathe, and kiss her like the night will never end.

WE'RE ALL AWAKE and restless at dawn. I doubt any of them slept more than I did. I feel alert and alive, full of determination, my nerves held at bay by the stunning things Lark and Lachlan said to me. It feels like a great weight has been lifted off my shoulders, and I am buoyant, energized.

All I have to do now is launch an attack-and-rescue mission on the most tightly guarded place in Eden.

Our plan is simple—just walk in. Lark says she has brought other kids to the Center on several occasions.

"Ever people from other schools?" I ask her.

She hasn't, but there's a first time for everything. "It will be plausible," Lark says, hopefully. "Chief Ellena wants to see any promising candidates, but she didn't specify just from Oaks."

Our scheme is to all dress in Ash's old uniforms, posing as kids from the Sahara School. It's not quite as lofty as Oaks, but it is a very good school, and Chief Ellena would probably be interested in candidates from those wealthy, important families. They are elites, too.

Her philosophy seems to be co-opt the wealthy and educated, and crush the lower classes.

We're all in Ash's old golden sand-colored uniforms. Angel seems to have a moment of confusion when she looks at herself in the mirror. Is she remembering her old Oaks uniform? Or, if she's not remembering, is there just some small spark in her brain that tells her something is off? I wonder if she'll ever get her memories back. I think brains are too resilient to be beaten down for long.

The clothes are too short for Carnelian, but passable. Mira loves her outfit. "Perfect for climbing, or fighting!" she says of the fitted tunic over leggings.

The only difficulty is Flame. She is small and trim, and easily fits in one of Ash's old uniforms . . . but she is obviously in her forties. She'll never pass for a young woman.

"I can be the suspicious parent," Flame suggests. "The one who assumes you'll be taken advantage of."

"No, having an adult there will raise alarms," Lark says. "Isn't there anything we can do to make her look younger?" She holds up her hands quickly, afraid of offending the woman she is relying on to fix her addled brain. "Not that you look old or anything . . ."

Flame snorts. "I own my age, thank you very much, kid. But you do have a point."

Angel has been studying her. "Do you have any makeup? I think . . . I don't know why, but I just have a feeling I can do something."

"The Pearl is coming out," I murmur to Lark.

When I check the drawers of Mom's mirrored vanity, though, we find something even better than makeup. It's a device with the same sort of simulator that kids use to give themselves tiger stripes or snake eyes. But this one is marketed for adults. Concealed in a headband is a highly sophisticated projector that creates the illusion of youth without surgery. When Flame pushes it down over her red hair and turns it on, her skin is immediately dewy and youthful, the lines around her eyes smoothed. The illusion is perfect—she looks no more than eighteen.

"God-like technology, and this is what we use it for," she gripes, looking into the mirror. Yet, I see her smile at her own image, even if she tries to hide the fact. "At least if I die on this crazy mission, I'll make a beautiful corpse."

Though our nerves are all on edge, we can't leave right away, and the waiting is the worst. Over and over, I climb the inside wall of the courtyard and cautiously peek at the surrounding circles of Eden. For a long time, everything is quiet—unnaturally quiet. The streets are empty, and I wonder if the Center sent out a notice keeping people inside, or if it was some tweak of the mind control, making the populace so indifferent that this morning they don't even bother getting out of bed.

Finally, I hear a sound coming from the direction of the Center. I duck back and beckon the others over, then peer over, reporting what I see.

"The bots are coming first," I say. "Securitybots." These used to be mostly sentinels, keeping an eye on things to make sure there were no crimes. They would report, and at most apprehend. But more recently, all securitybots were armed. They are supposed to be under the control of human handlers. They aren't supposed to be able to make independent decisions about lethal force. But at this point, I'm not sure. They might be programmed to open fire without specific instruction.

Bots wouldn't have any problem slaughtering the outer-circle rebels. They will simply do what they are told.

Of course, until we manage to interfere with the mind control, the Greenshirts might well do the same thing.

"The Greenshirts are behind them. I've never seen so many!"

"How many are there?" Lachlan asks.

"Hundreds!" I didn't know there were so many in all of Eden. And this is just one segment of this circle. They are expanding from the Center in all directions. "They must have been recruiting a lot more."

"There are thousands of rebels," Ash says. "Maybe they can . . ."

"We don't have many guns, Ash," Lachlan says grimly. "And too many civilians. You know that. If we don't succeed, the rebellion dies."

I watch in terrible fascination as the army approaches. The men march like machines, looking even more frightening than the securitybots, because I expect them to show humanity. I've seen and talked to Greenshirts, and though I've always been afraid of what they would do if they knew what I was, most of them have just been ordinary people, doing a job they thought was important.

Now this army of ordinary men and women in their green uniforms are marching out to slaughter children, to kill people who just want their freedom.

When they get near, I climb silently down. We can hear the sound of them marching by—just bootsteps, no talking, no singing. It is unnatural.

Crossing to the other side, I watch them until they cross to the next circle. It's time for us to move.

"There were so many," I marvel. "There can't be a lot of them left in or near the Center."

"I hope you're right," Lark says. "The way I go in, there's a security station, but there's usually just one guard. He likes me. Says my hair reminds him of his granddaughter."

We step out of my house with great trepidation. I feel like a deer entering a clearing, where a wolf pack might be waiting to charge me. But nothing happens.

We try to look normal, natural. Like kids heading to school. I'm sure we look stiff and weird, but there's no one to see. The streets are still deserted, and there isn't a single Greenshirt or securitybot to be seen.

One little cleanbot scuttles across the street in front of us, sweeping up detritus left in the wake of the army. It is the only activity we see all the way to the Center.

It's eerie. It feels like a trap.

"I almost wish they would attack," Lachlan says. "It's harder pretending to be casual, smiling like I belong here, than it is to fight. For me, anyway."

Mira, too, looks on edge, her fighter's body yearning for some activity.

We cross through the main Center gates without being challenged.

"This is just weird," Lark says as we walk across the open grounds, which are dominated by a statue of Aaron Al-Baz.

"All the guards, all the soldiers, are on the march," Ash says.

"And she's not at all afraid of attack?" Flame wonders.

"She thinks she's in complete control," I say. "She thinks she's won. What does she expect us to do, once we were routed, Mom captured? Why, run back to the rebels, of course. She'd never imagine we'd still be here. She'd never dream we'd dare attack. She feels perfectly safe."

"If she's even here," Lachlan says. "She might be leading the troops."

"Put herself in danger?" I ask. "I don't think so."

"Maybe we can just waltz in and do all this without any opposition," Mira says.

"Dream on," Flame mutters as we push open the back staff door and see a security checkpoint with a desk, and an empty chair.

As soon as I enter through the door, I hear a faint buzzing in my ears. Or . . . is it a vibration in my body? I don't know. If I was in Harmonia, I'd think it was a mosquito, a barely perceptible sound, a stir in the air, just at the periphery of my awareness.

I hate this place, Yarrow says, sounding small and frightened even in the safety of my head.

The Center is sterile, stark white, polished and shining. A pure, clean place where terrible things happen.

"The guard's not here," Lark says.

"This is crazy." I'm so suspicious. Is this a test? How could it be possible that, even in the middle of a war, we find this place undefended?

I hear a toilet flush, and immediately a portly, elderly Greenshirt emerges from the bathroom. Flame hunkers behind Carnelian so the guard can only see her youthful figure, and not get a good look at her face. Will the trick hold? Maybe, as long as the guard doesn't look too closely.

"Oh, Lark m'dear. What have we here? Enemy spies?" He sounds suspicious, and I see Lachlan's hand reach for his gun.

I touch his fingers with mine, stopping him. The old guard is just joking.

Lark laughs. "Same as always, Jasper. Bringing in the youth of today, the leaders of tomorrow, to take all your jobs." She raises her hand in a fist above her head. "Crush the old order!" She giggles, and Jasper gives a hearty laugh.

"Oh, we're in trouble now, missy!"

"You know it, Jasper. I'm going to have Chief Ellena's job before long. Better tell her to watch her back."

She winks at him, and he chuckles. It is obviously a familiar kind of banter.

"Okay then. That's the Chief's lookout. I'll just check

your friends' IDs and you can get on with your job of taking over Eden from us old-timers."

I feel a shiver of panic run through me, though I manage to keep my cool. The fake identification attached to out temporary lenses can hold up to an Oaks scan, or a street corner camera, but I think that a more sophisticated Center system will see through our deception.

We're going to have to fight, and I really don't want to have to kill this jolly old man.

What's more, if the fighting starts this soon, we'll raise the alarm. Even if there are hardly any Greenshirts and guards here, there must be someone. We have to get to the Center's control room before anyone is the wiser. And then, rescue my mother.

Jasper takes out a handheld scanner and approaches Lark. She leans in . . . then jerks her head back abruptly, a little sneer on her face.

"Jasper, I didn't hear the water running. I *know* you aren't about to scan us without washing your hands after you used the bathroom."

The old guard flushes the bright scarlet of a poppy flower and stammers awkward apologies. All at once their relationship has shifted. The easy camaraderie is gone. Lark draws herself up regally and makes it clear that she is an elite, rich and privileged, and he is no more than a servant, an underling. The jokes are over. He is beneath her.

Cringing like a beaten animal, he slinks away. As soon as we hear the water running Lark gives a shrill laugh and beckons us down the hallway.

"Oh, that just killed me to do that to Jasper," she whispers to us as we pass unchecked through the gate. "But he'll be way too embarrassed to call us back now. Oh, poor old Jasper!"

The fact that this upsets her is promising. She's still the original Lark, kind and considerate. I wonder how long it will last. Maybe forever, Flame said. Or she could revert to her nasty state at any moment.

As uncomfortable as it was for her, it is a boon to us. We sail through, and though we pass some people—scientists, bureaucrats—they assume we've already been vetted and don't question our presence. There aren't many people, though. Are they all involved in the attack, or are we just getting lucky? Maybe there's a meeting somewhere.

We move down the echoing, stark white halls, led by Lark for the first part, then Lachlan takes over. The faint buzzing in my head continues and I try to ignore it. I'm last of the group. My very feet seem reluctant to go any deeper into this building where I was tortured.

"What was that?" I gasp, alarmed, whirling to look behind me.

"What's wrong?" Lark asks.

I could have sworn I heard a whisper from just behind me. But there's nothing there. I shake my head. "Nerves," I say.

"It's right up ahead," Lachlan tells us a moment later. "Are you ready?"

We all have weapons, small, easily concealable guns. The lethal kinds. Since this was originally just supposed to be a quick infiltration of Oaks, I voted we all have stun guns. It was Lachlan who insisted on real, deadly weapons, just in case. We don't want to use them, he said. But if we have to, it is going to be serious—our lives or theirs.

He's been proven right. If we'd just had stun guns, Chief Ellena would have won. And we can be sure that if anyone opens fire on us in here they'll be using real weapons.

Lark is the only one without a gun. I argued that she's in

as much danger as we are. Flame reasonably pointed out that there is a very good chance that at any moment Lark might point the gun at us instead of our enemies. Even Lark agreed to be unarmed.

I take a deep breath, and Yarrow seems to as well.

"We go in hard," Lachlan says. "No hesitation, no mercy. Go!"

He flings the door open and charges in, aiming his gun, a grim look on his face. We follow close behind him. I've steeled myself for blood, for slick red against the stark white.

Inside there's a filing cabinet, a rolling table. A cleanbot whirs softly in the far corner, sweeping up dust. It swivels when we storm in, but since we aren't garbage it ignores us. There are no people.

When you're geared up for fighting and death, a lone cleanbot is kind of an anticlimax. All that adrenaline and nothing to do with it makes me feel shaky.

"It's not here," Lachlan says. "It's supposed to be here."

He consults the hand-drawn map, confers with Lark.

"It *was* here," Flame says. She points out places where the data storage blocks must have been, the power connectors and cooling systems of a significant control center. "She must have had it moved to a bigger room, once she started upgrading the system. She needed more output, more power."

"What are we going to do?" Angel asks.

Lark is biting her lip, deep in thought. "I haven't been all over this place, but there is one room, I remember I was there for a physical about a month ago. It was a big place with treadmills and medical devices, but it was in disarray. Stuff out of place, empty spaces. I thought at the time they were upgrading it, but maybe they were emptying it to relocate this control room there. It was definitely bigger."

"It would have to be not only big, but set up to use vast

amounts of power, to store vast amounts of data," Flame muses. "A medical room might take a lot of work to retrofit."

"Yarrow remembers something, too," I say before I even realize she's taking over. "When I thought . . . when Yarrow thought that the Chief was her mother, she went with her once to her private office. It was next to the prison wing—a huge room."

"It would take more than just space," Flame reminds me.

"She told me, bragging, that it was the most technologically advanced room in all of Eden. She said she had big plans for it, but when I was there it just had her desk and files. But I remember it was set up with extensive data access points, and I think it could have housed what we're looking for."

"We need to split up and check both," Lachlan says. "If we don't find it soon, we'll get caught. Flame, which do you think is more likely?"

She considers. "If I were the Chief, I'd want to execute my evil plan in the comfort of my own office. It's in the center of the Center, right under the dome, as far from the vexing populace as possible."

"And the most heavily guarded area," I say.

"Usually," Ash reminds me.

"So I'd guess there," Flame concludes.

"Then half of us check one room, half the other," Lachlan says. "Flame, you and I will go to the Chief's office, and . . ."

"I'll go," Carnelian says. It's the most dangerous of the two options.

"No, you need to be in the other group," Flame says. "Carnelian is the only one besides me who has any real tech knowledge. I explained to him how to shut down the mind control, once we use the seed to activate the access. Carnelian knows what to look for. You others would just see a big room with wires and think you hit the jackpot."

"I'll go with Carnelian to the medical room," I volunteer.

"I should go to the Chief's office," Mira says.

"No, I want you near me," Carnelian says.

She pats his cheek. "I know, sweetie, but with all modesty, I'm the best fighter here."

I see Flame raise her eyebrows in surprise.

"Seriously, she is," I say. "You have no idea."

"And here I thought all you wild-living outsiders were useless," Flame says wryly. "Okay then, Mira's with us."

"And I'm with Rowan," Lark says immediately, looking at Lachlan, challenging him to object. Lachlan only raises his eyebrows.

"I'll go with Lachlan and Flame," Ash volunteers, and though I'm desperately afraid for him, I beam with pride. Not too long ago he was a shy, quiet boy. His only close friend was Lark. Physically, he was always weaker than me. Born with lung trouble, he has chronic asthma and other breathing difficulties, which can be set off by stress. But since going to the Underground, and then joining the rebels— and maybe since falling in love with Angel—his health seems to have miraculously improved. He is stronger, more purposeful.

I still feel the need to protect him, but when I look at this boy who suddenly seems more like a man I think maybe I don't have to anymore.

"I'll join them, too," Angel says softly, and I know that if there is any protecting to do, she'll be as fierce as I ever could be. I'm glad my brother found that kind of love. Strange that it took torture, imprisonment, and a bikking civil war to bring them together.

"But there's only one seed," Carnelian says. "If the medial room is the new control center . . ."

"You come and get us," Flame says. "We'll take the seed

to the most likely place. If you check the med center and it's not there, hurry back to us."

"Hurry to us either way," Lachlan says. "And be prepared for a firefight. Come to help us hold the place while Flame works, or cover our escape. We've been uncannily lucky so far, but our luck is bound to run out soon. There's no way the Chief's office is unguarded."

We listen at the door until we're sure the hallway is clear, then we split up. The cleanbot gives a contented little hum as we leave it to its labors. I want so much to hug the others, to give them a real goodbye just in case. But it will only slow us down. And I don't need more emotion right now. I make do with a farewell smile at Ash, who winks back at me in return and sets his school cap at a rakish angle. Lachlan doesn't even look back. He's utterly intent on the task ahead of him.

Carnelian, Lark, and I walk as casually as we can toward the medical wing. I want to sneak and creep, but when I look a little furtive as we pass a trio of medical students, Lark gives me a pinch of reminder. Then she starts talking loudly about what a bore it is to volunteer at the Center, but how much it will help our careers later. She nods offhand to the medical students. As we pass, I see them roll their eyes at the privileged, elite young people who will have everything in life handed to them, even top-notch Center jobs.

I sigh with relief when they've passed. Soon we come to the former medical center.

Or rather, the current medical center. It is abuzz with activity—people on treadmills with wires on their chests, other people sliding into scanning machines, lab techs checking samples, and bots gliding from station to station. All the equipment looks shiny and new.

"It was only being renovated after all," Lark says.

"We have to get back to the others!" I say, and we hurry

out. But when I lead the way around a corner, I see several Greenshirts hurrying down the corridor. I duck back, and we have to hide in an empty office until they pass. It is several minutes before we are safe enough to emerge and seek the others. Once we do, I run, and the others follow.

I run, because running is the easiest thing for me. I run, because I want more than anything to run away from this place of pain and torment, of indignities that reach right into a person's brain and strip them of their most precious thing, their self.

But instead I run toward the danger, deeper into this treacherous pit. I run to the lair of my worst enemy, the person who killed my identity, who stole my parents. The woman who is taking away the freedom of millions.

We are in the heart of the Center now. The green faceted dome is above is, tingeing the bright white walls and floor an algae hue. There are no guards outside Chief Ellena's door. That's lucky, I think as I fling the door open.

That's because all the guards are inside. Ten of them, along with Chief Ellena. Mira, Lachlan, Angel, Ash, and Flame lie on the ground, on their bellies with their hands clasped behind their heads. They were waiting for us. They knew we were here. Could Lark have . . . ? No, she's herself again. I trust her. There must have been a scan that we missed, something. Or bad luck.

It looks like our team was ambushed as soon as they entered the room. In that short time we were apart, everything went to hell. The Greenshirts keep their guns pointed at the prisoners.

Chief Ellena raises hers to point it at me.

I don't dare reach for the gun at my hip. If I do, I know the Greenshirts will open fire on all of us.

Then I feel Lark's fingers brush against my flank. *No,*

you beautiful, heroic girl, I want to scream. *Don't try it.* She's behind me, where the Chief can't quite see what she's doing. Under cover of my body, she's slipping my gun out of its holster. If she can shoot the Chief, maybe we can rush the Greenshirts, and . . .

I feel the cold gun muzzle against my temple.

"Poor, stupid Rowan," Lark says as she presses the gun to my head. "Always ready to believe the best about people. A few tears and kisses and I had you totally convinced."

She steps away from me, toward the Chief, pointing the gun at my face now. She looks at me, a smile quirking her own face as she tells the Chief, "I'm pretty mad at you for abandoning me back there at Oaks, but I don't hold a grudge. Look, I brought you a present."

She goes to stand beside Chief Ellena.

"Good girl, Lark," the Chief says. "I'm very proud of you."

Lark beams under her praise.

It's over. The troops will destroy the rebels. We'll be brainwashed or killed. Eden will be ruled by a madwoman.

We failed.

That buzzing in my head grows louder . . .

28

"YOU ARE ALL so much more ambitious than I gave you credit for," Chief Ellena tells us. "Particularly you, Rowan. I think I can take some of the credit for that. You were such a nothing of a person before I went into your brain and tweaked you. I gave you strength and confidence in your persona of Yarrow. And now look at you—you think you can do anything! Unfortunately, your overconfidence has gotten your friends killed. Guards!"

I think she's going to give the command to fire, and I step forward. "Don't you want to know how I did it?"

"How you survived the Underground blast? Not particularly. You'll just give me some tale about life outside of Eden. We all know that is a pipe dream. There is only Eden, and only us." She sighs. "That is why it is so frustrating to me that you don't understand why I'm doing all this."

"Why do you care what she thinks?" Lark asks with scorn.

"I have a soft spot for all of my experiments," Chief Ellena says. "Including you, my dear. Every teacher, every parent feels the same thing, as they mold the future generation into a useful form. And it is so terribly disappointing when a promising student like Rowan fails so miserably. Why, Rowan?

Why did you and your little band of hapless rebels come to my office today?"

She still doesn't know, I think, a spark of hope igniting in me. She doesn't realize why we are here, or know we have a seed. If she did, she'd gun us down outright. Now maybe I can keep her talking, make her think it is better, or more amusing, to keep us alive. While we live, we might still prevail.

"We came to rescue my mom," I say, hoping she'll believe it.

Lark bursts into uproarious laughter. "Do you think I'm not going to tell her?" she asks when she's caught her breath. She studies my face. "Oh, you poor little fool, do you still believe in me? Do you still think I'm the old Lark you knew and loved?" She laughs again. "She's dead! Look at me! I don't even look like that deluded little do-gooder anymore. Do you think I love you? That love conquers all? I ought to shoot you now." She shakes the gun at me, but Chief Ellena pushes her arm down.

"Don't be hasty. We have all the time in the world. And they—they have nothing." With her free hand she reaches into her jacket pocket and takes out something small, pinched between her fingers.

It is our hard-won seed, the only way to reprogram Chief Ellena's mind control.

"Lark doesn't even have to tell me, though I know she would have. Do you think I wouldn't have my prisoners searched? Do you think I wouldn't put two and two together when I found the seed, and all of you exactly where it can be put to use?"

Though the Chief is talking, I glare at Lark. How could I have trusted her? How could she have betrayed me?

"How clever of you, Rowan," Chief Ellena says. "How

resourceful, to discover exactly what you needed. A seed. Isn't that beautiful? So symbolic. And you got your hands on the very last seed in Eden, the only chance to override my controls and reprogram the mind link to every person in Eden."

She holds the seed up, examining it. "This seed would put the control in your hands. You could rule all of Eden, make every man, woman, and child left on Earth your slave. Or you could erase the program, freeing the minds of the citizens of Eden. That's what you want, isn't it?"

She sighs. "I was like you, Rowan—long ago. Idealism is an illness of youth. I understand. You believe in the rights of the individual. Self-determination. Freedom. All very pretty ideas. But do you know what people do with those things? They destroy—first themselves, and then their world."

"Not necessarily," I say. "Not if they have guidance . . ."

She laughs. "What do you think all this is?" She spreads her hands, indicating the complex system that dominates the room, the flashing buttons and intricate circuits that let her reach into the mind of almost everyone in Eden. "I *guide* the people of Eden."

"No, I mean education, knowledge. If people are given all the information, they make the right choices."

"Sure, like our ancestors did." Chief Ellena scoffs. "Before the Ecofail, humanity was at its technological height. They could have made the world a sustainable paradise. And do you know what we were doing instead? Spewing out so much plastic that the very oceans choked. We poisoned our air so we could power the screens we stared at all day. We cut down forests for palm oil to give our snacks longer shelf life. And even in that advanced state, we fought wars with everyone whose beliefs differed from ours. With all that wealth and education, we allowed poverty and ignorance to flourish. With the power to create heaven, we made the world a hell!"

She's breathing fast, passionate about what she is saying, and her words make my skin crawl, because she's right. And I know what she's going to say next.

"How can creatures like that—like us—be left to our own devices? Like children, violent and undisciplined, humans need a firm hand to keep them in check. To keep them safe."

"You're about to kill hundreds, thousands of rebels!" I shout at her. "You're not keeping anyone safe."

"On the contrary," she says. "I'm keeping the species safe. EcoPan and I have the same goals: preserve humanity without destroying the Earth. Neither EcoPan nor I care about a few individuals when the fate of the whole species is at stake."

She takes a step closer to me. "You know what I say is true. If I were to stop the mind control completely, if the second-child laws were rescinded, if people could drive cars, use all the power they wanted . . . Eden would collapse. Maybe not right away, but eventually. And with it, the last of humanity. We can't have rebellion in a closed system. We can't have individualism. I know what I'm doing seems harsh, but it is the only way to preserve our species."

I want to argue with her, tell her that people can be trusted to make good decisions, to not poison their own environment. We've seen what can happen. We've learned from our mistakes.

But part of me can't help but think she's right, in a twisted way. In fact, Chief Ellena herself is living proof that humans can't be trusted with technology or power.

She bends down and places the seed on the ground. Then, taking a step back, she fires an energy pulse into it, obliterating it in a puff of smoke and a burning stench. Every one of us gasps, and I can tell that Lachlan is going crazy under his forced submission. He's just waiting for his chance to turn the tables and attack. But with all the guns pointed at us, we wouldn't have a chance. And now our only chance of saving the rebels, and freeing every citizen of Eden, is gone, burned to cinder and smoke.

"There, that's taken care of. No more seeds in all of Eden. No more worry about little rebel brats trying to interfere." She checks her watch. "And soon, no more rebels at all. My troop should be at the outermost circle border by now. Your friends will be utterly wiped out within the hour. Now, as for you . . ."

She begins to stroll near the people on the ground. She points her gun at Flame's head, then moves it away. "Do you know, I think I won't kill all of you after all, as satisfying as it may be. At least, not yet. You've accomplished far more than I would have thought possible, and I want to know how. Flame, you had a good job once, the respect of your peers. What happened? Who brought you into this criminal life?"

"I won't tell you anything," Flame snarls.

"Oh, you will."

Flame rolls her eyes up to glare at Chief Ellena. "No, in fact, I won't. I've figured out how to block all of your mind control. I've had the surgery done myself. Nothing you do can alter my mind, or make me believe any of your lies. My memory, my thoughts, my soul are all my own. Same for all of us in this room."

Except me, I think. My surgery was the first, and only partly successful because she was still figuring out the process. There might, theoretically, be a faint EcoPan connection in my blind eye, though none of us have seen any proof of it.

"How fascinating," Chief Ellena says. "But I'm afraid I plan to get my information the old-fashioned way. Torture. Maybe you can withstand my brain manipulation, but you won't keep your secrets when I flay you, peeling off an inch of skin at a time. When I starve you, then burn you, so that your own flesh smells like sizzling meat. I can torture your body and mind in ways that don't require brain surgery or programming."

Chief Ellena rubs her hands together in eager anticipation, and walks to stand over Lachlan now. She caresses him with the muzzle of her gun. "The body is full of sensitive nerves, and I will play yours like a master conductor until you scream a symphony. All of you. Believe me, you will tell me whatever I ask, and more, and beg me to end your life."

"This is insane!" I scream at her. "You don't want to save humanity—you just want power. If you would just think about what you're doing . . ."

"Don't condescend to me, schoolgirl!" she rages, charging forward to press her gun to my forehead. Peripherally, I see Lark shift closer to her. Does Lark want the chance to kill me herself? If this is my final moment, I'll go with dignity. I stand straight and lift my chin.

"You, I will torture in any way I can. Even if all you do is spout nonsense about the outside world." She leans close. "I will make sure you live a very long time. Before I'm done with you, you'll watch all of your friends die, one by one. Your mother, too. Your torture will be watching them be tortured. You will die a little more each time I kill one of them. You love them all, don't you, stupid girl? Which do you love the most?" She smiles, an evil curl of her lips, and whispers, "How about your sickly brother? He is a drain on society anyway."

All this time, our best fighter has been biding her time. Outnumbered, with her new friends in peril, she has pretended to humble herself, lying on the ground as if she is beaten and meek. But she's only been waiting for her chance, and she finds it when Chief Ellena is distracted by her own cruelty. Everyone is looking at the Chief, at Ash, waiting to see what will happen.

In an instant, Mira flips from belly to back and sweeps the legs out from under the nearest Greenshirt. With brutal efficiency she crushes his windpipe with her elbow before angling herself with a kick that breaks another's knee.

As soon as they see she is in action, the others are up, too. Lachlan tackles one Greenshirt, slamming him to the ground and getting his gun. Carnelian lunges for another, and all of us are fighting.

None of us move with a fraction of Mira's beautiful, deadly efficiency. There's gunfire now, but it doesn't distract her from her purpose. She's up on her feet, catching a third Greenshirt's gun before he can think to fire, twisting it out of his hand and delivering an uppercut that snaps his head back. Even before he falls, her leg shoots up high without obvious effort, kicking another Greenshirt in the face.

Then with her teeth bared in a feral snarl she turns to Chief Ellena.

Who shoots her in the chest.

I see Mira's look of confusion. She learned a different kind of fighting, a more noble kind—body against body. She knows in theory about guns, but when she thinks about doing battle they don't instinctively enter the equation. She fights like a panther, like a wolf, with wild passion.

She touches the wound on her chest, and looks at her bloody fingertips as if she's not quite sure how they got that way. The world seems to grow quiet and still as I see my friend fall.

"No!" I scream, and lunge for Chief Ellena as she laughs at Mira's death. There's a second bang, and Chief Ellena collapses even as I try to attack her. Her face is a ruined, bloody mess, that maniacal smile frozen on it as she dies instantly. She sprawls on top of Mira, and I just have an instant to see the look of rage on Lark's face before she opens fire on the other Greenshirts.

Catching them off guard, she shoots the Greenshirts in rapid succession until only we rebels remain.

Numbly, I look at the death all around me. Victory, for having defeated Chief Ellena and her Greenshirts. Defeat, because a beautiful soul, my brave friend, lies dead. Senselessly dead.

The seed is gone.

We've won the battle, but lost the war.

I DON'T *WANT* to go on.

But I *can* go on.

Elder Night told me that animals and humans each have special gifts. Humans have imagination. We can plan ahead. And so we can create civilization, prepare in summer for a winter we know is coming, give up the now for the future.

But with a few exceptions, animals only know *now*. A wolf with its foot caught in a trap won't think that if it waits some miracle might save it. It is trapped, and does what it must to be free . . . even if that means gnawing off its own paw. An animal that sees its family swept away in the flood won't give into despair. It will keep swimming, trying to save itself. No matter what happens to an animal, the struggle goes on.

The human in me wants to cradle Mira in my arms and never stop weeping, never leave her side. It wants to accept that all hope is lost, to give up, to wait for the end.

The animal in me pushes me forward, numbly, blindly, to do what we have to do. I think everyone is shocked that as I stand over Mira's body it is not martial Lachlan or brusque practical Flame, but me that says, "We still have a job to do. We rescue my mom, and we escape from the Center. The rebellion goes on."

"What rebellion?" Angel asks, looking up at me with livid eyes. "They're all dead, or will be soon. There is no rebellion anymore."

"There's us," I proclaim grimly.

Lark hands me her gun. "I thought I could be fast enough, when the time came," she says miserably. "I never thought she'd shoot anyone. I thought she'd want to take you all prisoner. I should have acted sooner."

"What do you want me to do with this?" I ask her as I take her gun.

She shrugs. "You can use it on me, if you need to. I never betrayed you. Not when I knew what I was doing. Not in my heart, ever. I took your gun and made Chief Ellena think I was still on her side. I thought it was the only way I could turn the tables, catch her off guard. I should have shot her right away, but I thought . . ."

Suddenly she crumples to the ground, a wounded bird. "Shoot me, Rowan. I can't go on like this," she says with her head buried in her hands. "I swear I pretended to be on her side to help you, but once I had the gun in my hand everything she put into my head came back, and for a second I hated you again. I didn't want to, but her voice was there, whispering evil in my head. That's why I didn't shoot her right away. I was so confused. I can't live like this!"

I think any other person in that moment would believe Lark was lying. At the very least they would question: Did she betray us? Did she change her mind again and again to try to stay on the winning side?

That never even crosses my mind.

"Lark, you were my first and truest friend. You showed me the world that had been hidden from me all my life. You helped rescue Ash from the Center, sacrificed yourself to the nanosand for my brother. You infiltrated Oaks to save me."

I pull her back to her feet, wipe away her tears. "I trust you with my life. You might have been manipulated by Chief Ellena, but I know that if there is ever any drop of willpower left in you, you will be on my side."

I think I'm not completely broken down right now because I expect all of us to die here today. What hope do we really have? In a way, Mira's death is not a shock. It was inevitable, once we chose this desperate course. Carnelian is the walking dead now, all hope stripped from him. I know that he'll be heroic until it kills him, because he has nothing more to lose, and in the end he'll welcome death. Then it will be me, or Lark, or Lachlan. And whoever is left will carry on, striving and hoping.

And very likely die, too.

I give Lark back the gun, and take one for myself from a fallen Greenshirt. I shove it down the back of my pants, another down the front, and take a third in my hand.

"My mom must be in one of the cells in the prison wing. It's adjacent to the Chief's office. She wanted to be close to the prisoners, her victims, so she could . . ." I gulp. I hope with planning the attack on the rebels she didn't have time to do anything to my mom.

Lachlan, Lark, Angel, and Flame take as many guns as they can carry. Flame has the foresight to take Chief Ellena's access card.

"Come on, Carnelian," I say, but he barely glances at me.

I see Lark start toward him. "Lark, no," I whisper, trying to hold her back. But something in her look makes me release her.

She stands over him where he kneels by his love's body, and touches his shoulder. "There's nothing to gain by staying except your own death. If you love her, live for her."

Carnelian looks up at Lark. "You brought death here," he says in a numb, flat voice. "It's your fault my Mira is gone."

What can I say to ease his grief? There's nothing, so I bow my head. I hardly feel like I have the right to mourn for my dear friend. I've known her for a few months. Carnelian has known her, loved her, for all his life. And because of me, she's been taken away from him. From all of us. Her bright light was extinguished on what may turn out to be a hopeless mission.

"She should be buried on a hilltop, under the sun she loved," Carnelian goes on. "She should be laid to rest some place where birds sing and gentle breezes blow, not this cold, artificial place." He looks down at Mira.

"That's what I want for Mira," Carnelian says. "But I need to do what she would want." He bends over her and kisses her pale cheek. Then he rises, pale but resolute. "I'm with you to the end. I'll do whatever it takes to destroy this terrible government, to set the innocent free. For Mira."

"For Mira," Lark echoes. She never even knew Mira, but I can see the grief in her own eyes. She feels as culpable as I do.

I'm overwhelmed by Carnelian's strength of character, by the sacrifice it takes to leave the body of his love behind in this den of strangers. Wordlessly, I thank him with my tears.

No one comes to challenge us when we leave Chief Ellena's office. I think it is strange, until I remember how she once bragged about her private space being completely soundproof. She designed it so that no one outside could hear the weeping and screams of her victims. Now she was doomed by her own foresight, and none of her remaining guards have heard the gunfire that ended her life.

When we meet no one in the hall, I begin to think that there are no more guards.

It makes sense. We're in the inner sanctum of the Center. What few Greenshirts aren't on the front lines of the attack are probably guarding more vulnerable areas. But here, in the prison wing, everyone is so tightly under lock and key that there is no threat. They think the cells are too deep in the Center to be vulnerable to attack. So if guards have to be pulled from anywhere to make up for a scarcity, this is the place that will be left unguarded.

We're approaching from a different route than when Lark, Lachlan, and I rescued Ash from the prison cells. But now, on the upper story, I can look down on the scene I once viewed before. Below us is the white lobby area, clean and inviting, with the azure waterfall cascading down beside the shell-like spiral staircase. Some gray-clad bureaucrat walks below, his nose buried in some files. He doesn't even look up, and we make it to the prison wing unchallenged.

Is this going to be easy? Now, when it hardly matters, are the barriers removed? I desperately want to rescue Mom, and any other prisoners here. But it almost doesn't matter, does it? It is like a final defiant gesture to the system that controls us. You can beat us down, but we won't stop fighting while there's life in us.

Maybe we'll get her out of the cells, but what then? Maybe we'll even get out of the Center. But what then?

Be an animal, Yarrow counsels me. *Don't think about the future or you'll be paralyzed with grief and doubt. It's like a party, when you're totally bikking high and you don't care about tomorrow. Just go, and never stop until you crash.*

I can't believe a party girl is giving me advice that, twisted as it is, is actually helping me carry on.

There's no one at the place where two guards once stopped and questioned us. Only a gate, which slides open when Flame inserts the Chief's card.

I remember the smell when I step into the corridor—like a too-harsh chemical trying to cover up an unpleasant odor.

There's an animal scent to this place, too, something primal that clashes with the steely walls and scrubbed floors. The visceral smell of fear.

"This place gets worse and worse," Carnelian mutters. I try to see it as he must see it. Prison is already terrible for us. How much worse it must seem for someone who scarcely knew walls for his whole life.

When I was here before, the cells were full. Once, when I came for Ash, with political prisoners. Later, after the Underground was burned, every cell was filled with second children. Now I'm first relieved to see that every cell we pass is empty. That has to be good, right?

Then I realize it is because there is no one left to imprison. Except for the outer-circle rebels, all dissent has been eliminated. The Center is so close to total control. Even with Chief Ellena gone, one of her minions will probably step in to carry on her mission. Or the chancellor, until now a political figurehead, will fill the void left by the Chief. Under a corrupt government, it is definitely a bad sign when the prisons are empty. It means the government has won.

We finally find her near the end. Flame releases Mom, and Ash and I envelop her with love.

"This family has lost each other so many times," she whispers. "When will it end?"

"Let's go," Lachlan says. "We might be able to make it out of the Center if we hurry."

"Hold on," Mom says. "We have to take Old Leo with us."

"Who's Old Leo?" I ask.

There are only a couple of more cells past Mom's. All of them are empty, except for the last one.

Flame opens the door, and I see a ragged shape crouched in the corner. It's the man from the nanosand cell. A pair of bright, birdlike eyes glitter at me in the dim light. A man with matted hair and dusty clothes watches me as he rolls something around in his mouth.

"Ah," he says in his strange, ecstatic voice. "More ants to carry the seed."

I step into the cell, and finally see what it is that he's carried in his mouth all this time, hidden from every Center official. The thing he said a bird dropped at his feet one of the many times this madman tried to cross the desert.

It is an apple seed.

A seed of hope.

⸻

MY SKIN IS tingling when we run back to Chief Ellena's office. I can't let myself believe it might be possible. But hope surges through me like tree sap in spring.

Flame isn't one for ceremony, but even she pauses and closes her eyes, taking a deep breath and maybe saying a prayer to the Earth herself before she types in the right codes and gestures for me to lay the seed on the scanner of Chief Ellena's control panel. With trembling fingers I place it in position.

I flinch back as a blinding light scans the seed . . . and obliterates it.

For a moment I think it is a trap, that I put the seed in the wrong place and our one chance is ruined. But then I see a long chemical analysis appear on one of the screens. The system is analyzing the contents of the seed, verifying its authenticity.

The faint buzzing that has been plaguing my brain grows in volume, one bee turns into a swarm, and with a dizzying sensation that constant undertone in my head resolves itself into a voice.

"Welcome."

The voice fills the room.

I recognize that voice. It is the same one I heard inside the silver globe that saved me from the explosion. The same whispered voice I've heard inside my head before. Everyone else hears it broadcast in the room, but I hear it inside my head, too.

It is EcoPan.

"You are authorized to make changes to the system," it says. "All prior authorization has been overridden."

"We're in!" Flame says. "The system is under my control, at least until the next person with a seed comes along. Carnelian, come here. I need your help, too. Let me give equal access so you can help with the reprogramming." She settles down with intense concentration to rewrite the program that is controlling the minds of everyone in Eden. *Are you going to stop us?* I ask, and it takes a second before I realize that I'm not asking this aloud, but in my head.

Why would I do that? EcoPan asks in return.

You let Chief Ellena do this. You'll just let us undo it all?

You should know by now that I don't interfere with the affairs of humanity. That's bikking nonsense! I only step in when things have gone too far.

And brainwashing a million people into compliance and passivity isn't too far? I scream at him in my head. *Slaughtering thousands of rebels isn't going too far?*

I swear I hear EcoPan chuckle in my head. *You're here, aren't you? You're stopping it.*

At that very moment Flame cries, "Got it!"

A pulse seems to travel through the air, as if something just rippled through my brain. We look at each other, not sure what will happen next.

Then suddenly the communicators come alive. Twenty different voices try to break in on different channels. I hear screaming behind the voices, the periodic report of a gunshot.

"We need intel!" someone shouts.

"What's going on? We need orders!"

"What are we doing? Where's the enemy?"

It's the Greenshirt commanders. Without their mind control, they're now utterly confused. They've woken up from a nightmare to find themselves pointing guns at their fellow citizens, the very people they have sworn to protect.

Flame gets on the communicator, broadcasting to all channels. "This is the Center. All forces stand down immediately. I repeat, put up your weapons and cease all hostilities."

"By whose authority?" one of the Greenshirt commanders asks.

"By your own," Flame says. "Your brain is free—now use it!"

"The ants are marching!" Old Leo sings, capering behind us.

We can't see what is happening. We don't know how many people were killed on either side before we stopped the mind control. But I know in my heart that by freeing the people, we've bought at least a temporary peace.

"Someone has to get out there fast and let people know what is happening," Lachlan says.

"There should be a hypertube system that leads directly into the Center," Flame says. "Let me see what I can find."

I feel the awareness still in my brain, though it says nothing, only watches me. The Center's mind control may be destroyed, but somehow EcoPan still has a connection to my brain. As it must still have one to everyone in Eden who has or ever had lenses.

"No," I say, looking out over the glittering lights of Eden, this beautiful prison of ours. "We are not free. As long as EcoPan exists, we will never be truly free. We need to destroy EcoPan."

THE SILENCE HANGS heavily in the room as soon as I utter those words. It's like when a predator comes into the forest, and the entire ecosystem, every bird and insect, momentarily goes quiet, waiting to see what will happen. In the forest you don't notice half of those little animal sounds until they are gone. The same thing is happening in my brain. Yarrow is silent. And that other presence, one which I hardly noticed but which seems to be almost a constant whispered echo to my own thoughts, a vague and mysterious other, is now hushed, too.

I think that they're just shocked by the audacity of my statement. We've been taught from our earliest days that we need EcoPan. Lark's eyes look glazed. With shock? Mom's face looks blank, too. Even Flame, with her clear-thinking scientific mind untroubled by superstition or tradition, has a numb look on her face. Have they really never considered that possibility before? I know it sounds drastic, but . . .

"She's right," Lachlan says, and I think, thank goodness, at least one person who isn't shocked. "EcoPan might keep Eden going, but we don't need Eden anymore. We don't need to be monitored and controlled."

"Humans are natural things," Carnelian says. "We shouldn't

be at the mercy of a machine. Even if that machine is supposed to protect us."

"But how?" Lark asks.

"It might rule over everything we know, but it is still a computer program," Flame says. "It is still basically code."

"So if you could access the code, you could rewrite the program, or destroy it entirely," I say. "But you can access the program from here, right? You shut off the enhanced mind control."

"That's different," she says. "These are localized systems, controlled by EcoPan but separate from it. I can control all city systems, like transportation. I might even be able to shut down the desert from here. But EcoPan is a separate entity." She spends some time at the terminals, but doesn't look hopeful when she's done. "It looks like there is some remote location where the essence of EcoPan is stored. We'd have to find that and rewrite it, or destroy it completely. But how could we ever find it?"

We think for a while, but come up with nothing. It looks like this will have to be part of our long-term goals, maybe just a pipe dream we can never realize. We've done something great here today, but I can't help but think it will all be for nothing if EcoPan can still hop in our heads whenever it likes. Ellena is gone, but EcoPan is a more insidious, enduring influence.

"I want to take her back," Carnelian says as he kneels beside Mira's body. "She doesn't belong in this dead place. I'm going to bring her back to her garden. Her soul will rest easy there."

I think, but don't say, that her soul will rest a lot easier if her body isn't lying under the statue of Aaron Al-Baz. Maybe we can knock it down, replace it with something more beautiful.

"I guess I'll get to work on shutting down the desert," Flame decides. "Carnelian, I'll need your help."

Heavily, he rises and tries to pay attention to her instructions. I take over his vigil, rearranging Mira's clothes so the terrible wound is less visible, smoothing her hair away from her face, closing her staring eyes. *I'll bring you home*, I silently promise her. *You are a child of nature. Your heart is in the wilderness, and I'll make sure your final resting place . . .*

Oh great Earth, can it be? The Heart of EcoPan. Is it possible?

My prayer to Mira has sparked a connection in my brain. I pull out the notebook and scan the chalky shadow of Aaron's final words.

There is no mention in the history books of Aaron having a family. Who else would his child be but his master creation, the EcoPanopticon? When he was on the verge of death, he wanted to be buried with his child. With the Heart of EcoPan.

And what is the heart? I look at Aaron's words: the language of EcoPan's existence, the code of his creation. Of course! He must be talking about where EcoPan's program is stored. I think of Aaron's statue in the garden, a garden with strange, exotic flowers that don't grow wild near Harmonia. A garden with a fountain at the statue's feet. I remember the way Aaron seemed to walk on the water.

He even gives the prophesy of doom in his last words: *When my child is no longer needed in this world, it is there that he will die.*

With renewed hope, I stand up and slap the notebook on the table.

"I know where EcoPan's programming is stored!" I say. "I know how to destroy EcoPan once and for all!"

I start to tell them as they gather around. The room is strangely quiet.

"Flame," I ask. "Is it even possible? Flame?" She's staring, not at me, but into some middle distance. I exchange a look with Lachlan. Something is definitely wrong.

He snaps his fingers in her face, but gets no response. I call Lark's name, but she doesn't react either. They're like blind, still statues. With a mounting panic I reach to shake Lark out of her spell. All of a sudden she draws in her breath.

They all do.

Then, in perfect unison, everyone except Lachlan and Carnelian speaks. "Activate priority defense mode!"

They all speak with the voice of EcoPan. It booms through the room, through my brain, and with a heart-sickening realization I know what will happen next. For another second they are still in a daze, their brains fighting for control. While they are vulnerable, I wrap my arms around Lark, pinning her own arms to her side so she can't reach for her gun. "Get them outside!" I scream to Lachlan and Carnelian as I haul Lark to the door and shove her out. She falls in a confused heap.

"Everyone with lenses," I yell. "They're turning on us! EcoPan is fighting for its life!"

I grab Angel next. "No!" she growls at me, in a voice that isn't quite her own. "EcoPan is sacred."

I shove her out, too, leaving Lachlan to take Flame. EcoPan's control is growing, and she punches and kicks at Lachlan. "Sacrilege!" Flame screams as Lachlan tosses her out. She tangles with Angel and Lark, and in the confusion Carnelian gets Ash outside, too. Old Leo doesn't seem affected. He's just sitting in a corner, rocking and singing about ants.

I slam the door before they can fight their way in again. Which just leaves Mom.

Pointing her gun at me.

"Mom, please," I beg her. "You're not thinking clearly."

"On the contrary," Mom says, aloud in her own voice, but

somehow inside my head, too. EcoPan has her firmly under its control. "You are the one who is not thinking clearly." Outside, Lark and the others are pounding on the door. "Eco-Pan is our savior, the one thing that has kept humanity alive for a thousand years. EcoPan is connected to every one of us."

"Mom, please put the gun down. Think about what you're doing."

She hesitates, looks at her gun, then at me, and her face is aghast. Trembling, she puts the gun on the ground and kicks it away, looking at it skitter across the room as if she can't believe what she is seeing.

"Oh, Mom," I say with relief. "For a minute I thought you were really going to . . ."

Then all at once her face twists in feral intensity, and she springs on me, wrapping her hands around my throat in a vice-like grip.

"We will stop you," she hisses as she squeezes, just as if she never loved me. "The people of Eden are a hive, with Eco-Pan at the center. We will protect EcoPan. We will kill you!"

As I fight her, I can see the struggle within her. EcoPan is vying for control, but Mom is strong. Her love is fighting EcoPan's power over her.

For now. Her fingers press into my throat. EcoPan is winning!

"I love you, Mom," I say, and for a second she seems wholly herself again, looking utterly confused at her own hands on my throat. Then there is a whirring sound in the room as Carnelian activates one of Flame's disruptors. Mom falters, and I shove her off me, beating her to the ground so hard she hits her head on the floor. Her eyes roll back in her head, and a trickle of blood rolls across the cold floor.

"No, Mom!" I weep, cradling her, sure I've killed her. But Carnelian checks her pulse.

"She's fine, just unconscious," he says.

"There' so much blood!"

"Scalp wounds always bleed a lot, even when they're relatively minor," Lachlan says as he crouches to check my mom also. "You did what you had to do." He stands up, and pulls me up, too. "Now, you tie her up. We have work to do, if EcoPan hasn't shut us out. Carnelian, can you shut down the desert from here?"

"I . . . I think so," he says, and gets to work.

"Rowan!" Lachlan snaps. "Hurry, before she wakes up."

I'm just looking at my unconscious mom in shock. "She turned on me," I say in disbelief. "EcoPan can control anyone. It didn't even need Ellena's programs." I can hear my voice rising to a hysterical pitch. "It can get any of us! Whenever it wants to. We're just puppets to EcoPan. It lets us imagine we have free will, but it can control us anytime it wants to!"

Lachlan rushes to my side. "Not me," he says as he takes my hands. "I never had lenses, so it can't control me. I'm always on your side, Rowan. You can always trust me."

I take a deep breath. One person on my side. And Carnelian, too. And the other second children, the ones who never had lens implants.

At best, a few hundred people who don't want to stop me. That leaves, what, almost a million people under EcoPan's control.

But what about me? Why aren't I affected? Flame and Angel and Ash had the surgery that was supposed to sever EcoPan's connection, same as me. They succumbed, but I didn't. Why?

Because of me, Yarrow says, and suddenly her awareness seems to overwhelm my own. *Let me take control, and I'll keep EcoPan out of your head.* She's separate from the

Rowan part of my brain, and unconnected to EcoPan. Usually I make an effort to keep the Yarrow part of me subdued.
I—Rowan—never want to feel like I'm out of control. But
EcoPan can access Rowan. He can't get to Yarrow. I relax the
mental control that usually keeps Yarrow partially contained.
Immediately I feel EcoPan's presence diminish. I can't tell if it
is completely gone, though, or just hiding, lurking.

I look out the window to the concentric circles of Eden,
the well-ordered streets. There are people on the streets—a
lot of them. They aren't going to work. They aren't shopping
or socializing.

They're marching.

Directly toward the Center.

"They're coming for us," I whisper.

"Who?" Carnelian asks distractedly as he struggles to understand the unfamiliar programming.

"All of Eden."

Lachlan stands at my side, staring at the citizen army
coming inexorably toward us. Under EcoPan's command,
they will stop us. They will tear us apart to save EcoPan. It
seems hopeless.

Unless . . .

"Can you access the transportation system from here?" I
ask Carnelian.

"I thought you wanted me to take down the artificial desert," he says. "I'm working on that. We need to free everyone,
right?"

"Humanity will never be free as long as EcoPan is operational. We've been in prison long enough. It is time for all of
us to be completely free. And that means destroying the Eco-
Panopticon. We need to get to Mira's garden."

"Flame cued up the controls for Chief Ellena's private
hypertube," Carnelian says, "so getting to the outer circle

should be easy—as long as EcoPan doesn't regain control. And as for the desert . . ." He types in a few commands. "Well, that was easier than I thought. There's basically an on-off code. Okay, I have the desert down."

"Then lets get out of here!" Lachlan urges. "They're converging on the Center to stop us. We're trapped!" Carnelian presses a button, and a section of floor on the far side of the huge room opens up. A pod rises and the gull-wing doors open.

"But won't EcoPan take over control?" Lachlan asks.

"Even a supercomputer can't do everything at once. I think it is taking all of its resources to manipulate the population right now. The city is on a separate system from Eco-Pan's main programming. I can still access the basic systems of Eden. For now."

"We better hurry then," Lachlan says.

Before we go, I kiss my unconscious mom, then walk to the door, where I can hear someone banging on the other side. The door is secure, though—Chief Ellena made sure of that—and almost completely soundproof so that even though I can hear the faintest muffled shouting, I can't tell which one of them it is. Still, I press my palm to the door, then lean my cheek against it.

"I don't want to say goodbye," I whisper. "Not yet. Not ever. I'll find you again, Lark. I promise. No matter what happens, I'll be with you again. And Ash, take care of yourself. If I don't make it back, I know you're strong enough to survive. I love you."

I kiss the door, hastily wipe away a tear. I see Carnelian deliberately break his eyes away from Mira's body. If he kisses her, if he holds her, he might never manage to let her go.

At the last moment he goes back. "I can't leave her. I have to bring her home, to the wilderness she loved."

I nod. It's the right thing to do, without a doubt.

We get into the transport, and when the doors close Carnelian sets the coordinates to take us to the outermost circle.

It is a harrowing journey. All the while, I expect the transport to lurch to a halt, for security bots to tear the capsule open and rip us to pieces. But we travel unmolested beneath the city until the transport comes to a halt.

"End of the line, apparently," Carnelian says.

"I'm not sure exactly where we are," Lachlan admits. "Hopefully we're in the outermost circle." We climb the ladder to the afternoon sunlight, not knowing what we might find.

We're not quite where we hoped to be. There, before us, is one of the bridges across the narrow waterways separating each of the circles. On the other side is the outermost circle, with our allies and friends, the second children and rebels. The second children at least must be free of EcoPan's control. But what about the others? The disruptor we had with us wasn't enough to keep Lark, Flame, and the rest free once EcoPan decided to take over. But maybe that was what kept them confused for a while. Maybe that was what helped Mom fight the control long enough to not shoot her own daughter. And out here, with more complete saturation, maybe EcoPan's inflence is likewise limited.

Whatever we may find with the rebels, right now we have to deal with the remnants of Chief Ellena's army.

The Chief is dead; they have no leadership, no orders. They have ceased their attack, but are holding position. Chief Ellena no longer controls them. But EcoPan still has access to their brains.

"Stop right there!" one of the Greenshirts shouts when he notices us. At once, thirty of them, all the forces guarding this bridge, have their guns trained on us.

Although we're hopelessly outnumbered, Lachlan and I aim our guns, too. It's an impossible standoff. We might take down several of them, but there's no doubt that they'll slaughter us. For a tense moment we all hold this position. Carnelian carries Mira's body, looking hopeless.

Then I lower my gun. "We surrender!" I shout.

"What are you doing?" Lachlan hisses.

"They'll drag us back to the Center!" Carnelian says.

"Trust me," I insist.

After a pause, Lachlan drops his weapons along with me. We hold up our hands, but as the Greenshirts move in to take us into custody I move behind Lachlan and adjust the controls of Flame's disruptor, which he wears strapped over his shoulder.

Eight of the Greenshirts have approached. The odds are too great for us to fight. Except, as soon as they step within range, the disruptor takes effect on them and they holster their weapons, looking confused. They don't know what to do, but their own natures are fighting EcoPan's commands.

The ranking officer shakes his head quickly to clear it, his cap flying off in the process. "Who are you?" he asks.

"Citizens returning to our homes," I say.

"Let me check your ID," he says, and swipes a handheld scanner near our eyes. Our fake lens identities pop up, making us look like normal citizens.

"Okay," he says, waving us on. Just be careful. There's been some trouble around here. Not sure what yet. We're investigating."

Freed from all control, his muddled brain is doing its best to process the situation. He knows he's responsible for public safety, knows there's some sort of incident, but can't quite figure things out. So he reverts to training and after a polite check sends us home to clear the streets.

The eight near us act like that, respectful public servants. The twelve or so beyond the range of our disruptor are still pointing guns at us.

"Halt!" they shout to us.

"Stand down!" the freed eight shout back. "They've been cleared."

Now none of them know what is happening. The ones between us and the bridge yearn to aggressively challenge us, just like EcoPan wants. Except, I don't think EcoPan can give them precise instructions. Right now, it seems like it has altered their adrenaline and testosterone levels, boosted their levels of aggression and excitement to make them meet every threat with maximum force. But they aren't as controlled as people were under Chief Ellena, so when their superior tells them to stand down, but something in their brain is telling them to attack, they don't know what to do.

Slowly, nonthreateningly, we walk forward, and I can see the change that overwhelms them as soon as they come in range of the disruptor. The aggression melts; they are friendly, courteous . . . while those behind us suddenly become angry and aggressive again when they fall out of range.

We keep a bubble of passivity around us, and it is enough to get us to the bridge, and beyond. The rebels have built a makeshift barrier of furniture and garbage and broken bots, anything they can find to hold off the attack they thought was coming. We find a way through, and are met by none other than Rook, Lachlan's brother, looking haggard and weary.

"What happened?" he asks, looking sadly at Mira's body, Carnelian's raw grief.

Lachlan hugs him, and quickly explains what is going on.

"EcoPan can't touch us out here," Rook tells us. "We have full saturation of the disruptors. This is a safe zone."

"At least, for now," Carnelian says grimly, and explains

how EcoPan is busy rewriting its programming to counteract all of their resistance. "It can't be long before EcoPan figures out how to break in."

"The desert is down," Lachlan says.

"What do you mean, down?" Rook asks in confusion. We explain that it is all a creation of EcoPan that can be deactivated with little more than a flip of a switch.

"But it might come back online any moment. We have to start evacuating rebels out of Eden. Away from the city, Eco-Pan's influence might be weaker."

"No," I say. "The first priority has to be destroying Eco-Pan once and for all."

"We can still get the rebels out, though," Lachlan says. "With the citizen army swarming, we have to keep them safe."

"The rebels will be safe," I say. "It's us that EcoPan is after. Right now, we can't risk taking everyone out with us. The disruptors might keep people with lenses free from Eco-Pan's commands here in the outer circle, but once we cross the desert, we don't know what will happen. If we have people with lenses with us, they might turn on us as soon as we're out of the disruptor range."

"What about portable disruptors?" Lachlan asks.

"No, she's right," Rook says. "They're only truly effective when there are a lot of them in close proximity and they make a feedback effect. We could take some with us across the desert, but even the people who have had the protective surgery—like me—might succumb."

"I hate to say it, but we can only bring the second children," I tell them.

He smiles with wry regret. "Looks like I stay behind on this adventure, little brother."

"Gather up as many of the second children as you can," Lachlan tells him. "We need to cross as soon as possible. Tell them not to pack, not to hesitate. This is their once chance at freedom." He grips his brother by the shoulders. "And I promise you, Rook, if we are successful, we will come back and free everyone."

"And I promise you in return," Rook says, "even if you fail, I will never stop fighting to free our people. I fight for all of Eden!"

We run to the barrier made of the refuse of past generations, the wall of garbage that divides the outermost circle from the desert. While Rook gathers the second children, we find a place where most of the trash has been pulled down. People have been trying more and more to cross the desert. Trying, and failing.

It doesn't take long before they are gathered. I can't tell if all of the second children are here, but I see all the familiar faces I'm looking for—Iris, the children, and most of the adults I knew in the Underground. I stand on the remains of the rubble heap, waiting for everyone to be ready, assuming Lachlan is going to make an announcement. But I realize with a shock that they are all looking to me.

"You brought them the journal, the truth about Aaron Al-Baz," Lachlan whispers. "You crossed the desert to the promise land, and returned to lead your people forth."

"You did just as much as me," I whisper back.

Lachlan shakes his head. "This is all because of you, Rowan. You are their inspiration—their prophet. Speak to them!"

Shy Rowan who has spent most of her life alone, behind a wall, quails at the prospect. But I look out at all those hopeful faces, and somehow manage to find the strength to climb higher and address them. Yarrow, who has no problem being the center of attention, certainly helps.

"Eden forbids siblings, but you are all my brothers and

sisters," I begin. My voice falters at first, then finds its strength and I go on.

"Some of you were born free, never to have the lenses that this society uses to monitor and control you." I look beyond the cluster of second children to the rebels behind them, the regular citizens of Eden. "Some of you chose to fight for your freedom, to strip away EcoPan's control as much as you could. We are all battling for the same thing, and now, at last, we have a chance to win our freedom from EcoPan once and for all. Today, I take the second children across the desert, where we will destroy EcoPan!"

There are cheers . . . but there are just as many worried, even angry murmurs. "EcoPan isn't the problem," someone shouts. "Other people are the problem!"

Part of me wants to agree. EcoPan might have the ability to control us, but it is other people—corrupt leaders, cruel policies, ignorance, ambition—that combine to make things truly bad in Eden. Still, EcoPan is the best target. Without its meddling, we have a chance to prove that humans have learned from the lessons of history.

So I press on, ignoring any doubts I may have. At this crucial moment, they need inspiration, not confusion.

"We need to be free!" I declare. "There is a whole world out there, full of life and space, full of plants and animals, just waiting for us!" I shudder at the thought of what will happen to all that pristine beauty if this goes wrong. "Today, I call upon the second children to join me."

"What about the rest of us?" someone calls from the back.

I look sadly across the sea of faces, and explain to them that however dedicated and trustworthy they may be here, once they are outside of the disruptors' influence they may not be able to control themselves. "Anyone with lenses could turn on us. My own mother tried to kill me when I decided to take down EcoPan. She was ordered to, and had no choice. I hate to do it, but we have to leave you behind for now." I echo Lachlan's words to his brother. "But I vow to you, if we succeed, I will make sure that every man, woman, and child of Eden finds freedom in the living world beyond the desert! There will be no more inner and outer circles, no more elites, no more second-class citizens or rejected children. This is not just a matter of life or death—it is a question of freedom or slavery! We must all be free! We are all the chosen people!"

They break into shouts and applause, and Rook takes the stage.

"The rest of us will stay behind and cover your escape. We'll hold off the citizen army as long as we can, to give you every chance to destroy EcoPan. Every rebel here would die to keep their freedom, to keep other people and machines out of their brains!"

And I can't help but wonder, Is death better than slavery? What if EcoPan got it right, if its mind control and monitoring were more benevolent? Would that still be worse than death?

For myself, I know what choice I'd make.

But how could I make that choice for anyone else?

A SHORT WHILE later, we move swiftly through the forest of bean trees. It is a small army, maybe two hundred people. Even the youngest children have come. I was torn about that, but decided that there was danger both before us and behind us. This might be their only chance at freedom.

And now the desert looms before us.

A cool, pleasant desert, a beach lacking only the ocean to make it perfect.

"I can't believe it," Iris says as she tentatively puts a booted toe into the sand. "This has kept us trapped in here for generations. People have died trying to cross it, or been swallowed by nanosand. And it was all fake? It could be turned off?"

As she looks across the now cool desert, I can tell she's realizing keenly how much everything she knew was a lie, an illusion.

"What can I trust now?" she asks.

"You can trust us," Lachlan says, putting a gentle arm over her shoulders and helping her across the loose sand.

"You've done this, Rowan," Lachlan says as our group marches. "You changed everything that everyone in Eden has ever known. Nothing will ever be the same again."

A crow flies overhead, curious about this new expanse it could never explore before. It is miraculous how nature will fill any available niche. As soon as the desert is passable, animals want to explore it. The crow flaps lazily over our heads toward Eden. A moment later, though, it returns the way it came, flying at top speed.

What it found was not compatible with the quiet life it had known.

I think of the million people in Eden, what they must look like to the crow. What would happen to that bird, to all of the wildlife, if everyone in Eden poured out?

With certain misgivings, I take Lachlan's hand, and together we cross the desert. Carnelian and the second children follow closely behind.

We haven't quite crossed the halfway point when I feel an ominous tremor beneath my feet. My first thought is of an earthquake, which I once experienced not far from here. But then there is a soft whooshing sound, and suddenly the desert becomes a furnace of dry, searing heat.

"EcoPan brought the desert back!" one of the second childrn shrieks, and she and several of the others start to run back the way we came.

"No, press forward!" Lachlan cries. "It's almost as far either way, and if we make it, better to succeed than fail!"

Oh, great Earth! My skin is burning already. This must be hotter than any natural desert. My eyes feel parched, my skin breaks out in a sweat that evaporates instantly in the dry heat. Three of the second children have taken off back toward Eden. We can't go after them. If we did, we'd doom ourselves.

Together we run, helping each other when we stumble but never ceasing our momentum. My feet feel like they are on fire, there seems to be no moisture left in my body . . .

Then, as suddenly as it came back on, the desert shuts

down. In the space of a few seconds the heat dissipates and we are just under a pleasantly warm summer sky.

We look at each other and giggle nervously. EcoPan must be really overextending itself.

Nice to see a godlike omniscient computer goof up, Yarrow says.

We don't waste this opportunity, but hurry toward the growing patch of green.

"Trees!" one of the second children gasps. "It really is real!"

They came out here with hope, not faith, and their hope has been rewarded.

Finally we come to where we can make out the trees clearly, see the expanse of flowery meadow before them. Even if the desert comes back on, we can make it from this point—a little scorched, maybe, but alive.

It comes back on. But it isn't the heat that gets us.

The second the heat reactivates, a patch of nanosand materializes under our feet. It swallows four of the second children, and traps another who tries to help. I run toward them, too, but Lachlan pulls me back. "You can't help them. You'll only get trapped yourself."

I shout to him and the others that the nanosand isn't lethal, it just takes them to a holding cell where they'll be retrieved. If we succeed, then they'll be set free. If we fail, they will be imprisoned, but at least alive. I shout that we'll try to rescue them, if we can.

The mission goes on, even with casualties. The losses only make us more determined.

Lachlan, Carnelian, and I run the rest of the way and collapse the moment we escape the terrible heat. Ah, how cool the grass feels against my cheek! How I missed the rich smell of the earth, the pure and natural colors of the living world. I hear the exclamations and signs of the second children as they behold the glory and wonder of the natural world.

"It might be easier now," Carnelian says when he finally pulls himself to his feet. "With no technology, maybe EcoPan . . ."

We're far enough from the edge of the desert that it doesn't scorch our skin, but close enough that I can feel instantly when the heat shuts off again.

"At least EcoPan is having problems," I say, standing to look back over the desert. I see a dark line on the horizon, separating itself from the rows of giant bean trees. For a moment I stare, uncomprehending.

Then I realize. "It shut the desert off on purpose this time," I say as I stare.

Lachlan shades his eyes to look. "It's letting them across."

Marching from the edge of Eden come thousands of people. Maybe hundreds of thousands. Maybe everyone.

"EcoPan is setting them free?" Carnelian asks, confused.

I shake my head. "I don't think so. He's sending them all after us."

An army of our friends, our families, our enemies and our allies, all marching inexorably across the cooling sands to stop us from destroying EcoPan.

Lachlan looks at me in concern. "What are you smiling for, Rowan?"

My smile only gets broader. "This means EcoPan is scared. It's sending absolutely everything it has against us."

Lachlan catches my meaning. "It means EcoPan thinks we can actually succeed."

Buoyed with hope, I look out over the meadow to the tree line I remember so well from when I was first released from Eden. I check the sun, remembering Elder Night's lessons, and calculate in which direction Harmonia lies, and where the nearest hypertube access is. It should be no more than a mile away. We can travel through the meadow.

"They can't catch us," I tell them with confidence. "Look, they still have all that to cross, and we'll have reached the hypertubes long before that. They won't have any idea where we went."

"But EcoPan can tell them," Carnelian says. "Or stop the hypertubes, or . . ."

"EcoPan has its limits," I tell him. "We just don't know what they are. If it could stop the hypertubes, why would it send an army after us? Come on, we have a head start but we don't want to squander it."

I lead them into the meadow, confident that we have time to escape the citizen army behind us.

Until the army in front of us steps out of the forest.

There are three or four dozen people, a pitiful number compared to the army of Eden. But they are close. They carry spears and clubs. They are made up of people I got to know and love in my three months of freedom.

Standing at their head, a knobbed club in his hand, is Zander. He's raised a militia.

His two brothers are at his side, of course—the ones who held me down while he broke my fingers. But joining him are other people who never showed any signs of hate or violence. Morgan the potter is there, looking dour. Several gardeners are in the group, clutching shovels and hoes in their callused hands. There's a mother of seven children, her bare arms painted with ocher. Just ordinary people, now the small army of Harmonia.

I skid to a halt, trapped between these two forces. Some of the second children are armed, but they're more refugees than an army. We outnumber Zander's militia, but I don't want to fight them. But fight or surrender, if we have to face the militia it will give the Eden army ample time to catch up to us.

"Stop right there," Zander shouts, and Yarrow pipes up in my head, *Idiot, we already stopped.* Just to show him, I take another two steps toward him. "You and that filthy city scum with you aren't wanted here."

"Zander, you have to listen to me," I begin. By the way he is focused on us, I can tell he hasn't noticed the people of Eden crossing the desert.

"I won't hear any of your lies!" he shouts at me. "Are you going to tell me how you heroically chased down that Eden scum after he escaped? That he's your prisoner? I know the truth. You and your traitorous mother freed him. After you escaped in the hypertube, we tracked you to the edge of Eden. We saw that you went into the desert, and I hoped we were done with you forever. But you Eden people are like rats. We've dealt with your kind before. My father still tells tales of how his parents were slaughtered by the outsider. I vowed I'd never let that happen again."

He slaps the club against his palm. "We posted guards at the border in case anyone else managed to sneak over. As soon as they spotted you they signaled the village, and we've come to make sure you and your kind can't corrupt our peaceful world."

"Peaceful?" I ask. "Who's the one holding a club?" We have guns, but they're in our packs right now. When Lachlan moves to draw his weapon, I stop him. We can't shoot the people of Harmonia. There has to be another way.

"I suffered you, at first, because EcoPan chose you. But that man from Eden was doomed from the moment he crossed the desert. And now you and Carnelian are traitors to your people. You'll die, with no trial but the trial of history. We've seen what people from Eden are capable of. I'll do anything to keep my village safe."

We could kill a lot of them—and I can't say that it wouldn't give me some satisfaction to shoot Zander—but there would be heavy casualties on both sides.

"We're not the threat," Carnelian says.

"They're a disease," Zander yells. "Now you've been infected, too. Get them!"

He charges at us, swinging his bat, and his two brothers follow. But to my surprise the others in the militia hang back. They aren't prepared for overt violence. They want to protect, but not attack. Cruelty isn't in their nature.

Zander attacks so quickly that none of us have time to draw our guns. I duck under his first swing, which would have caved in my head, and grab the club before he can swing it again. For a moment we struggle, four hands vying for control. But my grip is stronger from climbing, even if the rest of me is weaker, and I twist the club out of his grasp. Then I reverse it to jab at his face. He blocks it with his hands, sparing his nose, but I hear the satisfying crunch of finger bones snapping. Nearby, Lachlan and Carnelian are tussling with Zander's brothers, but I can't see how that's going, because my infuriated opponent dives for my legs.

I go down, and try to hit him again with the club, but with no room to swing it isn't effective. He doesn't even seem to feel the blow on his shoulders. I kick at him, but he pins both legs and straddles me. All I can do is use the club as a brace to try to keep him away. I hold it at arm's length, and he can't quite punch my face . . . for the moment.

"I'm not your enemy!" I growl at him between teeth clenched with effort. "You might hate me, but at least I'm human. I know how you hate technology. Do you want to be controlled by a machine?"

"Stop talking nonsense," he spits as he swings, and curses when his fist hits the dirt instead of my face.

"It's not people who are the danger. It's EcoPan. It controls the minds of everyone in Eden. It can take you over whenever it likes."

"EcoPan is a tool, created by humans, to keep diseases like you contained." He wrenches the club away and flings it aside. For a moment he gloats, sitting on top of me. "EcoPan is no threat to us. We will always live in harmony with nature. We will always destroy threats like you." With that he manages to get his hands on my throat.

"EcoPan isn't keeping them contained!" I gasp, just as someone in the militia shouts.

"Look!"

Confident in his victory over me, Zander pauses, barely squeezing, and looks first to the militia member pointing, then follows his gesture out to the desert.

He looks down at me in shocked hatred. "What have you done to us? So many . . . Don't you know what they'll do to this beautiful, wild place? There will be nothing left but ashes!"

"They're not coming for you," I gasp out. "They're not here to destroy Harmonia." I can hear the others fighting nearby, but can't turn my head to see them. "They're coming for me."

"For you?" He sits back on his heels. "Even your own people think you're a criminal?"

"EcoPan has taken over the mind of everyone in Eden. Think of it—humans, controlled by a machine. You love nature, believe that humans have a place in it. Will you stand by and let a machine invade your very mind? Take away everything you are in your very soul?"

I have no idea whether EcoPan will—or even can—take over the people of Harmonia. But I can tell the idea shocks Zander to his core. I play it up. Anything to get to the hypertubes.

"I know how to destroy it forever!" I go on. "Do you want a computer running your lives? Do you want this place overrun with bots? You rely on technology to some extent, but you still control it. If I don't stop EcoPan, the technology will control you!"

"I don't believe you!" he shouts. "You brought those people to destroy our way of life, to kill the Earth . . . Oh, great Earth!" He's looking over the desert again. The Eden army is closer now, and I can hear their shouts, hear a sort of grinding sound, of thousands of feet on sand. There's still time to get to the hypertubes before them, if we run right now.

"Trust me now! For the sake of humanity! We have to get to the hypertubes!" I cry. "If we can get to Harmonia I can stop this!"

"How?" he shouts back.

"EcoPan's main programming is in a secret spot there. I can stop this forever, but you have to help me! If I can destroy it, EcoPan can never enter a human's mind. Humanity can finally live at one with nature, without any technology to interfere."

I know he's confused, and scared. He wants time to think. But there simply isn't any time left.

The Eden army is almost here, preparing to attack.

"You can't fight them yourself," I say. "You need me."

He curls his lip in a snarl as he considers. "Remember the Fire Trial," I tell him. "You let your hatred of me overwhelm you so much you couldn't see what else was at stake. Will you let that happen again, when the test is real?"

"Come on," he says at last. "I'll get you to the hypertube, and the rest of us will try to draw their fire."

"No, you have to get the civilians to safety! There are kids!" He might be a bully and a brute, but this sways him, and he shouts for some of his militia to get the second children into the relative safety of the deep woods. Meanwhile, he leads us to the hypertube entrance.

"Don't think I like you, city trash," he hisses at me as I pass through the door. "We just have a common enemy. I'm helping you now to keep mechanical monsters like that out of Harmonia, to keep our minds free. But I'll die before I let that army of Eden scum befoul my world. When this is done, you pick a side. Those people belong in Eden. You know what they'll do to our world out here if they stay. There's nothing to control them. They'll tear down forests for fuel. They'll pollute the water. They'll start wars, they'll kill for no good reason. It's what most people do. You *know* it."

I do . . . or at least I know it is a possibility. We humans have terrible potential. But wonderful potential, too. I have no idea which will ever win.

I'm a little perplexed by his reasoning, though. "But you're helping me stop EcoPan. That's the thing that kept them contained inside Eden for so long."

"You don't understand me, do you, Rowan?" he asks.

"Er, no?"

"Harmonia isn't perfect," he says. "I know that. But humans aren't perfect. We're just doing the best we can. I hate those unnatural, plastic people from the city, those dirty, corrupt, lazy people . . . but I'm not such a fool that I don't know what made them that way. Machines. Reliance on a bot or an algorithm instead of thought or hard work. We have too much technology in Harmonia. We should be free of that, but the elders . . . I want to change that one day, return us to the way we're meant to be. Glass houses and electric lights? Crops shipped in from who knows where? It's unnatural. We're still separated from nature. With no EcoPan, the Elders won't have a choice. We'll have to be purely natural beings."

He sighs and rubs his temples. "I don't hate you, Rowan. Not really. I'm sorry for . . ." He glances at Lachlan. "For what I did before. But I know humans should return to a primitive, pure state—and I won't let anything stop me. You were a threat. Now you might be the only chance to stop a bigger threat. I never thought escaping EcoPan and its long technological reach was possible. But if this works . . ."

"If this works, all of humanity will return to a primitive state, like it or not. You'll have everyone in Eden to deal with. Not to fight, but to help. They'll be scared, as clueless about surviving in the wilderness as I was. They'll be relying on people from Harmonia to help them."

"Even people from Harmonia will be afraid if we pull this off," Carnelian says. "They think they're living so close to nature, but what will they do without the comfort and ease that electricity brings? How will they grow crops without crystal resonance to keep the pests away? Life will be different, and a lot harder. Have you all even thought of that?"

I bite my lip and look at my knees. Lachlan takes my hand. "What if you were a slave in a rich household, Rowan? They treated you well, gave you delicious food, you played with their children, and read their books. Your chores were light, maybe cooking, or childcare. Something you enjoyed doing. Your life was easy and comfortable . . . but you were still a slave. If you went to your master and told him you wanted to move out, or try a new career, he'd laugh at you and tell you to get back to work."

Lachlan looks at Zander. "You and I have had it easy in many ways. I was hunted, persecuted—sure. But I was never cold or hungry. You have to work harder than us, but when you want a light, you still just flick a switch, just like I did. But we're both slaves—slaves to technology. We think it serves us, but we would be almost helpless without it. You've kept it in check better than we have. Eden does a better job than our Prefail ancestors. But we are all at its mercy. We are all its minions. That was bad, but now that we know EcoPan is in our heads, how can we call ourselves fully human anymore?"

Zander nods. "Destroying EcoPan is the right thing. It will lead to hardship, to suffering even. It will take humanity a long time to learn to live without EcoPan's help. People will starve, they'll freeze in winter, they'll fight over scarce resources. But I think you're right—with the help of the people of Harmonia, all humans can eventually learn to live as one with nature, without any technology whatsoever."

He bids me good luck, and goes back to try and slow the onslaught that EcoPan is sending after us.

Carnelian gently sets Mira's body down and programs in the code that will take us to Harmonia, where we will hike to Mira's secret garden. We will lay her to rest there at the same time we try to destroy EcoPan once and for all.

Carnelian frowns. "Something's wrong. I think EcoPan is trying to take control."

"Can we still use the hypertube?' I ask.

"I think so, but . . ." He swallows hard. "I'm going to have to stay behind. I can't access the controls from inside the transport, and if EcoPan manages to take over we'll just be trapped underground.

He looks down at Mira's body, and I know what he is thinking.

"She belongs there," I tell him. "If you have to stay behind, we'll take her. I'll lay her to rest with love and dignity, and when this is all over, you can visit her in the most lovely garden on Earth."

He nods in wordless thanks, and falls to his knees beside Mira. I don't hear what he says, but when he rises again there's a look of hope on his tear-stained face. "Make this world a better place, Rowan," he says. "For Mira' sake."

With great reverence, Lachlan picks up Mira's body and we ride toward Harmonia. As we travel, I think about EcoPan. It seems like such a contradiction most of the time. Sometimes I believe that it is truly benevolent, that it is struggling with the limitations of its wires and chips to truly understand humanity and do what is best for it. Yet there is a corruption in EcoPan, too. There is something so calculating and cold, so indifferent. I feel like in a perfect world, EcoPan could really make the Earth a paradise.

But there's something wrong with it. It's had a thousand years, and the best it could do was Eden and Harmonia.

Yes, destroying it is the right thing to do. It must be.

If only so there aren't quite so many voices in your head, Yarrow quips. *One alter ego for you to listen to is quite enough, thank you. I'm just glad I don't have to listen to that computer yammer in my brain.*

"*My* brain," I murmur, and shake my head when Lachlan asks me what I said.

The whole time I'm expecting the hypertube to screech to a halt, for securitybots to tear open the walls and attack us. But nothing tries to stop us.

We emerge, far enough away from Harmonia so they don't know we are there, and a little bit of orienteering and a short hike later we are at Mira's secret garden.

"We have to be ready," Lachlan says. "EcoPan must know what we're doing. It will try to stop us."

I do my best to shield my thoughts in case EcoPan can listen in. I feel Yarrow hoarding the information, building a wall around herself, and I try to banish from my own mind everything we are about to do. I can feel EcoPan in my brain, a silent presence, lurking like a toad in the mud.

I start to open the door hidden in the tangle of rhododendrons. "It's fitting that you're the one finally destroying
EcoPan," Lachlan says. "All of this is because of you."

I know he means it as praise, but his words strike me
painfully. *All of this.* All this death, all this torture. And the
change, which we hope to achieve . . . will it be for the better?
For all its failings, EcoPan has kept humanity alive, and the
Earth clean and healthy. When EcoPan is gone, what will stop
humanity from destroying itself again? It did its best to ruin
its own civilization, even inside Eden. Only EcoPan kept the
whole thing from collapsing, by stepping in and resetting society when things went too far wrong. Part of me feels like we
went so wrong because we were in a false society. Prisoners
can't behave like normal people, no matter how hard they try.
The system limits them. I think—I hope—that when people
are free they'll do better. But what if they don't? History tells
me that they will fail, as they have before, over and over again.

And what about the natural world? Without EcoPan to
regulate them, with the freedom to roam, to use the world as
they see fit, will humans pillage and plunder the Earth again?
I share Zander's fears about that.

How much do we learn from our mistakes?

But I am convinced that we should be given a chance to
try.

I take a deep breath. As I turn the key I say out loud,
"EcoPan, thank you for serving humanity. But now your time
is over."

32

FOR JUST A second, we have time to marvel at the beauty of Mira's garden. How glad I am that we have brought her here for her final resting place. Even if this garden hides EcoPan's programming, it is the most beautiful spot on Earth. Once we disable EcoPan, this garden will have a new purpose—to honor those who gave their lives so that humanity can be free.

We lay Mira down on a bed of feathery foliage that sprouts pink puffballs of flowers. It is called a sensitive plant, and the responsive leaves curl at every touch. Now it seems like they are embracing her, welcoming her to the Earth.

I see jeweled movement around us, and at first I don't react. It's the little bug-bots, the tiny caretakers of this place. One flies toward my face, bumping me, and I gently shoo it away . . .

And feel a small searing pain in my hand.

And another on the back of my neck!

I swat at it, and a small crumpled piece of machinery crumples to the ground. I hear Lachlan yelp in pain as he gets stung, too. The bug-bots are attacking us!

Small but legion, they are desperate to defend their sanctuary, and EcoPan's programming. We're inundated by wave after wave of the minuscule attackers. Each wound they inflict is minor, but eventually we'll die the death of a thousand cuts.

"Where is the programming stored?" Lachlan shouts as he shields his eyes from the attackers.

"Under the statue somewhere, I think. It says where the colossus treads on the water." We fight our way through the bugs and I stare at the statue.

There are no control panels, no place for a key or a code. If there's anything hidden here, how do I access it?

"Aaron's notes just make it sound like it is right under the statue's feet," I say.

"Maybe there's a lock or a switch?" Lachlan suggests as we fight off the attacking bugbots.

I can't find anything on the statue, but plunge my hands into the water. Finally, my fingers find a knob sticking out of the smooth marble. I grab it and pull, and suddenly the waters part before me. The statue slides back, and a steep, narrow flight of stairs is revealed.

"Go!" Lachlan urges, and I scramble down, with him right behind me. Together, we descend, until I find the glowing golden heart of EcoPan.

It doesn't look like much. There's a control panel against one wall, with a lazily flashing light. In the center of the room are two oblong . . . tables? Boxes? I can't tell. Whatever all this is, if what Aaron Al-Baz wrote is true, everything that makes EcoPan what it is, its heart, its soul—if it has one—is here.

I creep closer, and realize that one of the oblong objects is a marble sarcophagus. It is clear on the top, and when I look down I see what I first think must be a model, plastic or wax, of Aaron in repose, his eyes closed, his hands folded across his chest. Wires connect to his body. Etched on the tomb, opaque against the clear, are his name and the words: *A colossus among men, the epitome of humanity, savior of the Earth.*

What an arrogant son of a . . . Yarrow begins, but I stop her. We have work to do.

The other raised chamber is empty. I turn to the control panel, the only other thing in the room.

"I wish Carnelian were here," I say. "At least he had some idea how all this might work." I know how to use the technology of Eden, but I never learned the science behind it. Lachlan knows a little more, but not much.

"We should have brought explosives," he mutters.

"No, look here," I say as I peer at the control panel. "Are you seeing what I'm seeing?"

Amid the other buttons is a larger switch, contained under a clear, protective box. Written beneath it are the words "Delete: Permanent."

"It's a trap," Lachlan says, frowning. "It has to be. Who would create a master program to control all humanity and then give it a kill switch?"

"Maybe someone who, for all is arrogance, realized what a monster his creation might become," I say softly.

"Don't touch it," Lachlan says. "It might be rigged with a weapon."

"Lachlan, we've come this far," I say. "What choice do I have?" And before he can stop me I flip open the protective panel and touch the switch.

Instantly I feel like electricity is coursing through me, paralyzing every muscle in my body. As I fly backward, my last coherent thought for a while is, *bik, why is Lachlan always right?*

Then the world grows hazy for a while. For a moment I can hear Lachlan's worried voice, very dimly. Then it disappears, replaced by a new voice.

A voice I recognize.

Somehow, I'm not on the ground anymore. I'm standing, or floating, in a weird amorphous place without color or form. And then I see him. The air in front of me shimmers, and there's a man standing before me.

I know him. From statues, from images in our school vids. From my dreams. More than that, though, I know him because he's been in my head. Part of EcoPan, but separate, too. Ever since I got my lenses, someone has been watching me. I realize that now. Perfectly hidden, I could feel him nonetheless. It was his voice that spoke to me in my head. Not like Yarrow, a part of myself, but an alien thing, an outsider, probing stealthily where it was not welcome.

"Aaron Al-Baz," I say.

The man smiles. "Only partly. I am the creator and the creation. I have the thoughts and memories, the hopes and dreams, the savagery and mercy of Aaron Al-Baz . . . but also the logic and fixed purpose, the patience and foresight of a machine. I am EcoPan, but the memory of my creator lives in me."

"He was a madman! He exterminated most of humanity!"

"I know," the phantasm says. "I . . . he was a great man. But a volcano is great. A crashing meteor is great. All of them can wipe out a civilization, a species, an era. Aaron Al-Baz was flawed. But he is a part of me. I cannot function purely as a machine. As my purpose is to protect humanity, I need humanity within me."

"Please, let us go," I beg. "We're ready to be free of you."

The figure who looks like Aaron Al-Baz shakes his head. "I don't believe you are. You evolved to destroy. To take, and use, and ravage. If you were rats or roaches it wouldn't matter — you would limit yourself with your own destructive exuberance. But being so clever, you could avoid your own demise for long enough to do real damage to the world. If Aaron had not acted as he had, the Ecofail would have indeed happened. The story you tell your children would have been a reality. In another thousand years humanity would have made the planet uninhabitable to all but the most simple life forms. Life would have had to begin anew. He saved you from that."

"That's only what you think would have happened," I say.

"My calculations show it would have been inevitable. And now you want to begin the whole process again?" Eco-Pan in human form shakes his head. "I have been watching you, Rowan. From the time you were a tiny child I watched you through your parents' eyes, and through your brother's. Later, when you broke free from your prison I watched you through the citizens' eyes, through bots. I was inside Lark's head when she kissed you."

I shiver, feeling violated.

"And then," he goes on, "when you had the lens implants yourself, I was in your head. I could feel your thoughts, sense every motivation. Even after clever Flame thought she severed the connection, I was there, learning who you were. Since then I have been with you all the time."

"Why me?" I ask, baffled. "What is so special about me?"

The man laughs. "There was nothing special about you, Rowan! Not at first. Do you think I only watched *you*? Foolish child, I watch everybody! Every single human in Eden is within my reach. And most of them are not worthy of attention. I have seen you kill for what you believe in. I have seen you risk your own life for your cause. I have even seen you put your dearest companions at risk of death and torture to do what you think is right."

I close my eyes in shame, remembering how I all but forced my friends to follow me into the nanosand.

"Rowan," he intones gravely, "I will let you destroy me. I was created for a purpose—to serve until humanity could care for itself. I always knew there would come a time when a human would destroy me. Perhaps your advent is a sign that humanity is indeed ready to be free of me."

I stare at him in disbelief. "You'll let me delete your program?"

"Yes, but there will be a price," EcoPan goes on. "Flame thought she could completely sever the lens link, but as you know, she was wrong. However, the bond between humanity and me runs deeper than you realize. Once joined, it cannot be severed. If you destroy me, every mind I am closely connected to will be damaged beyond repair. If you terminate me, every human with eye implants will die. The second children, the people of Harmonia, anyone without a lens, will survive. Of those who have lenses only you, because you have learned to block me enough with the Yarrow part of your mind, will survive my termination."

My hand drops, and I gasp. "You couldn't be so cruel! You might be a machine, but . . ."

"I have no choice," he says. "It is a consequence of the link, and beyond my control. My task is to save humanity. Not individual humans—humanity."

"I can't do that. You know I can't. So everything will remain as it is?" I ask miserably. "You'll keep ruling over Eden, keeping people as virtual slaves . . ."

"Is it so bad?" EcoPan asks me. "Most of humanity was happy and safe and well fed most of the time. There has never been a period in human history when this was so."

"But we weren't free." And now we never will be.

The little what-if portion of my brain considers the alternative. Delete EcoPan, and a million people will die, including some of the people most important to me: Mom, Angel . . . and Lark. But Lachlan will live, and little Rainbow, and all of the second children, and the people of Harmonia who never had lenses. Those few hundred people could start a new civilization, completely free. If I asked each one of those condemned people *Would you give up your life so that humanity could be free?*—I bet a lot of them would say yes. I would give up my life for their freedom, no question. But individual sacrifice is different than mass slaughter.

I'm not Aaron Al-Baz.

I see the man smile, and remember that he is in my head, knows what I was thinking just now. It makes me feel dirty. I can't shut him out anymore.

"No," he says. "You are not Aaron Al-Baz. But you may be the savior of humanity. Rowan, I give you a choice. End me, free a few, and kill a million. Or let things continue as they have. Things will get bad, as they always have, because that is the nature of the beast that is called mankind. But I will always snatch them back from the brink. Or, there is one final choice." EcoPan in human form steps closer.

"For generations, I have been searching for a human to replace Aaron Al-Baz as the humanity within my program. You worry so much about Eden, about Harmonia, but you do not realize that for more than a thousand years I have been conducting experiments—city after city, civilization after civilization—searching for the right people, the right combination to make humanity fit to live in the world without killing itself or the planet. Nothing worked."

"You mean, there are other cities? Other people?"

"One of the many failings of humans is that they all think they are unique, instead of meaningless biological blips in the long millennia of evolution. Yes, Rowan, there are many more cities—from industrialized metropolises like Eden to primitive hunter-gatherer villages, from vegan communes to nomadic herding societies. Each one is contained in isolation so I can observe it. The city of Three Rivers to our north, the flooded city you explored, was one such experiment. But all were a disappointment. So, I changed tactics.

"For a while I thought I could merge man and machine, create a hybrid that would fulfill the letter if not the spirit of my mission. So I made robots like that woman you saw in your first test. But they were never human enough, never real—only copies of the original. They could not fulfill my prime directive."

I imagine a world of those not-quite-right creations, filling the Earth, pretending to be humans. No, that would just make a mockery of humanity. EcoPan goes on: "I realized that humans can never be allowed to exist without some kind of guidance. But for some reason, I could never get it right. I had to humble myself, to realize my limitations. I simply could not understand humanity on my own, not well enough to guide it to salvation. And Aaron, a psychopath, was not the man to help me."

At least EcoPan is human enough to realize that, and to see its own limits.

"My heart is broken, Rowan. Aaron Al-Baz was never fit to be my heart. So I began searching for a replacement. After hundreds of years of watching, after millions upon millions of candidates, I chose you, Rowan. You shall be my new heart."

I try to take a step back, but we're in my own mind, not a real place. There is nowhere to go.

"I gave you obstacles, to see how you would overcome them. I gave you losses, to see if you would lose faith. And I allowed you to come all this way, when I could have stopped you with a mere thought, to give you this final test. You have the future of humanity in your hands now, Rowan."

"I don't understand," I tell him. "You want me to replace Aaron Al-Baz? But how?"

"Merge your humanity with me, Rowan. Give me your

heart, your soul, yourself. Let my program join with your biology to create a benevolent guardian of humanity. Alone, I have failed. With Aaron, I have failed. But I believe that with your compassion, your strength, your humanity to guide me, humanity can be saved."

"But I will be lost," I whisper.

"On the contrary," he says. "You will be joining all of humankind. And all of the Earth. Rowan, if you could only see the world as I see it, in all its myriad subtlety! Your brain is too limited to appreciate all but the tiniest fraction of life. But linked to me, you will stretch across the Earth, touching every living thing. You will feel the vast oceans at the same time as you touch the mind of a newborn baby. For I have evolved to the point where I do not need the lens implants to touch life. I have found out how to merge life and artifice. What is my program but code? DNA is also a code. What are thoughts and memories but electricity in the brain? So are signals in a computer system. The planet is nothing more than a huge computer, and I have accessed all of its systems. I can sense all life on this planet, Rowan. I have linked to the Earth itself."

It is all too baffling, too sudden. EcoPan looks at me with pity. "I'm sorry. I do not wish to cause you pain and strife. Sometimes I forget how small you humans are."

We fight for what we love, for what we believe in. But at the core of every animal—and what are humans but clever animals—there is a deeper atavistic urge to fight first and foremost for our own lives. Life wants to live. What is born fights death as long as it can. It is our nature.

"If I join you, heart and soul, what will happen to my body?" I ask.

"You will not need it. You will inhabit a program that spans the breadth and depth of the Earth itself."

"You mean I'll die?"

"Your consciousness will transfer to the EcoPanopticon, the all-seeing guardian. There will be no more electrical activity in your brain."

My eyes grow hot, but I blink the tears away. I would jump in front of a bullet for any one of my friends, for a stranger even, but this . . .

"What about my friends?"

"They will live. They will do whatever it is that humans do. I will not interfere." The man chuckles. "You will not let me, I'm sure."

I consider this. "I can control you?"

"You will be me, and I will be you. There is no separation."

"So Lachlan could return to Eden, lead the people out to start a new civilization in the wilderness?"

He nods. "Unless you decide to stop it."

"And the other cities you told me about? I can help them?"

"Of course. Your purpose will not change. It has always been the same as mine: to protect humanity and the Earth."

I've made my decision. "How do I give you my heart?"

"I will revive you, and you will enter the chamber beside the body of Aaron Al-Baz. There you will merge with me, leaving your living body behind."

I nod. "Wake me. I need to tell Lachlan goodbye."

"Are you sure? He will not understand. And it will make your transition harder."

"Please. I can't let him go through life not knowing what happened to me." And Lark, oh Lark! Where is she now? She is lost to me again, and I can't even tell her goodbye, kiss her one last time.

He considers. "Very well."

Then the world comes slowly into focus. I'm lying on the cool floor, with Lachlan looking into my eyes. "I thought I lost you," he gasps as he pulls me to his chest, kissing my brow, my eyelids, and finally my lips. His love for me breaks my heart.

I realize that I can't tell him what I'm about to do. His love for me will be too strong to let me kill myself, even to save humanity. And I know he will see it as death. As for me, I think I'm beginning to understand that it won't quite be like dying. All the same, I'm afraid.

And I fear that if I tell him what I'm about to do, he'll convince me to listen to my fears. I can't turn back now. I can't let humanity down.

"I know how to stop EcoPan," I tell him. "Help me up. I need to get to that other table. I need to get inside."

"Are you hurt?" he asks. "Were you electrocuted?"

"I'm fine," I assure him, but my legs are shaking. Without his help I'd never make it to the empty oblong. You've done so much to be here, I tell myself. Don't falter now.

Still, I am afraid.

Lachlan is worried, so I give him a reassuring smile as he helps me into the chamber.

"Now stand back, and I'll explain everything," I say, forcing the smile to stay, trembling, on my lips. As soon as I settle into the chamber a thin clear layer slides over me, separating us.

With a panicked look, Lachlan tries to find somewhere to grip to open the casket. He searches for a switch to open it, but there is none.

"Rowan, can you hear me?"

I can hear him fine through the membrane. "It's okay, Lachlan. This is what I want. This is what I choose."

"What is? What's happening?"

"I'm giving myself to the EcoPanopticon. I'm taking Aaron Al-Baz's place as the heart of EcoPan." As tears run down his face I explain what this will mean for humanity . . . and for me.

"You can't do it!" he shouts. "You can't sacrifice everything you are to a machine!" He pounds on the clear membrane between us, but it is impenetrable. "I won't let you!"

I close my eyes to his grief, and hear EcoPan's voice inside my head.

"Do you agree, Rowan? Do I have your consent to merge with you? It won't work if you are not willing."

I think of the great and beautiful world I have only just come to know. The quiet beauty of my courtyard, where I would draw things I had always imagined. The tempestuous, confusing ecstasy of love. The serenity of a bee settling on a flower. The heartbreaking pathos of death and sacrifice. I am still new to this world. I don't want to leave it.

Very softly, like a comforting hug, Yarrow says, *You won't be leaving it, you'll be joining it. And you won't be alone. I'm separate from your consciousness, remember. Whatever he takes from you, he can't take me. I will always be the part of you that is free from EcoPan. Through me, you will always keep your own self, your humanity. You will not be lost in the machine.*

"Do it," I whisper to EcoPan.

Wires spring up from the sides of the chamber. I can feel them burrowing painlessly into my skin, and for a moment I panic and want to change my mind. It is too much like the torture at the Center!

I open my eyes, and catch one last look at Lachlan's anguished face. "I love you," I say as his fist smashes futilely on the barrier . . .

Then the world goes white. It is a light that sears me to my very core, not hot, not cold, but *consuming*. I am devoured by it. I squeeze my eyes closed, but there is no escape, and when I open them again I *am* that light, shining on the world.

Oh, great Earth, I can feel everything! EcoPan was right,

everything is connected, with energy, with DNA, every bit of life on the planet. And I am part of it! I feel it all! The heartbeat of a baby bird in a nest a mile away. The agony of the grass he's crumpling beneath someone's feet. All that, amplified by a billion. I feel the mind of every human on the planet. Some, I can enter fully—the people with lenses. I can feel the people of Eden, and others, unfamiliar, who must live in other cities EcoPan watches over.

I sense other people, too, but so very faintly! The dimmest shadows of awareness. They are the people without lenses. I reach for Lachlan, and detect a whisper. I try to speak to him with my mind, but he cannot hear me. He is lost to me forever.

And I remember . . . oh, I remember everything that happened for the last thousand years. Everything that happened to every person that walked the planet since EcoPan was created. It is overwhelming. I feel like I'm going mad.

"You will not go mad," EcoPan whispers to me. Or I whisper to myself. I cannot tell where I end and anything else begins. I am all things . . .

I reach out and find the people I love who have lenses. There, as if they are standing before me, are Mom and Ash. I can see them—and see the world through their eyes. There is Pearl, and Flame. I see Rainbow, watch her herding the other children through the forest, utterly in charge as always. I can never hold any of them again, but they are not lost to me.

Everyone from Eden is themselves again. No computers are controlling their thoughts or actions. I—we—are only with them, observing, experiencing. EcoPan is now operating with my heart and mind to guide it. It will never make harsh, mechanical decisions again. EcoPan has learned humanity.

I will help my people become what they are truly meant to be—a part of the natural world. There will be none of Aaron's cruelty, none of EcoPan's cold calculations that consider the good of the species more than the suffering of the individual.

And someday, when humanity no longer needs us, Eco-Pan and I will let our vital spark slip once and for all into the Earth, and people will be on their own again, to fly or to fall.

I have absolute confidence that they will fly.

And now, from among the millions of people whose minds I can touch, I've found Lark.

Carefully, lovingly, I enter her brain, see the world as she sees it. She is confused, grief-stricken, and so alone. Then I echo the words that EcoPan said to me so long ago.

"I see you, Lark."

And I feel her soul light up with joy as she realizes we will never be apart again.

ACKNOWLEDGMENTS

THANK YOU TO my readers for allowing me the opportunity and freedom to create this series. It's been the most rewarding experience to share the world of Eden with you all, and I am forever thankful for your support and love of this story, which I hold so close to my heart.

Thank you Laura Sullivan for guiding me through this entire process and for helping me bring the world of Eden to life, I could not have done this without you.

Thank you Rakesh Satyal for challenging me and keeping me on track over the past years while creating Eden.

Thank you to Lisa Sciambra-Steyn for being the best tour mom and taking care of us on the road, your support has meant so much.

Thank you to everyone at Simon & Schuster, Atria Books, UTA, and Addition for always supporting me and helping me achieve my dreams.

Thank you Whitney Milam for always being there for me when I don't know which way to go.

And thank you to my partner, Daniel Preda, for being my biggest supporter and always believing in me when I didn't believe in myself. You are my rock, I love you forever.

To you, I hope you never lose your love for playing make believe and using your imagination to travel to other worlds.

Until the next adventure, thank you.
Love,
Joey

ABOUT THE AUTHOR

JOEY GRACEFFA is a leading digital creator, actor, and producer, best known for his scripted and vlog work with YouTube. He is the author of the instant *New York Times* bestselling memoir *In Real Life: My Journey to a Pixelated World* and the bestselling novels *Children of Eden* and its sequel, *Elites of Eden*. In 2013, he produced and starred in his own Kickstarter-funded supernatural series, *Storytellers*, for which he won a Streamy Award. In 2016, he debuted *Escape the Night*, a "surreality" competition series for YouTube Premium that returned for a third season in the summer of 2018. Joey's other interests include his jewelry and lifestyle company, Crystal Wolf, and supporting various nonprofit organizations for literacy, children's health and wellness, and animal welfare. For more information, please visit RebelsofEdenBook.com.

Follow even more of Rowan's rebellion in *Children of Eden* and *Elites of Eden.*

PICK UP OR DOWNLOAD YOUR COPIES TODAY!